BIG RED'S DAUGHTER

It all starts with a road accident. Jim Work has just returned from Korea and is driving around Carmel. Buddy Brown cuts in front of him, they collide. And that's how he meets Wild Kearny, Buddy's girl. But the first thing Work sees when he gets out of his car is Buddy's fist. Buddy likes to make a quick impression. In fact, as Work finds out, Buddy likes to inflict pain in general. After they fight, and Work gets the worst of it, he follows them up to Wild's pad, the Zoo, where he meets her rich friends. Wild's hot-headed father is coming to town, and she asks Work if he would pose as her boyfriend so she won't have to introduce Buddy. She knows her father well enough to know they won't get along. Big Red Kearny isn't a man to mince words—if Work is the boyfriend, then Work is going to marry his daughter. But not if Buddy finds him first. And so begins the wildest weekend of Jim Work's life.

TOKYO DOLL

Mate Buchanan has fought in WWII and in Korea. He's paid his dues and been discharged without prejudice, but only just. Now they want him back. Back to Occupied Japan, where a Japanese scientist may have found a virus to heal radiation sickness. Trouble is, Dr. Tsumi hates Americans. So the plan is to work through the daughter. Mate is to marry her, and bring her and her father's secrets back to the States. It isn't his fault that he falls in love with Sandra Tann, a tall, golden girl and the Tokyo Doll of Far East airwaves. It isn't his fault that every move he makes is blocked by Colonel Barham, who is convinced that Mate is working for the Reds. Nor is it his fault that everyone who is looking for the virus believes it to be a killer rather than a cure—an ultimate weapon in the Cold War!

JOHN MCPARTLAND BIBLIOGRAPHY
(1911-1959)

Novels:

Love Me Now (1952)

Big Red's Daughter (1953)

Tokyo Doll (1953)

Affair in Tokyo (1954)

The Face of Evil (1954)

Danger for Breakfast (1956)

I'll See You in Hell (1956)

The Wild Party (1956)

No Down Payment (1957; filmed the same year)

Ripe Fruit (1958)

The Kingdom of Johnny Cool (1959;
filmed as Johnny Cool, 1963)

The Last Night (1959)

Screenplays:

The Wild Party (1956, from the author's novel)

Street of Sinners (1957)

No Time to Be Young (1957; with
Raphael Hayes, story by McPartland)

The Lost Missile (1958)

Short Stories:

The Night Is for Dying (*Adventure*, June 1955)

Step Down to Terror (*Argosy*, Nov 1954)

Non-Fiction:

Sex in Our Changing World (1947)

BIG RED'S DAUGHTER

TOKYO DOLL

John McPartland

Stark House Press • Eureka California

BIG RED'S DAUGHTER / TOKYO DOLL

Published by Stark House Press
1315 H Street
Eureka, CA 95501, USA
griffinskye3@sbcglobal.net
www.starkhousepress.com

BIG RED'S DAUGHTER

TOKYO DOLL

ISBN-13: 978-1-944520-21-2

Book design by Mark Shepard, SHEPGRAPHICS.COM

PUBLISHER'S NOTE

First Stark House Press Edition: May 2017

FIRST EDITION

The Many Faces of John McPartland

John McPartland by John Fraser
(from his blog, 2002)

She was the kind of woman a man noticed, mostly because of her eyes. Dark, almost black pools, they had a warmth that I felt could turn to fire. She had turned her head, looking over the shoulder of the man she was with, and we looked at each other. The third or fourth time it happened he noticed it and I paid some attention to what he was like.

He was a type. You find guys like him driving ten-wheeler transport trucks, or flying, or sometimes as chief petty officers in the Navy, on a sub or a destroyer. Square-built, tough tanned skin, big hands with knuckles that are chunks of stone. The type—what makes him recognizable as a wanderer, a fighter, sometimes a killer—shows in his face.

Big white teeth, yellow a little from cigarettes like his fingers, and he smiles with his teeth closed, talking through them when he's angry. A thin line of short black hairs for a mustache, sideburns of curling hair, hair black and curly, a face that is rough and yet young, and it won't change much if he lives to be fifty. The eyes are fierce, amused, hard.

It's a special breed of man, and the breed are men. Maybe a mixture of German, Irish, French-Canadian, with a streak of Comanche, Ute, or Cheyenne in there about three generations back. You meet men like this one in the truck-stop cafés along U.S. 40, with the diesels drumming outside; or you meet them walking toward the plane on the airstrip; or in jail, still smiling, still ready for a fight.

This guy was laughing as he swung off the bar stool. He was still laughing as he walked over to me.

—The Face of Evil (1954)

McPartland is that rarity, a writer of tough novels who feels tough himself. (Was Spillane a barroom brawler? If so, did he win?)

McPartland was one of the Gold Medal blue-collar writers; had served in Korea; obviously knew the black-market milieu of that war; came back and wrote raw, rugged, at times very powerful novels; obviously drank, lived with a mistress and illegitimate kids before it was OK to do so; and died young of a heart attack. He was the kind of person who knew what it meant to be in trouble with the law, doing dumb impetuous things, getting into fights.

What comes across again and again in his novels is his understanding of power, the hard masculine will to dominate others, break them, destroy them. His bad guys are some of the most frightening in thriller fiction: Southern rednecks, syndicate "troopers," the Mob. His fights are fights in which the loser can get hurt very badly.

When a black-marketing non-com says he's going to scramble someone's eggs with his combat boots (crush his testicles), or the middle-echelon syndicate enforcer Whitey Darcy tells the fixer Bill Oxford, "We're going to make you cry, feller," or when Buddy Brown, the twenty-year-old petty crook in *Big Red's Daughter* (1955) tells Jim Work that he's going to make him crawl, we know that's just what they intend to do.

They are hard men.

King McCarthy in *The Face of Evil* (1955) is a natural fighter. Buddy Brown wins his first two fights with the hero—knocks him down with a sucker punch; gets a painful lock on his knuckles and punches him in the throat while they're sitting drinking beer in a barroom booth. And the Syndicate, the Mafia, punish offenders ruthlessly. Oxford knows what it will be like to go to prison and have your kidneys smashed by an inmate, crippled with pain for the rest of your life every time you pee. Johnny Cool's end in *The Kingdom of Johnny Cool* is dreadful.

However, in most of the novels there isn't just violence, there's also love, and things work out all right in the end for the hero and heroine. They very easily couldn't, though. A strong, focussed counter-energy on the part of the heroes is necessary.

MYSTERY*FILE Review by Steve Lewis (2013)

JOHN McPARTLAND – Big Red's Daughter. Gold Medal 354, paperback original, November 1953. Macfadden, paperback, 1968.

> *She was one beautiful girl. Her body was graceful without effort. Her hair was a tiger gold, natural and lovely, her face was that of somebody's pretty young sister grown up to be a woman.*

Her name is Wild Kearny, and for young Jim Work, fresh out of the war in Korea and attending a small college in southern California, it is love at first sight. There are two problems, though, besides the young and hip crowd of friends she hangs out with, and the first is the man she is with, a tough guy named Buddy Brown, who is apparently a good friend, and as happenstance would have it, he makes quick work of Jim Work in a couple of very short rounds of fisticuffs.

Not the best impression to make on a first meeting, but Wild Kearney must see something in Jim Work who tells the story, because it is not Buddy Brown she takes to the airport to meet her father flying in from the East Coast. No, it is Jim Work whom she introduces to her father as her current live-in boy friend, a guy she has met only four hours earlier.

And her father is the second problem: Broadway Red Kearny, last of the big gamblers, an honest and tough headline-making fellow whom you know does not want just anyone making hay with his daughter. Ever meet the father of the woman you love for the first time? Double that, or quadruple it, and you'll know how Jim Work feels.

This all happens with the space of 22 pages, and to tell you the truth, it's the best part, but the rest of the book is no slouch ether. There's a murder involved, and while Buddy Brown may be the killer, it is Jim Work who is accused, locked up, and who with the help of a magician friend in the same cell, makes his escape, only to confront Buddy Brown again, and this time the tables are turned, which merely makes Jim Work's predicament all the worse.

Only this time he has Wild Kearny on his side.

The story is plagued with what seems like gigantic coincidences, but somehow or another, McPartland, a writer with a smooth and easy way with words, pulls all of the threads together and more or less makes a coherent whole of them, I think.

It would make one heck of a movie, that's for sure. From the cover, I'd say that Robert Mitchum might have made a good choice to play Jim Work, a young Robert Mitchum, though, and I'd to qualify that to say it would work only if you could ever picture a young Robert Mitchum as a serious-minded college student.

Take a look at that cover again. I'll let you decide who should play Wild Kearny, if you'd care to.

From Brown Pages & Broken Spines
By Larry Crawford (2011)

BIG RED'S DAUGHTER by JOHN McPARTLAND, c.1953

Here's another unfortunately-misleading title. It shoulda been Big Red's Daughter's Buddy 'cause, just as McPartland's later *The Face of Evil* has no face, the action and most of the fascination lies in the despicable and dangerous personality of Buddy Brown. He is Wild's—that's the daughter of the title, Wild Kearny—cold-blooded and criminal boyfriend. Oh sure, Wild's an immediate fixation for our hero Jim Work. He claims her as his "the one girl" (Fawcett Gold Medal #354, c.1952, p.9) within minutes of meeting her. But from the opening scene where Buddy causes an auto accident with Jim, then exits his rolled-over MG and un-hesitantly pops Jim in the face for a haymaker knockdown, our attention is on Buddy Brown.

And Jim may be watching Wild's "sleek, golden legs" (p.7) but it's obvious he needs to be more concerned with Buddy. As soon as Chapter Two, the boys are at it again, with Buddy sucker kicking Jim's legs out from under him. He never gets his footing back. Finally, "there was a sack full of pain and the sack was me" (p.12).

And so it goes until Buddy's got every aspect of Jim's life gasping for breath, even setting him up for a laydown murder conviction. Jim's pursuit of Wild turns into whining and pining. Big Red shows up. He's some sort of legitimate gangster from NYC bucking a toothless indictment. He tosses all concern for his daughter's choice in a future husband around like a 50-pound medicine ball. Everyone's respectful—and afraid—of him. He sticks around long enough to gorilla-grab Jim when he thinks he's hurt Wild, then provides a legal safety net when he learns he hasn't. There's a jail break involving magic. There's a big bag of Japanese heroin floating around that's got everybody salivating. And then there's that final brawl between Buddy and Jim where Buddy weasels by pulling a knife and Wild distracts him by entering the room dripping wet and naked "like a glistening golden... Valkyrie fighter" (p.122). A wonderful climax.

Overall, Wild is somewhat of a disappointment, but she's out of the bag and up the street compared to Nile Lisbon—another "new woman" from yesteryear's pipe dreams—out of author McPartland's later and more critically acclaimed book, *The Face of Evil*. Nile gets feral-eyed with some sort of psycho-sexual fixation and Wild, too, goes white-hot for "the cruelty, the madness" (p.66) of Buddy's domination. She's too aware that Jim has broken another man in physical battle and taken her as his own by that same sort of aggressive thinking. But she's more so-phisticated in understanding the dichotomy of female power—what male-dominated traditional Hollywood typifies as "the hooker with a heart of gold"—that undermines traditional machismo and hands Big Red's daughter the leash to newly-crowned Top Dog Jim's future.

I like this novel. A big part is because it's set on the Monterey Penin-sula, an old, much-revered playground of mine. But, more to the credit of the work, it effectively captures that lofty air of bored and privileged youth. Reveling in good looks and smug money, and bandying their draining brains while mugging liquor with drugs, they're trying so hard to be hip with bohemian banter and cool jazz. This is usually seen as the baggage of club 'n' cab-hopping city kids. But the Carmel fog wisping the polished contours of Porsches and Jaguars, the sharp sea breeze dulled by the smoke of "sticks", or the cypress trees backdropping the logoed polo shirts and cleated alligator shoes on Pebble Beach greens all seem to cant true with the nonchalant arrogance and hi-brow disdain of Wild Kearny's crew.

And all the rumbling is done with fists, then words, then more fists, instead of this hold-horizontal, pop gun bravado of modern street endgames.

As a postscript: For as contemporary as this novel reads, it's still 1953. A pre-Elvis world. Author McPartland is valving off some socie-tal steam that should have gotten our attention. Because the train's a-rollin'. Korea. The Cold War. Bay of Pigs. An' the crossroads up ahead. Vietnam. Then it's all sex, drugs, and rock an' roll from there to where ever here is, right?

Time Magazine's Milestones

"Died. John McPartland, 47, husky, bushy-haired chronicler of sub-urban sex foibles *(No Down Payment)*, successful freelance journalist; of a heart attack; in Monterey, Calif. McPartland, who once wrote, "Sex is the great game itself," lived as harum-scarum a life as any of his char-acters, had a legal wife and son at Mill Valley, California, a mistress at Monterey who bore him five children and who, as "Mrs. Eleanor Mc-Partland," was named the city's 1956 "Mother of the Year." Later, Mc-Partland's legal widow submitted the daughter of an unnamed third woman as one of the novelist's rightful heirs. (9/14/58)"

BIG RED'S DAUGHTER

John McPartland

Chapter One

He was driving an MG—a low English-built sports car—and he was a tire-squeaker, the way a wrong kind of guy is apt to be in a sports car. I heard the squeal of his tires as he gunned it, and then I saw him cutting in front of me like a red bug. My car piled into his and the bug turned over, spilling him and the girl with him out onto the street.

By the time our iron touched I'd swung my car to the right, so it wasn't much of a crash. I climbed out in a hurry, angry and ready to go.

The MG pilot was up and ready to go, too. The girl was beside him, brushing the skirt over her long legs. Nobody drew even a scratch out of the bump.

This was a tall, lean lad with a pale face and hot, dark eyes. I saw that much before his left fist smashed into my face. Not a Sunday punch—a real fighter's hard, straight left.

I was looking up at the cloud-rimmed blue sky. My face was numb; this boy had a solid, exploding punch. I tried to roll over fast—stomping on the down man's face is popular these days. I was right but I was slow. I saw the heel coming down and I brought my hands up. But the heel swung back from me and I pushed up into a low crouch.

The girl had him from behind, pulling his jacket down over his wide shoulders, her right knee high in the small of his back. This was a girl who must have seen action. She knew just the trick to keep her boy friend from grinding my nose into my teeth with his heel.

I was up and ready again, but he was satisfied with his one-punch job. He was laughing, his head back, his narrow face white, his teeth gleaming in the sunlight.

The girl had been talking to him, slow and low, and he nodded, turned his head, and smiled at her. Real tall boy, maybe six-four, slim, maybe one-eighty. She was tall for a girl, bronze-blonde hair cut short, and she looked smooth and fine, even now.

A dozen or so people were standing around us now and more were running up.

"I got a little hot," the tall boy said to me. "We'll go into it later. Let's get the stuff out of the street." The girl put her knee down and let go of his coat. He was smiling at me, but his black eyes were watching for the first flicker of a muscle in my arms and shoulders.

"We'll go into it later," I agreed, and our eyes met. Neither of us would look away. All I could see now were those black eyes of his, and I guess all he could see were mine, which are a kind of gray, I think.

Another ten seconds of staring and we'd have gone at it again. I was willing, breathing hard but with a loose, balanced readiness for him this time. A boy with a left like a rifle shot and the kind that finished you off when he had you down…. It would be interesting.

There was a mumble of talk around us and then the law came through the crowd. This was the fancy little town of Carmel-by-the-Sea in California, and the law is professional and competent, the way the law usually is when there are lots of millions of dollars around.

He looked away first when we heard the policeman's voice. I knew two things about the tall, lean, pale-faced boy now. He was a mean, solid fighter. He'd looked away first.

Three things. He was a show-off in a sports car.

And I knew another thing about him. He was with a fine, beautiful girl who had sleek, golden legs and some tricks of her own. Since I knew I was going to try him out again, I figured I might as well know her, too.

The watching citizens, the boy, the law, and I pushed the MG right side up again. It was a little crumpled on the side, nothing else. The girl was dusting herself off now, and I looked at her for a couple of moments before going back to my own car. The left fender was bent in against the front tire. I pulled it out.

By now there was a police car and the crowd was a lot of intent faces that watched the tall lad, the girl, and me as if we were a trained-dog act. The law was friendly. There was no real damage and nobody was hurt, so they took our names and statements and called it a day.

Her name was Wild Kearny. Not a nickname or something coy that a press agent dreamed up—that really was her name, Wild, after her mother's people, she explained to the officer. She lived in Carmel but home was back East, Connecticut.

The slim boy with the hard fists was a simple Robert Brown up from Los Angeles. Wild called him Buddy when she spoke to him, and that turned out to be what everybody called him—Buddy Brown.

I gave my name and the rest of it to the soft-voiced man in the uniform. Jim Work. Twenty-five. Home was Chicago. On the Monterey Peninsula to go to school. Three weeks out of the Army. Yeah, I'd been to Korea. No, I didn't think much of Korea. The officer turned out to have been there too. He didn't think much of it either.

Everybody was being nice to each other now, so the crowd drifted off. The law checked our drivers' licenses and the stuff on the steering posts, gave us that last up-and-down look, and then climbed back into the patrol car.

The three of us were comparatively alone now in the bright sunlight of a Saturday afternoon in January on the golden coast of California.

"Well, boy?" said Buddy Brown. He was smiling, as if he remembered the last time he'd been in something like this, and how much trouble there'd been, and how much fun it was.

"You don't drive an MG for sour bat splat," I said.

"Let's go somewhere and you show me how I should drive my car," Buddy said, and now his mouth had an eager twist.

"We'll go to the Zoo," said Wild Kearny.

I was going to have to take this Buddy Brown. Because Wild Kearny looked like the kind of girl that would be with winners, not losers, top winners in the top tournaments and never the second-flight or the almost-good-enough. Not the kind of girl that I'd ever known.

"You want to go to the Zoo and see the people, boy?" asked Buddy.

"Anyplace, any time," I said.

"Latch on." They slid into the buckets of the MG and Wild waved at me.

I got into my car. Buddy squeaked his tires and headed down the street. I followed.

It had been three weeks since the lieutenant at Fort Ord, a dozen miles away, had given me the few hundred dollars I had coming and the certificate that said I'd put in twenty-three months for my uncle. There was nobody back in Chicago except some of my dad's people, no job with any beat to it, no real reason for going back.

The Monterey Peninsula had a nice little college, some of the best bars I'd ever seen, a lot of action, three fine golf courses, and blue skies in January. You're twenty-five for only one year, so it might as well be a good year. I was going to use it up in the best part of the country I'd seen yet—around Monterey.

The red MG clipped around a corner and scuttled up a narrow, tree-wrapped road. I followed some twenty yards behind. This part of Carmel I liked fine—lots of trees, plenty of flowers, comfortable little houses nearly hidden away. Downtown Carmel was set up to make tourists say quaint, but up here in the hills it looked like good living.

Anyway, January in Chicago was never like this. Or Korea.

Buddy Brown whipped the MG into a short driveway and stopped. I pulled up behind him and watched Wild Kearny get out. She was one beautiful girl. Her body was graceful without effort. Her hair was a tiger gold, natural and lovely, her face was that of somebody's pretty young sister grown up to be a woman.

The slim, tall lad uncoiled his long legs, slipped out from behind the wheel, and stood looking at me.

"What happens now?" I asked, walking up to him. Wild stood there, cool, indifferent eyes on me. I was the stranger who'd bumped Buddy's car and then had been knocked flat in a one-punch fight. The stranger whose nose, teeth, and face bones she'd saved from being hash. Just some guy.

To me Wild Kearny was the one girl. A couple of minutes watching her and I knew that. She had the beauty, the fire, the elegance that only one girl could have for me.

"Nothing happens now," she said. "We go in and listen to some music. That's all. Another girl and I live here. We call it the Zoo. A cageless zoo."

There were two other cars parked next to the little house, a gray foreign car and a low, shiny-black two-seater Jaguar. My '49 Ford was an awkward elephant beside them.

They went ahead and I looked at the gray beauty. It was a Nash-Healey; I'd read about them, but I'd never seen one before. Jaguars and MG's were common around the Peninsula, but this Healey was new to me.

Wild's house was a board-and-bat cottage, weathered a soft gray, with lots of vines and flowers almost covering it. I followed her and Buddy down three stone steps into a sizable room with a fireplace. A girl and three young men looked up at us, and the girl waved a hand at Wild, then eyed me with mild interest. The girl was pretty without Wild's blood-heating beauty.

Wild passed names around casually. The girl was Pen Brooks. She smiled, checked my clothes, my build, and some intangibles that girls seem to know about, and looked away.

I don't remember the names of the men. One of them wore wrinkled cotton slacks and a turtle-neck sweater; one was in charcoal flannels; the third had on a gabardine shirt, jodhpurs, and boots. They were the crew-cut Princeton type. I knew what anyone would know about these three: They'd have money and know how to spend it, they'd have women, and they'd live in the casually expensive way most people only read about.

Buddy was watching me, and our eyes met. We sure didn't like each other, but he was one up on me. He could laugh at me.

Wild went into the kitchen, up a couple of steps from the living room, and came back with three tall glasses of beer. The other four went back to listening to the Stan Kenton record, not new, and not saying much. There were some golf clubs in a leather job on the floor, and on a bookcase was a Rolleiflex with a flash gun. The record player was high-fidelity, and the whole place had an easy air of the best being just good enough.

"You like Kenton?" Buddy asked, smiling.

"He's changed a lot," I answered. "Now he's saying something, or trying to say something, that I don't quite understand. Maybe he doesn't, either, but he's trying to say it anyway."

Wild was looking at us, listening. Buddy nodded. "That's very good, boy."

"Always the rat, Buddy," Wild said, standing up. She turned to me. "I liked what you said about Kenton." She knew she had me—a girl can sense that awfully fast—and I think she was a little embarrassed and maybe a little sorry for me.

"How about Dave Brubeck? What's he saying?" Buddy asked.

"I've heard him only a couple of times. I don't know."

"What are you going to do about my car?" The change of pace was intentional. His face didn't change at all. Now he was waiting for me to protest, to say he'd cut in front of me, to get off balance. Wild had been friendly to me and I knew that made him angry. To Buddy there was only one stage and the only person in the spotlight was him, and there were only women in the audience. Men were to fight and to whip, to be smashed.

"You got any insurance?" I asked.

"What's that got to do with it?"

"Maybe they'll pay."

"You broke? You don't have any money?"

None of the others bothered to watch or listen.

I could feel Wild's eyes on me. I wondered how many men she had watched being pushed around by Buddy.

"You don't know how to drive. You're a punk," I said. I waited for that snake-striking left. It didn't come.

He looked quiet and thoughtful. "There's a little space in back. Maybe you want to take your shirt and jacket off first?" He was untying his bow tie now, unbuttoning his white nylon shirt.

The boy in the hound's-tooth vest looked up and shook his head. "Killer Brown is loose again."

"You'd think it would bore him. It bores everyone else," said Pen Brooks.

I stripped down to the waist, as Buddy was doing. He was lean, with unusually wide shoulders and more muscle than most thin men have. Wild drank her beer.

"Good luck, fellow," said the turtle-neck-sweater guy.

"You have our very best hopes."

"Try not to be noisy." This was the boy in jodhpurs.

Brown and I went out in back. There was a cleared space of bare dirt. Brown kicked my ankle out from under me and hit me as I fell.

Chapter Two

He let me get up because he wanted to have fun. I was way off balance and he tagged me twice in the face, snapping my head back. He was trying to cut my lips against my teeth. I came back close in. This guy's long, rattlesnake arms would cut me bad if we stayed apart.

I got in close, all right; he lifted my head right up off my shoulders with the heel of his left hand coming up under my chin. This time while I was trying to get up, he kicked me in the head and the ribs a few times.

There was a sackful of pain and the sack was me.

Maybe he looked at me after he kicked me, maybe he just walked away. After some time I pulled myself into a sitting position.

There was no reason to curse Brown. He'd taken me. Tripping to start the fight was O.K. in his rulebook, a knife or a set of knucks would be O.K. in his rulebook, and I had to play his rules or get out of the game. I wasn't getting out of the game.

Pen Brooks and one of the boys came out and helped me up. Pen had a wet cloth and she washed my face a little. Not because she cared; I think she was curious to see what a beaten man looked like, and a little too stuffy just to come out and stare.

"You O.K., fellow? Can you make it home all right?" the man in the turtle-neck sweater was asking me.

"Yeah, sure," I mumbled.

"Buddy's certainly tough to beat." Pen was speaking to him, not to me. I could tell, because the tone was different.

The man didn't like it. "Yeah, he's a real tough guy."

Pen smiled. Her mouth was half open, her eyes were bright. She was excited, the way girls get. Not for me, though.

"Better have him come in the house for a minute or two. He looks like he's oozing around a little."

"He's kind of messy."

"That'll be all right. We can always clean up."

I felt stupid and clumsy. That hurt more than my face or the aching weakness around my kidneys. The turtleneck-sweater boy actually had to help me walk back into the house.

Wild Kearny was in a big chair, her long golden legs over one side, yellow skirt high over her knees. A George Shearing record was spinning in the player.

"I'm sorry," she said, looking up at me, "but this time you asked for it."

"I didn't do very good." It was hard to talk. My mouth was a little swollen and crusted.

"Go in there and wash up. Maybe a beer or something afterward." She looked away. The one girl in the world for me and her boy had just worked me over without even breathing hard. I turned and stared at Buddy Brown. He was standing by the fireplace and I could hear him talking to the man in the hounds-tooth vest.

"So these two Paris hipsters take the boat to America. They come into New York Harbor and they see the Statue of Liberty. One cat turns to the other and says, 'Dig that crazy Ronson!'"

The vest guy laughed. Brown looked across the room at me.

"Hello, punk," he said, and his face was quiet and serious. The laugh was inside.

I went to the bathroom and began to wash the dirt from my face and hands. One of the boys brought me my shirt and jacket. I put them on and looked at myself in the mirror. It's wonderful, I thought, to be twenty-five in a lazy town like Carmel and a sucker for a dirty fighter like Buddy Brown.

I went back to the big room. Wild Kearny was still in her chair, but Buddy Brown was gone. The others were sitting around drinking beer, talking a little, laughing, listening. This time it was an old Artie Shaw.

"Come over and sit down, if you want to," said Wild. "There's beer on the other side of that door."

A carton of cans of beer, cold with little trickles of dew, stood on the table beyond the door. I punctured a can and walked back to Wild. It hurt a little getting down to the floor beside her chair.

"Feel all right?" she asked.

"No good." The beer tasted fine, stinging a little on the cut in my lip.

"Buddy took off. He's going to try to find a shop open to pound out the dents. He won't drive a car that's not wedding-night perfect."

"Wedding nights are perfect?" It was a strange phrase to use about a car, I thought.

"It says so," answered Wild. She had enormous, lovely eyes.

"What's 'it'?"

She laughed. "You know what 'it' is. 'It' is what makes all the rules and says how things have to be. Like wedding nights, for instance, the girls, and how to play doubles tennis, or what to drink at what time."

"It's probably wonderful conversation, only I don't know how to talk it." I was beginning to know what Wild, Pen, Buddy, and these other kids were like. They drove Allards and Jags, sat around big, comfortable rooms, drank beer because they liked beer, and if they liked champagne they'd drink that. If the men went to Korea and were sergeants with a line company they'd be damn good sergeants, but mostly they'd be lieutenants and a surprising lot of them would get killed being damn good lieutenants.

Wild and Pen were their kind of women, good-looking and reckless and very bright.

Yeah, I could dig these crazy kids, a little bit.

Wild was still looking at me, with friendly compassion now. "We're all waiting, not patiently, for somebody to smooth out our Buddy. I think we'd chip in for a small loving cup to the man who did it." She turned her glass in her hands. "But Buddy would come back and kill the man that whipped him. Kill him or die trying."

The record was Billie Holiday now and her voice conquered the room.

"I'm going to have to try your Buddy again."

"Why? No point, is there?" she said. "He's too fast, too hard, too mean. Why be hurt? And if you did take him, what add does that give?"

"I have to do it, for one thing. I'm going to live around here, so I'll be running into him. I'm going to have to stop that laugh of his. And there's you."

"So there is." Her eyes went over me as if she were seeing me for the first time.

Billie Holiday's voice was with us like the wind and the beat of a heart.

"Let's you and me get out of here. Let's you and me go someplace now."

"Why not?" she said, and she swung around and up like a dancer.

I got up from the floor. I felt shaky and there were plenty of aches in me.

"Where, for example?" she asked, but she was walking toward the open door and the little flight of stone steps. The others paid no attention to us.

"Bar?" I followed her through the tangle of vines and bushes outside the little house.

She turned to look at me in the bright sunshine, a tall girl in a loose gray-green coat and a soft yellow skirt, a tall girl with tiger-gold hair and the softest, clearest eyes I had ever seen.

She smiled and it was a pretty kid-sister smile, white teeth and red lips, eyes suddenly bright and crinkles at the corner of her mouth. For a moment she wasn't beautiful, only sweet and lively, the kind of girl a man wants to be with, laughing with him at funny things.

I pulled her to me and kissed her. She gave a little in that kiss, gave a little both of the pretty kid sister and of a wild, passionate woman. Both, like a touch of sweet cream and a touch of brandy.

She looked up at me—not much, I'm barely six feet—and laughed.

"Jim Work, the boy with impulses," she said. "He gets in fights, he kisses girls, he has an interesting life."

"What's this Brown? What's he mean to you, Wild?"

"He's my man. He's funny and he's a nuisance. He doesn't have a lot, but then he has me."

Take off, Work, I thought. You're in the wrong ball game. They pitch too fast and they play different rules. Take off, Pal.

"Let's take my car," said Wild.

"Which?" But I knew. It was the Nash-Healey.

"Where?" she said. She was behind the wheel in one smooth movement.

It was a word game, so I said, "Why?" and she laughed again.

"Because maybe I've got plans for you." She tooled the low gray car down the narrow driveway to the blacktop road.

"And what kind?" The car had a machinist's beauty that made me almost forget her.

"A drink, maybe two, and I'll make up my mind. You probably won't go for it."

"I'll go for it."

She took the car through the little hills to the highway and over the ridge down to Monterey, a town nothing much like Carmel-by-the-Sea. Monterey was a fishermen's town once when Steinbeck was writing about Cannery Row; now it's a tourists' town and a soldiers' town, but still a good, pleasant place.

We hadn't said anything during the short drive from the Zoo to Tyler Street in Monterey. Wild was the kind of girl that enjoyed driving. I had nothing to say. My face and body still hurt, Wild had kissed me and then told me she belonged to Buddy Brown.

I was thinking: You fall in what you feel may be love damn fast, in minutes, maybe in seconds and there's no future to it.

"Are you married, Jim?" Wild was backing into an open space by the curb; this was the first thing she had said since we left Carmel.

"No. I'm just a broken-down G.I. college student."

"What do you like to do?" The Healey was parked now.

"What I'm doing. Just living."

She slid out of the car. "How's for the Mission Inn for our drinks?"

"Good." I knew the place. For three weeks I'd been getting to know the bars of the Peninsula, and this was a pleasant one—a small room with a prow-shaped bar and quite a lot of action, one big room with tables and quite a lot of comfort. We went into the big room, Wild sat down, and I went into the little room to get us some beer.

As I came back into the spacious room I looked at Wild. I saw a beautiful young girl sitting at a big table, her short, bronze-gold hair still ruffled from the wind. She saw an ordinary guy in jacket, sport shirt, and slacks, his face swollen, carrying two bottles of beer. We were alone in the big room and for a moment we looked at each other and somehow we knew each other in that moment.

She was looking surprised, then thoughtful, as I set down the two bottles and the two glasses. I poured her beer and dropped into the low-backed chair next to her.

"Do you know much about people like Pen, Smoky, Buddy, me—the rest of us?"

"Why are you asking, Wild?"

"You know why." That was the way she told me that she, too, had known what that meeting of eyes had meant.

I nodded. "I think I know something about you, Wild." I looked away. "What were these plans?"

"Plans?" She was thinking about things somewhere else, maybe that other dimension her kind of people live in.

"You said you had plans for me and I wouldn't like them."

She looked at me in a new way now, as if she were trying to see me as someone else might see me.

"I have to know a little bit about you first, Jim."

I shrugged. "There's not much. Chicago boy. Drafted two years ago. Sergeant with a line outfit in Korea. Signed up at Monterey Peninsula College when I got out three weeks ago. I'd never seen this part of the country before and it I like it fine. I don't know anybody here, I've got that Ford you saw, and I'm staying at a motel out on Fremont. Anything else?"

"What did you do before you were drafted?"

"Fooled around a little bit with television. I had a low-echelon job with an outfit that made TV films. They folded while I was in the Land of Morning Calm."

"Family?"

"Folks died in a car smash-up six years ago. Relatives in Chicago, nothing else."

"This is an odd question: What kind of drinker are you?"

I laughed. "If they'll sell it and I've got the money to buy it, I'll drink it. Nothing big. Beer mostly."

She nodded. "You look like a nice steady beer drinker. Temper?"

"Not as hot as your sweet man's."

"You're allowed about two strikes. You've just taken one." Her eyes were cool, her lips slightly parted.

"You allow me no strikes. You allow me nothing. I'm going along with your questions and—" I stopped. She had me and I'd been as gawky and obvious as I'd been at sixteen. "Sure. O.K."

"Thanks, Jim. Don't throw rocks at me. This is serious for me."

She reached across the table and took my hand. Hers was strong and warm with long, slender fingers and unpolished, well-groomed nails.

"I'm going to ask you a crazy favor and I think you'll be smart if you say sorry, but you're too busy. One more thing: Do you go the sticks route at all?"

"Sticks? You mean marijuana?"

She nodded.

"No. I saw a little of it in Chicago, a little in Tokyo. Not my style."

"That about does it, Jim. You're what I need, if you'll go."

"What going do I do?"

"Last night my father wired me from New York. He'll be here this evening—flying from New York to San Francisco and then taking a local plane down to Monterey. He's due at the airport about five-twenty."

"So?"

"So he knows I've got a man. He called me long-distance last week at eight o'clock in the morning, New York time."

"That's five here. A touch early."

"Pen answered, all knocked out with sleep. She didn't know who it was and she mumbled just enough so that my father realized I was out somewhere with some boy."

"This did things to him?"

"Not so much. He just wants to see the boy and make sure I'm not with bad people. He realizes I'm twenty-two, I've got a body. I'm somewhat pleasant to know, so a lot of boys and men try their luck with me. Somebody's bound to make out. He knows that."

"What about marriage?" There was a lot of sense to what she had said, but it wasn't the kind of pattern for living much in use back home.

"I like the way I live. I'm no wife now, maybe I'll never be a wife. At this curve in my road I don't see what I can give marriage or marriage can give me."

"Kind of selfish, aren't you, Wild?"

"That wasn't your second strike. Just a pop foul. How about some more beer?"

I walked back to the little room with the bar where the crowd was people I could understand, men with business in the neighborhood, reporters from the *Herald*, girls who worked and were having Martinis on a Saturday afternoon. The barman passed my beers to me and I walked back to Wild. I knew what she wanted me to do and I knew I was going to do it.

Chapter Three

"Why not have him meet Buddy Brown? Are you ashamed of him?" I poured her beer, and it foamed up and over the glass, puddling on the table. We were still alone in the big, quiet room.

She looked up at me. "It's a fair question, Jim. I'm not ashamed of him, but my father will know him. Not his name or who he is. He'll know *what* he is."

I sat down and looked at her sensitive, beautiful face.

"He'll look at him and know him. The kind of guy that has talent and feeling, maybe even has ability, but who buried all that a long time ago. The kind of guy who's a bad drunk, who borrows and cheats for money to live on, who beats up strangers at bars and parties because he's able to whip most men, who always has some woman like me around, most of the time three or four. A guy who likes marijuana, a liar, a useless guy, slightly psycho."

"Your guy," I said.

"My guy now. Not a month ago, maybe not a month from now. Right today, yes."

"And this particular stranger who got beat up by your man—what about me?"

"You're the man I take to my father."

"Why?"

"Why for you, or why for me?"

"Both."

"For me because I'm my father's daughter. I don't want him to feel sorry for me."

"I understand. Some of it, anyway."

"As for you, Jim, you'd be doing me a favor. I know you're going to do it and I know why. There's nothing much I can say about it."

I nodded. "That's it. What do I say to your father?"

"Nothing much. He'll look at you and he'll know pretty close to right what you are. I think he'll like it and he won't be sorry for me."

"So you say. Supposing he's a little annoyed that I've been bundling with his lovely blonde daughter and starts throwing his weight around?"

"No."

"I'll take the chance. And Buddy?"

"If he finds out, he'll think it's very funny."

"Great sense of humor, your Buddy."

She finished her glass of beer.

"Before we go to the airport you'd better fill me in. How long have we been playing house?"

She pressed her lips. "Three weeks."

"I met you the night I left Fort Ord, then, a free man. Where?"

"Mission Ranch."

"O.K. I know the place. And why did you go for me?"

"I liked you."

"What are our plans together?"

She shook her head. "My father won't ask that."

"Who or what is your father, by the way?"

"He's just a man. Office in New York. Our home is in Westport. Divorced my mother years ago. She's been in Europe most of the time. He has quite a lot of money."

It was a quarter to five. "Let's go," I said.

We walked to the gray car and got in. She handled it as if she loved it. It was all smooth, all gliding, all with power and speed. She was a gentleman behind the wheel, but a gentleman who was sure and confident. The heavy traffic on the road to the airport meant nothing to her and the gray car.

We didn't talk. I was conscious of her being there and my nerves were hot wires; this wouldn't be something to write off as a mixed-up afternoon. The smooth arms as she held the wheel, the ripple as she moved them, the long legs riding the pedals.

We were twenty minutes early at the airport and it was good. Somehow we found a cool closeness over a table in the airport café. Coffee and talk.

We talked about a book we'd both read a couple of years back, *The Catcher in the Rye*. We both loved it. And *The Caine Mutiny*.

Pictures. Both of us were solid for Alec Guinness, and we liked swimming, walking just to walk, riding. She could ski, I wanted to.

That kind of talk.

It was fine and I could feel what it was doing to me. I find the girl who looks and acts the way I've always wanted the girl to look and act, then I find she's a girl who enjoys life the way I do. What more? She's Wild Kearny and she's in love with Buddy Brown and I'm going to meet her father in a couple of minutes, because his plane is circling in now, and pretend to be the boy she's been living with.

We walked out to meet him. The ship came in smoothly, taxied around, and came to a stop about fifty feet from us.

He was the first man out. Wild said, "Father," as he stepped out on the stairs.

We stood there and watched him come toward us, Wild holding my hand. He was a big man and he looked like an important man, from the way he carried himself and the kind of clothes he wore.

I recognized him just before he reached us. His picture has been in *Time* and *True* had run a story on him. It was easy to understand what Wild had meant when she'd said her father wouldn't feel sorry for her if he met me instead of Buddy Brown. It was also easy to understand how much of a jam Wild had set up for me. Her father was Broadway Red Kearny.

Red hair mixed with iron gray. Six feet two, 220 pounds, with the broadest shoulders I have ever seen. Red face and ice-blue eyes. Broadway Red Kearny.

Wild loved him, you could see that. She threw her arms around him and stretched up for a kiss. There were a few moments when father and daughter were alone and there was no one else in all the world. Then he turned away from her to me and they were individuals again, the lovely girl with the tiger-gold hair and the big man with the ice-blue eyes, Wild Kearny and Broadway Red Kearny.

He had once killed two of Joe Adonis's troopers in a Fifty-second Street night club. He was acquitted because two hoods had had their guns and Broadway Red had had only his bare hands.

The ice-blue eyes met mine, and it was like picking up a bare 220-volt lead. You felt the vitality and the power of this big man, his knowledge and judgment of men, his ruthlessness, his justice. He didn't hold out his hand to me; we looked at each other.

True magazine had told of how Broadway Red had once knocked down big Jimmy Dorich in a sudden flare of anger one night at Toots Shor's. That was when Jimmy was the toughest detective on the Broadway beat and a tough man in a fight. They shook hands five minutes later.

The big man didn't make up his mind about me. I wasn't in, nor was

I out. He wasn't sure about the man his daughter had brought to the airport, a kind of ordinary guy but one whose eyes had met and held his. We both looked at Wild at the same time.

"Is this your boy, Wild?" he asked. His voice was soft and deep.

Now it was Wild who felt the pressure, and I knew that she had not told many lies to this big, soft-voiced man who loved her. She was going to tell one now and she despised herself.

"This is Jim Work," she said, and the lie was unspoken but there.

"My name is Kearny, Work, and that's the way we'll talk to each other."

"Right, Kearny," I said.

Broadway Red, last of the big gamblers, straight, smart, tough. He was not in the Syndicate, but the little rats of the Big Combination scuttled when he came by, because he had his troops too, fast, merciless gunmen from the dockworkers' local that he controlled, the local that he had built when he was a brawling longshoreman thirty years before. Most trouble Broadway Red could handle with his powerful hands, but the rats knew that if anyone dared cut down Broadway Red, his boys would hunt the lords of the Syndicate and slaughter them, in East New York, along the West Side, in Brownsville and Miami, in Las Vegas and Beverly Hills. The writer in the magazine had shown a respect for the man that you seldom find for any man, who walks today on Broadway or across on Fifty-second.

"You feel like eating?" he asked. "I think I could chew on a live wolf right now."

"Steak, Red?" said Wild.

"Is there any other kind of food proper for men?"

"Let's go to the Hearthstone, Jim," she said, and she couldn't meet my eyes as she spoke to me. I hoped her father didn't notice.

The three of us got into the Healey, and it was a tight squeeze. I was against Broadway Red's biceps and they were big and rock-hard. This was a lot of man.

It was getting dark and the bright warmth of the day was gone when Wild parked the car on the main street of Carmel. We walked to the Hearthstone, a simple, pleasant place where they have good, big charcoal-broiled steaks.

As we followed the host to our table, I saw the other diners turn to look at Kearny. Ordinarily both men and women would have turned to look at the blonde perfection of Wild, but with her father there they looked at him and wondered who he was. He was used to the turning heads; he walked with a curious softness and a gentleness.

It was sirloin for Wild and me, porterhouse for Broadway Red. After the steaks he ordered brandy, and it was over the brandy that he talked to us.

"You're a grown woman, Wild." There was a sudden flash of rebellion across her face and I thought I could understand a little of this father and his daughter. She loved and idolized this man, but she had to find her own love in a man, a man who could somehow humble and defeat the power of her father. In some perverse, night-haunted way, this might have led her to the lean evil of Buddy Brown.

"You're a grown woman," he repeated, "and right now you're fine and pretty and full of pride."

He took two cigars from his coat pocket and offered me one. They were cased in aluminum with no brand name, probably his own specials. I lit his with my lighter and I noticed him glance at the regimental crest on it. We both sent out clouds of blue smoke, and Wild sipped her brandy.

"You've seen some of the girls at Palm Beach, up in Maine during the summer, around midtown New York," he went on, and there was still a touch of brogue in his speech. He was talking to Wild, but he wanted me to listen, too. "The beautiful girls a few years older than you are now. You've seen them, and you must have noticed the little lines, the little hardness in their eyes, the meanness around their mouths."

He took a drink of brandy.

"I've been watching the lovely girls change for many, many years, and it's not a pretty sight. They're fresh and fine like you now, and then, little by little, they're neither fresh nor fine any more. You've seen them, Wild, and you know what I mean.

"I don't want that to happen to you. I'd rather see you get big and fat, with round arms and red hands, like my mother, and have the look on your face my mother had. Life was a good thing to her, hard but good. Not the emptiness that these girls know. I don't want to see your eyes get so hard they don't see any good in things any more."

Wild was watching him and I could see that she knew what he meant.

"You've got everything in your hands now, and it can all turn to sand on you and run through your fingers before you even know it. Maybe I'm going to be making a mistake now, but at least it will be an honest mistake.

"This man has been good enough for you to want, and I don't blame him for wanting you. Good or bad, strong or weak, you've given him the one thing that only you could give him. Maybe there've been others, maybe you're cursed with hot blood like your Aunt Kitty, I don't know and I pray not. But now you're old enough and smart enough to pick your man, and you've picked him. So you're going to be married to him." Wild and I looked at each other. He watched us with those ice-blue eyes.

"I'll give you nothing but my blessings. A young man and a young woman should want nothing more than each other and what they can make of life together, and that's the way it'll be for you two. I'll give you no money. If the young man wants a job, I'll see that he gets one fitting his abilities and no more.

"If you love each other and do well together, if the Lord sends you children and you're happy, in a year or two I'll make it different. Then you'll have the best and lots of the best because I'll know you deserve it. Not until then.

"But married you'll be, and by a priest, and as soon as I can arrange it, which will be soon indeed. You're not Catholic, are you, Work?"

"No, Kearny, I'm not."

"D'you have any objection to being married within the Catholic Church, assuming of course that we can satisfy the priest as to the rightness of it?"

I had several choices. I could explain the truth and that would be the end of that, not only for Wild and me, but maybe for Wild and her father. I could keep on pretending to be Wild's man and try to wiggle out of this sudden marriage. I could go along with Broadway Red and marry his daughter.

I looked at Wild again and tried to guess what decision she was making. We had met each other less than four hours ago.

Somewhere, probably not far away, was Buddy Brown.

Chapter Four

"I've already asked your daughter to marry me," I said quietly. Odd, I had a quick picture of a junior-college football game—me with the ball and three big mugs from the other team converging on me. I had tossed a lateral. This time the lateral was to Wild Kearny.

The big man's eyes were hard on me, deep into me. Inside of me, somewhere, I must have been telling more truth than lie, because he was satisfied.

"That's a good thing to hear, Jim," he said, and then he looked at his daughter.

"And I will have none of it." Wild's voice was low. "I am a grown woman, as you say. When I give the vows of marriage it will be because

I mean them, because I want to give them."

"You don't want to marry Jim?"

"Every girl adds up a column of mistakes," she answered, her clear eyes looking into his, "and I'd rather have a lot of little mistakes than one big one."

His voice was softer than ever now and the brogue was stronger, and these were signs of anger. "They weren't big mistakes that turned those pretty girls' mouths and eyes hard and mean, it was year after year of little mistakes. You'll marry Jim Work and that's the end of it. You'll be a good wife or you'll be no daughter of mine!"

"I'm the man," I said, "and as the man I've got something to say. When Wild wants me, we'll be married. Not before."

His big hand closed on my wrist. There was iron strength there.

"And until then you'll toss her on her bottom, and afterward you'll tip your hat and be on your way whistlin'. Is that the way of it?"

Wild stood up, and she was as angry as Broadway Red.

"Here are the keys to the car you gave me for my birthday. You've forgotten it was my twenty-first, I think. As for your money, I don't want it. As for your advice, I don't need it. Go back to New York, where you can boss people around. You won't boss me!" The keys hit the table and she strode out of the restaurant.

We watched her go, each of us with his own thoughts. His fingers left my wrist. "That's the way of it," he said.

We were silent, and then he said, "Who's been working on your face, Jim?"

"I had a fight."

"Win?"

"Lost."

He didn't say anything, but I don't think he'd lost many fights in his fifty years. Not by anybody's rules. "What will we do about our girl, Jim?"

"We'll work it out. Wild and I."

"It won't be like that." The soft voice had power in it now, not loud, not hurried. "I came here to see her married. Either that or break the neck of her man."

His hands were before me, open, the fingers ready. They were well manicured, but still the stubby fingers of a longshoreman, a bare-fist fighter, a killer.

"If he hadn't been a man, if he hadn't the right stuff in him— But no matter. I'm satisfied with you. I'll take the two of you to the church and then you'll be on your own. If you do well I'll see that you do better."

The big fists closed again on my wrists.

"Now we'll go out and find her, and if I have to I'll carry her under my arm to the wedding, but a wedding there'll be. If you give me trouble, I'll give you the back of my hand till the teeth fly out of your mouth."

I put a twenty on the waiter's plate. It was one of my last six twenties but I wanted to pay this tab. Not to impress Kearny. Those weren't the things that meant anything to him. I just wanted to pay this one.

"What do you do, boy?"

"Three weeks out of the Army. Korea."

"An officer?"

"A sergeant."

He nodded. "And what kind of a sergeant, Jim?"

"Line outfit. Infantry. Nothing fancy."

"What are you going to do?"

"Go to college here. It's a good chance to go."

I was reckless, angry, ashamed. Lying to this proud, red bear of a man, pretending something that I wanted to be true, and knowing there was nothing there.

The waiter brought the change. I left a couple of bucks, and we got up.

"You're sullen, boy. Why?"

I looked at him, looked into the cold ice-blue eyes.

"You're Broadway Red Kearny," I said. "You're big, tough, and rich. I'm not big, not tough, not rich. My name's Jim Work and I stopped taking orders three weeks ago."

He chuckled. "And more power to you. In everything except this marriage. Here are the keys to her car. Let's find her."

Outside I fumbled around a little and then got it started.

It was quite a feeling to drive the gray car. It felt different than any car I'd ever driven before, lighter, surer, quicker. Wild must have been plenty angry to toss the keys to it back to her father.

I had a fair idea of where the Zoo was, but only a fair idea. Carmel is full of private village jokes—no street numbers, no street lights. I'd have to poke around up and down the black streets until I found the right little vine-covered cottage in a good-sized town made up of hundreds of vine-covered cottages.

After five minutes or so Broadway Red asked, "Where are you going, lad?"

"Wild's house. It's around here somewhere."

"Boy, stop the car." There was something to the big man's voice that made you decide not to argue. I swung the car over to the side of the road.

"Why have you been lying to me?"

I didn't say anything.

"You didn't know how to start her car. You aren't sure of where she lives. You've acted like a stranger in a family quarrel. You're not the boy she's been fooling with, are you?"

"No, I'm not. I met her this afternoon." That felt right. You don't like to lie or act a lie to men like Broadway Red Kearny.

Now he was silent for a long time. I felt sorry for the big guy.

"Who is the fellow? Do you know him?"

"I've met him."

"Why did you pretend to be him?"

"I just sort of got into it."

"She asked you to do it."

I didn't say anything. There are two kinds of relationships that are strong. One is the thing I had for Wild Kearny, and there's a loyalty, a pride, and an understanding in it. Or there should be. The other is one between men as men, and I could feel that with Broadway Red Kearny. Not exactly friendship, we weren't friends. Maybe a dignity, something that has to be honest and straight or you feel that you're cheating and weak. "Why did she?" His voice was soft, very low. "Why did you say you'd asked her?"

"I'm not sure."

"Something wrong with this man of hers?"

"I don't know."

"Do you think you can find her place?"

"I'll try."

About two minutes later the headlights picked out a driveway, then gleamed over my Ford. The Jaguar was gone but the MG was there. I pulled up behind it, turned off the ignition, and handed the keys to Kearny.

"That's my car there. Nice to have met you. See you around." I got out.

"Jim." The big man climbed out of the Nash-Healey.

"Yes?"

"Running out?"

"I never was in."

"I see. All right, Work." I had liked having him call me "Jim."

And I was still in this on a double count. I wanted to tangle with Buddy again. And I had a feeling about Wild that wasn't quite being in love with her, the way diving off the high board isn't quite being in the water— but you can see it in front of you, coming up fast.

"Probably nobody in there wants to see me, but I'll go in with you,"

I said.

"As you say, Jim."

I led the way down the three stone steps and pushed open the door. There was a record playing. Gerry Mulligan maybe.

Buddy Brown was holding Wild in his arms. Her head was back, her body tight to his. If we had come a few minutes later it might have been a little rough on everybody. It was plenty rough on me just the way it was. There was no sense to my wild blaze of jealousy, but sense had nothing to do with it.

Wild must have taken a cab and come straight here and Buddy must have been waiting for her. They heard Kearny close the door and they turned to look at us.

I wanted to say, "Hello punk," to Buddy, to try him again, right there and then. But up behind my eyes something was saying, play it cool. You'll look like a jerk and he'll probably take you in three punches.

I said, "Hello, Wild. Hello, punk."

"What did you do? Bring your old man?" Then he sensed the tension between the girl and the big man. "Oh, wrong old man. Hi there, Red."

Kearny walked across the floor and hit Buddy Brown in the face. The tall, thin boy crashed back into a chair, toppling it over, and rolled to the floor.

"You'll call me Mr. Kearny when you speak to me."

Wild looked at her father for one blazing second and then she went to Buddy. He was trying to get up and blood was spurting out of his nose, trickling from his mouth.

He made it up but he was shaky. He took the white handkerchief from his breast pocket and wiped at his face, pushing Wild away from him with his left hand.

"All right, slugger, all right," he said thickly. Wild dropped her hands to her sides and stood there. The room was a kind of stage now with three of us standing there, Kearny, Wild, Work, and the spotlight on the tall, pale-faced boy wiping the blood from his face. Buddy Brown had that trick of being the center, the one the rest watched.

The Gerry Mulligan record ended, the player buzzed, and it was the old Artie Shaw again.

Buddy Brown straightened his shoulders, crumpled the bloody handkerchief into a ball, and threw it into the fireplace. Then he walked by Kearny and me, up the three steps, and into the darkness outside. Wild watched him go, her hands still at her sides.

None of us said anything. We heard the whir of the MG's starter and the rustle as its tires spun on the gravel and dirt.

"That was your man?" Kearny asked.

"Yes."

"I'll go now," I said. Nobody answered. I felt awkward and stiff-legged as I turned and left the room.

I closed the front door behind me, walked over to my Ford, got in, and started it. I backed it down the dark driveway, curving around the Nash-Healey, and drove out into the street. The MG was parked there, its motor running. I recognized it in the blackness by its headlights, low and close together.

I straightened out the Ford and headed toward the road to Monterey. The MG followed. That was fine with me.

Chapter Five

Saturday-night traffic was a river of light over the hill and down to Monterey. I would have looked back over the whole crazy afternoon and evening, picked over the jagged pieces, but they scattered in my mind because what I was thinking about was the man following me.

I didn't try to lose him but he took no chances. The close, low lights of the MG were never more than twenty yards behind me, sometimes as close as five. I turned off Munras and went down Tyler to the Mission Inn. The MG pulled up to the curb along the now nearly empty street barely twenty feet from where I parked.

He was waiting for me when I got out of my Ford.

"Don't shoot, boy," he said to me. "I want to kiss and make up."

"So?" We were alone on the dim street. The Mission Inn was bright enough, but the doorway to the bar was solid and the only light came from three portholes in it.

"I lost a one-punch hassle back there. You're probably satisfied, and I want to talk to you."

If I told Buddy Brown that I didn't want to talk to him I'd sound like a sulking kid. If I swung on him I'd be in a street fight and not at all sure what I was fighting for. Those were the only choices that occurred to me.

I said, "Why?"

"You came back with that overage slugger."

"Yeah?"

"I want to talk to you about Wild." He held out his hand. "Let's have a drink."

I didn't take his hand but I pushed open the heavy door that led to the little barroom of the Mission Inn and held it for him. He went through and I followed.

Henry, the evening barman, looked up as we came in, and after a moment he smiled a little. I knew Henry slightly from visits during the past three weeks; he was a very sharp and observant guy.

"Third round over?" he asked. He was a beach-browned man who looked much like a Spanish nobleman. I didn't understand the "third round" thing until I saw Brown's face. His mouth was swollen, and so was mine. Both of us looked a little beat up. Both of us were.

"Beer here, Henry. You?" I looked at Buddy.

He nodded. "Roll you for them," he said, reaching for two dice boxes.

We rolled and I won. Brown paid for the two beers, reaching into his pocket and pulling out a few bills, mostly fives, wadded together.

"Let's sit back where it's quiet," he said.

I was a little curious about Brown's sudden interest in me, and though the two of us were apparently natural-born enemies, the kind of men who fight on sight, I took my bottle and glass into the big room where Wild and I had sat hours earlier. It wasn't empty now. A fair man and a big, handsome dark-haired woman were drinking highballs at one table, at another a very fat sergeant was smoking a pipe and playing chess with a harassed-looking middle-aged man who had a big nose and shell-framed glasses.

"Now what?" I said to Buddy when we were seated at a table in the corner.

"You met Wild for the first time today? When we tangled cars?"

I nodded.

"But you knew Broadway Red before?"

"No."

His eyes were black, bright, and hard in his white face. He didn't believe me.

"Does he know she's hooked?"

I looked at him. I knew what he meant, but I didn't believe it of Wild Kearny. Not that clear-eyed, proud girl. He bent toward me, sitting loose in his chair, a lanky, long-boned, sinewy man, his swollen mouth still twisted into a mocking half-smile.

"I don't believe it."

"Do you think I'm hooked?"

I looked into his shining eyes, at his white face, at his hands.

"No. I've seen men on heroin and morphine. Not many, but some. You're not on that stuff. Marijuana, sure, but nothing that would hook you."

"You're real smart."

As long as the two of us were within sight of each other, we were set to go. I had to let him move first, but I hated it, because his first move would be something I might not expect, maybe a beer bottle in my face. I was tense and my hands were cold again.

"I'm trying to find out if you know Broadway Red or not. You say not, and probably you're a real honest boy. But still—Broadway Red is a little bit important to me."

We looked at each other. It's a hard thing to say you want to kill a man, but I've killed men—strangers in quilted uniforms in the early mist on the Punchbowl ridges; killed two carefully and slowly with my M1, killed one in a panic fight, smashing his skull with the butt of my M1. I wanted to kill Buddy Brown and I was angry with knowing that he didn't care one way or the other about me. He might kill me, but not because he hated me more than any other man. He didn't, and the burden of hatred was all mine.

"You don't know Broadway Red at all, maybe you've never been to New York, stuff like that?" Buddy asked again, spinning his glass between his slender fingers.

I looked across the table into his mocking face. "This has been a goof-off afternoon for me. From the time you cut in front of me in Carmel to right now it's been goof-off. You want to talk, Buddy, let's talk. You don't want to talk, then let's go back in the alley and try it again. O.K. with you?"

He lit a cigarette before he answered. "You're a real hairpin, boy. Always willing. I like that about you. But I don't want to fight you. I'm your friend. Like a fraternity brother. You just keep calling me Buddy, because that's what I am—your buddy, buddy."

This was the man who had Wild. This was the man she was ashamed to show to her father because she knew that Broadway Red would pity her, seeing Buddy Brown.

"Let's talk like a couple of friends," Buddy went on. "About music. Maybe you like Dixieland. You're probably a real Dixieland fiend. Or maybe we can talk about sports cars, and you can tell me how you're saving up to buy a Jag or a Riley. But then, you're probably a Cadillac man. Then we can get down to talking about women. You like blonde girls, kind of tall? Maybe you're saving up to get a blonde girl. Let me give you the word, don't bother. I've got some spares, I'll loan you one. I'm your buddy."

"Broadway Red get you kind of mad, Buddy?"

He waited a moment or two. "That's right. It upsets me to have some old gentleman give me a Sunday punch in front of you and the blonde. It upsets me so much that I'm probably not very good company, am I boy?"

"You're a punk."

"You keep calling me that, boy, but you don't stand up to it very good. I'll tell you something. I'm going to make you crawl across the dirt to me begging me not to hurt you any more. Crawling and begging. Can you see it? Is it a picture to you?"

"Let's go back to the alley."

He laughed. His left hand snaked across the table and he had the second finger of my right hand in his fist, bending it back, holding my palm hard against the table. His right hand thrust his cigarette toward my eyes and I ducked my head back. Still torturing my finger with his left hand hard on my right, he moved up like a cat and his fingers laced into my short hair. He pulled my head way back and I tried to reach him with my left hand. He let go and clipped me across the throat with the side of his right hand. A hard clip on the Adam's apple.

It was all pain. I couldn't breathe. I couldn't move. I was in the chair, my head hanging forward, loose, holding myself up on my elbows. I could see the puddles of beer on the tabletop, I could feel the frantic pounding of my heart.

Maybe nobody noticed. It happened inside of ten seconds. I was sick and weak, knowing only the ultimate desperation of trying to get air through my paralyzed throat to my lungs.

He didn't say anything until he thought I could hear him again. Then he said, "You're probably a good man, a real good man, fighting boys like yourself. Don't feel bad. You don't have it, that's all. In about five minutes you'll be able to talk again. Then we'll talk about Broadway Red, where you met him, how well you know him. Then we'll talk about Wild, about how she's crazy about me. Then we'll go to some quiet place and I'll work you over until you crawl to me. Then we'll say good-by and that will be the end of our friendship. You can write to me if you want to."

I was there in the chair, my head hanging forward, the pain easing a little.

Somebody had walked up to the table.

"Is your friend all right?" It sounded like Henry's voice.

"He choked on something. Swallowed his beer wrong."

"You all right?" It was Henry. I tried to look up at him. I nodded.

He stood there a moment, uncertain, and then he walked away.

Buddy Brown spoke to me softly. "Probably now you're thinking about getting a gun or a knife, or jumping me from behind. Think nice thoughts, boy. After I'm through with you you won't think about those things. Just hearing my name will make you cry and try to hide. Do you know why I'm going to do that to you?"

I was able to lift my head now. I looked at him.

"Because you like to call me a punk."

This was a nightmare worse than any lonely night in the quiet, deadly darkness of Korea. I was all hate and anger, sick and weak; he was talking to me in a low voice and laughing at me.

"You won't get rid of me tonight, boy. I'll be with you until I'm through with you. You want to ask the police for help, boy? Something like that? Are you scared, boy?"

This snake-quick sadist had me. Three times today he'd taken me, knocked me down, kicked me, hurt me. I had forgotten Wild now, forgotten everything except the hate and the fear that were like bitter ice in my blood.

"You're not one of Broadway Red's people. You're not tough enough or smart enough." Buddy had brought his face close to mine. "But you met him somewhere tonight and brought him to Wild's house. What is he on the Coast for? Where is he staying?"

The glittering eyes were deadly intent now.

I guessed that Wild had told him nothing of her father. He hadn't known that Kearny was flying west. Yet he had recognized him almost at once and now he wanted information. Information about a man who had deadly enemies.

The first time I tried to say something there was no voice at all and my throat tightened with a sudden aching. After half a minute I tried again, and produced only a hoarse squawk. I didn't have anything to say, anyway. All I wanted to do was get out of there, away from Buddy Brown.

There was a sound of quick steps across the wooden floor.

"Hello, Buddy. Buy me a drink?"

I turned and saw Pen Brooks.

"Hi, kid. How'd you find me?"

"I saw your car and I peeked in the window."

"Great." Buddy smiled. "We're busy. Take off."

Pen Brooks pushed back the empty chair at the table and sat in it. She was a pretty girl, not striking but with good eyes, a good mouth, a good body. Some nice family's nice daughter, a Pasadena kind of girl.

"I said take off, Brooks." Buddy was still smiling.

Pen looked at me. "Oh, hello. I thought you two were feuding and making muscles at each other." Then she looked at Buddy. Then hungry desperation was pitifully open. "I've been looking all over for you."

"Did you just come from the Zoo?"

"A little while ago. Then I drove around Carmel looking for your car. I tried Monterey and there it was. You'd be surprised how far away I can spot your car, Buddy."

"Who was at the Zoo?"

"Wild."

"Who else?"

Pen Brooks hesitated. "Her father."

"You knew he was coming. Why didn't you tell me?"

The snarl and the smile were both there now.

"We haven't been together in three days, Buddy."

"You should have told me this afternoon."

"Wild asked me not to tell you."

Her hands were across the table on his wrists, the fingers grasping at him. She was either a little drunk or high on marijuana.

"Listen, Brooks, go out and pick up some boy somewhere. If he isn't sure you're worth the price of a motel, have him call me and I'll tell him you're great. Now get out of here."

"Buddy." Pen Brooks's mouth was imploring. "Buddy, I'll meet you somewhere later. Anywhere. I've got plenty of money, Buddy. Please."

A pretty girl from a nice family. This afternoon at the Zoo with the three boys she had looked so right, as if she found the world a pleasant place of young men who drove Jaguars and played good golf and liked Gerry Mulligan records and drank beer and eventually married nice, pretty girls.

"Get out of here, bum, or I'll throw you out." Buddy was still smiling.

Pen looked at me. She laughed, pretending to me, to Buddy, to herself, that this was all fun, boy-and-girl insults given in laughing sophistication.

She got up. "Well, if you won't buy me a drink, where'll you be later, Buddy? Mission Ranch, maybe?"

"Get out of here, bum."

She smiled and walked out, head high.

Chapter Six

"You told that cop today that you'd been a soldier. Just got back from Korea." Brown lit another cigarette. I watched him, trying to gauge the strength that was coming back slowly to my body as the ache in my throat eased. This was strange—to know that I'd met the man that was the final one to me, the one you killed or died trying to kill. Met him the same day that I'd met the girl I wanted for the rest of my life. I wondered if he had called her "bum"—yet.

"When you were in Korea you probably thought lots about women. You're young and healthy, no girls around much over there, you probably thought lots about them. Too bad I didn't know you so I could write you letters and send you pictures. Now tell me about Broadway Red."

I stood up.

"Sit down, boy."

I knew I wasn't ready to try Buddy Brown yet. A hard blow to the throat is a bad one to take, paralyzing, strangling, and you don't come out of it quickly. I walked through the door to the smaller room, still alive with talk and laughter. There were half a dozen men at the bar. Henry glanced up at me; he had the good barman's intuition about people and he had known that things weren't right. I sat on a stool.

"Brandy."

His eyebrows flickered. "Any trouble?"

"No trouble, Henry."

He poured the brandy and set the glass before me. His eyes looked beyond me, through the door to the larger room. I didn't turn around. Brown didn't follow me.

"Pardon me, but didn't we meet this afternoon?" There were two empty stools to my right and then on the last one was the boy from the Zoo, the one in the turtle-neck sweater who had helped me after Brown had worked me over back of the house. The whole damned afternoon and evening seemed to be Brown working me over.

"Yeah, you're Pete. Right?" I said. He smiled and slid over the two stools.

"I didn't mean to seem brutal this afternoon. After that fight, I mean."

"That's all right. You helped me enough." I looked at him. He was wearing a dark blue jacket now, and narrow bow tie.

"You're Jim…."

"Jim Work."

"And I'm Pete Barrow."

"Glad to meet you again." We shook hands.

"Sorry about that fellow Brown. He's a lot of fun, but he's got a nasty temper."

"Yeah."

"He's not really one of our crowd."

"No?"

"Wild met him a few weeks ago. He seems to have a fascination for women."

"Sure does." I looked around, bent over to get a better view into the big room. Buddy Brown was gone.

"Wild's a fine girl." He ordered another round of the same for each of us.

"I don't know her well," I said. "I'll roll you for the drinks."

"Fine."

We rolled the dice and I won.

"Pen Brooks is a fine girl." Pete's conversation seemed somewhat limited.

"She was in here a while back," I said.

"Where?" The smooth pleasantness of his good-looking face rippled for a moment.

"Back in the big room. Brown was there, too."

"With you?" He had slipped off the stool to look into the other room.

"In a way."

"They're not there now," he said. "Were you all together?"

"She just stopped by. I don't know what happened to Brown."

"Oh." He seemed to turn over his own thoughts for a while. "Pen and I are engaged."

This time I said, "Oh." He hadn't been more than twenty feet away, on the other side of the wall, when Pen Brooks had been there. "Didn't you notice Brown's MG outside?"

"This place is crawling with MG's," Pete answered. "How long ago was Pen here?"

"Ten minutes, maybe."

"Darn." He was the kind of guy who said darn. "This is the first Saturday night in weeks that Pen and I haven't had a date. She said she was going to stay at the Zoo and do some work."

"Work?"

"She's an artist. Wants to be, anyway."

"She said something about going to the Mission Ranch." It was none of my business, and when I'd said it I regretted it, but I'd been thinking about other things.

"Just by herself?" He seemed shocked.

"I don't know. Maybe she was talking about some other time."

"She's been terribly restless these last few days."

"Who is this Buddy Brown?" I asked.

Barrow shrugged. "Wild met him and brought him around. He's from Los Angeles, that's about all I know. Maybe his folks have money, but he doesn't seem quite like that. He's just around—a little golf, sports-car rallies, those things. Wild seems to like him. The rest of us take him because of her, I think."

"And Wild herself—who is she?"

His carefully tended caste consciousness buzzed on that one. Young men like Pete Barrow talk about women only to their friends. He might unbend a way to me, but he'd already set up all the friends he'd ever have, back at prep school or at Santa Barbara or at Bar Harbor and Mount Desert.

"She's from the East. Very nice girl."

That would be it from Pete Barrow. It looked to me as if Buddy had taken Pete's girl away just for practice, the way a guy like Buddy Brown will do, and apparently Pete hadn't noticed at all.

"Our crowd isn't too happy with this fellow Brown," Pete said. "He really isn't one of us. Pen wasn't with him, you say?"

"No. She just dropped by."

I wondered if Brown were waiting for me outside. He wasn't going to let me go tonight, I knew that. There was a mutual hatred between us that was extraordinary. I'd never felt that I would have to kill a man until tonight, and now, away from the guy, the feeling seemed childish and crazy. But I knew that when we saw each other again it wouldn't seem childish or crazy.

"I'll be moving on," I said to Pete.

"Good to have seen you."

I walked outside. The MG was gone. I opened the door of my Ford and she stepped out of a doorway that led to the hotel part of the Mission Inn. Pen Brooks, hurrying across the sidewalk to me, taking my arm.

"Could I talk to you?"

"Pete Barrow is in the bar there."

"Lord." She lifted her head, looking up at me. "Would you take me somewhere, anywhere, and talk to me a little bit? Please?"

"Sure. Get in."

She slid into the front seat and I walked around to the other side, got in, and started the engine. As I pulled away from the curb Pete Barrow opened the door of the bar and stood there looking at his girl and me driving away.

"I sounded pretty awful back there, didn't I?" said Pen. Somehow I had the feeling that she found a strange pride in this self-torture of hers. She hadn't seen Pete standing in the doorway, looking at us.

I shook my head. "Where to?"

"Anyplace. I don't want a drink. I need somebody to talk to. I don't have anybody that I can talk to. Not anybody."

The car rounded the corner to the Carmel road. "You know a lot of people. Why me?"

"Can you explain Buddy to me? Can you?"

"What's to explain?"

"You came to the Zoo this afternoon. You and Wild and Buddy. You know about me? I'm Wild's best friend. I'm engaged to Pete. Know something else? I'm crazy about Buddy. Could you tell that Wild wasn't the only girl there this afternoon that was having a big thing with Buddy?"

"It's your life."

"Not any more. When a girl once knows Buddy, really knows him, she's like a slave. Wild pretends that she isn't, but I know better. Why is it, tell me, why is it?"

Her hand was hot on mine, dry and hot, and I could feel the nerves that made her fingers tighten in spasms.

"You tell me what he's got," I said. "You know."

"He takes off the mask. He tears off your mask. Maybe you look smug, or pretty, or cool. It's a mask. He knows it, and then you're there, and your face isn't pretty any more, or cool, or smug. Maybe you're beautiful, if passion is beautiful, but there's nothing left for you to hide behind."

It was horrible and I knew it was true.

"Nothing's really changed. I know what he is. I don't have stupid, silly plans of changing the guy. He's cruel and rotten. I love him."

"Wild talks that way too, a little. She doesn't say anything about love, though."

"She's talked to you about Buddy? What did she say?"

I was climbing the long hill to Carmel now. "The hell with it," I said. "Both of you are fascinated by a punk and you make a big thing out of it. Women have been going for his kind for a hell of a long time. Your story is no different from any of the others."

"You don't understand. I've got to do something about this tonight."

"Why?"

"I can't stand it. I've got to break off with Pete. I have to find someplace where Buddy will meet me. I don't care if he has other women."

"Why didn't you go with him in the MG instead of waiting around for me tonight?"

"Because he wouldn't let me."

"So you decided to pounce on me and make me listen to your soap-opera romance?"

"You know him. You were with him. You could tell me what to do."

"Drown yourself."

"You're a smart character, aren't you?"

"I'm sorry. It's just that you can't get me wound up about your mad passion for Brown. He and I don't get along."

"You're a little bit like him. More than Pete or the other men I know."

"Thanks."

I made the right turn to Ocean Avenue, Carmel's main street.

"Where can I drop you?" I asked. Pen Brooks had seemed like such a pretty, easygoing girl this afternoon, drinking beer and listening to records. Now she was just that worst of all nuisances, a girl telling you what a heel the guy she loves is and how much she loves him.

"Do you know where Buddy was going?"

"No, but I can tell you where Pete Barrow is."

"Where?"

"About fifty feet behind us in his Jaguar."

"Lord."

"Suppose I pull over to the curb and let you ride with him. You've got more to talk with him about than you do with me."

"Oh, Lord." Her vocabulary was a little limited. I edged over to the curb and stopped. The low, sleek Jaguar pulled up behind me. I got out, Pen stayed in my car. Pete ran up to me.

"What are you doing with Pen?" he asked.

"Turning her over to you."

He was a nice guy and he didn't know how to react. He was angry, hurt, and puzzled, so he swung on me. He was in fine physical shape and big enough, but I'd been pushed around enough for one quiet Saturday, so I stepped in close and gave him the knee. He looked terribly surprised and just for the hell of it I clipped him as he doubled up. He went over backward.

If Pen hadn't slipped in the grass she would have brained me with the heel of her shoe. The first I knew about it was when I turned to go back to the Ford and I saw a white arm in the darkness bringing something down toward my face. I ducked and she slipped. The heel of her shoe, which she was handling like a blackjack, got me on the shoulder instead of in the temple. I slapped her with my open hand and she went back. She came forward again like a fury, swinging the shoe with one hand, clawing for my eyes with the other. I batted her once more and she tumbled across Pete, her legs white in the light of the Jag's headlamps.

I went back to the Ford, feeling a little like Buddy Brown.

Chapter Seven

The fight had happened on a dark, tree-lined street, slanting downhill toward the lights and shops of Ocean Avenue, three blocks away. Other cars had gone by during the flurry but none of them had stopped.

I drove toward the lights.

What did I want? I wanted a girl, and Wild was everything I wanted in a girl. I wanted to straighten myself out about Buddy Brown. Now, away from him and alone, I felt that if I could beat him soft, smash his pale face, that would be enough. Killing a man sounds insane except when the insanity is exploding inside you.

This first afternoon with Wild had been too violent. We could never have the easy growth of love, not any more. I couldn't be the overgrown schoolboy, off to classes, looking forward to a date with his girl in the evening. In three or four years I could maybe think about marriage. Do you marry a girl like Wild Kearny?

I would.

What would she find in me? Not the evil, quick violence of Buddy Brown. Not the smooth certainties of wealth, family, and backround that Pete and the other men had. She wouldn't find very much in Jim Work.

I felt lonely and empty.

I parked my car near the Pine Inn and got out. I didn't want a drink, I didn't want to talk to anybody, and I didn't want to be alone. I thought about going back to Chicago.

I went past the glitter of the shops in the Pine Inn, across the street, and on past the flutter of flames in the window fireplace of the Hearthstone. Then I saw him walking unsteadily toward me. Buddy Brown, drunk. He must have poured it down fast during the hour since I'd seen him.

"H'lo there, boy. 'Member me?" He stood there, rocking a little, his mouth half open. I had him if I wanted him. He was almost helpless.

He stood there on the light-splattered sidewalk, his long, thin body rocking, his mouth half open and wet.

"Take off, punk," I said.

"You're right. I'm a punk. You're so right." He looked at me and there was no mockery in his face.

I started to walk by him. He put a hand on my arm. "Don't go, boy. I have to talk to you."

"Again? You talked to me before." I pushed his hand away.

"This is serious. Dead serious. Gotta talk to you."

"About what?"

"About the mess I'm in."

"You'll always be in a mess. Big man with the babes, big man in a fight, nothing else. Take off. I want no piece of you."

"You fingered me to Red Kearny."

"You're off your rocker."

"He's gonna kill me."

"Great."

"'Strue." His hand was on my arm again, to steady himself and to hold me there. His face looked old and there was no glitter in his eyes. His voice was a soft whisper.

"So he kills you. Who weeps?" I didn't believe any of this. He was half stupid with alcohol.

I walked on down the sidewalk. He stayed with me, weaving, his hand still clutching my jacket.

"You fingered me. Now you save me and I'll give you five thousand bucks."

"You haven't got five thousand. You're crazy drunk, that's all."

"Come a li'l ways with me and I'll show you the five grand. I'll give it to you if you can save me."

"How could I save you?"

"You know Red Kearny. You found me for him. You can get me away."

"You weren't hard to find. You were on a love beat with his daughter."

"That was the big joke. That's what was so funny—until you fingered me for him."

I was beginning to get the idea that somewhere there was some truth to all this. Buddy Brown was drunk, but he was also in a panic of fear.

"You weren't scared when we walked into the Zoo and found you with Wild."

"I didn't recognize him for a second. Then I bluffed. But I've been scared ever since. Scared all the way."

"We'll get some coffee. You need it." I wanted to know what Buddy Brown had to say.

We walked a block. Brown was silent now, still holding to my jacket sleeve. We went into a small café with deep booths, and I ordered a couple of coffees.

"Now what's the deal?" I asked him when the waitress turned away.

He looked down at his cup and then raised his head slowly, looking beyond me.

"I was hunted once, when I was a kid in New York," he said. I waited.

"That was ten years ago. I was fifteen then." He sounded almost sober now, his whispering voice slurred some of the words, but what he was talking about was so real to him that his drunkenness slipped away from him like a heavy, smothering cloak that he had pushed back for a little while.

"Three of us caught the girl at the edge of Central Park. She was with another girl, but we just wanted the one because her guy was the wheel with a big gang down the street. We held her skirt up over her arms and head so she couldn't do nothing but yell, and then we beat her up a little and ran away. We were all laughing when we did it because we were high on sticks, but after a while the sticks wore off.

"We were just punks. We didn't have any loot and we all lived with our folks. Next day we were afraid to go to school or be seen on the street. We knew what was going to happen. The wheel and his gang got Lee—that was one of my friends—at his house. They gave him the business while his old lady was there and his kid brothers and all. They left him alive and that was all they left him. I don't know what happened to him after that, maybe he died. He had nothing left, nothing. You know?"

He looked across the booth at me, his bruised, pale face a little twisted.

"Mick and me, we run off from home. The boys came to my house and worked over my old man to tell where I was. He didn't know, so they gave him the big *schlammin.* He's never going to get over it. They caught Mick downtown somewhere and they took him out on Long Island, tied him up with wire, and burned him. You know, with gasoline. He was a very sharp kid, good dancer, lot of laughs when he was high on sticks. He got burned up."

The slender, drunken boy was talking in his soft whisper, his eyes far away from mine, talking with a clear earnestness as if he were living it all again.

"I've never forgotten that year. I hid down near the produce market, sleeping in the daytime, going out at night to scrounge rotten fruit and stuff. The big rats would be out at night and I'd carry a stick and a sack of rocks. For two months I hid like that. Then it cleared up. The wheel got sent up for armed robbery and the other guys forgot about it. But I remember that year."

He drank his coffee and looked away, beyond the little café in Carmel-by-the-Sea.

"You want to know what happened after that?"

"I'm listening."

"My old man was sick from the beating. He worked in the shipping room at Macy's but after it happened he couldn't work there any more. The family went on relief and they wanted me to work. They got me a job at Macy's, like my old man.

"What kind of clothes can you buy on a deal like that? What can you do at night except hang around the corner and wish you had a buck? What kind of broads can you make out with? So you know what I did? I left them and went out hustling.

"What can I hustle? Who do I know? Nothing and nobody. I went back to the school where I used to go and where I knew the kids, and I hustled sticks—you know, the weed. I made enough bucks for clothes and stuff. It was a big school, maybe five– six thousand kids. Nothing great, but at least I didn't look like a jerk in cheap clothes. I found out if you live right and go along with the big men, you make out good. I never got picked up, I never had any trouble. But I'm eating my heart out all the time. Six years on the hustle and I'm nobody. I live in a hotel on Forty-ninth, I dress fine, I know a million dumb broads, I get to know a little about music and modern stuff, the big acts in show business, good cars, things like that. But I'm nobody.

"I get some real fine-looking broad with class, maybe, and I take her to the Copa. The big men are there and some of them know me. Sure, they know me as a punk hustler doing a two-bit business in weed and they wouldn't even say hello to a punk like me. I don't have it and I know it.

"So I go out to the Coast. L.A. A village, believe me, a village. New York people stand out like diamonds in L.A. I hustle. A million guys are selling weed in Hollywood and it's starvation so I do other things. Girls, mostly. A month ago I make a little score and I'm sick of L.A. so I came up here where I can be with nice people.

"I know how to talk to nice people, I dress right, I drive a right car. Nobody figures me for a punk until you come along and say it. I was going to kill you. Do you know I was going to push you around all night and then maybe kill you? I was going to find out why you fingered me to Red Kearny and what the score was and then work you over like no guy was ever worked over before. That's what I was going to do."

The thick cloak of drunkenness was slipping over him again. The whisper was louder now and he waved his hands while he talked.

"You walked away from me back in that bar. I waited outside and then it struck me. That was Broadway Red Kearny's girl that I'd been making out with, and Kearny would find out who I was—a punk, like you said, a punk. Do you think Kearny's going to let a hustler, a guy who peddles weed to school kids, make out with his daughter? It was like when I was fifteen again, only Kearny isn't just a wheel from a tough gang down the block, he's Red Kearny, and he can find me no matter where I hide. Do you understand, boy?" He half stood up on the other side of the narrow booth. "It's like when I was fifteen again—only worse. Do you understand?" He wasn't wrong. Kearny would kill him if he knew the truth. If he knew the truth, he'd find him no matter where the lean, evil boy hid.

That soft-spoken man I'd met tonight loved his daughter, and he knew the slime of the night world. He wouldn't live with himself until he'd cleansed his daughter by killing the man who had dared bring the slime to her.

Buddy was quieter now. "I didn't know who she was. I was at the Mission Ranch alone. She was dancing, sitting at the bar. I asked her for a dance. They always say yes when I ask them for a dance. I made out like a jet plane with the girl. It was just some more of this top-drawer stuff out here, as far as I knew."

He lit a cigarette, stubbed it out a moment later.

"This Brooks thing. She knows what's with Wild and me, she knows Wild is on the big beat for me. This makes it nothing but easy. Right in front of everybody, when her guy is pouring the drinks and playing the records, I ask her with the smile and the eyes. Bango! She comes whispering the time and the place to me. It was something brand-new to her, too."

He laughed. "They're pigs. All of them. Remember that and you'll make out every time. And then you'll hate them too, buster, you'll hate them."

His eyes were glittering, and he was almost sober again. He lived in a flame of intensity, and alcohol hit him fast, but burned away almost as quickly.

"Forget it," he said, standing up. "Buddy Brown's not afraid of anybody. If you see the old slob, tell him that. Tell him I'm no punk. Understand? I'm no punk."

He walked toward the door. There was somebody waiting for him there. A big man, not so big as Kearny. Brown must have seen the man, and the man must have first noticed Brown in the booth of the bright café.

I got up and paid the check. By now the two were together outside the door.

"Looking for you all over town. What gives?" the stranger was saying. He had immensely wide shoulders. He seemed in his middle fifties, with thick white curly hair.

Brown looked down at the powerfully built man. "It isn't all here, Sandodera. I wouldn't cross you, you know that."

"Yeah, sure, I know." Sandodera chuckled. "All your life you cross people. You crossed your own mother. You know how? By being born."

His laugh sounded jovial until you saw his eyes.

Brown noticed me in the door. "Let's get away from here. The place is crawling with crumb-bum squares."

Sandodera sent one quick look at me.

"You just stumbled into the deal back there, buster, and you've taken some pushing. You don't belong with the sharp people. Come on, Joe." Brown had spoken to me, then taken the heavy man by his thick arm.

I watched them walk into the darkness.

This time I was able to find the Zoo in the lacing of dark hill streets. I was going back there because of what Buddy had said: "You just stumbled into the deal." He was right, I didn't belong in the deal. I wasn't a hard, smart guy who could work for Broadway Red, I wasn't a guy with three generations of rich family and all the right stuff like Pete and the others, I wasn't a guy who could make out with Wild Kearny the night he met her. I had the feeling of the other dimension again; I had stumbled into a world where I didn't belong. It was brighter, with blacker shadows, it was brittle and filled with a music I could almost understand. But I didn't belong there, and unless I hung on I'd wake up in my motel room tomorrow out of it forever.

I might see these people on the streets, in bars, but I couldn't get back in their world again. And that was the world where the girl I loved lived. So I drove back to the Zoo.

The Jag was there, the Nash-Healey was gone. I walked along the path through the bushes, went down the three stone steps, and pushed open the door.

Pete Barrow was sitting on one of the soft chairs in front of the fire. When he saw me he didn't stand up, but he waved the hand that wasn't holding the tall drink.

"I'm sorry," he said. He reached to the leather golf bag and pulled out a driver.

I walked over to him. He looked up and I could see that my being there wasn't important to him. For a moment I'd thought the driver was trouble, but it wasn't.

"I was kind of nasty myself," I said.

"Forget it. Everybody fights like that now. I had it coming, swinging at you before I knew the score." He fiddled with the golf club, nervous.

"Do you know the score now?" I asked.

"Yes, I think I do." He took a long drink. "Pen had a big scene with me after our hassle. Funny, I didn't know the girl at all." He dropped the club to the floor. "Sometimes I think my mother is the only person in the world I understand. But, of course, none of this is really your business, is it?"

"No."

"Just the same, do you know what the girl I was going to marry wants to do? She wants to move in with Brown. Very simple. No problems. Can you understand that?"

"A little."

"She called Wild's father and told him about his daughter. She wanted to get Wild out of the picture. Quite a girl, my once-intended bride."

We looked away from each other.

"Is Wild here?" I asked.

"In the bedroom with Pen. Just walk in."

I went to the bedroom door, pushed it open.

Pen was in pajamas, sitting on one of the two narrow beds in the small room. Wild was standing next to her. She was in her slip.

"Jim! It's all right. Come in."

There are moments in a man's living— Well, this was one of them. I walked into the room and nothing was easy for me to do, right then. Not even breathe.

Chapter Eight

I closed the door behind me. Pen was looking at the floor, Wild and I were looking at each other.

Her body was supple, smooth-limbed, small-waisted.

Her face was friendly, but she didn't smile. "Pen and I've been trying to get straight. It hasn't been working out."

She stepped across the room, picked up a cigarette and her lighter.

"Why don't you two go somewhere and leave me alone?" Pen said. Her face was tight and sullen.

Wild sat on the bed, crossed her long, golden legs. "Why did you come here, Jim?"

"I wanted to see you." I guess I smiled, because she did.

"And now?"

"We did pretty well together for a little while this afternoon. Want to try some more of it?"

"I've got to do something. It hasn't been the finest day in the world for me."

"Go out with this peasant. He's your kind—not Buddy." Pen's voice was as empty as her words.

It flooded through me with bitterness that I was standing there listening to two of Buddy Brown's women talk about him, and one of his women was the girl I'd fallen in love with.

"It's female stuff, Jim. I've been trying to tell her that jealousy is self-hate. I'm not jealous of her because I don't really hate myself. If I did, I'd be a biting, scratching wildcat of jealousy."

Pen looked at her with pure venom. "What's one man to you? Right now you're showing yourself off to another one."

Wild still sat on the bed. "One man can be important to me, Pen. There haven't been many important men to me. But believe me, I know him. I know what he is inside. It's not good. It's rotten."

"So what?" said Pen. "You're still crazy for him!"

Wild snuffed out her cigarette in a tray on a night stand. "Let's not talk any more, Pen."

I was blazing angry. "I'll tell you what I'll do. I'll take you around in my car until we find lover-boy and you can have him, and he can have you, and the hell with you both."

Pen laughed.

"I'm sorry, Jim," said Wild. I knew she meant it.

She stood up, took a wheat-yellow linen dress from a closet, and pulled it over her head. Then she ran a comb through the bronze-gold hair.

"Let's go." She stood there, regal, lovely.

We went into the big room with the soft chairs and the fireplace. Pete was still there, another drink in his hand, a George Shearing disc on the player. He'd been fooling with the Rolleiflex camera this time; it was on the floor.

"She could use a little friendship, Pete," Wild said.

"So could I. But not hers. See you around town later. Ranch, maybe?"

"Maybe. 'By."

"'By, Wild."

We walked out into the bright purple night.

"Tough for the guy," I said.

"Not so tough. He's been trying out all the lonely women at the Ranch and the Blue Ox." Wild slid into the right front seat of my Ford.

"That doesn't figure, does it?" I asked, getting behind the wheel and starting the car.

"He's a little bit afraid that he's gay—or maybe he's afraid that people will find out that he is. I don't know."

"Aren't there any nice, ordinary people in your crowd?"

She only said, "We're all off the road somewhere."

My anger and jealousy were gone. I wanted to be with her, forget the crazy Saturday, forget everything and everybody except her.

"Your father took your car?"

"He drove back to the airport to get his luggage. He'll stay at the Pine Inn."

"Then what happens?"

"He thinks his daughter is sort of stupid, sort of cheap. I don't know what happens. I know that I agree with him."

"You mean you're a woman again—you belong to yourself and not to Buddy Brown?" I turned to look at her.

She was watching the road ahead, her chin high, her full lips open. There were seconds, and I had to look back at the road. Then she spoke.

"I'm his. I don't know why. Women are like that sometimes."

I kept driving.

"Why talk, Jim? How can you talk about a man with only words to use? Words like 'rat' and 'punk' and dirtier words than those. I know all that, you know it, Red knows it.

"I know where Buddy belongs. In a bottle of gin or a half-smoked stick. With a bitter woman who hates him but who can't leave him."

I could see the picture her words made. It had reality.

"Or maybe in a cell in San Quentin. Or dead. Jim, I know, believe me, I know. But a woman doesn't live by what she knows."

It had to be said. "What about Pen Brooks?"

Her laugh was quick, scornful. "Forget it, Jim. You're a nice boy, but you don't understand this sort of thing. Pen was easy for him. Most women are. I was. Let it go at that."

Ahead was the long hill road and beyond were the lights of Monterey. I knew what I wanted for this night. Noise, and the riff of jukebox music. Drinks and darkness. This girl.

"I'm going to take you out to one of the joints near Ord. I'm forgetting everything else, Wild. A Saturday-night date in a juke joint. O.K.?"

"O.K."

We swung toward the neon fires of Seaside. I wanted to be in Seaside with Wild Kearny, in a brawling juke joint where the air would be thick with the smell of whisky and the clatter of voices with the rasp of Oklahoma or the high softness of Tennessee and Texas. Some soldier hangout where the juke would be loud and bright, spinning Rosemary Clooney or Frankie Laine, the kind of place with the kind of people I knew best and liked best.

There was the right kind of place on the side of the road and I swung into the jammed parking lot. Two soldiers were fighting near the entrance, two girls were screaming at them, and the MP's would be along in a minute to take care of them.

We found a booth inside and I ordered a couple of 7-and-7's because that was the wine of the country. The waitress was hot, sweating, and happy, pushing a wisp of too blonde hair back from her forehead, her head turned to shout something at two fat first sergeants in the next booth. I felt relaxed and easy for the first time this day.

Wild and I could find each other fast when we were alone together. I felt like a guy with his girl, the one he's been going with for a year, the one he's going to marry in June. She had that warm, knowing closeness for me when we were together.

I guessed how she felt, too. Jim Work, O.K. and fun to be with, maybe the kind of man she could fall in love with, slowly, if she wasn't Wild Kearny. That was the bitter taste at the back of the drink, the other rhythm, strange and faraway, that you could hear behind the music.

Enough 7-and-7 highballs might wash knowing how she felt away. I was going to try it.

It was almost two and both of us were high and happy and her hand was warm in mine as we walked out to the car. We drove back on the highway toward Monterey and the motel signs were dancing in golden and scarlet neon.

"Stay with me tonight, Wild." I was watching the road ahead and my fingers were easy on the wheel.

"No, Jim. We're not like that."

"We were when we were dancing."

"I know. But I don't sleep around. I never have."

"What do we do tonight? Say good-by?"

"Probably. I don't have anything for you, Jim. Maybe I wish I had, but I don't."

She had everything any woman could ever have for me. She was mine, this girl. If I lost her I'd never be a complete man again; I'd have no pride in my maleness.

I swung the car to the right on the rutted road over the dune, toward the surge of the waters of the bay.

It was a finding without a knowing. There had been a typhoon in Tokyo once when the wood-and-paper buildings ripped before the fury.

This was a typhoon between two people—a man and a woman who thought she belonged to another man.

Then it was a knowing as enemies who were once friends might know each other.

After that it was a silence between two people who should not have been silent. We both knew now, we understood each other. We should not have been silent in that way.

At last I held her in my arms again, and there was no storm, but there were no words.

She lit a cigarette, and the flame of her lighter was bright on the face of the most beautiful woman I would ever know.

"Take me home, Jim."

I backed the car over the dune, turned, and drove into the quietness of sleeping Monterey. We went along the night roads and came to the driveway beside the little house in Carmel that Wild had called the Zoo.

"Thanks for not talking. There was nothing I could have said, Jim."

She opened the door and was outside the car. I was out and we stood there together. I brought her to me, but she was not with me. A tall girl in my arms, a lovely girl, a girl behind a frozen wall, a girl who did not speak.

Wild stood there after I put my arms down, and then there was a kiss, and we were close and warm there in the darkness, kissing as lovers do when the good-by could be forever. Perhaps Wild thought it would be.

It was over, still without words, and she went down the steps and pushed open the door. There was a rectangle of soft light just before the door closed behind her.

I was halfway in the car when I heard the scream.

The Zoo door wasn't locked. I pushed it open. The big room was empty but the bedroom door was open and that room was bright with light.

Buddy Brown was there, standing, looking at Wild. She was kneeling by Pen Brooks, and Pen was sprawled on the floor, her pajama jacket pushed up, her bare stomach streaked by a stream of blood. Wild held the scissors, the blood-covered scissors.

She looked up and saw me in the doorway.

Our eyes met. She shook her head slowly and threw the scissors to the floor.

Chapter Nine

The important thing to do was to take care of the wounded girl. I went to her, bent over, and carefully, gently, quickly touched her skin above and below the wound. There was too much blood coming from it; the girl would die if she was not already dead. It's hard to tell sometimes.

Pen's lung had been cut. That's the way it looked. Her eyes were closed.

"Clean cloth," I said. Buddy stood above me, looking down at the girl.

"Let her die." His voice was thick.

"Here," said Wild. She handed me a stack of clean linen handkerchiefs. I made a pad, pressed it against the wound.

"Call a doctor, then call the cops. The doctor first."

"Is she alive?" Wild spoke in a thin whisper.

"Get the doctor!" She saw my face, angry, intent, without patience for any wasted second.

Wild turned and Buddy grabbed her arm. Whatever rage had brought him to stab Pen was still in him. "You stay here. I'll handle this!"

She pushed at him, tried to break away from him. He brought the heel of his hand up hard and fast against her chin and her head snapped back.

Pen's blood was flowing from around the pad. I straightened up and Buddy turned to face me. I hit him, a short left to his breastbone with my weight behind it. His mouth opened as if his face had been torn in two.

Wild had fallen backward when his fingers freed her arm. I saw her hit against the bedroom wall, slump to her knees. I stepped close to Buddy and tried with a right that was coming up with my whole body lifting it but he buried his chin against his right shoulder and I felt his thumbs jab into the arteries of my neck.

You didn't have many seconds when the carotid arteries are stopped. You feel pain, but that's a little thing; the big thing is the panic that explodes through your body when your life arteries are bursting against the relentless dams. Not many seconds—but you're taught in the dust of a sunny afternoon in basic training what you must do in those seconds before the death panic turns your muscles to slop. Arms up in front of your face and out, as if you were diving into fast water.

The terrible thumbs were shoved away.

Both of us tried the knee at the same time, but I was the one who hooked my foot under his and threw him backward. In his second off balance I got him in the breastbone again, and over the liver with the strongest punch I will ever throw in my life.

His thin, snake-whip body couldn't take it. I knocked him against the wall and he tried for my eyes with his thumbs as I came into him. This time the stiff hooked-arm right coming up got him on the side of his jaw. His head banged against the wall and my hand felt as if all the fingers were broken.

He wasn't out, but he was hurt. I was seeing a funny thing—the wooden tabletop at the Mission Inn with the circles of moisture on it, the way I had seen it hours ago when I was helpless with my throat paralyzed. He got the knee this time the way the pictures in the hand-to-hand combat training manuals show, which is the same way you learn on the streets of Chicago. As he slumped I caught his hair and pulled his head back and the hard ridge of the side of my left hand hit his throat like a thick, dull cleaver. I let go and he went all the way down, face to the floor.

I stood there, and all I had left now was a heart like bass drum and lungs that were trying to push my ribs apart. Then I bent over Pen Brooks again. She was still bleeding around the pad. I did what I could for her, but my hands were shaking and my lungs still felt hot, dry, and empty. I looked around. Where was Wild?

Just then she came back into the room and knelt next to me and Pen.

"I called a doctor. He'll be here in a couple of minutes. How is she?"

I tried to speak but my lungs weren't ready for it yet. I shook my head. Then our eyes found each other.

I remembered the man, a little guy, a kind of Mongolian pony of a man in a dirty quilted uniform. He was looking at me as he died, his hands pressing into the torn wetness of his belly. There was hate in his eyes, and fear. There was a look as if he had a big question to ask, but mostly it was pain and hate. That was the way Wild Kearny was looking at me now. Pain, fear, hate, a big, bewildered question of some kind.

What she saw in my eyes I don't know.

We both looked away. There was too much, now, between us, too much that we had shared in passion and defeat.

"Is there anything we can do for her?"

"Wait for the doctor. Keep the blood inside of her." I could talk again, husky and gasping.

She turned her head and saw her man trying to push himself up from the floor. That was the way I thought of it, "her man." She watched him as if he were very far away.

He did it slowly, getting one knee up, resting his arm on that knee. I kept pressing the bloody pad to Pen's body. Wild stood.

"Did you call the cops?" I asked her.

Brown put one hand to the wall, leaned against it as he straightened his body.

"I called my father."

"Better call the cops."

Brown walked slowly, like a man made of wooden sticks tied together with rubber bands, one hand against the bedroom wall. He walked to the doorway, stood there a long second, and then lurched out of the room.

Wild watched him, her head turning slowly as he moved.

"Why did he do it?" I asked her.

"Goddamn life," she said, her lips tight and bitter. "Damn life, damn life to hell!"

"Wild...." My hand kept the pad firmly on the wound, but I wanted to be standing, holding Wild Kearny, telling her that she was loved, loved completely.

I had beaten the other man. I did not have to be ashamed. I had taken my woman by strength, I had broken the other man by strength. Now was the time to be gentle.

But instead I held the bloody cloth pressed tight and said only, "Wild...."

"But it's no use damning life," Wild said, her voice low and clear. "Life damns you."

She opened a drawer, took out a stack of small, soft towels.

"Here. The doctor's hurrying. What else, Jim? Boiling water? Anything?"

"Boil some water. Maybe he'll want some. What is—" couldn't say the name. "What's that punk doing?"

"I don't know. I don't think I care, either."

Pen moved, her mouth hanging open. I held my wrist watch in front of it. The glass misted slowly.

"I'll get the water boiling," Wild said.

I changed towels and watched the dying girl. All I could do for her was hold a pad against the wound. Minutes later Wild came back.

"How is she?"

"Still alive."

"He should be here now."

"Maybe he can save her. What happened here tonight, Wild?"

She shook her head. "I came in. He was standing there, she was on the floor. The scissors were still—"

We two, who might have so much together, still were half enemies, half lovers.

"I wish I could cry for her. I can't."

"Because of Brown?"

Her lips curled. "No. I never felt any jealousy, I never hated her. I don't see why she had to be killed. I don't understand it."

"But you're not sorry for her?"

Wild shook her head. "I'm sorry that any woman can destroy herself, but I can't pity the woman, I can't weep for her. If we destroy ourselves, no one should weep, least of all ourselves."

I didn't quite understand. "Do you think she stabbed herself?"

"No. Pen wouldn't."

"The punk?"

"I don't know why he did it. He's got a wicked temper. I know."

There was something strange, distant in her voice. It was the voice of a woman who could look at herself, with passion gone. Look at herself without pity, but with a shamed knowing that somewhere still inside her she longed for the cruelty, the madness that would not be again. I felt it, and tried not to know what I felt.

We didn't hear the doctor's car but we heard his voice. Wild went to the front door. I heard his footsteps, and then I saw him, a square-faced, square-built man in a gray suit. His eyebrows were thick and white. He had his case open by the time he reached her. He lifted the bloody pack, snapped on his stethoscope, and without removing the earpieces, prepared a hypodermic, swabbed her skin, and gave her an injection.

"She's barely alive. Have you notified the police?" His eyes were cold.

"Not yet."

"Afraid to?"

"I didn't stab this girl."

"Call the police." He had gone back to work on her, his stubby fingers setting a sponge in the wound.

"O.K." I started for the big room.

"Don't try to run away."

"I won't."

Wild stood near the fireplace. As I looked at her I realized that the whisky of the night was still hot in my blood and my brain. I realized that for hours now I must have been drunk. What had happened in the car, the fight with Brown, all of this was misty now. I had been drunk, with the kind of drunkenness that lets you look all right and talk all right, while the madness stays hidden inside.

"Got to call the cops." Now my voice was sounding thick.

"Is she alive? What did he say?" Wild asked.

"He said she's barely alive. He told me to call the cops."

"My father will be here. He'll handle all that. He knows how." It was strange, the mixture of pride and bitterness in her voice on the last words.

"I'm here. I'll handle it."

I went to the phone, dialed the operator. As I waited I remembered Brown.

"Where's Brown?"

Wild shook her head. I put the phone back on the cradle just as the operator answered.

"Is he trying to get away?"

"I don't know. I'm awfully tired." As she spoke she dropped her arms to her sides and fell straight forward to the floor. That's the way men fall in a Fourth of July review on the parade ground when the sun has baked their brains—straight forward like a tree toppling. You don't fake it.

I was there beside her, lifting her head, talking to her. I don't know what I was saying, maybe telling her I loved her, maybe angry with her for passing out. I don't know. The whisky I had drunk was with me now, swirling through my eyes and my mind.

There were rapid footsteps behind me and square, stubby fingers grabbed my neck.

"What are you doing?"

"She fell over."

The doctor pushed me away. I was shaky. Then I saw the golf club on the floor where Pete or somebody had left it. When Wild had fallen she had fallen right on the club. I went in closer. The doctor was putting his stubby fingers gently on a great, swelling bruise close to Wild's temple.

He lowered Wild's head to the floor, got up slowly, warily. He didn't say anything to me but he walked quickly toward the phone, his head turning so that he could watch me as he moved.

He lifted the phone, his finger spinning the dial.

"Operator! Get the police to a small house…." His voice was muffled as he brought the mouthpiece to his lips, but his eyes never left me.

I knew what he thought: that I had hit Wild with the golf club. I was a dangerous murdering maniac. It didn't bother me. I could explain as soon as he hung up the phone. Wild would be conscious again in a minute or two.

"Wild!"

It was Broadway Red Kearny, coming through the door, across the long room to where his daughter was crumpled on the floor.

As I had done, he lifted her head, spoke to her, and then he looked at me.

"What's happened, boy? Is she hurt bad?"

The doctor answered first. "This man just clubbed her after stabbing another girl. Who are you?"

Broadway Red Kearny came up like a great bear.

"You did this?"

"No!"

"He did it just a minute ago. I came in from the other room just after he assaulted her with that golf stick."

Kearny had killed men with his hands before. I lifted my hands and he was on me, one fist swinging toward my face like a sledge.

I suppose the police saved my life. They arrived a minute or two after Kearny, and by that time the big man had me unconscious and he was choking me to death.

Chapter Ten

When I came out of it the place was very different. It was still the big, easy room with the fireplace and the record player, the room that had fitted around the four young men, the two girls, the beer, and the music yesterday afternoon. But now it was very different. It was the scene of a crime.

They had me sitting, my head back, in one of the big chairs. The watchdog of a doctor was rubbing my throat with his blocky fingers, and there was a taste of something in my aching throat, a smell of something high in my nostrils. Some kind of stimulant, acrid and metallic. I could hear a siren, going away.

As I came back the first thing I did was look for Wild. She wasn't on the floor, and the golf club was gone, too. There were three uniformed police in the room and a couple of sleepy-looking men in ordinary clothes. Broadway Red was across the room from me in another big chair. He was looking straight at me and I looked into his ice-chip eyes for a second.

"He's all right," barked the white-haired doctor, standing away from me.

I tried to lift my hands to rub my throat myself. I discovered I was handcuffed.

"What the hell's the idea?" I croaked. I waved my arms, shackled together at the wrists.

"What's what idea, son?" asked one of the men in uniform. He was blond, heavy, and he sounded tired, annoyed, but very much interested.

"Why the cuffs? Ask Wild—she'll tell you what's been happening here.

I'm not the guy—"

"Suppose you tell me what's been happening here."

"Do you want to do all that here, Clyde, or take him into the station at Monterey?" asked one of the sleepy-looking men.

"Better hear his story now," said the one they called Clyde.

"Where's Wild? Is Pen Brooks all right? I mean, is she alive?" I brought the fingers of both my hands to my throat, easing off the pain of talking.

"Just tell us what happened here."

He was close to me, in front of the chair, bending over a little. One officer stood by Kearny and I could guess why. More than anything I wanted to straighten the facts out with Broadway Red. I liked the big, tough old guy and I could see why he was looking at me out of eyes filled with murder. He didn't know the story. None of these jokers knew the story if Wild hadn't come out of it yet.

"Did you see a tall, skinny guy—real tall—around here?" I asked.

The blond officer shook his head.

"His name's Brown, Buddy Brown. He's the guy that stabbed the girl."

Clyde looked at the doctor. The doctor shook his head. "Just this fellow and the girl when I got here. Besides the victim, that is. I guess it was the girl that called me. Nobody else."

"Start at the beginning, Mac," said Clyde. He wasn't talking tough, but he wasn't friendly, and I could sense the hardness in his voice.

"Wild and I were out. We came here. She went in. I heard her scream. I ran in. Buddy Brown was in the bedroom and the girl was on the floor bleeding."

"This the girl you call Pen Brooks?"

"Yes."

"Then what happened?"

"I tried to help her—first aid. Brown and I had a fight. I worked him over. He went out of the room. Wild called the doctor while we were fighting. When the doctor got here I came out to this room. Wild fainted—she'd had kind of a rough night—and when she fell her head hit the golf club on the floor. That's about all I know."

There was silence while each of them chewed over my story.

"What do you mean, she had a rough night?" Clyde asked.

That was the tough question. Across the room Kearny was watching me with a cold glitter in his blue eyes.

"We'd been drinking."

"Much?"

"Quite a bit."

"Where?"

"A place in Seaside."

"Just liquor?"

"What do you mean?"

"Marijuana? Anything like that?"

"No. Where's Wild? She wasn't hurt bad, was she? She can tell you the whole story."

"She's hurt bad enough. Was that all you meant by saying she'd had a rough night?"

The tough question again. I thought for a moment. Wild had faced the bitter problem of her father and Buddy Brown yesterday. Maybe it was a problem a lot of girls have in their lives, sometime, when they know their fathers will see the cheap, dirty truths about the guys they're nuts about. For Wild it was bigger than for most girls; Broadway Red Kearny wasn't an ordinary father, Buddy Brown was dirtier than most men.

Then the good evening we'd had. After that it was Pen Brook's blood, and the rest of it. Half drunk, with whatever I had done or we had done together, with the painful emptiness she had caused between her father and herself, with the shock of the stabbing—it had been one hell of a rough night for any girl.

But how do you explain all this to a policeman who is waiting for you to speak up?

"How bad is she hurt?"

Clyde pursed his lips. "She's unconscious. Concussion, maybe a fractured skull. It's plenty bad, son."

"She wasn't hit," I explained. "She fainted, fell straight on her face. The club was on the floor."

"What about that, Doctor?" Clyde asked, turning to the square-faced man.

"Girls don't faint much," said the doctor. "Passing out from alcohol— that's something else. But you slump when you pass out, as if your legs turn to rubber, and you don't fall hard. The kind of injury she has looked as if he'd hit her a glancing blow with that golf stick."

"What do you say about that, son?"

"She fainted. A lot of things had happened to her today. She'd drunk a lot, and she got a big shock when she got here."

"But she waited to faint until after this fight you say you had, and all the rest of it, calling the doctor and everything?"

The doctor interrupted. "That part is logical, to be fair about it. After auto accidents, any kind of shock like that, both men and women faint sometimes, minutes later, when everything's over. But this was a big, strong, healthy girl. I don't think she'd topple over, no matter what happened."

Clyde nodded. "Thank you, Doctor. Want to change your story, son?"

"No. This fellow Brown roughed her up when she started to call a doctor, a lot of things happened to her. You better find this Brown quick. He stabbed the Brooks girl."

"Why?"

"Because he's crazy-tempered and he hates women. He's psycho."

"You been in the Army, son?"

"Yeah, just got out."

"Related to anybody around here?"

"No. I'm alone. Going to stay here and go to school."

Clyde looked a little sad. He had me sized up as a young man in bad trouble and he was a little sorry for me. He was thinking about my future in terms of San Quentin, maybe, and not Monterey Peninsula College.

"About this Buddy Brown—"

"Yes?" The other officers were grouping around Clyde now.

"He was sort of involved with this Brooks girl. They must have quarreled and he lost his temper. I beat him up. He won't be far. Very tall, thin, pale."

"You say you didn't harm either one of these girls? You didn't stab Brooks, you didn't hit the Kearny girl?"

"No, sir." The Army training hadn't left me yet.

"Son, we'll find this man Brown, all right, and we'll check into your story very carefully. But—"

"Yes?"

"I don't believe you."

"I'm telling you the truth. Look for fingerprints on those scissors, on that golf club."

"Well, son, I don't believe you. One girl dying, one girl beaten with a golf club, and nobody around but you. You're pretty drunk right now, maybe you've done things you don't even remember. You'll get a fair shake, son, but it looks like you've got yourself into big, bad trouble."

Clyde went over to one of the men in civilian clothes and they talked in low tones.

"All right, son, come on. We don't have a jail here in Carmel so we're going to take you to Monterey and hold you there until Monday on an open charge. Then, the way things look now, you'll go to the county jail in Salinas. You can call a lawyer tomorrow if you want to. And you know something, son?"

I stood up, the cuffs heavy on my wrists. I was dizzy; some from the whisky, some from Red Kearny's big hands around my throat. "What?"

"You better pray those two girls don't die."

"I want to see Wild. You can take these cuffs off, too, because I don't have to run away."

"Both girls are at the Monterey Community Hospital. You won't be seeing them, not right quick, anyway. We'll leave the cuffs on. A boy who's been drinking a lot might change his mind about running away."

"How about those fingerprints? How about Brown?"

"We'll take care of everything, son. We're real careful about things."

Broadway Red Kearny got out of his chair and walked up to me. The other men closed in around him nervously and he pushed one of them out of the way.

"You didn't harm my girl?"

"No. I love your daughter."

"You didn't know her until today."

"I was pretty sure of it before we met you at the airport. I'm dead sure now."

These were cold blue eyes that had looked into the core of many a man. There was a long searching and the others in the room were quiet and motionless.

Kearny's face was like reddish rock. "Yes. I'll back your play."

I had one man who believed me in the room, and he was the only one that mattered.

They led me out, up the three stone steps, past my Ford, and to the open rear door of a police sedan. The front seat was protected from the rear by a screen of heavy wire. Two of the uniformed officers got in back with me; one of them was Clyde. The driver got in, started the car, spoke into the radio telephone briefly, and then backed the sedan into the street.

"You were kind of lucky," said Clyde.

"Yeah," I said, "this is my lucky night. My girl's in the hospital, I'm in jail."

"You could be at the morgue. It took three of us to pull that Kearny off you."

"He's a good man. He just got the wrong idea when he walked in."

"You always drink this much, son?"

The car was climbing the long hill now. Carmel was dark and sleeping.

"No. It wasn't an ordinary day. A lot of beer in the afternoon, some stuff at dinner, whisky at that place in Seaside. Brown was drunk, too. Earlier in the evening. He got drunk fast. He's dead scared of Kearny."

"Why?"

I didn't say anything. It wouldn't be easy to explain that the one girl in the world for me had been sleeping with a man so rotten that he was afraid her father would kill him for his rottenness. It wouldn't be easy.

"I'm not sure. Like I said, he's a psycho."

"How long have you known these people?"

"Just today, yesterday. Saturday."

"How'd you get involved?"

"There was a little car accident. We got to talking. Wild introduced me to her father. Later I went to the cottage and we went out."

"Who was there? This Brown?"

"No. Another man. Pete Barrow. He was engaged to Pen Brooks."

"But she was playing around with Brown?"

"Yes."

"And when you came back with the Kearny girl, Brown was there with Miss Brooks?"

"Yes, sir. She'd been stabbed. Brown said to let her die."

"But you tried to help her?"

"A little. I've been in Korea. Sometimes you have to help a guy until the medic can get to him."

The car whistled through the blackness between the great trees at the crest of the Carmel hill. In front the police telephone rattled in a faraway voice at intervals.

"You know how it is, son," Clyde said. "You tell a pretty straight story, I'll say that. But you didn't call the police, even after the doctor told you to. The girl may have fainted, but nobody thinks she did. Girls don't faint, not girls like that one. They'll be in there pitching when the average boy is frazzled down to his socks. You were pretty drunk tonight. There's only your word, so far, about this Brown. One girl stabbed, one girl slugged with a golf club, and you were the only person there. You understand how it is, don't you?"

"Yes, I understand how it is," I said.

Take it cool, I told myself. Kearny believes you now. He liked you from the beginning. When Wild wakes up, she can tell them the rest of the story. I spend a night in jail, so what? I've told the facts a couple of times, all the facts. All the facts except that Wild Kearny used to be Buddy Brown's girl. All the facts except that a couple of hours ago I found that she was mine, and never Brown's again.

Through the mesh of wire I could see the lights of Monterey and Seaside with the light-flecked shimmering of the bay beyond.

The police car turned off the main highway as we came into Monterey, the old part of Monterey where many of the buildings were once the homes of the great Spanish families a century and more ago.

We swung past a small park and the car pulled in behind a large building and stopped. I could see a naked electric light over a wooden door in a frame shed and another building, a low, one-story stone structure. Beneath the light was a sign, "Police and Prisoners Only." That was us. We had a ticket.

Clyde led me through the doorway.

"Got one for you," he said. "Book him open."

The man behind the desk was in uniform shirt sleeves. He yawned, scratched his head, and came over.

"Figure Carmel wants to spend the ten bucks?"

Clyde laughed. "For this one, yes. But if he asks for a blanket, be sure and lock the cell after you give it to him." He turned to me and put his key to the handcuffs. He was chuckling. I got the idea that he had begun to believe me, a little. "Carmel has to pay Monterey ten dollars a night to keep our prisoners in their jail. A while back a Carmel prisoner asked for a blanket and the lockup forgot to lock up. Prisoner just walked away."

The handcuffs fell open and away. "Carmel and Monterey are still arguing about the ten bucks," Clyde added. "We say we don't owe for a full night since they didn't have him in the morning. They just want the ten bucks. Fingerprints now, son."

They inked my fingers, one at a time, and rolled them off on a card.

"You aren't wanted someplace else for something, are you?" asked Clyde.

"No."

"Might as well speak up if you are, because we'll find out about it by Monday anyway."

"What about my car? It's parked back there at that house." I wasn't much concerned or interested in the procedure of booking me. I knew that by Monday I'd be back in normal life again, normal as it could be considering that I was in love with Wild Kearny.

"Got to check over your car a little. It'll be here waiting for you if you get out. Which brings us to your keys, money, billfold, all that stuff. Get everything out of your pockets and put it in this envelope."

I emptied my pockets. The man in shirt sleeves sealed the envelopes. He took out another card and had me spell my name, my address, my Army history, previous addresses, the whole works.

"We're going to run lab tests on his clothes," Clyde told the desk officer.

"O.K. there, fellow. Start taking your duds off."

He went into a back room while Clyde watched me. The officer came back, tossed me a faded denim shirt and a pair of patched denim pants. I put them on. "How about my belt? These damn things are ten sizes too big." I pulled them out from my flat stomach.

"No belt. How do you get along with fleas?"

"No good. They like to chew the hell out of me."

"You going to have a scratchin' good time tonight, then, bub."

They led me into the one-storied stone building next door. The old prison had smells stacked up on each other. Sour smells of ancient sin, dirty smells from Saturday-night drunks, acid smells from disinfectants.

A heavy key creaked in a heavy lock and a heavy door was pulled open and shut behind me. The key creaked again. I was in jail. The first flea bit me and I began to scratch.

It looked like a bad night, the hour or so that was left of it.

"Hey! You sober?"

I could see a head peering down at me from the upper bunk. The cell was big enough for one double bunk.

"Yeah, I'm sober. Pretty much."

"Good. Was figuring it was just about time for them to put a hootin' and hollerin' drunk in here, being Saturday night and all." I could see the face a little now. It looked like a pixie out of Walt Disney in the bad light.

"What are you in for, pardner?" The voice sounded young, and it had a twang that was maybe Texas or Oklahoma.

"Nothing. They got me mixed up with another guy."

"Good boy! I like being in with an old-timer. You always learn something."

"No, seriously. On the level. It's just a little mix-up."

"That's my pardner talking like I like to hear him talk. What's your name?"

"Jim Work. No kidding, fellow, it was another guy. I'll be out tomorrow."

"My name's Dooley. Billy Dooley. Glad to meet you."

"Here, too. These fleas bother you?" I was scratching energetically now.

"Fleas? Pardner, a couple years ago when I first hit the road the fleas ate all the meat off my bones. When a flea climbs my frame now he just slides off disgusted-like."

I sat down on the bunk. Right now I felt pretty damn miserable. There was the liquor wearing off, and my sore throat and general aches all over.

But it was mostly Wild being in the hospital. I wanted to be with her, to wash the hate and bitterness out of her clear eyes.

"What they got you in for, Dooley?" Might as well talk. The night was terrible in its loneliness.

"Curiosity, mostly. This part of the country is running wild with sports cars. They've got MG's for the peasants, and they've got Jags like Oklahoma has rabbits. I kind of tried out a Jag for size, a little. Weren't mine."

I stretched out on the bunk.

"I'm a magician," Dooley said. "That's my trade. Miracles and stuff."

"What do you mean, miracles?"

"You know, like a magician does. Things you can't believe that you see right in front of your eyes 'cause I make 'em happen. The unbelievable, the impossible."

It was a strange conversation in the solitude of the cell, yellow-lit from a dim bulb. Outside was the quiet of the night, nearby the jailer was probably sleeping, a few miles away two girls were in hospital beds. Somewhere in the outer darkness was a lean, hard-muscled, hot-eyed man named Buddy Brown.

"Where do you do your magic?"

"Anyplace. Taverns and cocktail lounges. Sometimes schools. Wherever I am and there's an audience. Freest man in the world, pardner, that's Dooley the Fantastic."

"Not now, you aren't."

Dooley laughed.

"Where are you from?" I asked.

"Tulsa, Bartlesville, Rincon. Places like that. I move along, mostly."

"Why did you steal the Jaguar?"

"I'd never driven a Jag, and it didn't look like I was saving money fast enough to buy one real soon. I was just samplin' it, kind of."

"How'd the cops catch you?"

"I guess maybe I didn't look like the Jag type. Just going by in a police car and they looked at me, and then they looked a little more, and then they said, 'Hey, you, pull over.' Didn't sound like they figured a li'l ol' country boy like me belonged in it. Didn't have a report on the car or nothing. 'Bout an hour ago or so. I think I'll try to grow a mustache. Might help."

I didn't answer and we both were quiet. In a little while I heard Dooley snoring gently. He sounded like a nice kid.

Chapter Eleven

The night loneliness engulfed me. I thought of Buddy Brown.

They'd find him somewhere tonight. Walking on a dark street between the hills. In his bed. Sitting alone in his room with a bottle. Sitting alone and laughing, with the brown cigarette cupped in his hand, the weed-sweet smell thick in the room. Maybe now an officer, hand on his holstered gun, was walking toward Buddy Brown in the lonely Greyhound waiting room at Salinas while the heavy-eyed soldiers and huddled Mexicans watched. Maybe a state highway patrol car was flagging down the MG on 101. Night thoughts. Night thoughts on a bunk, scratching flea bites.

They wouldn't find him. It was a night truth, one of those things that you know as you lie awake toward dawn. Maybe they'd look for him, but they wouldn't find him.

I moved restlessly on the sagging bunk.

If Pen Brooks died, only two people would know who killed her. Wild Kearny was one, and I was the other. If Wild Kearny died....

Nights thoughts. If a snake whip of a man went to Wild's hospital bed tonight in the darkness, a man who would know the simple trick of killing an unconscious person without leaving marks or traces—the simple trick of the soft pressure through folded cloth on the carotid arteries until the brain died, blood-starved—then it would be Jim Work that would inhale the gas in that little room in the big house above San Francisco Bay. There were no other witnesses against Brown.

Wild was in danger. That was the alarm bell that exploded through the night thoughts. I swung out of bed, pounded on the heavy door.

"What's the trouble, pardner? Want a better room? I don't figure they have any."

I didn't answer Dooley. I kept pounding on the door.

"Hey you, you crazy or something?" The jailer's voice was gruff, complaining. He came up to the heavy door.

"I've got to talk to the Carmel police. It's a matter of life and death."

"Get back in your bunk. You're going to see plenty of police tomorrow."

"Then call the hospital. Tell them to put a guard on Wild Kearny."

"Why should they? We got you in here."

Clyde must have told him the story after they'd locked me away.

"This fellow Brown. If he kills her, he can beat this."

"Get back in your bunk." He walked away.

I pounded on the door until my bruised hand was hot with pain. He didn't come back.

I tried to think. Brown wouldn't know what had happened. He wouldn't know that I had been arrested for the stabbing of Pen Brooks. He wouldn't know that Wild Kearny was unconscious or in the hospital. I pushed the night thoughts back into the shadows. I'd blown my top.

But the night thoughts returned insistently.

Brown wouldn't know yet what had happened, but he would think as I did when he learned the whole story, and his plans would be more subtle, more dangerous. He would act for reasons of which I knew nothing.

Even as the deep fear for Wild circled through my head and the fear for myself, I slid into sleep while the January dawn moved across the hills in the east.

I was jerked out of it by the jailer's voice.

"Chow time. Wash up."

Billy Dooley slid down from his bunk. In the morning light he had the face of a freckled Irish pixie out of Oklahoma, and eyes laughing as if he were just about to push the outhouse over behind the school with the teacher inside it.

"Hi, pardner. Wanna see some magic?"

They hadn't taken Dooley's clothes. He wore almost skin-tight jeans, a red and white checked shirt, a green bow tie, and scuffed, high-heeled cowboy boots.

Before I answered Dooley waved his hands, passed one over the other, and there was a rose in his palm. It was a paper rose, and a little beat up. His hands moved and he was holding an egg, a rubber egg with a Scotch-tape patch on it. He clapped his hands, there was a little bright flash, a puff of smoke and the egg was gone.

"Fantastic, ain't it? Of course, it's a little more fantastic if you're kind of farther away." He was smiling like a proud but bashful kid.

"You mean they left you your magic stuff?"

He dug one boot against the other. "It's kinda hard to search a magician real good. Practically takes another magician to do it, and these John Laws aren't magicians. Except at figuring out guys that don't belong in Jags at three o'clock in the morning."

"Hey, you, we're going out for chow." The jailer was pushing the heavy key into the door. He swung it open, slapped his pistol holster in a very broad hint, and motioned us along. We washed up, and he took us out into the morning brightness of Monterey.

He took us across the street and around the block to a pleasant little café. We had a stack of wheat cakes and a cup of coffee apiece. It tasted fine, in spite of a hangover and plenty of bruises that bounced around my body.

"How about a phone call?" I asked the jailer. He was a fat man with a good-natured face, not the one who had booked me the night before.

"Who you going to call?"

"I want to call the Community Hospital."

"'Bout them girls you beat up?"

"Make it easy on both of us," I said to the jailer. "I don't know what the night man told you, but I'm being held on an open charge. I didn't beat up or hurt any girls, and if Wild Kearny is conscious I'll be out of your flea circus in an hour. How about calling?"

"You got any money in your envelope?"

"Enough."

His eyes narrowed and his good-natured face clouded up. "I didn't mean that. If you got a dime for the phone, that's all you need. I'll loan it to you now. Use that phone booth, and I'm lettin' you in there with this dime to call your lawyer. Understand?"

"I understand. Thanks." He gave me the dime and watched me go to the booth.

There was a slim phone directory in the booth. I found the hospital number and dialed it.

"Monterey Community Hospital, good morning," a woman's voice said.

"I'm calling to find out the condition of Miss Wild Kearny."

"One moment, please."

I scratched a flea bite and waited.

"Yes?" This was a nurse's voice, coolly pleasant but with plenty of conscious authority.

"How is Miss Wild Kearny, please?"

"Who is calling?"

"Jim Work."

"Are you a relative?"

"A friend." It was a funny word to use, but what else? Lover? The guy who's in the jug accused of slugging her? A friend.

"She's doing well."

"Is she conscious? Is she awake? Could I talk to her?"

"She's doing well. No visitors or phone calls."

"How about Pen Brooks?"

"We are not permitted to give any further information." She hung up.

It wasn't much of a dime's worth. I walked out of the booth and the fat man slapped his holster again and paraded us to the door. We went back to the jail and he put us back in the cell and closed the heavy door.

"Won't work you boys much, 'cause it's Sunday. Got a couple drunks in the other tank to sweep up and mop. Do 'em good." He rumbled away.

I stretched out on my bunk and went to sleep. Billy Dooley was disappointed: he'd planned to give me a magic show. He was practicing with a deck of cards as I sank into sleep.

Chapter Twelve

It was after twelve when they came for me. The jailer opened the cell door and shook me awake. This time it took a few seconds before I remembered where I was and what it was all about.

I slid out of my bunk, rubbed my eyes, and yawned. Billy was asleep in the upper bunk.

"Come on," said the jailer.

"Lunch?" I was going to wake Dooley.

He shook his head. I had the feeling things were bad.

"More important than lunch. Come on." This time he held my arm as he closed the door and locked it. For a fat man he had strong fingers.

He walked me down a corridor, up some stairs, and into a room, holding my arm tightly all the while.

"Here he is," he said to the three men in the room. Clyde, who was probably the chief in Carmel, was sitting at a table with a man in civilian clothes. A uniformed officer was standing near the door.

"Sit down," Clyde said, motioning to a chair. His voice had changed since last night. It was cold and businesslike now.

The uniformed officer closed the door and stood in front of it.

"This is Mr. Gloster from Burr Scott's office," said Clyde. "Burr Scott is the district attorney for Monterey County."

I nodded. The other man didn't nod back.

"Tell us exactly what happened last night. Start yesterday afternoon or evening. Tell it slowly and don't leave out anything." Clyde spoke carefully, coldly.

"Have you picked up Buddy Brown?" I asked.

"Just tell your story," Clyde said. He wasn't calling me "son" today.

"I'd like to know about Brown. Wild Kearny is the only witness outside of myself, and if Brown's loose she may be in danger."

Clyde shook his head. "She's in no danger from Brown. Now tell your story." He meant it.

"It started with an accident yesterday afternoon. On Ocean Avenue in Carmel. My car turned over Brown's MG. Not much damage, nobody hurt."

Clyde nodded. "I saw the report."

"Brown and I had a little fight. One punch. His." The D.A.'s man was making notes.

"Then we went to the home of Wild Kearny. She lived there with Pen Brooks." I went on with the story. The fight back of the house. Wild and I going to Monterey, to the airport to meet her father, leaving out the reason. The dinner at the Hearthstone. Later, the incident at the Mission Inn, Pen Brooks and Pete Barrow. Meeting Buddy Brown, drunk. What he had told me of himself. Going to the Zoo again.

"We went to a juke joint in Seaside. We drank and danced. Talked about things. Then...." I wondered if my face showed anything, if these men could notice.

"Yes?"

"Then I drove her home. She went inside. I heard her scream and ran in." I told them the same story I had told Clyde the night before.

"That's all of it," I said.

"You're sure? Nothing left out?"

"Nothing."

"You'd swear to it?"

There was the squeeze. I'm pretty tough-minded; it's a tough world, where the best you can do is take care of yourself. But an oath is important. I didn't feel like lying under oath.

"Speak up. Will you swear to it?"

"Not right now."

I was aware of the speculative stares of both men. "What role did you play with Miss Kearny and Miss Brooks?"

"I knew them slightly. Pen Brooks, that is. I spent several hours yesterday with Wild Kearny."

The laugh wasn't friendly. "Yeah, I'll bet you did. You meet her yesterday, last night you take her to the Corral in Seaside, and the waitress remembers you as a sweet couple. That's what she called you. She recognized a picture of the girl and described you."

"So what? Maybe we are a sweet couple."

"The Corral closes at the regular hour. Then what did you do?"

"We talked in my car."

"What did you talk about?"

"We talked about the foreign policy of the United States."

"You think being smart's going to help, kid?"

I didn't answer.

"Why didn't Miss Kearny phone the police?"

"She phoned her father."

"Did you ever talk about foreign policy with Pen Brooks?"

"No."

"How did Wild Kearny get along with the Brooks girl?"

"Fine."

"In spite of the fact that both of them were in love with Buddy Brown and possibly with you?"

Damn. I waited, silent. People's lives were never meant to be naked in the cold machinery of law. But what else is law for?

"Did Miss Kearny stab Pen Brooks?"

"No. It was Buddy Brown. If you want co-operation from me, you'll have to tell me if Brown has been caught."

I was going to have to fight. Not for myself; I didn't feel afraid or worried. I wasn't fighting to save Wild Kearny, either. I wasn't worried about their suspicions. I was fighting evil—the dirty, snakelike trail of Buddy Brown that festered into corruption behind him. I was fighting for the hope of something decent and good for Wild Kearny and Jim Work together.

"We're still looking for Brown."

"Thanks." It was a bitter word as I said it. "Is Wild conscious yet?"

"We found out why she fainted. Sometime—maybe from this Brown, as you say, or maybe from you, earlier—she received a bad blow on the back of her head. If your story is true, Miss Kearny was helping you with the Brooks girl, making her call to the doctor and all that, in intense pain, fighting off unconsciousness. She is still unconscious."

The heel of Brown's hand snapping Wild's head back, her head hitting the wall behind her. I remembered.

"We'll hold you here for arraignment tomorrow, Work. Then you'll be taken to Salinas. You are being charged with the murder of Penelope Brooks. She died this morning."

I stood up and the policeman behind me stepped forward, one hand on my arm.

"Then Brown's your murderer. Wild will tell you that."

"We don't know what Miss Kearny will tell us. There are some things we do know. You were with this girl for a long time somewhere last night. Then the two of you went to her house. Sometime later the girl calls a doctor. Then the girl is slugged. Nobody calls the police until the doctor does.

"What we want to know is this: Are you trying to cover up for the Kearny girl?"

"No."

"Just for fun, supposing this happened. Supposing you sell the Kearny girl a big line of goods yesterday. Bigger than Brown's. You go out and have fun. You come back. Brooks threatens to tell the old boy friend about the two of you. There's an argument. Maybe Kearny stabs Brooks, maybe you do.

"Then the doctor comes. You're scared. You tell the Kearny girl to help you frame Brown. She refuses. You slug her. How does that sound, fellow?"

"Lousy."

"It's lousy, all right. Damn lousy. But it happened that way, didn't it?"

"Have you found Brown?"

"He'll be picked up. We'll check out your story. But the only fingerprints on those scissors seem to be the girl's. The only people we know were there were you and the girl."

"Wild will tell you the truth."

"So you say."

"What are you holding me for, right now?"

"Suspicion of murder. You'll be arraigned tomorrow. It's up to you what Burr Scott will ask for."

"How do you mean?"

"We're thinking about first-degree murder. How does that sound to you?"

"Fine."

"What do you mean, fine?" The eyes were hard, and the faces moved closer to mine.

"Find a tall, thin man with a pale face. Charge him with murder and you'll have two good witnesses."

"You, for one?"

"I didn't see him stab the girl. Otherwise, yes."

"Try this one for size, fellow. Let's say Brown really was there."

"He was."

"You don't go in with the Kearny girl. She went in, found Brown and the Brooks girl—well, let's say she found them talking about American foreign policy. You know how women are, don't you, fellow?"

I kept my mouth closed, my teeth hard together.

"Sure you know how women are. You do real good the same day you met one. The fact that she's been finding out how the night air feels with you maybe doesn't keep her from thinking that Pen Brooks should keep her hands off her other boy friend. So she stabs her. How does that sound?"

It didn't sound very good, but I didn't say anything.

"Well," Gloster said, his fingers drumming on the table, "let him stay here in storage until tomorrow morning. If things haven't changed by then we'll charge him with murder. Do you have a lawyer, Work?"

"No, and I won't need one." I was thinking about money. Fifty dollars at the least if I asked some attorney to represent me. I wasn't nervous or worried, and fifty dollars was a lot of money to me.

Gloster looked at me, shoved his lower lip over the upper one. "O.K. We'll see." He nodded to the policeman behind me.

The officer opened the door and led me back downstairs. The fat man put me in the cell.

"What's the story, pardner?" Dooley asked.

"Giving me a bad time," I said.

"Trouble?"

"Some. My girl's in the hospital unconscious. They think I slugged her and killed another girl."

Dooley's pixie eyes widened. "You don't look mean."

"I'm not." I told Dooley the whole story, everything. There are times when the best thing you can do is open up to somebody else. This was the time. I needed to say a lot of things out loud, not because of Dooley, but because when you say them to someone else they make more sense to you.

"Best this girl of yours gets well fast. Until she does, these boys are going to twist your arm good. Too bad you didn't work that Brown down a little more. Shouldn't have let him move out like that."

"I was busy with the Brooks girl. Brown didn't look as if he could walk ten feet."

"Skinny ol' boys got a lot of grit in their craws," said Billy. "Want to see some magic?"

"Go ahead, Houdini."

The kid did tricks for an hour. When he'd been booked he had sleighted a small box full of magical equipment and a sack with some more stuff. It was amazing what he could do—card tricks, ventriloquism, disappearing objects, everything. I liked it and I never asked how the tricks were done, so he knocked himself out entertaining me.

The good-natured fat man took us out to lunch and Billy bedeviled him with ventriloquism at the café's lunch counter. Then Billy made a puppet out of a couple of paper napkins, two spoons, and two knives. The little puppet bawled the fat man out for spilling his soup, made fun of his double chin, and flirted with the waitress.

When we got back to the jail Gloster was waiting for me. He had another man from the District Attorney's office with him. The jailer put Billy into the cell and took me back upstairs with Gloster. They closed the door.

"I've met some pretty crumby specimens in this job," Gloster said to me, "but you're the prize."

"What the hell do you mean? Is there something about working for the District Attorney that gives you a license to pop off any time you want to?" I was ready to swing at him. I knew that they'd handle me rough if I did, but I was plenty angry.

"Work," said Gloster and he spat out the words, "a reputable witness showed up at the Carmel police station at noon and explained that he'd heard about the Brooks affair on the local news broadcast. The news broadcast said that the police were searching for Buddy Brown.

"This witness is willing to swear that Brown was at his home from midnight until nearly four this morning playing records and drinking coffee. He's also willing to bring in another witness of the highest character to affirm that Brown was there during those four hours. Now what do you have to say?"

"Who is this witness?"

"You'll find out in due course. We're satisfied as to his reliability. His story knocks out not only your clumsy attempt to frame Brown, but also your dirty attempt to smear the dead girl."

"What do you mean?"

There was no doubt of Gloster's contempt for me. He didn't bother to answer me.

"Do you want to tell the truth now? All I want to know is who actually did the stabbing, this Kearny woman or you? Everything leads me to believe that she killed Miss Brooks except for your attack on her later. We're not going to bargain with either of you now. One or both of you are going to be tried for murder in the first degree. If you didn't do it, you'd better get out from under in a hurry, because there's going to be a conviction in this case and we're going to ask for death. Understand?"

"Your witness is lying," I said.

"These witnesses belong to one of the oldest and most respected families in Pebble Beach. Their testimony is unimpeachable. You can stop this pretense now, Work. The rest of it is up to you. If you did it, I guarantee you'll go to the gas chamber. If you didn't do the actual stabbing, this is your last chance."

There was no point in my talking to Gloster now. He was sure of himself, angry and contemptuous.

"Brown did it. I don't care who your witnesses are, they're lying. Either Brown has something on them or he's bought them. I want to know two things: How is Wild Kearny, and have you found Buddy Brown?" I spoke evenly, without passion.

"I'm not here to answer your questions. You'll do the answering."

"Then there's nothing to say."

"Do you want an attorney?"

"I don't need one. I'd like to talk to Mr. Kearny."

"If he wants to see you, he'll have to get permission from Mr. Scott."

"Can I call him?"

"We'll call an attorney for you. You're entitled to that, and you'll not get one damn thing from our office except the strict legal rights any prisoner has. You're facing a murder charge and you have damn few rights."

Chapter Thirteen

Even the cheerful fat man had changed when he took me back to the cell. He knew that Burr Scott's office was sure of me now, sure that I'd been involved in the nasty murder of a young woman. There was no warmth for me; he took me to the cell as if he were a mechanical man, chill and unapproachable.

Dooley was asleep.

The jailer locked the door. "I've got special instructions on you, Work," he said. "You don't go out to eat any more. I'll bring your meal to you in the cell. If you decide to call a lawyer, you're to tell me and I'll do the calling." He walked away, righteous, unemotional.

What I had in my mind were the night thoughts, the night truths again. The strength of evil. A Buddy Brown is not weak or helpless; he has secret strengths, secret dark helpers. He's not especially smart, maybe he's even a little stupid. His own life is empty and terrible. In the end, always, he will destroy himself. But while he lives, because he is evil, he has dark strengths. Everything that is weak in a decent person, every lust or abnormal desire, gives power to the Buddy Browns.

I sat on my bunk and looked at the truth. It wasn't important that Brown had found witnesses to lie for him. It wasn't even important that I was in a bad jam. The big thing was that here and now I was face to face with evil in a showdown battle.

Let's get practical, boy, I said to myself, and pushed the deeper thoughts away.

Brown knew the score now: Wild still unconscious, suspected of the stabbing, with her fingerprints on the bloody scissors; Work in jail; police hunting for Brown. Sometime on this Sunday morning he had found a way of making respected people lie for him.

Absolute safety for him still meant Wild Kearny's death. She might even know or guess the kind of pressure he had used to get his witnesses. If she lived, her father would believe her, regardless of what the law and the courts did. Believing her, he would hunt down Buddy Brown, and he would find him.

Kearny had tamed the forces of evil. He knew them and he could use them. The people of the night world would hunt Buddy Brown for Broadway Red Kearny. The weary hustlers, the worried little crooks, the whole web of the night would be spread across the continent for Buddy Brown. They would all know that Broadway Red Kearny was looking for a tall, thin pimp and reefer-pusher named Buddy Brown. Kearny would get him and that would be the end.

Broadway Red wouldn't kill him. He'd break him and turn him in, sobbing, spilling his guts in confession. I knew that. Brown would know that, too.

I tried to imagine that I was Buddy Brown.

How would I kill Wild Kearny?

It would have to be fast, before she could regain consciousness and talk. It would have to look like suicide. Wrists slashed with a razor blade, maybe. Or maybe Brown would have some other scheme, a surer one. But no matter what his scheme, he had to kill Wild Kearny, and quickly.

It wouldn't be an easy thing to do. Her father would be there, maybe in the room, and there would be either a police matron in the room or a policeman outside her door. The whole routine of the hospital would be there to protect her. No visitors except maybe her father. He'd be a hard man to get around. A girl in bed with walls around her, with guards around her, watched by nurses. It looked as if she should be safe.

But Brown had no choice. He had to find a way, and he would.

The cell around me seemed to close in on me like stone fingers. For the first time I felt imprisoned, helpless, trapped.

Brown was probably free to move. If the police had found him, they would have brought the two of us together. Now, with his alibi, they wouldn't even bother to pick him up.

Wild might still be unconscious. Tonight, maybe sooner, Brown would try to kill her. I was in a cell, behind a heavy door.

As I had last night, I pounded on the door.

The fat man came to the grille. "What's the matter?"

"I've got to explain something."

"You do your explaining at court tomorrow morning. You don't explain nothin' to me."

Like the guard last night, he turned away.

"Let me talk to Gloster, anybody. Let me make a phone call!"

He was gone.

They wouldn't believe me, anyway. Brown had his Pebble Beach alibi. No matter how I explained things, they wouldn't believe me. I was an unknown, unimportant ex-soldier. I'd been found drunk in a house with two girls, one dying, one knocked out. I'd accused a man who had brought respected witnesses to testify that I was lying. They wouldn't believe me.

"You really like pounding on that ol' door, don't you, pardner?" said Dooley, peering down at me from his bunk.

"I've got to get out of here. Somehow I've got to get out of here."

"Sounds reasonable, pardner. This place really don't have much. Not a good neighborhood, practically no conveniences, and confining as hell. Don't much care for it myself." He slid down from the bunk. "Howsoever, here we are. Might as well make the best of it and quit bashing your hand on that door. That ol' fat man ain't fixing to come back no matter how you pound."

Helpless, trapped. It was the first time in my life that I had felt completely trapped. Nothing to fight against except the iron bars and stone walls. The hours would go by, and somewhere outside Brown would be moving toward Wild Kearny.

I had to get out of this cell. I had to go to Wild. I had to find Brown and do myself the job that Kearny would do if Wild could talk—break him, bring him to the police, confessing the truth that would destroy him.

"What you puzzling over, pardner?"

"I'm going to try to escape, Billy." I hadn't meant to tell him.

"I'm going to have to take you home and introduce you to my folks."

"Why?"

"They got the idea that I'm crazy. I want to show 'em the real thing."

I sat on my bunk, looking at the door.

"Pardner, these walls are mighty thick and those bars are mighty strong. Ol' fat man got him a big roscoe on his hip and I believe that man knows how to use it. Got shootin' eyes. You cause him trouble and he'll mess up your insides with those slugs. Maybe I'd better do some magic for you."

"Billy, I've got to talk. I've got to explain to somebody why I've got to get out of here."

I told him what I thought Brown would do. He listened carefully, shrewdly, and the pixie face was serious when I was finished.

"Believe you're right, pardner. This mean-tailed boy Brown's got it cold in front of him. If this girl talks—especially to her old man—Brown has had it. He's a gone pigeon. If he knocks the girl off, he's got a fine chance of going on his way whistling. The answer is, knock the girl off fast."

We both were on my bunk and for a little while we were silent.

"Maybe I could call this Broadway Red Kearny on the phone for you."

"See if the fat man will let you."

Billy went to the door. "Hey, what do you want me to do with all this whisky I found back here under the bunk?" he yelled.

The fat man came huffing to the door. "What whisky you talkin' about?"

"I want to phone my lawyer. How's about it, huh?"

The fat man was peering into the cell. "Hell, there ain't no whisky in there. No, nobody calls nobody today any more. I got my orders. Nobody calls nobody and nobody talks to nobody. Nobody." He went off, puffing a little.

"When we go out to eat—" began Billy.

"I'm not going out. I'm a bad one, so I get my meal brought to the cell."

"This cheese is sure binding, ain't it?"

"I'm going to try a break. When he brings in my food."

Billy looked at me, his face excited and happy. "Can't be an escape act with Dooley the Fantastic around unless Dooley is in it. You know that, pardner."

"Billy, there's no reason for you to break out. You'd only get in more trouble. You pretend you're asleep when I try it."

"Pardner, I'd never live it down. I'm supposed to be a magician, escape artist and all that. How would it look if an amateur like you escaped and a professional magician like me stayed cooped up? Besides, I want to get out of here before I have to face that ol' judge in the morning. That ol' boy is likely to say something silly, like 'Five years.'"

"They won't give you five years for borrowing a car. Probation, most likely."

"Seems I've been in a little trouble before, here and there, for this and that. If that ol' judge takes a notion, he could get real silly. Best that I leave these parts."

"No dice, Billy. You stay here."

"Pardner, I've got to go. I'm goin' to go. Curtain."

I was thinking. I had to break out, and I knew that if I did, Billy would go too.

"That key is on a big ring. What can you do about that, Billy?"

"I can get it off. Slick as chicken guts. But that won't do no good, pardner. Only time I could get it was when we were out eating, and he'd need it to open up and let me back in."

"If you're going to try to break out too, Billy, I don't want to use force. We've got to outsmart him."

"That fat man's in the jail business. Probably pretty smart about his own business. A magician generally would use misdirection of some kind, making you look there when the gimmick is being worked here. Got to make ol' fat man look where we ain't."

"When you were showing me those tricks, Billy, how did you make that bright flash of light and puff of smoke?"

"These papers. Most magicians use them." He took some thin tissues from his little box of equipment. "There's a tiny cap at one end that explodes when you hit it, then the rest of the tissue burns real quick. It's a kind of guncotton."

"Could you fix some of them so that when he opens the door, they'll go off at the hinges?"

"Easy, pardner."

"If you could get that key off the ring, maybe you could lift his gun when he wasn't looking? I mean, could you ease that gun out of his holster?"

"Love to."

"O.K., Billy. Fix those flash papers at the hinges. Then we sit tight till he comes to get you for supper. That'll be around four o'clock, maybe. The fat man's relief won't show up until maybe six. Set the papers so I'll know how to do it. Then we unset them again. He takes you over for supper, brings mine back. When he opens the door the flash will go off."

"Going to kind of surprise him."

"You try to lift his gun as soon as you get in the building, before he gets to the door."

"If he don't make me carry the tray. Having met the law socially pretty often, I'm going to guess that I carry the tray."

"In that case, we'll have to risk his having the gun. The door opens, the flash goes off, he turns to look with the key still in the lock, I pull him in, slide out, you slam and lock the door. What do you think?"

"It's simple enough. Might work."

"We'll have to run. He'll start shooting and there's a whole nest of cops next door. After that I don't know what happens."

"I'll tell you one thing that'll happen," said Billy.

"What?"

"Your pants will fall down."

I'd got used to my loose jailhouse pants, making the holding of them with one hand a habit. They'd be clumsy to run in.

"Something else, Billy. We both look pretty rough. No shaves. These prison clothes I'm wearing. If we have to run for it we don't have a chance."

"Looks like ol' fat man goin' to have to go to sleep for a while."

"I hate to use force. I'm a completely innocent joker, but if I muss up a cop in a jail break they'll put me away for a year on general principles even after I'm cleared on this other stuff. Same way with you. I hate to do it."

"We'll come back from the café before four-thirty, the relief comes on at six. We could use that hour and a half, pardner."

"I'm just guessing at the times."

"What about those drunks in the other cell? They've been sleeping all day. I thought he was going to put them to work. When do they get fed?"

"All we can do, Billy, is try it."

"O.K., pardner."

Billy folded the flash paper into the hinges, showed me how to set them so that the turning hinge would pinch the small caps and set off the flash. Then we went to our bunks and waited. If the fat man came by he wouldn't see us talking together.

The drunks in the other cell finally woke up. They began yelling, so the fat man came and took them off. I guessed that they'd be mopping up the police headquarters in the big building next door. It must have been about four when he came back to our cell.

"Work, you stand at the rear wall. Don't make any moves." He opened the door and motioned Billy to come out. I was being treated like a real dangerous character. As far as they knew, I was.

When they had disappeared I went to work, setting the flash paper in the hinges. Once, back at the Punchbowl, I had felt like this. My squad had been at one end of a steep, narrow valley. The Reds had come down the slope behind us and we were going to have to fight our way out. It was the same tense feeling now.

The flash papers were ready. When the door opened the hinges would crush the tiny caps. I sat on my bunk and waited. A couple of years went by.

Then I heard footsteps and the fat man waddled up to the cell door.

Billy was behind him, carrying a paper bag. It looked like scant rations for me.

The bolt squeaked and the door began to swing open.

There were two pops, two bright flashes of light.

"Hey!" The fat man turned his head and I was on him, pulling him by his shirt in one quick jerk. I swung past him and slammed the door. He was reaching toward his holster as I turned the big key. I started to run.

"It's O.K., pardner. I got it." Billy waved the jailer's gun.

We ran to the room at the end of the hall in the shed between the old jail and the building where the police offices were.

"Want to try that phone?" whispered Billy, pointing to the desk.

"Can't risk it. Goes through the police switchboard. Leave the gun there."

"How about looking for your clothes and stuff?" Billy put the gun on the desk.

"Take too long. We'd better get out of here."

Back in the cell the fat man was yelling. He had a big voice, but the walls of the ancient jail were thick.

We went out the back door. Two empty police cars were parked there. I looked inside the nearest one. The ignition key was in the lock.

"We might as well go first class," I said, swinging open the door.

Chapter Fourteen

We climbed into the car. I started it and eased it as quietly as I could away from the curb. The clouds were purple-gray above us, and the cool darkness was edging over Monterey.

The first law officer that saw us would blow the whistle. All the car could do for us was to get us away from the jail fast. Then we would have to ditch it.

Back streets—and I didn't know the tangle of dead-end roads in this hundred-year-old part of Monterey.

The telephone on the dashboard muttered something about Franklin and Tyler Streets, then quieted into a buzz again. I headed the car toward the downtown section.

"You fixing to go to the hospital or you going to phone?" asked Billy. He knew the desperate urgency of time now.

"If I could phone Kearny, maybe at the hospital—"

"You don't have even a dime, do you?"

"No." I wheeled the car into a shadowed street.

"Me neither. But I can get maybe four-five bucks quick."

"How?" We were three blocks from the jail now. Time to ditch the car. I pulled it to the curb.

"Got to go downtown. Can you make out with those pants?"

"Have to." I pushed open the door and got out. The street was empty, a tired old street between tired old houses. We walked toward the glow of lights that was Alvarado, main street of Monterey.

"Where's this money?"

"I'll show you. Kind of a trick, too. Let's cross the street to that big hotel and you'll have phone money faster than a preacher can forget about a banker being drunk."

As we went alongside the stuccoed walls of the hotel, Billy reached high above his head to a ledge over a window. He brought his hand down, a half dollar between his fingers.

"See how easy it is?"

"What the hell—" I began, but I was reaching for the money. We might have an hour, we might have a minute before the silent air around us was filled with police radio alarms and the squad cars would begin their search for us. For Wild Kearny it might already be too late. I was half running toward the entrance of the hotel. Billy hurried along beside me.

"When I first hit a new town, if I have any scratch I put a few bucks in silver all over downtown, high up where it can't be seen. It's like a sort of bank. Usually I remember all the places."

The clerk looked up as we entered the lobby. He didn't seem too surprised at my flopping denims or Billy's jeans, shirt, and green bow tie. Lot of sport fishing in Monterey, and even nice people dress oddly there. There was a row of booths near the newsstand. I got change from the girl at the stand and went to a booth.

It was hard to dial the number.

"Monterey Community Hospital, good evening."

"Is Mr. Kearny there? His daughter is a patient."

"One moment, please."

It was one pure hell of a long moment.

Another voice. "Who is calling?"

This was no time for nonsense. "Work. Jim Work."

"Oh." There was a long silence.

The nurse's voice again. "You want to speak to Mr. Kearny?"

Something sounded wrong. "Yes."

"Are you calling him for his daughter?"

"Isn't she there at the hospital?"

Long silence, more whispering, and then, "If you have any information on Miss Kearny, or if you know where she is, you'll have to tell us. It's most important."

"She isn't there?"

"She disappeared more than an hour ago. Where are you calling from?"

"Is her father there?"

"No."

I hung up.

She'd run away. She'd been forced to leave either by violence or by some kind of argument. Her father had taken her away. One of the three—it had to be one of those three explanations.

Which one? And what do I do now?

I pushed open the booth door, stepped out. Billy was showing the rose and egg tricks to the girl behind the newsstand. She was giggling.

"Everything O.K., pardner?"

"I don't know."

Billy put his tricks back in his little box.

"Better be moving along, maybe?"

"Let's go," I said. Go where?

I could walk back to the jail, turn myself in. Then the stone walls would box me in again and I would be helpless. As long as I was out, no matter how loud and close the hounds, I wasn't completely helpless.

"You're on your own now, Billy," I told him as we walked into the cool evening darkness outside.

"Did you reach the hospital O.K.?"

"She isn't there. They're looking for her."

"Maybe her old man gimmicked her out."

"I hope he did. But if he didn't—"

We walked toward Alvarado again, not speaking.

Billy stopped about a hundred feet from the corner. "Here's another spot." This time he brought down three quarters that had been hidden behind an awning bracket. "We better do something about getting away, pardner. This town's going to heat up awful fast for us right soon now."

"You take off, Billy."

"Hate to leave you, pardner."

"You want to get out of town. I've got to stick here and find out—"

"O.K., Jim." Billy held out his hand, and as I shook it he gave me his three quarters. "I got lots more around. Just remember Dooley the Fantastic."

He walked away, bowlegged in his tight jeans, a giant elf who would never let the world mean more to him than an audience to be amused. I stood at the corner for a moment watching him. He was more than a hundred feet away when the police car coming toward him pulled sharply to the curb. Two officers were out, guns toward Billy, before the car stopped. Some woman on the sidewalk screamed. Billy stood there, hands high.

I turned back on darker Franklin, not running. I had maybe ten or fifteen seconds to get out of sight. At the corner I turned right and ran past a used-car lot, past the rear entrances of the Alvarado Street bars.

There was a wooden stairway leading up to old flats above the stores on Alvarado. I went up the stairway.

This was a back porch, two windows and a door opening on it. I tried the door. It was locked. A searchlight swept across the store fronts on the other side of the street. The police car, with Dooley inside, was hunting for me now.

One of the windows was half open. I climbed through it just before the searchlight swept across the porch.

This was a tiny bedroom, empty and dark. I opened the door in the far wall.

"Well, I'll be damned. A burglar!"

Two girls were looking at me. One of them, a full-bodied redhead, was wearing a man's pajama coat, much too large for her, with the sleeves rolled up on her arms. She was holding an opened can of beer.

The other girl wore a half slip and a bra. She had crisp, black hair and a delicate, sculptured face.

They weren't frightened, only annoyed, a little amused maybe. The redhead put down her can of beer and stood there looking at me, her hands on her hips.

"What's the idea, guy?"

"I'm sorry. I'll go." I was surprised at the calmness of both girls.

"Damn right you'll go. But what the hell did you come in here for? You look like a bum. What are you, prowling for food or money or something?" The redhead walked up to me, her hands still on her hips. I thought she might be drunk, but she wasn't. Just annoyed and curious, more curious than annoyed.

"Give the guy a break," said the slim, dark-haired girl. "He doesn't look tough, just kinda scared."

"Walking in on us like he owned the joint. I ought to call the cops," said the redhead. She was in her middle twenties, with everything a little big in her face, big eyes, big nose, big mouth, but handsome.

"I made a mistake." I started to close the door and the redhead grabbed it.

"Just a minute, fella. You come in here. We won't bite you."

The dark bedroom behind me brightened for an instant. They were still hunting me, the squad car's searchlight fingering across the shadowed porches.

I shrugged. "The cops are looking for me." It was only a question of seconds anyway.

"Yeah? Why?" The redhead motioned me into the cluttered living room.

"My name's Work. They think I killed a girl."

The two girls looked at each other. "In Carmel, last night?"

"That's right."

The dark-haired girl picked up an iron from the table behind her.

"Tell us about it," said the redhead. Her face was inches from mine, her big eyes wide.

"Didn't do it. Long story."

"Are the cops hot after you now?"

I motioned toward the street back of me. "Out there."

The dark-haired girl put the iron back on the table. "Shall I call 'em, Dee?"

"What do you think, kid?" asked the redhead.

"Give the guy a break. Let him move on out of here and we forget we saw him."

"Want a can of beer, fella?" asked Dee.

"Sure." These were sort of Chicago-style girls, the kind you find behind the Twenty-six game in the taverns. I could understand why they hadn't been frightened or excited when a stranger walked in on them. They were completely confident of their ability to handle almost any situation.

"You girls in show business?"

Dee nodded. She was opening another can of beer, taking it from a carton of six on the table. "I sing. Not too good, but plenty loud. Marcy's cocktail waitress. Here's your beer, fella."

"Thanks." I drank it from the can and it tasted fine. Dee walked past me into the bedroom. Marcy got out of the chair and came over to me.

"What's with the elephant-sized clothes?"

"Jail clothes," I answered. "I broke out a few minutes ago."

"We don't want to be rude or anything," said Marcy, "but after you finish the beer maybe you'd better travel. The law might take it wrong if they found you here."

Bang-bang-bang. Somebody was knocking on a door in the front of the tiny apartment, at the end of a short hall.

"Hell," said Marcy. "Duck, kid. I'll answer it."

I went into the bedroom. Dee was pulling on some clothes.

"Now what?" she said. "Will you kindly stop roaming around our apartment?"

"Somebody at the door. Marcy answered it."

"Probably the cops. What's she going to tell them? That you're here?"

"I don't know."

"I guess not. She's too damn kindhearted for her own good. This place'd be crawling with stray dogs, cats, and wounded birds if I let her."

"Figure me as one of the stray dogs. I'm no wounded bird."

"Are you going to stand there and watch me get dressed? I'm a singer, not a stripper, laddie-boy."

I went back into the living room. Marcy was closing the front door. She put a finger to her lips.

"Who was it, hon?" called Dee.

"Cops. Warning us there was a desperate killer maybe in this block."

"This fella? Maybe it's those crazy pants, but he doesn't look desperate to me."

"Finish your beer and take your time, now. Better give the law a chance to go somewhere else," said Marcy.

"Where you from, guy?" asked Dee. She was looking at her face in the mirror.

"Chicago."

"Good town. Kind of dirty, but the people are fun. Used to sing at a tavern out on West Seventy-Ninth." She was exploring her mouth with a finger. "Gah cavvy," she mumbled. Out came the finger and she smiled. "I said I've got a cavity. Better I should see a dentist."

"You've been saying that for six months." Marcy laughed. "Hey, I'd better start dressing now. I go to work at six. Another night of shoulder-grabbers and fanny-patters. Ah, me."

I finished my can of beer. "You girls got something I could use for a belt?"

"Hell," said Marcy, "I'll give you a whole outfit, and I think it'll fit you. Some of my damn ex-husband's stuff. Glad to get rid of it."

"Where's he at?"

"Jail. Where else?"

"Hell of a charming guy," said Dee. "Marcy was kind of crazy about him, in a kind of crazy way, I suppose. But he was a real lush. Never could understand a man who liked whisky better than women."

"I can," Marcy called from a closet. "Some whisky and some women." She came back with a coat and trousers. "Here, try these on. I'll get the shirt and the rest of the junk. You got the stuff on underneath that frantic outfit?"

"Suppose you give us the real scoop on what happened last night," Dee said.

"It was a man named Buddy Brown."

"The radio didn't mention Buddy Brown," said Dee, "Do you mean a tall, wide-shouldered, skinny guy with real black eyes?"

"That's the one. You know him?"

"Damn right I know him."

"Here?"

"L.A. He a friend of yours?"

"We each hate the way the other guy breathes."

"That's nice," said Dee, smashing out a cigarette. "He's a real fine person—to hate."

I began to change clothes.

"Go on. Tell us the story," Marcy said. "I'll whip us up a few corned-beef sandwiches and some more beer."

"It started yesterday. I was in Carmel...."

But as I talked, the question was pounding within me: Where is Wild?

Chapter Fifteen

The sandwiches were good and I needed mine. They listened to the story carefully, asking questions now and then.

"You're really all gone for this girl?"

I buttoned Marcy's ex-husband's shirt. It fitted well, a wine-red tab-collar job.

"I'm gone for her."

Dee was pulling on her stockings. The three of us were finishing dressing, eating our sandwiches, drinking beer as I talked. We could have been three people in a carnie, not bothered, not bothering.

"Why?"

"She was exciting from the second I saw her. She's never stopped being exciting, and she never will for me. That good enough?"

"I get guys excited, but it never seems to last," Dee said.

"You don't mind about this Brown?" Marcy asked.

"Of course I mind," I answered. "Plenty. But that's got nothing to do with us. I love the girl."

"So now what are you going to do?"

"Find her. Get the facts so the law will leave us alone."

"Sounds all right if you don't have much else to do tonight."

I finished tying the knit-silver bow Marcy had picked for me. It wasn't bad. I looked a little too sharp, but it was better than the tent-sized denims.

"Do you think she's got much interest in you?" Marcy asked.

"If a man starts worrying about that—" I began.

Marcy shook her head. "Don't bother, kid. You're right."

"You're a dreamer," Dee said, putting down her can of beer. "I've heard about this Broadway Red Kearny. He's loaded. He'll hide her out in some fancy resort hotel until his lawyers and private dicks handle everything. Then off to Paris for his daughter. There'll be no more loving for you, poor dreamer. What you've got, kid, is memories. Memories and a mess of cops on your tail."

I didn't say anything.

"This Brown," she continued, "that's different. It couldn't happen to a sweeter person, what's going to happen to him. Kearny'll have his boys kill him like a farmer kills a rat.

"I'll tell you about Brown. I used to sing in a joint way west on Santa Monica down in L.A. Place got a big play from a bunch of kids who thought they were real cool hipsters. Brown hung around there and picked them off like grapes—the girls. Sometimes one of these kids would have a boy friend or something who'd get sore when he found that Buddy had turned the girl into a dopey-eyed hustler. Brown loved that. I'll give him credit, he's plenty tough. He'd work the guy over like a butcher. One of the girls told me the only time she'd ever seen Buddy look content was when he was marking a boy up for life. She'd done plenty herself to try to make him look that way, but it never worked. A girl can't do it for him."

"You'd better shave," said Marcy. "There's a razor and things in the bathroom."

I went in. I found the razor and pushed the drying stockings out of my way so I could see the mirror.

"I've known a lot of bad ones," Dee called toward me, "but Brown is the pure quill when it comes to being bad."

There was a man's face in the mirror. A tired face. Jim Work, who hadn't had a worry in the world thirty-six hours ago. But he hadn't had Wild Kearny then, either.

I started to shave. The razor pulled like an old rake in high weeds.

"Personally, I don't think a girl who's fooled around with Buddy is ever much good afterward," said Dee. I could hear Marcy trying to shush her.

"He seems like a nice guy," Dee said to Marcy, "and he's in a big enough jam right now without having to eat his heart out over one of that rat's tomatoes. I've seen too many of them."

I finished shaving and went back into the other room. Marcy had finished dressing and she wore a lacy black evening gown. Dee had on something in green, off the shoulders; she was good-looking in an easygoing, strong-bodied way.

"You got a phone?" I asked.

"Sure. Want it private?" Marcy asked. There was something in her eyes as she looked at me that said she'd wait around until I was out of my jam and maybe in the market again. Then she'd be there.

"I'm going to call the cops," I said.

"Not from here, you aren't, honey," said Dee. "I think you're in a bum deal and we're glad to help you. It's real interesting. But you don't get us in no wringer with the law. If you want to call the cops, do it from the drugstore—and when you leave here, please remember to forget that you ever saw us. O.K.?"

"Wish my goddamn husband could see you in that suit," said Marcy, putting her hands on my lapels. "He always looked like he needed some more padding on the shoulders."

"What you want to call the law for, friend?" asked Dee.

"I figured a gimmick. I'm going to say I'm calling from the city room of one of the San Francisco papers."

"And you want the latest scoop on the Brooks killing. That's kind of clever."

"If they know where your girl is, for example," said Marcy.

"I want to know who this witness is. Then I can do me some action."

"Call away. Better let me pretend I'm the long-distance operator."

The phone was on a table in the corner. Dee looked up the number and dialed it.

"This is San Francisco," she said when she had an answer, and her voice was changed now, it had the mechanical quality of a telephone operator. "I have a call for the chief of police at Carmel." She waited for a few seconds, listened, and then said, "Here is your party. Go ahead, please." She handed the phone to me.

"Hello." It was Clyde.

"*San Francisco Examiner*," I said, speaking crisply.

"Yes?"

"What's the news on that Brooks affair?"

"There's a lot of news," Clyde answered. "The man we think is the killer escaped from the Monterey police an hour or so ago. You've got his name?"

"James Work. That the man?"

"Right. He and a cellmate, a kid who stole a car, broke out. They captured the kid—William Dooley, a transient—about half an hour ago in downtown Monterey. Work is still on the loose."

"You're sure he killed the Brooks girl?"

"Looks that way. You know he accused a fellow named Brown?"

"We got all that this morning."

"Brown's got a solid alibi. He's clean."

"Who is his alibi?" This was the big question.

"Couple of people. What makes it solid is Mrs. Worton Henderville." Clyde spoke as if I'd know the name.

"I see. Anything else?"

"Lots. This thing is getting very odd. The other girl involved, Wild Kearny, disappeared from a local hospital this afternoon. Apparently just walked away. You'd think somebody would see her—tall, beautiful girl with hardly any clothes on, just a hospital nightgown. But she walked away."

"Do you think her father is involved in that?"

"No. That's another odd thing. You know who he is—a New York gambler and union boss. Not a hoodlum, but with lots of hoodlum connections. Very rich. This afternoon, just about the time his daughter was getting ready to do her vanishing act, we got a telegram from New York to take this man Kearny into custody."

"Kearny?"

"Yes. We arrested him this afternoon and took him to Salinas for the U.S. District Marshal. He'll be on his way back to New York tomorrow to face income-tax-evasion charges."

"With his daughter missing and mixed up in a murder?"

"It's tough, but we had to do it. When Uncle Sam says to arrest 'em, we just go out and bring 'em in. It took three deputies to put the cuffs on Kearny, too. He was like a crazy man."

"Yeah, I can understand." I said.

"But this case is still breaking. You've got the picture? A girl from a rich Eastern society family murdered. The killer escaped from jail. The girl we suspect was involved in the killing escaped from the hospital. Her father arrested for income-tax evasion. Now we find out that this fellow Work is involved in the biggest dope ring on the West Coast."

"What?"

"That's right. This ex-soldier just back from Korea smuggled in a big load of Japanese heroin. At least five thousand dollars' worth at wholesale prices—maybe would sell to addicts for fifty thousand or more. We've got a man hunt started for that fellow that will sew up the Monterey Peninsula tighter than a rat trap. Shoot to kill, if necessary."

"Give me the story on this dope angle. That's brand-new."

"Sorry. You can say that we know he's involved and that's all. We've got the evidence and we're holding back until we can get the rest of the gang."

"Can't you give me anything more?"

"Sorry. Try the folks at the Federal Narcotics Office in San Francisco tomorrow. They're hot on it and we're playing ball with them."

"Thanks," I said, and hung up. Five thousand dollars' worth of narcotics! Me—a dope smuggler!

"What's the matter, dreamer? You don't look happy."

I turned to Dee and Marcy. "The law's got me pegged for being a dope smuggler as well as a murderer," I said.

Dee's big eyes narrowed to slits. "You mixed up with that stuff?"

"No. Flat no. Never."

"Why do the Dick Tracys think you are?"

"They won't say. But they sounded awful sure." I sat down.

"Did you find out who the witness is?"

"Never heard of her. A Mrs. Worton Henderville."

Dee's eyes widened. "Marcy, we've been taken. This guy is guilty as hell."

"Hey!" I said. I could see that she wasn't joking.

"Look, guy," said Dee. "I know Mrs. Henderville. She comes into the Gilded Cage with her friends and sometimes she asks me to do special numbers for her. She's nearly sixty. She's very wealthy—has a big house in Pebble Beach. She's a nice, smart, decent old lady who never told a lie in her life. If she says you're lying, then you're lying."

"Take it easy," Marcy said. "I still believe the guy." Dee lit a cigarette, blew out smoke. "Mrs. Henderville is the alibi for Buddy Brown—is that right?"

"That's what the cops say. She'll testify that he was someplace where she was around three o'clock this morning. That's when I found Brown standing over Pen Brooks in the bedroom."

Dee stubbed out the cigarette. "It doesn't figure. Mrs. Henderville isn't the kind to be mixed up with Buddy Brown, not for one second. She's too nice."

"Could she be on a dope kick?" asked Marcy.

Dee shook her head. "When she comes to the Gilded Cage she's always with a party of rich old folks like herself. One of them is her family doctor. He'd know if there was anything wrong with her. There isn't, I guarantee that."

"But she's lying." I said.

"She doesn't lie."

"Then she's been fooled."

"That would be one hard old lady to fool."

"What's the news on your girl, Wild?" asked Marcy.

I stood up. "No news. She walked out this afternoon in her nightgown. Nobody's seen her since. And her father's in jail in Salinas on federal income-tax charges. He can't get bail here and they'll take him to New York tomorrow."

"You sure don't go around with a very nice crowd, do you?" said Marcy. "Two of you on the lam, one in the cooler. You turn out to be the biggest hoodlum since Mickey Cohen, and the chief witness that you're a liar is the nicest old lady west of the Statue of Liberty, according to Dee, who doesn't fool easy." She opened three more cans of beer. "If you didn't look so sweet in my damn ex-husband's clothes, I'd be in favor of yelling for the cops myself."

Dee drank her beer, wiped her lips. "O.K., buster. You're on your own. If it wasn't that Buddy Brown's mixed up in this, I'd be blowing the whistle right now to have this place belly-deep in cops. But even Mrs. Henderville will never convince this girl that Buddy isn't the dirtiest rat in California. So take off, buster."

I walked toward the hallway.

"Got any idea what you're going to do?" asked Marcy, following me.

"I know what I've got to do." I took her hand. "You girls have been great. If you hadn't gone along—"

"Skip it," Marcy said. "When you aren't hot, look me up sometime. I'd like to see that technique of yours in action."

I walked out the front door and down the stairs to the street. At about the same place on the Alvarado sidewalk where Billy had been picked up a police cruiser passed me. The officer on the right side looked at me and looked away.

In my pocket was about a dollar in coins that Dooley had given me. I knew where I was going and what I was going to do.

Chapter Sixteen

Five thousand dollars' worth of Japanese heroin. That's what Clyde had said. Last night, when he was drunk and panic-yellow, Brown had talked about five thousand dollars. It was only a mixed-up thought as I went along.

I turned off Alvarado and walked to the Bay Rapid bus station. Twenty-five cents would get me into Carmel. It was a thousand to one that Wild Kearny was in Carmel, and I had to find her fast.

Fifteen minutes after I got there the big white Carmel bus rolled into the station, and I got aboard. I watched the neon signs of the stores flashing red, yellow, and green as the bus moved toward Carmel.

In no time at all, it seemed, the bus was on Ocean Avenue in Carmel. I got off and crossed the street to Whitney's, a red-and-white-fronted restaurant and bar. The bar was in front, small and U-shaped, with tables around the walls. Maybe fifteen people were in the place.

"Beer," I said to the barman.

As the barman poured the beer I said, "I'm looking for a fellow named Buddy Brown. You know him?"

The barman looked at me with open curiosity. "Yeah, sure. He comes in here sometimes."

"Know where I can find him?"

The place was completely silent.

"You a friend of his?"

"No."

"Newspaperman?"

"That's right."

"Yeah. You might be wasting your time; the story around town is that he had nothing to do with that murder. He was somewhere else."

Carmel is a little town where people in the half-dozen or so bars spend much of their long drinking days talking about each other. The stabbing of Pen Brooks would be a big, big thing to the talkers in the bars. In one way and another they'd know most of the story by the time their second Martini was down to the olive.

"He was?"

"Yeah. Rich old doll and her son say he was with them last night until about four this morning. She's the kind of old doll everybody believes. You know the girl and the guy both escaped?"

"Yes. We got a flash on it."

"Damnedest thing you ever heard. She was in the hospital with a cop outside the door—I'll be right with you, sir—and when the nurse came back the girl was gone. Took off in her nightie."

"Find her yet?"

The barman mixed a Martini. "Nope. She's wandering around like that, barefooted, practically nothing on. You'd sure think somebody would spot her."

On a stool around the corner of the bar a big man chuckled. "That's one beautiful girl, but she never did seem to like clothes too much. During that warm spell a little time back she used to come down Ocean in shorts. Real short shorts."

"Had real long legs, too. Gorgeous legs. Don't blame her for wearing shorts. Ought to be a law requiring a girl with legs like that to wear shorts," said a sandy-haired man in a loud sports jacket.

"You're the boy to notice 'em, Jackson," said the barman. Everybody laughed except me.

"Where can I find this Buddy Brown?"

"You rented him the place," the barman said to the sandy-haired man.

"Yeah. About a block from here, down Carada. Right next to the corner where the big ravine cuts through. Redwood, green shingles."

"Thanks." I finished my beer. There was no way of even starting to look for Wild, but if Brown was home....

It was dark off the main street on Carada. I was worried about a police stake-out at Brown's house. They might figure me to come here, even figure Wild to go to Brown. Cautiously I walked along Carada, passed the house on the corner. There was a light behind drapery-covered windows. No cars nearby.

I walked through the tangle of flowers around the side of the small house.

Wooden shutters covered a side window. I stumbled over a heap of branches and climbed a low stucco wall. Now I was at the rear of the house. A steep ravine cut off the ground here, and I could see the lights of houses at the bottom, twenty feet or more below me.

The window at the back of the cottage was a large single pane of glass, without curtains or draperies. I could see into the long main room of Buddy Brown's home. There was light from a lamp near the door, and I saw bottles on a coffee table near a big couch, a couple of chairs, another couch that was probably a bed in the corner. One corner of the room near my window was cut off by a wall, and I guessed that the bathroom and whatever kitchen he had were behind this wall.

The big room was empty. I waited outside in the darkness, the brush-tangled ravine behind me.

This was my only point of contact. I could try the mysterious and respectable Mrs. Henderville, but she lived in Pebble Beach, behind the guarded gates of Del Monte Properties, impossible to get to without a car.

I could try to search the hundred black streets of night-shrouded Carmel for a barefoot girl in a hospital nightgown, but the police were doing that.

This was the only point of contact I had.

Maybe it was an hour. It was a long, measureless time in the cool, purple dark. Then some animal was coming through the winter-dried brush of the ravine, slowly. I turned to look for it and I saw her, a slim ghost.

Wild Kearny was climbing the side of the ravine, ghost-pale in the faint light from the houses.

She couldn't see me against the darkness of the wall, but now she was close, coming over the tall grass at the edge of the black incline.

I could hear a car stopping in front of Brown's cottage. "Better give it another check all around," a man's voice called. A flashlight beam brightened a circle of bushes behind the corner house.

"I still don't think that girl could make it over here in her bare feet. It's a helluva cold night!" answered the man with the light.

Carmel police hunting for Wild Kearny at Buddy Brown's—and they were right. Somehow she had come through the wooded hills of the night-black village toward the house of the man I knew would kill her.

She saw the light, heard the voices. The slim ghost vanished against the edge of the ravine.

The beam of light traversed the bushes beyond the stucco wall and then it flickered out.

"Damn!"

"What's the matter?" the man in front yelled back.

"Light's gone sour. I think it's the bulb."

"I've got a spare in the kit."

I could hear the officer tramping through the pile of branches next to the house. Bending low, I half ran, half crawled to the place where Wild was flattened against the ground in the high, dry grass.

"It's Jim, Wild," I whispered.

Her face was a faint silver oval. I straightened myself on the ground next to her, one hand on her back. "It's Jim," I whispered again.

The muscles of her shoulder were quivering. We were side by side in the tall, crisp slivers of grass; by lifting my head I could see the glow of the window in the rear wall of the cottage. The flashlight beam came again, wavering as the policeman stumbled along the side of the cottage, climbed the wall.

"Don't talk, don't move," I whispered close to Wild's ear.

The flashlight swept across the grass at the top of the ravine, searched out the wall, the bushes. We could see him, like a shadow, across the window glow as he peered in. He called something back to the man in front, and then went around the side.

In the still, cool blackness we could hear the police car start and pull away.

"Wild, are you all right?" I tried to see her face.

"I'm terribly hungry," she said as she pulled herself up.

I stood and took her by the shoulders. "Why did you run away from the hospital? Had the police talked to you?"

"There was a doctor. He wouldn't let me talk to anybody. They said my father was outside, and then when I asked for him they told me he was gone. I had to get away."

"You've been out—like this—for hours?"

"There were French doors on my room. I just walked out and then I knew I would have to hide. There was a garage behind a house and I hid there until it was dark. When it was dark I started to walk here, hiding in the bushes and behind trees if there were cars on the roads. Now I'm hungry."

"Why here, Wild? You know he killed Pen." I was still holding her by the shoulders as we stood in the dry grass above the houses in the ravine. I could see her face in the glow from the window.

"Nobody would tell me anything. How Pen was. You say she's dead. I didn't know. This was the only place I could go. I had to find out about Pen. About my father. About Buddy. I couldn't go to the Zoo, never again. But there would be a phone here, and I could find out. They wouldn't tell me at the hospital. They wouldn't tell me anything."

"Pen died today. Your father is in trouble—income taxes. Buddy is free and on the town."

"Buddy? With Pen dead? Did they think it was an accident?"

"They think either you or I stabbed her."

Her body was still trembling. I could feel the thin, harsh hospital cotton nightgown on her shoulders.

"I broke out of jail, Wild. I came here to get Brown before he could kill you."

"Buddy—kill me? Why?"

"He was gone before the doctor or the police arrived. He's got a witness to say he was never near the Zoo that night. He's afraid the police might believe you, and most of all he's afraid of your father."

"My father—where is he?"

"I told you. In trouble. Held by the federal marshal in Salinas on tax charges."

"He knew that was coming. That was one reason he came here—to make sure I'd be all right if there was trouble. He'll get out. He always does." She sounded very tired.

"But Wild, you're sick. You've got to get warm, get some food, have medical care."

"I can take care of myself. I'm going into Buddy's house." She pulled herself away from me. "One thing I remember, Jim. I remember you."

"You said you hated me." We were standing a little apart, facing each other.

"I was in that hospital bed looking at the ceiling for a long time today. There were things to think about. Buddy. Pen. You. I don't hate you, Jim. It was all pretty dirty. I wish you had met me three weeks ago. I wish I'd never met Buddy. I wish a lot of things."

I went to her and took her in my arms.

"Most of all, Jim, I wished it hadn't been a lie to my father yesterday. If it had only been true, things wouldn't be dirty, would they."

"We'll make out," I said, and I kissed her.

Her slim, strong body in the torn rough nightgown wasn't trembling now.

"I'm going to break into Brown's house. It's the only thing we can do. I'll call somebody who can get us help. Pete Barrow or somebody who knows you. Once they understand what happened last night, we'll be fine."

We climbed the top of the ravine and I went to the big window. It was hinged from the top so that it could be swung up and open. I hit it with the heel of my hand until I broke the catch and then I pried it open. I lifted Wild in my arms. She pushed up the window as I held her and slid in, dropping to the floor. I climbed through after her.

Now we were together in the light. Wild's nightgown was badly torn, very dirty. She was rubbing the soles of her bare feet, and they were dirty, too.

"You walked barefoot?"

"It wasn't bad. In the summer I usually do. Tough feet." She managed to smile. "There's only one thing that will do me any good now—a shower."

I took her in my arms again. What I had known by instinct yesterday was certain now. This was the only girl that would ever be important to me. For better or for worse.

I let her go and for a moment she looked away from me, looked at Buddy's room. She shivered and her head turned.

"It's all right, Wild," I said.

She looked up at me. "All right, Jim."

She put out her hand, we each felt the pressure of the other for a moment, and then she went into the bathroom.

I heard the splash of the shower and I stood alone. We'd fight our way out of this. It wasn't a bad jam once it started straightening out.

The front door clicked, swung open, and Buddy Brown was there. We stared at each other.

I moved toward him and he dropped his right hand to his pocket. He came forward with a thin, long knife ready for me.

"Sucker," he said in a bitter voice. "This was the last place you should have come."

He'd kicked the door shut and we faced each other. The splash of the shower was the only sound.

"I'm going to kill you, sucker." He heard the sound of the water now and I could see his body tighten. I moved toward him; we were maybe ten feet apart now. The knife was bright for a moment as it caught the light, a four-inch, slender blade pointed forward and upward.

"She's here," he said. "It has to be her." The black eyes searched out mine. "I'll kill you and then I can handle her, sucker. I'll hurt her and she'll love it. I know her, and I know she loves it."

We were six feet apart, both of us moving very slowly, both of us on the balls of our feet. Both of my hands, fingers open, were chest high, a little forward. I was trying to get his eyes again, but they would flicker up for a moment, look down.

"I know her, sucker. She's crazy about me when I kick her around. Crazy for it."

This was the time now. We were close enough, four feet apart. The knife was lowering a little, pointing flat and straight toward my belly now.

"Sucker!" he hissed, and struck.

I went to the left, chopping down with my right hand toward his wrist. The knife missed and I swung in with my left hand, trying to find his wrist with my right. The knife was coming forward and I fell back, stumbled, went over.

I kicked him away. He was standing, knife ready, smiling. I was on my back, looking up at him.

He was in no hurry and I had to wait for his move.

He was a knife fighter; he would know how to handle himself against an unarmed man flat on his back. I could kick, grab, roll, try to throw myself up—but that blade would find my belly, my throat.

He picked up a silver cigarette case from the low table with his left hand and threw it at my face. I rolled and the box hit my shoulder heavy and hard. He was on me. I kicked and missed as he came down, knife arm close to his body, left hand reaching for my face.

The knife caught me at the top of the throat, just the bite of the point as my head went back, my hands grabbing his wrist. He leaned on me, putting his weight on his stiff right arm, and the point bit hot and wet.

My hands and wrists fought his arm, fought his muscles, fought his weight, a tight, close struggle of breath-deep fractions of an inch.

And then his black hot eyes looked away and over his shoulders I could see Wild like a glistening golden statue above him, a statue of a Valkyrie fighter.

I twisted his hand back against his wrist as his weight lifted for a moment, brought my left fist solid against the bridge of his nose. The knife slithered away and I rolled with him, locking my right arm around his head, twisting myself to get above him.

His whole body jerked once, and I let him fall away from me, his eyes wide, white now. I pushed him and his head fell against his shoulder.

We still looked each other in the eyes as he died there, his neck broken.

Chapter Seventeen

My hand was against the cut in my throat. She was standing back, hands at her sides, her golden body wet, her head down.

He was dead. The few nervous, hot-blooded years, the twisted hungers, the caged-animal hate—all over.

"How badly did he hurt you?" she said, looking up, her hands out to me.

It took a moment to talk. "A cut. Nothing. He's dead."

We both looked at the man. He had meant a kind of love to her, a terrible thing of passion-whipped senses. A dozen nights of laughter and white-hot nerves, hot black eyes and a mocking mouth. But love.

He had meant hate to me from the moment we met. I shook my head the way a fighter does after a bad round.

Her arms were around me, sensitive fingers touching the bleeding hole in my throat. "It wasn't really killing," she said.

"I would have killed him with my hands, with a knife, with a gun, with a whip."

For a long time we were silent, but we were close.

I dropped my arms from her and pushed her back.

"You'll have to get away from here, Wild. I'm going to call them before they come here again, looking for you. You'll have to be gone—and you never were here, not tonight."

"How bad is this, Jim?"

"Real bad, Wild. I'll get a lawyer and maybe somebody will believe me—I don't know. They were pretty sure that one of us, you or I, stabbed Pen. With Brown dead, what can I say now? I killed him."

"If you hadn't, maybe I would have done it," Wild said, and she pointed to the floor. "When I heard the noise over the splashing, I looked out and saw you on the floor, and he had the knife over you. I brought that from the shelf."

It was a straight-edged razor, bright and deadly, on the floor.

"You would have killed—him? To save me?"

She pointed again to the razor and then she began to sob, covering her face with her hands, dry, soundless sobs that shook her body.

I waited for her to be done. When she was ready for my arms she put down her hands. I held her tightly, as if I could bring us together above flesh or life, and she said, "That's the way it is, Jim."

"That's the way it is, Wild."

A tiredness of cold, liquid lead was rising in me, as if I were a grotesque, man-shaped empty bottle slowly being filled with it. I fought it off. Wild and I would have to work for our lives now. We were looking into short weeks and endless years, the two of us. Short weeks to the tiled room at San Quentin with the curious, terrible faces looking through the thick glass window as I waited on my chair. Endless years in stiff, shapeless prison clothes for lovely Wild Kearny.

"Get some clothes on," I said to Wild, and I spoke sharply; there could be no tenderness of love for us until there was nothing, no other hope, left for us.

"I—have some here, Jim."

"Get them on, and hurry." There was no time for jealousy of a dead man.

While she dressed I went into the little bathroom, turned off the shower, closed the razor, and put it back on the shelf. I put a Band-aid on my throat.

She would leave, I would wait a little while and then call my friend Clyde. I wondered if I would see Billy Dooley again. Probably not, unless it was in a jailhouse corridor.

Wild was dressed now in a deep-toned print dress, a pattern from the Islands, and very pretty.

"You look wonderful, Wild." It was a good thing to say. She needed words like that.

"Jim, you say my father's in Salinas?"

"I guess in the county jail, being held for the federal marshal. They'll take him to New York tomorrow."

"If I call him from here they might trace the call."

"It doesn't matter. I'm going to call them anyway."

"Couldn't we escape, Jim? Get away from here? Once my father's in New York, he'll get out on bail. He'll hire the best lawyers, use influence. It would be better if you could hide someplace until they know the truth."

"The truth that I killed him?"

"That was self-defense. He had a knife, he would have killed you. There are fingerprints, the wound on your throat."

"They'll say I faked them, cut myself. It would be easy to do."

"Jim, you said Buddy had a witness. Who is it?"

"Some rich old lady in Pebble Beach who's got a better reputation than an archbishop. Her name's Henderville. Mrs. Worton Henderville."

Astonishment opened Wild's mouth, widened her eyes. "Mrs. Henderville?"

"That's right. Know her?"

"Pete Barrow is her son by her first marriage. She says Buddy was with her?"

"I pretended I was a newspaper reporter and called the Carmel police. That's what they told me."

"But Pete and Buddy weren't even friends, not even before Buddy—" She didn't finish the sentence.

"The chief said there were two witnesses. They would be Pete and his mother."

"Jim, we'll have to see them. Tonight. It's a chance."

"They'd just call the cops and that would be it. You get out of here, Wild."

She didn't answer. She went to the front window, pulled the drapes aside enough to look out, and shielded her eyes against the light from the lamp. Then she walked back to where Brown was crumpled and I saw her lift her chin high, close her eyes, clench her hands, breathe deeply once. She let the air out in a soft sigh and bent over Buddy. Her hand went into his trouser pocket and came out with a jingle of keys.

"The MG is in front. Let's go, Jim."

It would be better than calling, waiting for them.

We turned out the light and left the cottage.

"I'll drive," Wild said. "I know the way."

She pulled away from the curb and almost up to Ocean before she turned on the headlights. "While we're driving, tell me what happened after I fainted last night."

She was hearing about Billy Dooley by the time we climbed the hill. It was exactly nine o'clock then and she turned on the car radio for the news.

"He must be a swell kid," she said. "We've got to help him as soon as we can."

"—and the top local news story is the desperate escape of a murder suspect and a young car thief from the Monterey jail late this afternoon," said the pleasant, mildly enthusiastic voice of the newscaster. "James Work, a recently returned Korea veteran, was held on suspicion of the murder of Penelope Brooks, young artist, in Carmel last night.

"Work, who is believed to have masterminded the smuggling of fifty thousand dollars' worth of heroin from Japan, is still being hunted by Monterey Peninsula authorities. The car thief, William Dooley, was found walking on Alvarado Street in Monterey shortly after the jail break. When questioned about Work's movements after the escape, Dooley told police, 'I'm a magician. I made him disappear.'

"The Japanese heroin was brought over on the troopship *General Hanford* by another soldier. Work, who also returned from the Far East on the *Hanford*, is believed to have picked it up after landing. The heroin was discovered hidden in his car during a police search following the stabbing of Miss Brooks.

"Other news—" I clicked it off.

"Buddy," said Wild. "He had a package in the Zoo he asked Pen and me to keep for him. He must have put it in your car when he walked out last night."

"He didn't have much time."

"It was next to the door in a cabinet."

"He figured the police would search the house anyway, and I guess he thought my car would be safe. It was only worth five thousand wholesale, but that must have been the big score he was talking about."

"Now all we have to do, after we get Pete and his mother to tell the truth, is to tell the police that this was Buddy's package," said Wild, swinging the car into the stone-towered gate of the Del Monte Properties.

"They won't believe you," I said.

Wild stopped the car for the guard and the last two of Dooley's quarters went to him. We didn't dare have him call the Henderville home and ask them if they were expecting guests. Otherwise it costs a half dollar per car to enter the private barony that includes Pebble Beach and the Del Monte Forest.

Wild put the car in gear.

"They won't believe you and these people won't change their story." I felt low. What I had done tonight was with me now and there was no escape from it. Self-defense? Sure, but I felt sick and dirty inside. The clouds had rolled away from the moon and the night was bright with silver now, too beautiful, too unreal.

I knew what reality was.

Around us, almost hidden by the trees, rising up on the hills above the moon-streaked Pacific, were houses warm with lights. Pleasant, secure, comfortable houses, the kind I'd thought about for myself someday.

Wild swung the little car into a short driveway curving before a long, low house built mostly of glass, surrounded by Shasta daisy bushes that seemed to be explosions of white in the moonlight.

Pete's Jaguar was parked behind a Chrysler Imperial, both of them shining with streaks of moon fire.

"We'll play it straight and hard," I said. "They're lying. We know it. Their lies could kill us both—so it's straight and hard."

"We're together, Jim."

Up the broad, low fieldstone steps to the long panels of glass. Wild knew the house. She went to the left, pulled a panel that rolled quietly aside. We went into an enormous room done in gray and green with a round fireplace, hooded in copper, in the center.

Pete Barrow was in a low chair made of shaped wood. He was looking through the glass wall on the other side of the room at the silver, shimmering Pacific. He had a bottle and a half-filled brandy glass on the table beside the chair.

"Hello, Pete," Wild said.

He sat completely still for a long moment and then he stood up and faced us.

"Hello, Wild. It's good to see you," he said. Brush-cut hair, the kind of modern handsome man's face that isn't pretty or soft—rugged lines and tanned, big, tall, muscular body, white teeth, and an automatic smile. The smile was on now, and his eyes moved from Wild to me.

"Did you get out of your troubles, Work?" The laws of his breed made him look at my clothes, the sharpie time-payment clothes of Marcy's ex-husband, and I knew that Pete Barrow would not have worn such clothes even to escape from a pack of bloodhounds.

"Is your mother at home?"

"I don't believe you know my mother." The smile hadn't changed, the voice was pleasant; the remote coldness seemed to seep out of him invisibly.

I took a handful of his soft cashmere sweater, pulled him toward me, and slapped him hard across the face. He pumped three or four short rights and lefts at my body and I swung him into a wrist lock.

A Japanese houseboy peered around a door at the end of the gray-green room, squeaked, and came pattering to his master's aid.

"Hideo!" said Wild sharply. "You get Mrs. Henderville, *hayaka!*"

Hideo stopped in mid-patter, looked thoughtful and worried, then pattered out of the room. Pete was wiggling. I dropped the wrist lock and put the works into a right that went an inch into the muscle over his heart. He said, "Oof!" and sat down on the floor.

I'd killed a man with my bare hands within the last half hour and the feel of it was in my blood.

"Hello, Mrs. Henderville," said Wild. I turned to look at the woman who stood for a second in the doorway. Dee might call her a nice old lady, but it was a bad description. She was the kind of mother you'd expect to see with her tanned son in the society-page pictures of the horse show or the Pebble Beach sports-car races. Slim, silver-gray hair, a face much like Pete's, tanned, with lines of strength and experience. She was wearing a dark blue suit of something soft and tailored, a pearl-colored sweater of Angora, a necklace of Mexican silver.

She looked at her son, sitting on the floor, and I felt that even when he was a little boy and was hurt she would do as the books said and not rush to him with alarm or sticky sympathy.

"What's the trouble, Pete?" she asked him, still at the end of the room.

"This is the fellow the police want, Sue," he said. He got up, one hand on his stomach.

Sue Barrow Henderville looked at me briefly, to see what I looked like, and then spoke to Wild.

"I believe you're ill, Wild. Do you want to go upstairs and rest?"

"Did you tell the police that Buddy Brown was here last night until four a.m.?"

"Certainly. Why are you interested?"

"Why are you lying?" I asked her.

She didn't bother to look at me, or indicate in any way that she had heard me. I knew that this would be true always. To Mrs. Worton Henderville, Jim Work did not exist.

"You don't talk to my mother like that, fellow," said Pete.

I moved toward him and he stood his ground. He'd try, I'd give him credit for that, he'd try until he was bloody hamburger.

"Hideo!" Mrs. Henderville called sharply. The round brown face peered around the corner as she spoke, and he pattered to her, bowing.

"Call the sheriff's office. Tell them to come here at once."

I grabbed him by the mess jacket and slapped him across the head, and the little cuss tried some judo. Pete came in from behind me and the three of us went sprawling across the floor, knocking over a table. Hideo got the hand chop on the throat—it seemed kind of popular today and it seemed only right that he'd get put out of the ball game with a judo cut—and Pete and I wrestled. He was stronger, bigger, and knew more about it until I got an elbow into his face. Use an elbow like a hammer, and bones and teeth go. After the first one, he took the others limply.

When I stood up Pete was holding his broken face and Hideo was rubbing his throat and trying to swallow air. I was fighting madness, kill madness. My hands were working, clenching, unclenching, and I couldn't breathe enough air to satisfy my blood.

"Goddamn you to hell," I yelled at the Henderville woman, "start talking or I'll tear this kid of yours apart!"

She was a sportswoman; she belonged to those strangers who lived in another dimension from mine. With her son trying to spit out blood and broken teeth, holding his hands to his smashed cheekbone and nose, she made no gesture of sympathy to him. She stood a few feet from Wild and looked at her.

"You're obviously mad or ill or under the influence of dangerous drugs, young woman. For your own sake it would be well if I called for help. Will you see that this thing here doesn't molest me?"

Wild came to me and put her hands on my face. But in the need to destroy that had swept through me I almost struck her as she touched me. Then it was gone, and I was myself again.

"I'm all right now," I gasped.

"Mrs. Henderville, please," said Wild, looking over my shoulder at the cold, gray, remote woman. "We know you lied. We're trying to find out why."

"There was no lie. Mr. Brown was here with my son and myself until nearly four this morning. Our house-boy served us coffee and brandy at intervals until then. I am, of course, prepared to state this under oath."

Hideo scuttled like a crab, and was out of the room. Pete pushed himself up from his knees with one hand, the other still held to his smashed face. He stumbled away.

Wild and Sue Henderville were fighting a wordless conflict of eyes, and neither looked away. "You're lying because of your son," said Wild. "Brown had something on him. Is that right?"

"My son has been injured. You can prevent me from calling for help only by further violence."

She turned and started to walk away. Wild grabbed her, spun her around. "It's no good, do you understand? It's no good. You can't win. Start telling the truth or you'll get your violence!"

Sue Henderville tried to break away.

"I'm fighting for my man. I'll rip the truth out of you if I have to!" This was Red Kearny's daughter, not something elegant from a Connecticut finishing school.

"It's the truth!" Sue Henderville's voice was high and frightened.

Wild slapped her hard.

"You're lying. What's Brown got on you?" She stopped suddenly.

Hideo came back into the room, holding a big, black Army .45, pointing it at me. He was using both hands.

"I kill him," he squeaked, and the room was a blast of sound. There was a clattering tinkle of falling glass somewhere.

"Come on, Wild," I shouted, grabbing her arm and pulling her toward the open panel.

We got to the opening and there was another blast.

Some of the glass ten feet from us shattered and fell. Down the steps and there was a third one. God only knows where that slug hit.

We were in the MG and Wild gunned it up to sixty in fifteen seconds, with the rear wheels sliding on the first curve.

"The sheriff will be here in a couple of minutes. We've got to get away!" I said loudly.

"I tried, Jim, I tried," she said.

I bent over quickly and kissed her. We wouldn't have much time together now, and these few seconds in the car, high above the moonlit Pacific with the pine scent rich in the air, were unbelievably precious.

We had so little time, we had found each other so quickly and in such violence.

"All the strength is in that woman. I know her kind. She'll die before she lets the world look down on her or pity her. Wild turned the car up a steep, hill-circling road.

"Who is your father's best friend in New York? Better if it's a lawyer."

"Max Schoenberg. Smart, honest, and a good friend."

"We'll find a phone and you call him collect. Our only chance now is to have friends."

"Right, Jim. I'll find a phone."

"The sheriff will try to block off the Peninsula. They'll probably catch us within minutes. If you can call, give Schoenberg the whole story, step by step. Right up to the Jap shooting that big forty-five."

"If they catch us before I can call, then what?"

"We'll try our best to keep from getting caught. If they do—"

"If they do it will be the both of us together," she said. "They can't beat a team that keeps fighting, Jim."

"We're going to have to dump the car. They have the license. If from nowhere else, they have it right in the Carmel police accident file for Saturday." I was trying to think against the police now, the way an officer leading a patrol in enemy country has to think against the enemy. We needed those minutes to get a call to Max Schoenberg, to get our story—the true story—to somebody with strength.

"I know the Forest pretty well, Jim. We're going to come out above the Presidio, where the Army Language School is. We'll park among all the cars in the lot there, and we can walk down through the Presidio to Fishermen's Wharf. We can go into a restaurant and put in our call."

Suddenly the Forest was behind us, and Wild swung through the gate and down a broad, straight residential street. A few blocks down she turned to the right on another wide avenue. In the distance now we could hear sirens screaming through the night.

The Presidio is a small Army post set on a hill above Monterey Bay. Wild drove the MG down the main road and took us into a big parking lot for the military students.

A minute later we were walking down a steep, curving road toward the lights of Fishermen's Wharf.

"When you put in the collect call to Schoenberg, who will you say is calling?"

"Why, Wild Kearny, of course. Oh, I see. The operator would recognize the name, maybe."

"If she reads the Sunday papers she will."

"I'll say Miss Kearny—that should get by. Do you have any money, Jim?"

"About a nickel."

"I stopped being hungry back there in the cottage, but I think we both need a drink. A double shot, straight."

We walked out of the shadows of the Presidio into the lights of a big service station. A block away was the Wharf and a clock in the station showed nine-forty-five. It was about the best part of Sunday evening in a warm, fine January on the Monterey Peninsula. For a moment I forgot that I had killed a man tonight, that I had maimed another man's face, that we were hunted as psychotic killers by the police.

Chapter Eighteen

The wharf is a jumble of sea-food cafés, bars, and a little theatre, and scattered among them are good, honest fishermen's shops that sell the heavy tackle of ocean fishing. It's a few hundred feet long, as wide as a street, and it smells the way it should.

Wild and I walked through the wandering groups of winter tourists and I tried to pretend we were what we were not until the lights in front of the Wharf Players showed me the blood on my coat sleeve from Pete Barrow's face.

"It hasn't been a night of very good surprises for you, has it, Jim?"

I thought Wild had seen the blood. "No. There've been a lot of surprises, and only one of them was good—you."

"I've got a nice little one. Come with me."

We went into a little hole-in-the-wall bar. An elderly Portuguese lady was sewing on something colorful and lovely behind the bar. When she saw Wild she stood up smiling, waving her arms, welcoming her in Portuguese.

"This is my good friend," Wild said to me, "and she doesn't speak English very well. Not well enough to hear news broadcasts or read papers. Best of all, I often come in here with a crowd and pay her at the end of the week."

The lady was smiling at me and she looked as if she liked me. Wild sat down on a high stool.

"What do you want, Jim?"

"A double Scotch straight. Water in a glass, please." Wild pointed to the bottle, indicated a straight double.

The drink washed away a lot of strain I hadn't known I had. Things shifted into perspective. It was going to take explaining to get me out of the shadow of that thin body with the broken neck. It was going to take strength to crack the steel will of Sue Barrow Henderville and make her tell the truth.

The clock behind the bar pointed to two minutes after ten. I reached toward the corner and turned on the radio. There was music.

"I'm going in back and phone," said Wild. She slid from the stool and walked behind the bar. She pointed to the cash register and made a writing motion. The lady smiled and nodded, as if paying for drinks were not very important at all.

Wild and I looked at each other before she stepped through the curtain to the room in back. It was a look between a man and a woman who knew each other and liked what they knew.

I sat on the stool and stared at my empty glass. The lady made filling motions but I shook my head. The double had done the trick. I knew where I was in the world, what I had to do.

A fat man in a gaudy shirt came into the little bar from the Wharf. The lady looked at him with a mixture of dislike and respect. He had a big, red face, with a halo of curly white hair around his bald head. His bare forearms were thick and strong, covered with tight-curled black hair. There was a nest of mixed white and black hairs like springs rising up from the open shirt.

He put a hand on my arm and smiled. He was smoking a thick black cigar that he had to take away from his mouth before he could smile. I remembered him from somewhere.

"I'm your friend," he said. "I know who you are. When the girl comes back I want to talk to you."

"Who are you?" Even as I asked, I knew. Carmel, Saturday night, with Brown.

He kept smiling, the cigar close to my face, his arm on mine. He had an immense stomach, but behind the fat was a fisherman's muscle.

"I told you. I'm your friend." He laughed.

It was the damnedest laugh, almost like a baby's laugh.

"Where do you know me from?" This big cupid with the halo of white hair and the net-hauling muscles didn't bother me much. Wild was in the next room talking to Max Schoenberg. It was one o'clock in New York, he'd be home, and she had said that he was tough, smart, and a good friend. That was what we needed.

"I don't know you real well, but we have some good friends." He laughed again.

The music on the radio stopped.

"We bring you a news bulletin. James Work, escaped killer of a wealthy society girl in Carmel last night, has apparently added another victim. A Carmel resident known as Buddy Brown was found by police tonight in his cottage dead from a broken neck. Fingerprints found in the cottage indicate that James Work may be the killer.

"Work had tried to implicate Brown in the murder of the girl and made his escape after witnesses offered an alibi for Brown. Police say—"

The fat man turned off the radio.

"Broken neck. You're real strong for a kid your size." The thick fingers hooked into my arm like gaffs and the hard eyes were dead cold and small. "Why'd you kill the punk, huh? Talk. The old lady doesn't understand."

Wild came through the curtain. She saw the fat man and stopped. They knew each other, I could see that. "Hello, Joe," she said.

"Hello, princess. I was just talking to your boy friend. Your new boy friend, I mean. Ha-ha."

"It's fine, Jim. I talked to him. He's flying out on the early-morning plane. He says if we want to we can give ourselves up, but he'd rather be here when we do it. He's wiring five hundred dollars tonight to me as Mary Cash, waving identification. He says not to worry about anything. He'll be here tomorrow afternoon, late."

She was trying to tell me everything while she had the chance.

"This is Joe Sandodera, Jim. I met him several times in the last few days with Buddy. He and Buddy had a deal."

The fingers stayed deep in the flesh of my forearm. I had to take it. I couldn't risk trouble.

"You didn't have to introduce us, princess. This boy and I got good friends together. You want to come along, huh?" He chuckled around the cigar.

I got off the stool. The Portuguese lady looked worried and Sandodera spoke to her.

"Her old man's the bartender. The law says a woman can't serve drinks, but she don't know about that law. They don't have it in the old country. Ha-ha. Let's go." The last two words were flat; he meant them.

Wild walked from behind the bar. She looked at me and I shrugged.

"Funny thing," said Sandodera. "I wouldn't have known my pal here if I hadn't seen you sitting in this joint. Right away I put two and two together—this is the fellow I want to meet and everything's george. Funny, huh? All the cops looking for you, and who finds you? Me." This time he really knocked himself out laughing. He ended up coughing.

"Want to go with this clown?" I asked Wild.

"All I know about him is bad," she said.

"Ha-ha." Then the fingers really went to work on my arm. This man was a giant of muscle.

"Schoenberg says give ourselves up tonight?" It was hard to talk because of the pain, but I was trying to act as if Sandodera were only an annoying barroom drunk. Not easy with his big red face close to mine, his gaff-hook fingers in my arm.

"He says better not until he gets here."

"O.K., clown. We'll go."

"Everything's george, huh?" Nothing seemed to make Sandodera angry. The three of us walked out of the bar into the wind-swept coolness.

He led me with his arm. Wild followed. There were plenty of people around and now that Schoenberg was coming I wasn't worried. If I remembered the rules, he couldn't practice law in California, but he could give a lot of enthusiasm to some local law wheel. To hell with this muscular cupid with the polar-bear hair. I felt great.

"The boat's right below here." Sandodera pointed to a flight of wooden stairs leading down from the Wharf.

"What boat?"

"Go ahead!" He gave me a shove and I fell down half the flight until I caught the railings. Wild was behind me, Sandodera behind her.

I went down to a wooden platform. The boat, a small purse seiner, was bumping the pilings, her rigging banging gently.

"Get in. We're not going anyplace, don't worry."

I helped Wild over the side. The big nets were piled high on the short, broad deck. The cabin and pilothouse were forward, with a small flying bridge above.

"Sit down. We can talk private here. Want a drink? I got a couple bottles in the cabin." He motioned to some boxes on the deck. Wild and I sat on them.

"No. O.K., so you know I'm Jim Work. Now what?"

"Well, kiddo," he said, thumbs in his belt, standing over me, "I didn't know you were in this tough a jam. I didn't know you killed the punk. Why did you do it? Because of this tomato?"

I didn't say anything. A dozen feet above us was the Wharf, all around us were other fishing boats, and apparently we were alone on this one.

"Yeah, that's your business, kiddo. You're like me, like the great Sandodera. If you got to kill 'em, do it with your hands. Crack! Break a back, snap a neck. Take 'em out on the boat far enough, throw 'em to the eels. Ha-ha-ha-ha." He slapped me on the back. "But I wouldn't do it for a tomato. World's full of tomatoes. Sometimes I have three, maybe four of them on this tub, all trying to scratch each other's eyes out."

He lit his cigar, chuckling.

"I'm not from this port, kiddo. I'm from down south. That's what we want to talk about. How much you got for me?"

"How much what?"

"Uncut Japanese number-one white. Like the punk showed me a sample."

"Heroin?"

"Sure, heroin. What the hell did you think I wanted from you?"

"What makes you think we've got friends in common? You mean Brown?"

"Brown?" Sandodera spat. "Who calls that punk a friend?" He turned to Wild.

"Excuse me, princess. I forgot about you."

"Who do you mean?"

"The kid on the *General Hanford*. Who else? Ha-ha." I didn't say anything. The fat man was waiting. Then his hand slapped my face gently.

"There was maybe fifteen or twenty thousand bucks wholesale of uncut Japanese *ichiban* on the *General Hanford*. The kid brought it over, gave it to you. You gave Brown one box. I want the others. You can't peddle the stuff, you're so goddamn hot now you're blistering that box under you. I'll make a deal. Come up."

"Why do you figure me in this?"

"I called my finger at Fort Mason after I heard the news about the box they picked up in your car. My finger says you came in on the *Hanford*. The law finds one box in your car. Brown, the punk, said he had a box off the *Hanford* and he gave me a sample. Damn good Japanese heroin. That adds up easy. You've got two, maybe three boxes left. Brown said no other buyers but me were here or knew about the stuff. I want it—all of it, kiddo—and I'll deal good with you."

The festering trail of Buddy Brown. Wherever he went there was this.

"Understand, kiddo, you don't have any choice. You can't make a better deal because I'm the combination's man. I'm the buyer for the combination. I'll take care of you and the princess. She says some guy is flying here, not to get picked up until he's arrived. O.K., make yourself at home on the tub."

He spat out a piece of cigar. "Five grand a box. I'm not chiseling because you're hot. Five G cold for each box. Tell me where they are, I send a punk to pick 'em up. When I get 'em and they check out, you get the loot. O.K.? Everything george, ha-ha."

I was trying to balance the play in my mind. Sandodera was deadly dangerous, a child would know that. Immensely strong, cruel, selfish. Being with him was being in danger.

But it might not be easy to prove my innocence on Brown's box of heroin. The very closeness that Wild and I had found together was against us. I'd come from the port of Yokohama on the Military Sea Transport Service *General Hanford*. The heroin had been smuggled in on that ship. It had been found in my car.

A few other soldiers had tried the gamble—smuggling in a small fortune in Japanese narcotics, as easy to buy in the black market of the Shimbashi in Tokyo as liquor or women. I couldn't prove that I hadn't been one of them. They wouldn't believe Wild because she was in love with me. They knew that Wild and I had been lovers on the night of Pen Brook's death.

Schoenberg might find ways of getting the truth out of Mrs. Henderville and Pete Barrow. He might convince a jury that I had killed Buddy Brown in self-defense. But heroin brought over on the ship that I had been on, heroin found in my car....

"Howsabout it, kiddo?"

"What do I know about you?" I asked.

He slapped me on the back and laughed, holding his belly. "You're no punk, hey, kiddo, ha-ha!"

I spoke to Wild. "You know the picture. It's the gimmick about the car. This one might be the right one—but there's a risk. I'm going to go along for two reasons, tonight and the payoff. Understand?"

It was double talk. I had to hope she understood. Sandodera's eyes were closed to black, glittering lines.

"Brown was afraid of you," Wild said to him.

"Sure he was afraid of me," Sandodera growled. "He thought he was tough, but Sandodera was what the punk was praying to be. I kill with my hands, like you do, kiddo, and when I see a tomato I want—" He laughed and threw his cigar into the water. He poked me with a spike of a finger. "You knew the punk, you don't know me good yet. I'll tell you a story. You know who Sandodera is? Sandodera is the man from the combination.

"You know who your friend was? Nothing! A schnook! But a schnook with a cute racket. He'd find a young broad—just the right one—with a guy overseas. Then he'd sell the girl on a big story about how she could have minks and diamonds and a fancy car. All she had to do was get the boy overseas to smuggle a little Japanese heroin back to the States. The punk would tell the girls he'd find a place for them to raise the dough, and how to send it to Tokyo. When the kids came back he'd have the buyer with the big money ready. For a schnook it was a good scheme. All the C.I.D. could ever trace was the broads—if they traced anything."

He reached over and grabbed my arm, the spike fingers digging under the muscle. "I been waiting on this lousy tub for two days more than I figured. For a week the punk played around, giving me a sample, talking big, trying to up the price. He thought he could get in with the big boys through Joe, ha-ha-ha. I been walking the Wharf all evening waiting for him, and he can't show because you busted his neck. Ha-ha-ha. Good joke, but no more jokes. Where's the rest of the stuff?"

"How do you figure me in this?"

The fingers tightened.

"The combination ain't stupid, kiddo. We watched the punk operate. He got three girls to raise six grand from an L.A. shylock with the dough going to their guys in Tokyo. We traced that. Six G in Tokyo, American green money, buys twenty G's worth of heroin, at wholesale prices delivered here. Brown was going to pay the shylock eight and diddle the kids out of their share. We knew that.

"We know that four packages went on the *Hanford*. We contacted the three guys as soon as the Army brought them off the ship and to the separation center. They were clean. The stuff had been passed to another soldier, who was going to take it to the dealer, and the dealer was Brown. We couldn't find who was the other soldier, the guy who brought the stuff to Brown.

"Now I know who he is. You. What are you trying to do, kiddo? Figure some cute angle of your own? For you there ain't any cute angles, ha-ha."

Now I know enough of the story for the Army's C.I.D. and the Federal Narcotics Bureau to trace the whole lousy mess. Three soldiers who had been in Tokyo, who had wives or girls in Los Angeles, who came in on the *Hanford*. Out of the two thousand men on the ship, only a hundred, maybe, would fill those particulars. Out of those hundred, three were the greedy, stupid, dirty ones. They'd find them, thanks to the Los Angeles and Buddy Brown lead. And I would give them Sandodera.

For a man in a bad jam, I felt good. I'd never feel guilt for having killed a rat like Brown. The only girl I wanted was my girl now. I knew I could fight my way out of the jam.

I was through with Sandodera now.

"Get your crumby paw off my neck," I said.

"You tough, kiddo?"

"Get back on the Wharf, Wild," I said.

Sandodera put out a big arm to stop her. "I wasn't going to do this until after a while," he growled, and he grabbed her by the throat, his other hand still in my shoulder. He gave me a shove and, holding Wild by the throat he pushed her into the open cabin hatch. I was on his back and he turned, grabbing me with both arms like a bear.

Holding me in the bear squeeze, he threw me into the cabin. I was up fast but he was standing there ready for me. Wild was crouched behind me and there was no room for movement. I hit him three times. It was like hitting a bull.

I felt his arms go around me again in the rib-breaking, lung-smashing bear squeeze. I tried to fight him and Wild hit him with something that tore his forehead.

The big red face, the white halo of hair, the cold eyes were in front of my eyes and the thick arms were tightening on me. Blood was trickling down his face and Wild it him again but the arms kept tightening.

She stuck her thumb in his eye and the arms dropped but he threw a left into my belly like a sledgehammer and I went down. He knocked Wild on top of me and stood above us, one hand to his bleeding eye.

He was crying, his mouth twisted down like a bawling baby's and he was cursing us in sobs, cursing in some strange language.

Then he pulled Wild up by her hair and slapped her with his other hand, terrible slaps with his thick hand and his powerful muscles.

I kicked him from the floor and he was hurt. He dropped Wild and came for me. She fell against the cabin bulkhead. I got my heel into his face as he came down, pushing him back. I was still on the cabin deck and he was on me again, his hand grabbing for my foot as I tried to kick. He got my throat, pulled me from the deck, and hit me. That was it. I was still conscious, but my body control was gone. The sledge hammer got me on the side of my head and I was out.

I came back because of shock and pain. I had fallen into some kind of big box. I looked up at the cabin's beams. My knees were doubled up and the box wasn't wide enough for my shoulders.

I saw Wild's face above the box for a moment as I started to struggle to get out of it and then her face came down to me and the weight of her body was on top of me.

"Have fun, you," yelled Sandodera. Wild was pushing on my chest, trying to get up from me. "Have lots of fun. It's your last chance, kiddo. After a little bit I make you tell me where the stuff is, then I work this tomato, and then you meet some eels, a long way down." He closed the lid on the box and fastened it.

Wild screamed, the sound tearing into my ears. Maybe the tourists on the Wharf could hear her, or the fishermen on the nearby boats.

We could hear music, suddenly loud. Sandodera had turned on a radio, and then both the radio and Wild's screams sounded dull and leaden. He had thrown something, maybe a blanket, over the box.

"My fault," I said. It was already hard to talk.

"Couldn't help it," said Wild.

"Suffocate," I mumbled. It was hot and thick even after a few seconds.

"Little air from sides, not much. Don't talk."

I tried to move, but any movement I made pushed Wild against the sides or the top of the box.

"Love you." I knew it might be one of the last things I would ever say.

"Love you, Jim. We've had it kind of rough." And I knew she was smiling.

We didn't try to talk after that.

We lost consciousness slowly, as if our minds were running out, drop by drop.

Chapter Nineteen

Light above me and coolness. No weight on me. Terrible pain beginning to explode in my bones. This was consciousness.

He dragged me, sodden and limp, up and out of the box. Wild was on the deck, clawing at it with her hands. I couldn't stand erect either, and I fell, my body a sack poked by millions of blazing hot needles.

Like Wild, I gasped in great lungfuls of cool air. Cool, thin air with oxygen. I began to rub myself, tearing the wet, crushed clothes from my chest, rubbing my arms and legs. I had killed Buddy Brown. I was going to kill Joe Sandodera, slowly. Somehow I'd live to do that.

He was there in the little cabin, looking at us. His eye was blood-red and swollen, and there was a crust of blood on his forehead.

"Pretty soon my crew will be back. Tell me where the stuff is. Otherwise I throw you back in the box and take you to sea. You want to go back in the box, huh?"

This was the first time in these two days that I was afraid. I was more afraid of that box than I would be of death. I had to fight myself to keep from begging him, praying to him, not to put me back into the box.

"My crew are my boys. They'd watch me cut you both up into shark bait and laugh. I got something pretty nice for them here after I get done with her. What I mean is you'd better tell me where the stuff is goddamn fast."

I got up, holding to a bulkhead, tottering on my rubber, pain-filled legs.

"I'll tell you," I said.

"Where?"

That was a damn good question.

"In an icebox." I was trying to whip my sick mind into action, inventing a story.

"What icebox? Where?"

"In a little bar on Alvarado. The bartender thinks it's just a package. He's holding it for me." Now I knew what my mind had been trying to figure out through the fog of pain. I had wished for an answer, and my mind had followed my wish. It had brought out of the blood mist the words "In an icebox." An icebox that held a secret a bartender had told me a week ago.

"Will he give the box to me?"

"Only to me personally." I had to gamble on that icebox. It had an answer for me.

"It's twelve. The goddamn bars won't be open only two more hours."

"I'll take you there." If the icebox still held the same secret as last week....

His good eye was a narrow slit. "You got cute tricks, kiddo?"

"The only trick is if the cops don't spot me."

He looked at my torn shirt. "I'll give you a fisherman's shirt and jacket and cap. I want that stuff."

"How about her?"

"I tie her up good. My boys won't bother her until they know I'm finished."

Desperately I hoped that Wild wouldn't scream now, that Sandodera and I could get to the bar without being spotted by the police.

He rolled Wild over, tied her wrists behind her with a length of cord. He tied her slim ankles. "You won't scream, maybe, because of the cops, but I take no chances." He took tape from the wall cabinet and taped her mouth.

"Rest easy, kiddo," he said to her. "You have a good time after a while." He looked at me, went to a locker, and threw me some clothes. I put them on.

"You being too goddamn good, kiddo. What's the trick?"

"No trick. I'm whipped."

"Maybe. Maybe. Come on."

We went out of the cabin, up the stairway to the wharf.

"If a cop spots you, you got nothing to do with me, understand, kiddo?"

"Yeah. If a cop spots me I never heard of you."

We walked the length of the Wharf, quiet now, with only two or three of its cafés still open.

A block, going by the old custom house, an ageless adobe, and then into the Sunday-night brawl of Alvarado, where the soldiers from Fort Ord were trying to drown the reality of tomorrow's reveille in tonight's beer.

"It's this one," I said to Sandodera as we reached the middle of the block. An M.P. patrol sedan had passed us but we hadn't seen any police.

"O.K."

"You'll have to come up with the money for a couple of beers."

"O.K." He was wary, suspicious.

We went in. It was a small place, one girl, four or five soldiers at the bar. I had stopped in there several times in the last three weeks; the bartender remembered me and said, "Hiya." This was the one who had shown me the secret.

"Two beers," I said, sitting on a stool well beyond the soldiers. Sandodera sat next to me and threw a dollar on the bar.

"I'll get the stuff," I said. I walked to the end of the bar, where there was a sign, "Men." The bartender paid no attention to me. I stepped behind the bar, slid the cover from the icebox, and took out the .45 I knew he kept there.

Joe was standing about ten feet from me.

I'm not a killer. I blew his right knee to pieces. I'm a good shot with an Army .45. He spun around and fell over.

No matter what else happened, he wouldn't have a right leg any more. I figured maybe we were even. Now I would try to send him to prison.

I threw the gun on the floor and put my hands high. Everybody was yelling and screaming. I just kept my hands high. When the cops came I didn't want them to get worried about what I might do.

Good mind. I told my mind I wanted to kill Sandodera and it searched until it found the memory of this bartender showing me his gun and where he kept it in case of a holdup.

They grabbed me now, the bartender and the soldiers.

The cops got there and they slipped cuffs on me, pushed the crowd away. An ambulance was rolling up in front of the place for Sandodera. He was moaning.

"I'm Jim Work," I told the police. "Wild Kearny is in the cabin of a boat at the end of Fishermen's Wharf, bound and gagged. Better hurry."

They hustled me into the back of a squad car and sirened down the block and out to the end of the wharf.

"Quite a week end for you, Work," said the policeman next to me in the back of the car. "Kill a girl. Kill a guy. Escape from jail. Almost beat a man to death in front of his mother. Shoot another man."

"It's been quite a week end," I agreed.

"What a character!"

The car squealed to a stop. They hurried down to the boat and they were carrying Wild up the stairs just as the two members of Sandodera's crew arrived. They arrested them on general principles.

Wild saw me and smiled. They were going to take her to the hospital and that's where I wanted her to be.

They took me back to the jail and put me in a cell all by myself. I didn't try to tell them anything. Max Schoenberg was coming.

"Hi, pardner! Mighty sorry to see you back." It was Billy Dooley in the other cell, calling to me.

"You O.K., Billy?"

"Why, sure. I've got social security, if nothing else. But what in the name of jumping frogs have you been doing? Killing people?"

"Killing. Beating. Shooting. I broke one dope peddler's neck and shot another one. Billy—"

"Yeah, pardner?"

"What are you being held for now?" My mind was working real fine tonight.

"Now, that's a funny question, pardner. You know what they're holding me for? Vagrancy. Me, Dooley the Fantastic, being held for vagrancy. Of course, it ain't the first time."

"Not for borrowing that Jaguar?"

"The mark I borrowed it from wouldn't press charges."

"Where did you borrow it?"

"Off the driveway of some little place in Carmel."

"When?"

"About two o'clock in the morning."

"What was the man's name who owned the Jag?"

"Not sure I remember, pardner. The cop mentioned it, though. Barrow, I think."

It was all pretty obvious now.

Chapter Twenty

When Wild and I had left the Zoo, Pete had been there drinking. Pen, contemptuous of the man who had wanted to marry her, had been in the bedroom.

Billy Dooley had stolen the Jaguar sometime after two o'clock Sunday morning. Pete was still there.

Pete and his mother were willing to alibi Buddy.

Buddy Brown had come to the Zoo when Pete had just stabbed Pen Brooks, Buddy Brown saw a golden future. Get Pete out first, get away himself, blackmail Pete Barrow for the rest of his life.

When we came, finding him over the dying girl, Buddy wanted Pen to die. Alive, she was worthless to him. Dead, she was worth a fortune in blackmail. That was why he had tried to stop Wild from phoning the doctor.

He knew the house would be searched, knew that his place might be searched. He put the package of heroin in my car, walked to a cab stand, and took a cab to the Pebble Beach home of Pete and his mother. They kept him for the night, arranged an alibi.

What kept Pete from taking the easy road—blaming Buddy? It would have been one man's word against another's. There had to be a reason. I'd think about that one.

I went to sleep thinking about it.

Next morning they arraigned me in front of a judge who looked at me with sad wisdom. I pleaded not guilty to a long list of charges.

They took me upstairs and I gave them a long, completely truthful statement. I didn't tell them about Billy Dooley and the stolen Jaguar. That would be for Max Schoenberg later.

Naturally, my statement didn't sound so completely truthful to the police and the district attorney. They questioned me for a long time about it and then gave up for the day.

"I want to talk to Dooley," I said to the jailer as they were getting my stuff out of the locker before they took me to the county jail in Salinas.

"Dooley ain't here."

This was a punch below the belt. Dooley was a star witness against Barrow, and I knew that Billy would be hard to find once he left Monterey.

"Dooley got ten days for vagrancy and six months suspended for breaking jail. The judge liked the kid and he figured that you were the hardened criminal that made him go with you after you closed the door on Stevie. Dooley's out on the truck, helping keep the city clean. For the next ten days."

It was a habitable cell in the Salinas jail and I had a good long nap until Max Schoenberg arrived. The first thing he said was that Wild was doing fine.

Max Schoenberg was a wide-shouldered, rangy man with all the patience in the world. His hair was snow-white. The local man with him was quiet and friendly. He wanted to hear everything I could tell him.

Schoenberg thought about the Barrow angle for a long time.

"You're right," he said, "there must be some pretty strong evidence against Barrow somewhere or he'd have accused Brown instead of giving in to his blackmail. A picture, maybe. Young people like Wild and her friend would be likely to have a flash camera around. It's my bet that this Brown came in, saw Barrow bending over the girl, and just picked up the camera and shot the picture. From what you say, Pete would be no physical match for him, and Brown had the evidence against Pete cold in the camera. He probably left the camera there at the house when he ran out."

The quiet, friendly local attorney seemed impressed with the idea.

They left, I slept some more, and after supper Max came back. He was smiling. They took us to a conference room and he showed me a photo print. It was a good clear flash picture of Pete Barrow still holding the scissors and bending over Pen.

"Before we opened the camera we had the Carmel police take Brown's fingerprints off the shutter release, the flash bulb, and the focusing knob. I talked to Wild at the hospital—she's doing wonderfully—and she said that Brown liked to fool with the camera. It was on the bookshelf next to the bedroom door. This Brown seems to have been a fast thinker."

"Now what happens?" I asked.

"The Monterey sheriff has arrested the Barrow boy. When he saw the picture he broke down."

"How many things does that leave them holding me for now?"

He smiled. "Not so many. Sandodera has a long string of narcotics arrests. The police found about two pounds of crude opium in his boat, so he'll be on his way on a charge of possession, along with his crew. I hope he gets a long trip.

"I'm guessing that the coroner's jury is going to find that Buddy Brown met his death by misadventure. Miss Kearny's story corroborates yours, and the knife, again with Brown's fingerprints, was found near his body. In any case, it's clear self-defense, but the coroner's jury can save everybody a lot of time and money. That's the feeling I get from the county people.

"Neither the Barrow boy nor his mother intends to press charges on the assault. Nobody's angry about your shooting Sandodera except the bar owner, and I gave him a hundred dollars. He's happy."

"What are they holding me for, then?"

He laughed. "Nothing."

I got up from the chair. "You mean I'm free?"

"For a man who was arraigned for murder on two counts, narcotics possession, jail break, assault, and a few minor things, you've got yourself clear in world record time—about nine hours since you were in court.

"We'll go downstairs and get your things. My associate—your actual attorney—is downstairs with a writ from the judge. I'll drive you to the hospital to see Wild. She's expecting you."

"There's one thing," I said.

"Oh?"

"The legal fees and costs. That hundred dollars, your trip, the local lawyer...."

Max Schoenberg smiled again. "You worried about paying?"

I nodded.

"You've got a friend named Broadway Red Kearny. A real friend. Stop worrying."

"What's going to happen to him?"

"I know the story," the white-haired, vigorous Schoenberg said. "Kearny is straight. His taxes are paid. The Eastern combination played politics with a little man in the Internal Revenue office and the Treasury knows already—today, Monday—that they got off on a bad steer. Your friend is O.K."

"One thing more," I said. "There's still a lot of Japanese heroin loose somewhere."

He nodded. "I phoned your story to the Narcotics office in San Francisco. They'd been watching Brown and they picked up his contact in a hotel there last night. He'd mailed the rest of the stuff to Brown in Carmel. They found it in the Carmel post office."

The friendly, quiet man was waiting for us. The officers gave me my things and we left Salinas in the Monterey attorney's car.

"Poor kid," said Schoenberg.

"Who?"

"Barrow. Half drunk, angry, and the girl tormenting him. And then, before he quite realized what had happened, there was a bright flash and he turned to see this Brown there with a camera. He left the place with Brown hurrying him, only to find his car gone. He says he walked for an hour before he took a cab home. Brown was there, and his mother. Brown had told her everything except that there was a picture. He was pretty battered from the fight, Barrow says, and he had some vague idea of saying that you and Wild had stabbed Pen.

"In the morning the police brought the Jaguar back—that is, they had it at the station and Pete went there to get it after they phoned. He found out that you were being held for the stabbing, he phoned home, and the deal was set.

"This boy Dooley didn't know the address where he'd stolen the car, so the Carmel police didn't make any connection. Naturally Pete didn't press charges."

We were passing the green and white buildings of Fort Ord.

"Brown's number was up anyway. The Narcotics people knew about his smuggling racket, but they didn't know that Sandodera was in town or that he had a boat. Nailing him has made you kind of popular."

I thought of the terrible box, of the slug shattering the fat man's knee, of the fact that I wasn't a killer.

They took me to the hospital and I saw my girl.

Chapter Twenty-one

We drove out to the airport in my Ford. It was a beautiful February day on the Monterey Peninsula.

At the airport café we talked about a lot of things. College, mostly. We didn't have any classes together but we sort of shared each other's classes. Wild liked the school and it made it mean a lot more to both of us to be there together. So we had coffee and talked. It was wonderful.

When the plane stopped at the end of the runway we watched them roll up the stair and open the door. The first man out was Broadway Red Kearny.

Big man with the warmest blue eyes I've ever seen. He shook hands with me.

"Is this the man, Wild?"

"This is the man," she said.

THE END

TOKYO DOLL

John McPartland

Chapter One

It is a city in motion, a human typhoon.

Tokyo, third largest city in the world. They live there in slums and palaces, the eight million. They understand the refinements of cruelty. They are children, but they are terrible children of the Orient.

She was here, tall and beautiful as she rode through the street hordes of little brown men and their women. Her name was Sandra Tann, and the men who listened to her voice called her, in love, in friendship, and in desire, the Witch. And sometimes they called her the Doll.

They heard her voice, singing to them, from the transmitters in Korea. They clustered around their radios, their ears close to the speakers. They knew her voice, knew the whisper of velvet, knew the quick twist like the lilt of a violin that would make a word sung by Sandra different from the words of any other woman.

She was a tall, golden girl. She had a lean, supple body and she was beautiful. You don't see them like Sandra often, once in a year maybe. You turn your head for a girl like this and watch her, happier for having seen her, for knowing that women, sometimes, can be so splendid.

But she didn't belong in Tokyo, not in this third summer of Korea. Sandra was for New York or Paris, maybe London, or, regrettably, even Beverly Hills. Never in Tokyo, with its swirling millions of little brown people.

Tokyo was a town for the colonels and the sergeants, when we were gods in khaki, but we are leaving it, becoming strangers and alien again. Tokyo is a town for the shrewd, the merciless, the schemers; it is not a town for a tall golden girl.

She was a Department of the Army civilian, a DAC, singing a daily quarter hour over the American Far East Network, in a slot between the ball-game transcription and the news. At five each evening the corporal who announced her program would say, "Now the Far East Network brings you the lovely Witch of Tokyo, Miss Sandra Tann," and you would hear the whisper of velvet, the rich, vibrant voice.

I saw her first on the broad street between Hibaya Park and the Imperial Hotel. Three men were trying to burn her to death.

It happened fast. I was walking toward the street from the gardened courtyard of the Imperial. A group of men, twenty or so, some in the white cottons of laborers and three or four in the black uniforms of university students, were clustered around a speaker on the sidewalk that borders Hibaya Park across the street.

A blue Buick was coming toward them. The group seemed to hesitate for a moment and then the men ran out on the pavement. The Buick slowed down, then stopped. I ran toward it.

These things aren't too uncommon—a hit-and-run attack on an American car. The Reds strike, do their damage, and disperse, all in a few seconds. But in those few seconds a match can be thrown into the gas tank, or sulphuric acid may be splattered into a white face.

They had the car surrounded now. I got there as the car was turned over. One student turned and saw me. He came for me, his hands forward, low, spread wide apart. The Buick crashed on its side with a sound of metal tearing, glass breaking.

The student was planning some minor-league judo, but judo is slower and fancier than a straight-arm smash with a big left fist into the small bones of the face. He arched backward and fell into the crowd.

The next man between me and the car was stocky and round-faced, maybe a Korean. He wore a big grin—maybe because he was bringing a knife up in a sharp arc toward my belly.

My left hand was still numb but I reached out, caught his knife hand just above the wrist, and twisted it to the right, hard. As he started to go over, the edge of my right hand cut into his throat like a dull cleaver. The knife fell, the broken wrist dangled, and the fat guy went down.

There were shouts and the mob burst apart. I got to the car.

Three men weren't running away. One had a knife and he used it as the driver of the Buick, a Japanese, opened the left front door and climbed through it. He pushed the door up and as his head came out his throat was cut as if he were a butchered hog.

One of the other two had a paper torch and he was trying to light it. The third man had a bottle of acid. The rest of the mob had scattered. There were two people in the overturned car, a man and a girl. I could see her blonde hair through the windshield as I swung around to the acid man. He was smashing at the rear window with a short club and he was in too big a hurry to see me. The knife man looked down at the dead driver, then turned and began to run. The torch man threw his roll of paper down and ran, too. But I got the acid man.

I got him good, before he knew what was happening. The bottle was pushed into his face and I kept pushing though the stuff was spattering me. He screamed as he went down, the acid biting into his eyes and flesh.

I felt very tired as I got up. The Korean was trying to stand up now, holding his broken wrist with his left hand. The student lay on his back, both hands on his bloody face. The whole thing had lasted maybe ninety seconds. My wrist was alive with pain from the splatter of acid and my left hand was aching.

I leaned against the car and when the man inside saw me he unlocked the rear door and opened it. He pushed himself up and out, awkwardly, clumsy from fear. A gray-faced man, not young, breathing heavily. He was in uniform and he wore the eagles of a colonel.

First the golden hair, then her face looking up at me. Slender hands into mine, and Sandra Tann jumped down from the side of the overturned car. She was not frightened. She did not seem to notice me again as she spoke to the gray-faced colonel.

The police came. Maybe the men in the mob had heard the siren of the police truck and had scattered for that reason. They're good, competent, tough lads, these Tokyo police, but they hate Reds and know how to handle them. They had no mercy for the three they found. There were a dozen riot-squad experts in the first truck, each with a ready gun and a readier club. Two more trucks roared up and more police jumped off. Their cameras began to record the scene.

Sandra Tann looked at me to remember me, and asked if I was hurt. I said no. One of the riot squad had run off to his truck to get ointment for the acid burns, and I felt the fighter's shakes a little, but otherwise I was fine.

"I want to thank you," she said. "My name is Sandra Tann." She held out slender fingers to me, warm, soft, young.

"My name's Buchanan, Mate Buchanan. It's a name, not a rank." I smiled.

I'm not a good-looking guy at all. Figure me as looking like a fairly rangy tackle on some Southwestern Conference team ten years ago, which is true.

Sandra Tann was wearing a suit of raw silk, the stuff that looks like tweed mixed with fog, a scarlet bow tie, no hat. Lovely, American, and a million miles away on a star.

They were lifting the driver's body from the car now. Sandra's mouth softened. "He was a good man, and an *ichiban* driver."

Ichiban—number one, the best. He had driven for the Americans and he had died for it.

The Tokyo crowd had gathered around the police and the overturned car. A ring of faces, five or six deep. Hundreds of people. I looked at them, into dark, staring eyes that held mine for a second and then looked away.

The Colonel was talking to the precise, courteous police lieutenant. The two men nodded to each other in agreement and the Colonel walked over to me.

"Thank you, sir. I believe you saved our lives. My name is Barham." His eyes were direct on mine.

"Buchanan." We shook hands. His grip was hard enough to worry the little aches running through my left hand.

"I've just talked to Lieutenant Tanimoto of the police. They will want statements from us later, but for the time being I thought maybe we might go into the bar of the Imperial. We all could stand a touch, I think." The Colonel's face was no longer gray and his eyes were cold and bright now.

Sandra Tann waited for my smile and then the three of us walked away from the car, across the wide street to the old Imperial. There were a few people in the lobby, Japanese and Americans, watching us with the curiosity we all have for figures involved in sudden, public violence. The three of us strode across the deeply carpeted floor and down the brick steps to the bar. Barham held a chair for Sandra at a narrow wooden table and we all sat down. The bar boy hurried over. Sandra said to Barham, "Brandy."

He looked at me. "Canadian and soda," I said.

"Two Canadian and soda, brandy." The bar boy bowed and ran to the counter.

"Apparently, sir, you rescued Miss Tann and myself singlehanded. A remarkable act." The Colonel's bright cold eyes studied me as he spoke, and I studied him.

I saw the crossed pistols on his lapels. A bird colonel in the M.P.'s is a lot of rank, and in getting that kind of rank in the military police you also get some habits. One of the habits is finding out everything about everybody you meet. Especially violent guys that wade into a fight.

"Have you heard Miss Tann sing?" he asked to break off the silence. "She has a program on the Far East Network."

I looked at her for a long moment. "Almost a year ago. In Korea."

"The program had just started then. It was almost a year ago that I came to Tokyo." She was looking at me as if she were studying my homely face.

"You're in the service?" I could see the entry being made in the dossier on me now being kept in Colonel Barham's shrewd, remembering mind. So far it was short: name, Mate Buchanan; age, about thirty; nationality, American (?); skillful street fighter, used to violence; height, about six feet one; weight, about 190; reticent about self.

The bar boy brought our drinks. Barham picked his up and put down an empty glass a second later. Sandra spun her glass slowly.

"I was in the service then," I said.

"You've got the look of Army about you," said Sandra. "The look of an infantry soldier. You could be dirty and tired, with your boots muddy, a torn field jacket, angry, laughing, mean." Her gray eyes seemed to look into and beyond me and I felt the witchcraft and the magic. She had been well named, the Witch of Tokyo.

I nodded. I was wearing a soft gabardine and it probably didn't look right on me. She had me pegged: dirty, tired, angry, laughing, mean. I had spent more years of my life that way than I had spent months in pressed, neat suits.

A little man was standing by our table, a brown man in a worn blue suit with a glistening white shirt, slightly frayed at collar and cuffs. He was holding his Homburg hat in his hands, smiling, bowing a little.

"Excuse me, please. Mr. Suruki of the *Mainichi Press*. I would like to make an interview on the sorrowful incident with the Korean Communists, please."

Barham's mouth tightened and his eyes seemed to go colder and brighter. "Nothing. I'm sorry. Nothing. That's all." He turned to look for the bar boy and, seeing him, called, "Another Canadian and soda, boy-san. *Hayoka!*"

The little man didn't go away, but Barham paid no further attention to him. The bar boy came with the new drink as fast as his legs would carry him. The Colonel had said *hayoka*, and that meant hurry.

"We were coming from the studio when we had this trouble," Sandra said to me, "and I've got an appointment. But I'd like to see you again, Mate Buchanan."

I wanted to see her again the way a miser wants gold or a drunkard wants whisky, but there were some other things involved, too. Fifteen years of knowing show girls and waitresses in all-night cafés, playgirls, and good rough girls generally had kind of fixed my ways. I took care of my business first and then I took care of my drinking and my women. I wasn't planning on marrying anybody and that made things a sort of hobby, nothing more. But this was Sandra Tann and there was more horse power in those engines than I had ever tried to handle before.

I had known who the Tokyo Doll was, and I suppose I figured her as a beautiful DAC living in the Osaka Hotel and being squired around by colonels and generals.

"Osaka Hotel?" I gave her a man's look as I asked.

She had taken a cigarette from a silver case and the Colonel made himself busy lighting it for her. Mr. Suruki stood by the table, still patient, still smiling.

Sandra blew jets of smoke and smiled, and we both knew that I had a date with the Witch of Tokyo sometime early in the evening.

"Sorry to be trouble," said Mr. Suruki, and there was a curling edge to his voice, "but does Colonel Barham know that it was not only despicable Korean Communists in mob that tried to kill him?"

The Colonel looked into the bright, black eyes for a moment and it was the sharp, cold eyes that looked away first. He said nothing. He stood up, and Sandra rose to leave.

"Lieutenant Tanimoto will want to see you, Mr. Buchanan," he said. "Where can he reach you? I will be at his office in thirty minutes."

"I'm staying here at the Imperial." I was standing but obviously remaining.

"For long?"

I smiled. "It's going to seem long, probably, Colonel." I watched the long, striding legs of Sandra, strong and lean against the silk of her suit, until they were out of sight.

I smiled at Mr. Suruki before I sat down. Japan is a nation of smiles and cruelty. "Care for a drink, Suruki?"

A quick, brief shadow seemed to cross his face, then he lit up with pleasure. "Thank you. I would like to very much."

We ordered a couple of big bottles of Kirin beer. Our bottles were half empty before we did any talking, and then I got down to cases, fast.

"What's the story on that trouble out in front?" Suruki went into a small Oriental tizzy of surprise, confusion, and shock. This gave him time to figure out the best counter to my question.

"Excuse me, but newspaper reporter come to you for story," he said, but his eyes were no longer those of a fluttering sparrow.

"Who were they trying to get? The Colonel?"

He thought about that for a while.

"I think so, maybe."

"Who were they?"

From the look on Suruki's face, I was pretty sure he knew.

"Who are you?" was his answer to my question, and I was more shocked by his directness than he ever could be by mine. When they're as direct as this, it usually involves something like Pearl Harbor.

"My name's Mate Buchanan. I'm an American."

"Who do you know?" There was something here terribly and dreadfully important to little Mr. Suruki, or he would never have shown this feral directness.

We looked each other over carefully.

I was going to need somebody like Suruki on my own private business, but my business was pretty delicate too. I was a little bit scared to talk about it to any Japanese yet, but I was going to have to talk to a lot of them.

Suruki, on the other hand, had wanted to talk to a colonel, and even in these last days of the Occupation an American colonel had magic words he could use that might change a Suruki's life immeasurably for better or worse. What kind of deal did he want, and what kind of deal could he make for me?

"I know a few people, Mr. Suruki. What do you want to talk about?"

"Pardon me, Mr. Buchanan. I am very scared."

"Why?"

"I know something. I recognized some people."

The little guy had found out something bigger than he could handle and didn't know what to do. If he held on to it he might get hurt, and if he let it go he'd regret that he'd been afraid of his one big chance for the rest of his life. It's a tough deal for little guys. I had seen it before.

"I'm an American. I was an infantry officer. I'm tough. I've got a little money. Can I help you?"

He looked at me and then his eyes were attracted by a fly. He caught it with a dart of his thin brown arm. He smashed it between his fingers and showed me the crushed body. That was his answer.

Chapter Two

"Where can you go? Who can help you? The police?" I asked.

His eyes were filmed. He shrugged with the weariness of an old man and waited for me to get up to let him go.

"How about your story? The stuff you wanted from the Colonel about the trouble—you know, the story?" I wanted to help him, even a little.

He gave me a small smile. "That? Oh. I phoned all that to my newspaper before I came down to the bar. The desk manager gave me all the names, everything."

I stood up and he popped up immediately like a sparrow leaping to a perch.

"Thank you very much. Good-by." He bowed, turned, and was gone.

I put some money on the table next to the crushed fly.

Suruki had a little secret and he thought that it involved people who would crush him like a fly. Well, I had a little secret, too. And it would make things dangerous for me too.

Suruki-san, we belong to the same kind of club.

I walked back up the narrow stairs, across the deep carpet, down the wide stairway, and out into the plum-blossom rain of late May. It had come suddenly and Tokyo was wet and dripping. Now it was stopping and the air was almost luminous. As I walked down the broad street I looked over Mate Buchanan, the man with the hard, tough job.

A few months back it had been a different kind of job. I'd been Captain Buchanan then, commanding a line rifle company dug in at the base of a ridge in central Korea.

Two years before that, just before that thing in Korea had started, I was the promotion manager of a big-city newspaper in California. It had been a dirty, exciting, fast-moving job, and half the time I'd loved it, half the time I'd hated it. Between times I drank a little whisky with good friends in a dark barroom with lots of wood and no chrome, and had good times with plenty of women—none of them serious.

Before that there'd been the Southwest Pacific. Green wet leaves and tendrils of jungle, sweat, jungle rot, Japs, bugs, lousy food or no food. It had been kind of great, when I looked back on it from ten years away. Better than being under a ridge in Korea by a country mile. One night, back on some forgotten island, the battalion commander had come around and asked T/Sgt. Buchanan where in hell the company officers were. T/Sgt. Buchanan told the battalion commander that the company officers were with half of the company, the half that had been kissed by Japanese mortar fire and by the lonely bullets from the snipers who seemed to grow in the palm trees like coconuts. My own platoon lieutenant had gone about four hours earlier, a tall, blond kid who had worked hard at OCS for the brief glory of walking slowly forty yards into a jungle and into the target sight of a sniper.

The blond kid had seemed like a good officer for the few hours we had known him and I'd been standing next to him when he pitched forward. I lobbed a ready grenade I was carrying into the palm where the sniper watched. It worked fine, but it didn't help the blond kid any.

The battalion commander told me I was a lieutenant and to carry on.

"Yes, sir," I said, and saluted. So about eight years later I walked into my office at the paper I was working for and found a registered letter telling me to report to Fort Ord.

Next it was Korea. B Company, or, as they called it, Baker Company. We called ourselves the Jolly Bakers because we were the skinniest, meanest, and bitterest bunch of lads in the Eighth Army, with acid for blood.

Then one day the Jolly Bakers moved up that ridge, under orders from our colonel, and the Reds greeted us with mortars. The Japs used to be pretty good with mortars, but these guys were professionals.

We were racked. After two hours we stumbled back down the ridge and the aid men worked some of us back into shape. We brought all of our wounded and most of our dead back with us, and that was doing mighty well.

Two days later we got our replacements. Nice lads, trying not to look nervous and bewildered. I was supposed to take them up the ridge again that night. I didn't.

Two of my company officers, four sergeants, an old leather-and-bone Pfc who had been a master sergeant twice in his twenty-two years of duty, and I went up the hill instead of the hundred green kids. One sergeant, the Pfc, and I came back down the hill. Each of us carried a wounded man, the other three sergeants.

In the morning the planes out of one of the K bases came over and burned the two thousand Reds who had been waiting on the top of that ridge into contorted black corpses with napalm. If we'd gone up in company strength that night there would have been a hundred telegrams reaching homes back Stateside at about the same time as the first letters that said, "I'm here in Korea, but don't worry about me...."

So they court-martialed me for disobedience to a direct order, and they were right. If I had been the colonel I would have court-martialed the company commander, too. But I wasn't. I was the company commander, and I had one hundred green kids.

Maybe they regretted it too, but the colonel ordered the papers drawn for a court-martial and a few weeks later I sat before the board of officers. They found me not guilty and suggested I resign from the service, without prejudice.

I'd been wrong. The lives of the hundred green kids could not outweigh an order, and I knew that. So Captain Buchanan became Mr. Buchanan and went back to the States feeling very lonely and empty.

Then somebody found me. They were looking for a type and the records said I was that type. He had to have been a soldier and have known something of death. He had to be out of the service, willing to take on a mean job where he was on his own, with no one to back him up, no one to mend him if he got broken, no tears for his grave if he died.

There was a man in Japan and he had something the people of the United States might need desperately. This man alone had this secret and he hated the people of the United States. I was to get his secret from him.

Somewhere in Japan there was a doctor who tended a culture jar in which a virus lived, a submicroscopic kind of living substance, one of the tens of millions of viruses, but the one kind that by a chemical miracle might save the lives of millions of Americans in case of war.

When they found me, back in the States, I knew that viruses caused influenza and diseases like that. Otherwise I knew nothing about them, and didn't give a damn about learning.

I was in San Francisco when the strangers came to my hotel and asked for me. The desk clerk rang my room and told me some gentlemen were in the lobby. I didn't recognize the names but I thought it might be some old Army friends. I was only partly right; they were Army.

One of them was a great big joker, and anybody who'd ever been in the Army would know that he was Counter-Intelligence. The other fellow was small and neat and quiet. He was there to look me over and listen to me, like the top senior on campus looking over a possible new pledge to the fraternity.

"You're hotheaded," said the CIC man, who said his name was Johnson. They'd come up and into my room with handshakes and the small sample-sized smiles. Their business might be about a job, the big man said. Was I free? I was. Very free and mildly broke.

"Yeah, I'm hotheaded," I admitted. Why argue with the record?

"But you've done good jobs. Would you like to go back to Japan?"

"No." I could have written a book around that "No."

"Remember a girl named Akiko Tsumi?"

"Yeah. I know a girl by that name. Nice kid, good-looking. Not mine. She belonged to a major in GHQ."

"How well did you know her?" Both men were watching me closely.

"I was in Japan twice. Just after the war, and for a few months after the Korea stuff started. I met Akiko then. Hell of a beautiful girl, strictly Japanese. I saw her around, danced with her at the clubs, stuff like that. This major had her all tied up and he brought her around. A few of the officers tried to move in. I didn't. Nobody made out, as far as I know."

"What about her family?"

I shrugged a shoulder. "Who knows? What's with Akiko? Why the questions?"

The CIC agent shook his head. "We'll give you a rundown later, maybe. Just tell us as much as you can remember about Akiko Tsumi."

"She's a little doll. Really a doll. Delicate features, small slender body. Got more up here than most *musume*. She dresses Western style, of course, and very sharp. Her English is fair. I never got the idea she was too smart. Upper-class Japanese girl, maybe twenty-six or so. Fine dancer, but then, most Japanese girls are. That's about it."

"How would you like to move in on her?"

"Who, me? I never went for the short-legged women, and besides, she's already taken by that major I mentioned." The hell with this, I thought.

"Supposing she was free, and the major was out of the picture?"

"No, thanks. There are enough Americans who're crazy about *musume*. Find some other guy if you want to fix Akiko up. Before you go, tell me what the score is, will you, please? As you go."

The two men looked at each other and the little man winked. Then they got down to facts. The facts were pretty good, because I was in Tokyo now.

The facts began with a careful intelligence report on Akiko Tsumi. One sentence stood out for me: "Friends of Miss Tsumi say she was much impressed by a Captain Mate Buchanan. She told other Japanese girls that she felt this American was one of the few a Japanese girl could trust, although she loved Major Corbett."

I hadn't gone on the make for her; maybe that was why the big trust.

The facts continued. "As indicated in previous reports, the only nonofficial thread of contact with Dr. Tsumi is through his only child, Akiko Tsumi. When Dr. Tsumi disappeared, just before the Occupation troops arrived in September 1945, his daughter was with him. She returned to Tokyo in 1948 and in the following year she began associating with Americans and took employment as a clerk in the field grade officers' billet, the Dai Iti Hotel. Early in 1949 she was seduced by Major Corbett, with whom she has maintained a home since. Dr. Tsumi is known to be violently anti-American and it is presumed that he has cut off any connection with his only child since she became friendly with Americans.

"All other attempts by various agencies to locate Dr. Tsumi have failed. If he is still alive and has kept specimens of the RK virus alive, these specimens can be secured only by an official search for him with the assistance of the Japanese police, or through his daughter, who may know his hiding place even though there is no contact at present between them."

"What's this RK virus?" I asked handing back the flimsy carbons of the intelligence reports. They were stamped "Top Secret" across the front.

"That's the heart of this matter," said the wide-eyed little man, who looked as if he had a double portion of brains. "We won't go into that right now. I'll tell you this much and you can take my word for it. It may be the most important stuff in the world today. Probably all there is of it is in a few jars hidden somewhere in Japan.

"It was discovered by a Japanese doctor—the father of this girl Akiko—and he has a bitter hatred of Americans. We're pretty certain that if we make any open attempt through their government or through the Occupation authorities to get this stuff, he will destroy it before we can secure it. And once it's destroyed, we've got a hopeless task. There are millions of possible virus forms and each one is different. Right now more than a dozen big biological research laboratories here in the States are hunting for something like the RK virus. With luck we might run across the right kind in five years. Without luck, maybe never.

"We want to send a man to Tokyo to meet this Akiko Tsumi, gain her trust, and trace her father through her. If possible, this man will get into Dr. Tsumi's house and secure the RK virus cultures, by violence if necessary."

This wide-eyed little guy with the big forehead was talking about violence the way he might talk about taking a bus out to the zoo, and yet I knew he meant violence. Whatever RK was, it was as important as his immortal soul to him.

He continued, his big eyes staring at me. "Your name was on the report. We traced you and found you here. It's the kind of mission a man like you can do. You've already got this girl's trust. We'll take care of Major Corbett, and you move in. You find her father and you take the jars. Get them to us and the mission is accomplished."

"Now look, laddie," I said, uncrossing my legs and standing up. "I don't want to spoil your pretty little thriller here, but I've got a few sensible questions. First, who do you represent?"

The big man flipped his wallet and the stuff I expected from him was there. Picture, card, regular corps identification. I wasn't too impressed.

The little guy showed me a letter and a card. The letter was from the White House. The card told me who the little guy was. I was very much impressed.

"Good enough," I said. "Now why all this about a secret agent? You guys probably could get anything you want in the world this side of the Iron Curtain without too much trouble. Why bring me in?"

"You won't be the only one, or your way the only way. RK may mean a million lives, and maybe next year. We've got to have it." The scientist was quietly earnest. "You're just one attempt we're going to make.

"We need only a drop of the living virus. From it we can grow all we need. The dead virus is worthless. It would take Dr. Tsumi only ten seconds to kill it, and we don't even know where it is or what he's doing with the stuff.

"We dare not move openly because as yet he doesn't know that anyone in the world except himself, his daughter, and an idiot girl is even aware RK exists. We dare not trust it to any government as yet, except our own. We can't go through the official channels of the Occupation, we can't use our own official channels of the State Department, we can't use the Japanese government. We must move secretly.

"You're going to go to Tokyo. I'll be there too. You will have no contact with me until you bring Dr. Tsumi's culture jars to me, and that must be within twenty-four hours of the time you get them. The virus must be examined by a competent biologist who can determine what culture medium is used to feed it, and it must get the proper food at once or it will die. Do you understand?"

I understood, and I understood something else, too. He had said, "You are going," not "If you go," or "Will you go?"

"How much do you know about me?" I asked.

"Buchanan, we've talked to everybody who ever knew you, no matter how slightly."

"Why?"

"You may soon have something in your hands that Uncle Joe would give anything for, only we don't believe he knows it exists. You may be happy to know that you're cleared for the RK Project, and there aren't many people that have been cleared for it. You don't like Reds, you don't associate with any Commies, you keep your mouth shut. You're in."

So I was in. After about a week I found out what RK was and I was really in. The problem of the biological scientist who had come to my room back in San Francisco was not that of the people caught in the explosion of an atomic bomb, but rather that of the millions more who would be exposed to water-borne and air-borne radioactive materials, an immeasurably greater threat.

The secret of Dr. Tsumi had been learned through a strange chance—the idiot girl whom he treated with his virus as a control had been the ward of a Christian missionary. Dr. Tsumi's treatments had been completely secret, but in those weeks of chaos following the atom blast at Hiroshima and the surrender, the old missionary had seen both girls, Akiko and the idiot, before and after their treatment. He had taken photographs of his mindless ward. Those photographs, and the statement of a now dead doctor at a Hiroshima hospital on the nature of Dr. Tsumi's work with an unknown virus whose biological action was specific for X-ray burns, had been lost for six years. The missionary had died a few months after the surrender, the doctor was dead, and only Tsumi, his daughter, and the idiot were left.

We would never have known anything about it if the old missionary's few trunks of possessions had not reached a niece in California. Five years after she received the trunks she looked through their contents and found the photographs and the notes the old man had made in the hell of Hiroshima in the weeks that followed the world's first atomic attack.

She sent the notes to the Atomic Energy Commission. A top-priority intelligence project was set up. The best agents our nation has were sent to Japan. Everything was checked and everything checked out.

Dr. Tsumi was a leading specialist in virus and radiological research. He had found—by the kind of incredible accident that has produced so many scientific discoveries—that rabbits inoculated with an obscure virus resisted the tissue destruction of X-rays. The living virus in the blood of the animal caused tissue reactions that repaired radiological burns and poisoning. The Doctor had talked only to his professional friend at the Hiroshima hospital, had told him of the RK virus that he had developed from his original discovery.

Then came the atomic bomb. About one hundred thousand people died, thousands of them in the first weeks after the bomb. Most of these died from radiation burns and radiation poisoning. Tsumi had sufficient virus to treat the idiot girl and his daughter. The RK virus worked; the girls recovered in good health and with unscarred bodies.

With the RK virus, which could be produced by the ton from one original drop of the living substance, the greatest threat of Red atomic warfare on the United States would be countered. We could protect our people from radiation poisoning and burns by inoculating them by the millions with the virus.

There were two things I didn't like but that I had to take. There was going to be a clear field for me. Pressures had been applied gently and secretly so that Akiko's major had learned some bad news recently—his wife was arriving from the States. That was playing pretty rough with people's lives.

The other thing was that my instructions were to go all out in getting to Akiko. Anything—including marriage, if necessary.

And I had just met the wonderful blonde Tokyo Doll.

Chapter Three

Akiko and her major were to end their three years together. The major's wife figured to take care of that.

I was to move in fast. Mrs. Corbett's ship was due in Yokohama at noon tomorrow. Sometime in the next twenty or so hours I was to find Akiko and be ready to take Corbett's place.

If I could do it by conversation, that was fine. But if I had to make love to her, then the Buchanan body was as expendable now as it had been in Korea.

Akiko was one of the most beautiful girls I'd ever seen, as I remembered her. Small, fragile, delicate, with great dark eyes, honey skin, and blue-black hair. But now I wanted the supple, blonde, long-legged Sandra Tann. I wanted all of Sandra and none of any other girl in the world. That's how I felt.

It started to rain. I hailed a cab, a '37 Ford held together by wire and prayers, but clean as a kitten. Half a block before the tree-lined Ginza, the Fifth Avenue of Tokyo, the cab turned right into a bazaar alley bright with color and loud with music, voices, shouts, horns, and the scratchy singsong of recorded commercials played endlessly from sidewalk kiosks.

My driver edged through the people, his horn a banshee scream, and let me out by the stairway that led up to the Haji-basha, a tiny café run by Mr. Morning Sun, Asahi-san, a bad one.

There was a sign in English: "Upstairs. Nicest little place in Tokyo. On limits." "On limits" meant that the military authorities hadn't found Asahi-san's little nest too dirty or too dangerous for our men.

I went upstairs. A dance girl met me at the top. She gave me a smile. "Haro! Nice to see you!" My being in civilian clothes put me way up on the welcome list. She showed me to one of the Haji-basha's two booths and waited for my pleasure. It had been a year since I'd seen it, but nothing had changed.

The room was about twelve feet square, seated eight people, and was equipped with a big, ancient radio and record player, and with a service bar about three feet long. I was the only customer. Two other dance girls lounged in the other booth, giving me almond looks.

"Canadian and soda." I was thinking of Asahi-san, the owner, a repulsive homosexual.

"You buy me drink? You like dance?"

"No. You find Asahi-san. Bring him here."

She went and got my highball, then trotted off down a corridor behind the bar.

The girls in the other booth paid no further attention to me and I sipped my drink, waiting for Asahi-san.

I saw him waddle down the corridor and into the room. He was a big, fat man that looked like a big, fat, ugly woman with lots of powder and rouge and perfume. He looked at me, recognized me, and nodded. No big welcome. He was waiting to see what I wanted. He probably had the completely logical idea that the only reasons an American who had been in Japan in the military service would come back to Japan as a civilian were a Japanese girl or a scheme to make money off the Japanese. Neither of these reasons interested him very much.

We'd had dealings once before. A major I had known got himself a couple of million yen in one way or another and wanted to do something with it without going to prison for five or ten years. If the major could work a deal with his yen he'd have something like five or six thousand American dollars. Asahi-san had worked it for him. My part of the deal had come in when Asahi-san had pulled a so-sorry on the major and it looked as if my boy had had it for his two million yen.

Asahi-san and I had talked things over, and the major had got his loot. It made Asahi-san and me understand each other real well: He was smart and I was mean; we could work together all right.

"Sit down, have a drink."

His English was fine, which was one of the reasons I had decided to start the search at the Haji-basha. He asked me when I'd returned, if I was out of the service, and why I was in Japan. Then we got down to the sparring around.

"I'm going to write a book about Japan." I said this with much earnestness.

He smiled a prissy smile. I was either an idiot or a liar, and he was sure he'd find out which pretty soon, and he could smell money here for him.

"I'm sure you know Japan so well you will write *ichiban* book."

"I'm going to need some help," I said, finishing off my tepid highball.

He looked a bit alarmed, as if he was wondering if I really was intending to write a book about Japan and had come to him for some free assistance.

"I need a good driver with a new car, maybe British, French, or German. Not American."

He looked at me, but said nothing.

"Four thousand yen a day, thirty-day contract." I waved at a girl peeking from the corridor to bring us drinks. She'd know what to bring Asahi-san.

"Five thousand yen. In advance." Asahi-san wasn't bargaining toward a deal, I knew. He was trying to find out how illegal and illegitimate my enterprise really was. The way I answered, not what I answered, was what he was interested in.

"O.K."

Now Mr. Morning Sun had his answer. If I figured him right, his thinking would go along these lines: Anybody, even a stupid crook, will try to hide the fact that he's willing to pay more because he has an illegal deal in mind and will therefore at least pretend to haggle. The crookeder the deal, the more pretense of haggling. This hairy foreigner of an American doesn't even bother to pretend; therefore, he is so sure of himself he doesn't care what I think or what I may find out in the future. This is a hot deal and I better play along. But smart.

At least, that's how I hoped he was thinking. And if I had him pegged right, he would go a step further. He'd get me the best and most honest driver-interpreter he could find.

Asahi-san probably knew every pimp, black-marketeer, dope peddler, thief, pickpocket, counterfeiter, camera-case slicer, and policeman in Tokyo. He could have put any kind of cutthroat in the driver's seat of a car. But maybe this was really a hot deal, and he didn't want to be sold out of his end by any cheap crook.

He had to figure that I'd expect the driver to have a go-from-me-come-to-me relationship with the fat boss of the Haji-basha. The driver would have to pay Asahi-san a big split of his earnings from me. But the driver would also expect to get rewarded by Asahi-san for any information he could pass on to him. I'd be expecting this, so I would make my own deal with the driver. I would pay him more to give the old auntie false reports and information. And if the driver was a crook, he'd make the deal, double-cross me too, and bring in some sinister fourth party of his own, which would make things a little cloudy for Mr. Morning Sun.

Such is the way these things are done in the clattering side streets of Tokyo.

That kind of thinking is the advantage of dealing with somebody like Mr. Morning Sun. There's a beautiful logic to it.

"Hokay." He waved his head and the rouged dewlaps fluttered, the thick peach-colored powder on his skin cracking in little lines as he agreed.

The girl brought our drinks, a nice brown highball for me—if you seem to be a friend of the boss they mix your drink triple or more—a colored gooey mess for him.

"Hokay," he said again. "I got *ichiban* driver." Then he looked at me and said, "Earman mince."

I didn't get it right away. But I'd been in Japan before, so I worked on it.

"Hillman Minx?" As soon as I said it I knew I was right.

The Minx is a nice British car, about six sizes larger than a little red wagon, and just what I wanted. Going around in an American car wouldn't have been so good—it's like saying, "Your rich uncle's here and happy drunk!"

Might as well have wheels and a driver for my date with Sandra Tann tonight, so I said, "Get him here in an hour."

"Hokay."

I dropped a thousand-yen note to cover the drinks and left.

Down the shimmering, sibilant, screaming bazaar street. Over to the tree-lined Ginza and back toward the heart of downtown Tokyo. The rain had stopped and the clouds billowed up in the sky toward Fuji.

Around me the eight million moved restlessly and constantly. Tokyo is the movingest town in the world. All the homes, the offices, and the schools must be empty all day, because everybody is on the streets.

I passed under the viaduct of the main railway lines and crossed a narrow street. Facing me was the block-long building of the *Mainichi Press*. The police were pushing a crowd away from a broken body on the street, a small heap of clothes in a big puddle of spreading blood.

It was Mr. Suruki.

The white-helmeted M.P.s showed up in a prowl jeep. It was still the Occupation—the Military Police reported on all accidents and crimes that might touch, however remotely, the personnel of UN forces.

One of them talked to the police as Suruki's body was gathered up. Apparently the American, an M.P. sergeant first class, had a good working use of Japanese. As he stood by the jeep writing out his report, I pushed through the crowd and asked him, "What's the score, Sergeant?" The blue eyes shifted up to look me over. I was an American in civilian clothes, and soldiers were polite to Americans in civilian clothes.

"Guy seemed to collapse in front of one of our six-by's, sir. Fell right in front of it and the wheels went over his midsection. Killed instantly."

I thanked him and walked on past the long row of trucks lined up against the Mainichi circulation loading dock. I could hear the rolling rumble of the presses. Upstairs in the city room there must be a little desk where Suruki had sat, writing out his stories in flowing brush strokes, a brass teapot bubbling next to his ink jars. There was a Japanese bar across the street. I bent low to walk through its door, pushing away the long beaded cords that hung before it to give it privacy.

A few men were sitting around low tables on chairs that seemed built for children. A radio was playing a high, haunting minor-key Japanese melody that echoed like the wind chasing ghosts through a bamboo forest.

The proprietor popped out from behind the short bar, bowed, grinned, and gave me a mean look from his hooded eyes.

"Suntory, please," I said. Suntory is pretty fair Japanese Scotch, if you'll forgive the expression, and comes in three grades: very old, very old rare, and then some good stuff that goes for about the equivalent of sixty cents.

He nodded and went back to get me a slug.

I stood at the bar and sipped. It turned out to be the very old grade and I was going to be charged for the good stuff, but then, I was an American and didn't belong there in the first place.

So the little reporter had collapsed in front of a big G.I. truck and had been smashed by its wheels. Could be, but I remembered the crushed fly on the table at the Imperial. That's the way Suruki had called it, and that's the way he had looked, in the end.

The personal interest for me in Suruki's fast closeout was that the probable reason for it was his knowing who—not Reds—had tried to kill Barham and Sandra Tann a couple of hours ago. Somebody very daring was out to get either Barham or Sandra. Why?

The proprietor made a gesture of Japanese-American friendship by switching his radio from the local Tokyo station to Radio Tokyo, the Far East Network. Maybe he was an admirer of the Witch of Tokyo, because the announcer was finishing, "—Tokyo, Miss Sandra Tann!"

Even the Japanese in the bar looked up, and as they listened their eyes were warm.

I finished my whisky, paid the top price, and walked back toward the Haji-basha to see what Mr. Morning Sun had done for me.

It turned out that he had done fine. The shiny Minx was parked in the narrow bazaar street and a taxi was squeezing past it while the driver swore and honked his horn. Upstairs a young man sat on a straight-backed chair outside the miniature café, and when he saw me he started to smile, then decided it would not be good manners to smile until he had been presented to me.

He was a good-looking kid in his early twenties with an intelligent face. Asahi-san was waiting at a booth for his 150,000 yen. I paid it.

My driver-interpreter was named Ken Kimato and he seemed like a nice boy. I'd gone through all this monkey business with Asahi-san because of the way the Japanese like to run their country. They like to know everything that's going on, most especially if there's an American involved. If I had gone to a regular agency for interpreters or drivers a daily report on my activities would have been sent to the Japanese police. I didn't want that.

Because the perfumed and powdered old man of the Haji-basha believed I was up to some illegal deal, he would cover for me until he found a way to get his cut. This boy Ken, who was now holding the door of the little Minx open for me and smiling big, would give Asahi-san a daily report for certain, but the police would not find out that an American civilian was on mysterious affairs in Tokyo.

Ken closed the door and I told him to take me to the Imperial. I had time to shave and shower and maybe catch a tall, cool one before going over to the Osaka—provided I had a date. It was just about six, and when the little Hillman rolled past the fountain and under the brick canopy of the Imperial courtyard I was pretty eager about telephoning the tall, blonde girl.

I called her from my room. It took about a minute to get through to her at the Osaka.

"Hello?"

"This is Mate Buchanan, Sandra. Dinner tonight?"

"Dinner tonight, Mate Buchanan. Seven? Meet me here?"

"Seven at the Osaka, Sandra."

"O.K., Mate. 'By." We hung up. I like girls that use a telephone that way.

Then the phone rang back at me. It was the desk to tell me that Colonel Barham was in the main bar and would like to see me. I said I'd be down in twenty minutes. No colonel was going to interfere with a civilian's shower and shave.

He was waiting at a booth in the barroom.

"Good evening, Mr. Buchanan. May I order you a drink?" He gave me a tight smile.

"My turn," I said, and sat down. The white-jacketed bar boy hurried over and I ordered Canadian and soda for the two of us.

"As you know," began the Colonel, "we're very grateful for what you did this afternoon, although the police had arrived in time to disperse the agitators."

Well, bless me, I'm back in the Army again. I knew it was perfectly possible for the incident to end up officially as Mate Buchanan having started a drunken brawl with some Japanese civilians and causing all the trouble. "Disperse the agitators"—with the driver looking like a butchered chicken, the acid man banging on the window glass, and the fire man trying to get his torch lit.

I waited him out. Men like Barham are always counter-punchers: They let you lead with a statement and then they work on that statement like ants on a dead bird.

"However, in the press of events we temporarily dispensed with some formalities. Because of my rank, our Military Police officers yielded their responsibility to me in respect to statements, personal history, and other necessary information." Barham said all this evenly, as if he was used to talking that way all the time. What he said was actually: Look, boy, I want to get you on the record and if I hadn't been a bird colonel those M.P.'s would have kept you filling out reports and forms for hours this afternoon. So talk, bucko.

"Hmmm," I said.

"You are Captain Mate Buchanan?"

So he'd already taken time to check me out.

"I'm Mr. Buchanan, Colonel, as you probably know."

His lips tightened and were only two lines. "Yes. You were relieved of your command. Why are you in Japan again, Mr. Buchanan?"

"I'm going to write a book about Japan, Colonel."

His agate eyes didn't change at all. To him I was an ex-officer who had been court-martialed and had resigned from the service. He didn't like me and I was surprised that he would even drink with me.

"What kind of book?"

"I don't know what it's going to be about, Colonel. Just a book. Everybody wants to write books."

His lips tightened even more. "How did you happen to become involved in the disturbance this afternoon?"

"I have to have some exercise every day, Colonel, or I get flabby."

His cold eyes sparked blue. "You are in Japan under the authority of the Occupation forces, Buchanan, and you will conduct yourself accordingly. You will answer each of these questions without levity, sarcasm, or evasion. That's an order."

I was coming in again at the same place I went out. "That's an order—" had led to an interesting chain of events ten months ago. Now there was no point in bucking the system. He could have me on a boat tonight if he got his back up. I had to go along with him.

"It was accidental, Colonel. I was leaving the hotel just as the trouble started."

"You did not know Miss Tann previously?"

"No, Colonel."

"Did you know any of the indigenous participants in the disturbance?"

"I didn't know anyone in the riot."

"You remained and talked to the Mainichi reporter Suruki this afternoon?"

"Yes."

"What was the burden of the conversation?"

"He said he knew some of the jokers in the brawl, and they weren't Reds."

"What did he offer as proof of his contention?"

"Nothing. He just said it."

"What did he want from you?"

"Nothing. I didn't seem to have what he needed." I threw him a bird. "He was killed this evening."

"How do you know?" His response was faster than a stop watch could measure.

"Saw him. Just after the accident."

"What were you doing there?"

"Walking. Going to get a drink."

"You will stay at this hotel?"

"For the time being, at least."

"Notify the Provost Marshal's office before you change your address. That's all for this evening."

He got up and left. His drink was untouched. So he wouldn't drink with me after all.

Chapter Four

I walked out of the front entrance of the Imperial and Ken swung into the driveway to pick me up. I got in the rear seat of the pocket-sized sedan.

"Osaka Hotel, Ken."

"Yes, sir." The car slid away as smoothly as cream on a plate. Ken was a skillful driver.

The Osaka Hotel had once been an office building for one of Japan's big insurance companies. When we came in we made it a billet for civilian women employees of the Occupation. Does that sound drab and uninteresting? If the walls of the Osaka could talk....

Sandra met me in the lobby and the eyes followed us as we went out.

I took her to the club on the roof of what had been a nine-story department store in the Shinjuku district. The building housed an American engineer unit now and the roof garden was the officers' club. I'd known a guy there the last time and I took a chance on crashing the gate. It worked out fine. The guy was gone, but the corporal who checked membership cards remembered me.

We ate steaks, drank Martinis, and talked hardly at all. We danced and it was a woman in my arms, warm and supple, flowing with the music. Between dances we sipped at brandy. Neither of us needed much stimulation. The officers and their ladies—about two thirds of the ladies were *musume*—watched the slender, lovely girl who was the Tokyo Doll. The CIC came over, very apologetic. Would Miss Tann sing a number with the band?

She sang. If I hadn't known her, hadn't been with her, it would have been the same; I would have felt that the golden girl and I were alone on the roof under the stars together. Her voice did that to you, clear and cool with the warmth bubbling through like champagne. When she ended they were silent for many seconds.

They applauded then with hungry insistence and she gave them an encore. When she finished this time she laughed, waved once in thanks, and returned to our table.

"Sandra, why are you here?"

"In Japan?"

"In Japan, singing on the Far East Network, living at the Osaka."

"Because I like it. Not Japan, maybe, but the network, yes, very much."

"Patriotism, Sandra?"

"I like the audience, if that's patriotism. They're young men like we know back home, three or four hundred thousand of the best that America's got, and most of them are in Korea in a dirty, miserable war. I like to sing for them."

"How did you happen to come here?"

"I asked for the job."

"And where's home?"

"My home is where I wash my stockings. I'm in show business, Mate."

I tossed off my brandy. Sandra wasn't talking; pleasant brush-offs and no answers. Good enough; she didn't ask any questions of me and she wasn't giving any answers. For a man and a woman it's sometimes the best way to play.

Except that I had the feeling that every nerve and muscle in my body were more alive than they'd ever been before when I was with her, and that I wanted to tell her every damn thing about Mate Buchanan I could think of. I wanted to show my muscles and do handstands, I was breathless and I was mighty happy to be with her. All this stuff was new to me and I guessed that I was falling in love with the Witch of Tokyo.

"What's with this Colonel Barham?"

The gray eyes were clear and steady on mine, the way a woman's eyes are when they're going to lie to you.

"He's just here in Tokyo on some police job. I scarcely know him."

I lit a cigarette for her. The band was taking a rest and now the night was with us, clouds rolling across the purple-black, a breeze whipping the trees that edged the rooftop. "Did you know that Suruki, the reporter who talked to us at the Imperial this afternoon, is dead?"

She let the smoke curl slowly from her nostrils. "No, Mate, I didn't know." She was far away from me for long seconds and then she seemed to give a little shiver. "It was horrible. I've been trying to forget it ever since it happened. I'll never forget, Mate, the way you came tearing in. I'll want to remember that always, and forget everything else. All right?"

It had to be all right. There was a life of Sandra Tann's of which I was supposed to know nothing. The Witch had secrets, as witches are supposed to do. But I was still breathing hard. I'm not subtle, so I played it straight and said, "Sandra, I've never played house with any girls, not even when I was a dirty-faced kid. But I think I'd like to play house with you."

Her face, shadowed in the swaying lights of the roof garden, seemed suddenly lonely and longing. Whatever road Sandra Tann walked must have been a solitary road.

"This is only the first day, Mate. But I think it would be fun playing house with you. For real."

"For real, Sandra."

It was a wonderful moment. We were high above Tokyo in the night. Below us the neon fires played across the rooftops and around us were the rustling trees of the garden.

I felt someone looking at me. I turned and looked into the eyes of Akiko Tsumi. She was at a table with her major, barely twenty feet away. There was a welcome in the great, dark eyes of Akiko, and as we looked at each other she smiled.

"Sandra," I said, getting up, "I've got to speak to that girl. Please pardon me for a minute."

She may have been surprised, but she didn't show it. Her soft gray eyes were steady and she smiled a little. "Of course, Mate."

I walked over to Akiko. Major Corbett looked at me stupidly. He was drunk, his face a red puff. "Hiyah," he muttered, and picked up his drink; some of it spilled on his chin.

"Hello, Captain," said the ivory princess—because that's how Akiko looked. Perfect, exquisite, fine features on a small head, a fragile, delicate body. But I wouldn't have traded my strong-limbed golden Sandra for a score of ivory princesses.

"No captain now, Akiko. Just Mate Buchanan. How are you?"

Lie to her, make love to her, marry her. Anything necessary to have her lead me to her father. It was a lousy job, especially since I had found Sandra.

"I'm very good, Buchanan-san, but the Major—I am so sorry—he very stinko." Her words were tilted a little with an accent. It was charming and exotic, as was Akiko.

"I didn't think you'd remember me, Akiko."

"Not forget Buchanan-san. You different. Not like other men very much."

"If you get lonely, Akiko, I'm at the Imperial."

She looked shocked and hurt. "Buchanan-san!" Akiko may have been used to sly passes made by other officers when the Major brought her to clubs like this one, but she didn't expect them from me.

I shook my head. "Not like that. You and the Major both, maybe dinner, dance. The three of us."

You could see the relief flood her delicate face. Little Akiko wanted so terribly to be respected. Many Japanese girls of good family had entered into affairs with Americans, but each of them thought of herself as a wife, hoped frantically to find that her lover wanted marriage and would take her to the enchanted land across the Pacific. I told Akiko what she wanted to hear—that I was inviting her and the Major as a couple, as if she were his wife.

I wondered if she knew yet that the Major's wife was arriving in Japan tomorrow. But of course she would. The *musume* had one of the finest co-operative spy systems possible; they knew more about their men than G-1 or G-2 did.

"We like that very much," said little Akiko.

Her drunken major was looking at me as if he couldn't quite focus his eyes or hold his head erect. Not a bad-looking man sober, but one of those who had sunk into the swamp of Tokyo—the swamp of elegant bars and cheap good liquor, of the complaisant, worshiping *musume*.

"Would you care to dance?" I had to start operating. There'd be a climax for little Akiko tomorrow and I had to be ready to move in fast.

She was up and in my arms in the wink of a hummingbird's eye. I would have enjoyed dancing with this fragile child-woman, but Sandra was there, and though this feeling of love was developing perhaps too quickly, I couldn't help myself. Nor did I want to.

But Akiko was in my arms and I was a soldier in civilian clothes, a soldier on a mission of violence, with the safety and welfare of uncounted American women and children possibly dependent upon the success of my mission.

As we danced on that garden rooftop I looked down on the girl I held. Some top intelligence agents had worked on her, subtly and without disclosing their purpose, trying to discover where her father had hidden himself after the surrender. There were no other relatives. The Tsumi family, except for father and daughter, had been killed during the war. It was extraordinarily sensitive and delicate intelligence work, because no one outside of the selected few assigned to the RK project could be permitted to know that anyone was interested in Dr. Tsumi.

The agents had failed and had been withdrawn. Others were still trying, but I was the only agent assigned to Akiko.

"What you think, Buchanan-san?" Akiko was looking up at me and we were dancing.

"That you're beautiful, Akiko," I said. The Buchanan body was expendable.

She laughed and hid her face. "Never happen. Akiko very homely. No?" She was like many other Japanese; she would beg for compliments like a twelve-year-old.

"Akiko very lovely." My hands tightened gently. It was like holding a fluttering thrush. The dance ended and I took her back to her table. The Major was pouring another drink down his gullet. I could understand why the RK Project agents considered him useless to them. "Please call me at the Imperial tomorrow. The three of us could go out together very soon."

"Maybe the Major, he call," said Akiko primly. I knew that she would never have phoned herself. It was good and bad luck meeting them here on the rooftop tonight; good because it saved me the trouble of hunting her home on the Yokohama Road tomorrow morning as I planned, bad because tonight was my first night with Sandra.

Sandra's gray eyes were warm and friendly for me as I came back to our table. She was one wonderful woman. There were no questions about Akiko. Sandra considered me a big boy, an independent male.

After another dance together we left. Ken waited patiently for us in the Minx and it was getting to the hour when the chattering, clattering, moving, twinkling city of Tokyo runs down. I had her in my arms before Ken had wheeled the car away from the curb and she stayed in my arms until we reached the Osaka.

We didn't talk. There are things that cannot be said by words.

It wasn't a mere physical searching and closeness. We were as emotionally and as physically close as we could be until the time when we were not in the back seat of a car with a driver only inches away. When that time came we both knew we would be together until, when our bodies parted, each would forever have some of the other.

We didn't go to the Osaka. She went with me to the Imperial, proud and unashamed.

It was like a marriage. She said that to me as she walked her finger through the tangle of hair on my chest, and I said it to her as I tightened my arms around her.

The rooms of the Imperial are tiny, and this little room seemed to protect us, to be close and friendly around us. We would awaken and find each other and sleep again. When, at last, we slept deeply, we did not awaken until the bell of the telephone jangled us into the world again.

I answered the phone.

"Buchanan-san? Buchanan-san?" It was a tiny, faraway voice, racked with pain and terror.

"Who is this?"

"Akiko. This is Akiko. I need you. Please come, Buchanan-san. I need you."

"Where are you?"

"In the house with the red tile where the Yokohama Road makes two with the road to Tachikawa. You can find, Buchanan-san?"

"What's the trouble?"

"You must come quickly, please, quickly!"

The phone clicked and was dead. I put the receiver down and turned to look into the warm gray eyes of Sandra.

There was no question of not going. My mission was concerned with the Japanese girl, not with the beautiful woman who sat erect in my bed.

"Stay here, Sandra. Have breakfast sent up. I'll be back inside an hour." The hands of my watch pointed to ten after eight. Ken would be downstairs with the car by now.

She asked no questions. Instead her hand stroked mine as I stood there by the bed.

I showered and dressed in four fast-moving minutes. One deep kiss, then I left her and went downstairs. The Minx was in the courtyard, ready to go. Ken popped out and had the door open before I reached the car in quick, long strides.

"You know where the Yokohama and Tachikawa roads branch?"

"Yes, I know."

"O.K. *Hayoka!*"

"Hokay!" Ken grinned and the Minx rolled into the broad, busy boulevard.

I tried to get my balance back. Too much emotion and too much sense of desperate urgency. Sandra and I had wanted each other from the moment our eyes first met yesterday, and now we wanted each other for all of our time. But my job with Akiko could not be put aside. If I had to make love to Akiko to trace out her father, I'd do just that and Sandra would never understand why Buchanan had taken her and then thrown her away. I couldn't tell her about the RK virus, and any lesser reason would not seem big enough to explain what I had done.

Ken was driving along a wide street that was much like any Stateside street. We were headed toward a district of big homes, hidden away from the streets by walls and thick shrubbery. Just before we reached the intersection with the highway to Tachikawa I saw the house with the red tile wall. I told Ken to park the Minx near the gate and I got out and walked through the archway into the little garden beyond.

It was a Japanese-style house of the kind that had belonged to comfortable families before the war. Many of them had been rented to Americans during the Occupation years.

There seemed to be no one around. The sliding panel of wood and glass that was the front door was partly open. I pushed it back and walked into the house. Only a half hour had passed since Akiko phoned me.

For a moment the house seemed empty. I walked across the rice-straw matting to the wall of paper panels on the other side of the room and slid the center panel aside. Now I could hear a hushed, broken sobbing.

They were in the bedroom at the back of the house. He lay there on the *futon* mat, holding a bloody cloth to his loins. The hushed, broken sobbing came from him. His eyes were closed. She sat, Japanese fashion, close to the bed mat. She was in kimono without obi, the nightdress of Japanese women.

Akiko and her major.

"What's happened?" I asked, and she raised her beautiful oval face, her great dark almond eyes shadowed.

"I have hurt him," she said. I saw the knife then, a slender thing, still coated with a reddish gum of blood.

"How?" I bent over the gray-faced major. The *futon* was an ugly sponge of blood.

"He will not look for a pom-pom girl again." Akiko spoke softly, as if to herself. "He lay there waiting for me, his eyes closed. I made a little love to him, like all the time before. The knife was ready, and as he smiled I cut. So sharp, so fast. Like the farmer does to the young bull. He called out in a big voice and held himself but it was all over. He bleed and I give him the cloth. Then I go to the telephone and call you."

"Where's the phone, Akiko?"

Her small hand gestured toward the next room.

There was a Tokyo directory on the low table with the telephone. I found the number of the Army's Tokyo General Dispensary. While I dialed the number I tried to figure out what to do, after this first necessary thing was done.

"Tokyo General Dispensary, Corporal Burns speaking."

"This is an emergency. An officer has been cut with a knife and needs immediate aid. He's in the house with the red tile wall near the junction of the Yokohama and Tachikawa roads. Your ambulance can find it easily. He's bleeding badly."

"Yes, sir. Red tile wall, Yokohama and Tachikawa highways. What is the nature of the wound?"

"I think he has been emasculated."

There was a sharp bleat of sound. I'd been shocked, too, when I understood what Akiko had done. I hung up the phone. We had less than five minutes to get away from here. The corporal was probably phoning the Provost Marshal right now, and an M.P. jeep would be roaring toward the house in a minute.

I ran back to the bedroom and lifted Akiko from the floor, stood her up.

"We're getting away from here right now! Come."

"I cannot go. I am not afraid."

"Akiko! There will be doctors here soon. Police too, M.P.'s. You come with me."

"I do not have my obi on, I am not dressed."

I swung her off the floor into my arms and ran to the front room. Still holding her, I ran through the garden to the open gate.

Ken seemed a little surprised to see me coming toward the Minx carrying a girl in a kimono, but he was out and had the door open before we got to the car. I put her in, got in myself, and told Ken to get moving fast. He did.

"Why did you call me, Akiko?"

"He made noises like hurt animal. I was afraid and very lonely."

Ken rounded a corner into the wide boulevard to Yokohama. Two minutes later we passed an M.P. jeep, siren howling, headed toward the intersection behind us. It had been close. I was holding Akiko, one arm around her, but her head was erect and she was not trembling.

"Why did you do that, Akiko?"

"Because his wife comes today. I knew that many days ago. He did not tell me. Always a Japanese girl knows about her American man. We have many friends who work in your offices, other girls. They watch for reports and records. Always know."

"You were jealous of his wife, Akiko?"

"Not so. He made me shamed. I was a girl to sleep with to him. I was not such a girl to myself. Now I am."

"Why didn't you kill him, instead?"

"If he was dead, maybe Akiko would still love him."

"And this way?"

"Who can love him now? What woman?"

"Had he lied to you, Akiko?"

"Who lies to a pom-pom girl? I did not know, I thought I was like a wife, but to him I was just a private pom-pom girl."

"But you're no pom-pom girl, Akiko. You're a good girl, from a good family."

"Today he make love to me in morning, go to Yokohama at noon to meet his wife. He had found other man for me, he told me. A colonel, old and fat. He does this colonel a favor, he gives him his pom-pom girl when he is done with her. But now all he can give his wife is money, so she will be pom-pom girl, too."

"What are you going to do, Akiko?"

"You took me away from that place. O.K., I do what you want, Buchanan-san. You want pom-pom girl? Pretty Japanese girl named Akiko? Only one-man girl, almost good." Her voice was more sad than bitter.

Ken slowed the car and turned his head to me. "Excuse, please. Where you go? You not tell me."

Good question. If I'd left Akiko back there the police would have had her now and her father might learn of her arrest. If so, he might, in fear of discovery, destroy the only specimen of RK virus in the world. I had to stay with Akiko now until she took me to him, and I would have to find him within hours, because the hounds would be hunting this fragile, lovely girl.

Fragile, lovely girl who made love to her man while her fingers guided the knife.

"Haji-basha, Ken."

I wondered about Major Corbett. It had lasted three years, this thing between them. What had he thought of his ivory princess? Had she seemed like a real woman to him? Or was she just another Occupation girl to him, lovelier than most?

Oh, the hounds would be out, all right, were out now. The M.P. patrols, the web of the Tokyo Metropolitan Police would search Tokyo until they found her. A Japanese girl had turned on her American, and it would be a nasty problem for the high command tonight.

I had to hide her until I found her father, while back at the Imperial Sandra waited for me.

The Minx turned off the broad street that led to the Ginza and into the narrow bazaar alley of Ginza-nishi. It was early for this place. Most of the shutters were still over the store windows and the bazaar was quiet.

"Will the place be open, Ken?"

"Maybe. I go speak." The boy went upstairs and I thought about the situation. Mr. Morning Sun would know of some place to hide Akiko for a few hours or a few days. The price would be high and the danger of a double cross even higher, but where else could I go? The girl was silent, and what her thoughts were could not be guessed.

Ken came down. "It's O.K. You go up. Pretty soon Asahi-san come."

I led Akiko up to the little dance room. A round-faced pudding of a girl was scrubbing the floor. She did not look up as we came in. It was hot and sticky in the box-sized room, and the air was stale. I sat next to Akiko in the same booth where I had waited for Asahi-san yesterday.

Ken stood in the doorway.

"Tell the girl to get us some whisky, Ken. Two."

He spoke rapidly to the girl and she shuffled, barefooted, behind the bar.

"What you do with me, Buchanan-san?"

"Do you have any family, Akiko?"

"Just my father. I have not seen him for long time."

"Where is he?" Be lucky, Buchanan. At the easy, bargain price.

"I cannot tell." No luck, Buchanan. Keep trying.

"Why not, Akiko?"

"He told me I must never talk about him."

"But now you need him. Tell me where he is so I can take you to him."

"He told me, long ago, I must never talk about him. Never."

The round-faced girl brought us two glasses of straight whisky. Akiko picked up her glass and looked at the brown liquid.

"Akiko maybe get stinko. Akiko has heavy heart."

I looked at her. Despite my feeling of pity for this lost, fragile little ivory princess whose heart must be very heavy, there was a feeling of disgust and revulsion toward this woman whose slender, almond-tipped fingers had cut so surely and terribly into the body of a man.

Why feel sorry for her? She'd lived high for three years with a major, traveling first class. But maybe she'd loved him.

"Go ahead, Akiko. Get stinko. Maybe it would be a good thing."

A slender hand reached across to mine, closed warmly and tightly on my big fist. "Why you help me, Buchanan-san?"

I didn't answer her. I looked at her and my eyes must have been cold because she looked away and her soft hand left my fist.

She upended her glass of whisky and when she put it down she coughed, but the glass was empty. I took mine, too, and it was harsh and hot, tasting as if it had been distilled from the sins of the night.

I wanted to call Sandra. It had been more than an hour since I had left her so abruptly at the Imperial. But I couldn't call her until I knew what

I was going to do, until I knew that I could find Dr. Tsumi.

"More whisky, please, Buchanan-san. I want to get very stinko."

Maybe I could follow an old American tradition—get her drunk. I waved the two empty glasses at the plump girl, who was scrubbing the floor again. She got up and brought us two more whiskies. Ken had gone downstairs, presumably to wait in the car.

"I have a friend here, Akiko," I said. "He will know a good place for you. But I must find your father so that he can help you."

"Never happen," said Akiko.

Maybe I smelled his perfume over the stale stink of the place or maybe I felt his sin-steeped eyes looking at me from their powder-encrusted wrinkled pouches, but I knew he was there. I turned.

Mr. Morning Sun stood in the doorway, his smudged lips pursed into a pouting smile.

"Hello. You need some help, maybe?"

Chapter Five

For a moment I felt trapped. Asahi-san may have been repulsive and grotesque, but he was deadly dangerous as well. Giving him any hold on me was like letting an octopus wrap a tentacle around my body, but because of Akiko's act I had to bargain with him for a hiding place.

"Sit down, Asahi-san," I said, my voice crisp and unfriendly. This was no time to show hesitation or weakness.

He lowered his fat body into the seat across from us, his eyes never leaving my face.

"This girl is wanted by the police. I will pay well for a place for her to stay."

That was all he needed to know. He had the high hand, I needed what he had to sell.

"Why is she wanted?"

"She knifed an American officer."

He thought about that for a while. Then he shook his head and got up. I cursed him silently. He knew he had me and he was going to make me sweat.

"Never happen." He shuffled toward the bar. "Maybe better you go. Bring trouble my place."

"You speak how much," I snarled. He turned and looked at me.

"How much you got, G.I.?" It was the traditional question and answer of a pom-pom girl and a soldier in a Shimbashi alley, and both my question and his answer had been bitter sarcasm.

"I'll pay a hundred thousand yen."

Two hundred and eighty dollars. It was the amount of money a skilled worker would earn in six months.

"How long I hide her?" He shuffled back toward us.

"*S'koshi* days, a little while."

"This officer, he die?"

"No."

There was nowhere else for me to go and we both knew it. There was no hotel, no train or bus, nowhere on the island of Honshu where a hunted girl could hide, except a place provided by the professional criminals.

"Hundred thousand yen now, hundred thousand yen in three days?" He had a worry too, a worry that he wouldn't squeeze the last possible yen out of the deal.

"Hundred thousand yen now. We speak again in three days."

"Hokay. You come."

"Where do we go?" I asked, putting an arm around Akiko. She had a bewildered look and I figured she was going to start crying.

"I have nice place. Shimbashi district. Very nice."

It was guaranteed to be a very nice place if it was in Shimbashi. Shimbashi, the human sewer of Tokyo.

I held Akiko as we followed Asahi-san down the stairs.

She'd had about two double shots and they had got her well started. She clung to me.

Asahi-san's own car and driver were close by. He had a '52 Cadillac with the extra-long body, which showed that he belonged to the aristocracy of Shimbashi. Only the *zaibatsu*—the incredibly wealthy industrialists who by now were all out of Sugamo prison—and the black-market bosses had Cadillacs in Tokyo. You'd be surprised at how many new Cadillacs there were around.

It was only a five-minute drive through the clattering streets, across a broad canal of smelly, black-scummed water, and into the streets of Shimbashi.

The Shimbashi district by day is a business section of two-storied buildings with shops selling cameras, silks, and pearls, dried fish and strange fruits, every third one a *pachinko* parlor where dozens of men and women stood before upright pin-ball machines trying to win cigarettes and soap. It was a gaudy district clustering around Shimbashi station, much of it bright with gilt and scarlet, all of it noisy. At night it is the playground of the pimp and the prostitute, the black-market money trader, the thief and the killer.

The long black Cadillac stopped in front of a two-story stone-and-stucco building. There was a bar on the first floor, the Shamrock Bar.

We went in and it was a standard Shimbashi saloon—lots of chairs, low tables, a three-foot bar, all of it about as Irish as cold rice and fish heads. Asahi-san waddled ahead and we followed him upstairs. This was old-style Japan again, with a rack of felt slippers, rice-straw floors, and walls of sliding panels.

Asahi-san took us to a room at the end of a short hall. The room was barren; one wall of windows, screened by bamboo curtains, two walls of paper panels, one wall of sliding wooden doors behind which, I guessed, were all of the utensils for living: cooking pots, dishes, and sleeping rolls. It was a typical Japanese one-room apartment.

He slid the door panel closed behind us and said, "Now you pay, please?"

I had about twenty ten-thousand yen notes. I gave him ten of them.

"All right now. Pretty soon we speak more." He bowed slightly, opened the door panel, and shuffled out. Akiko and I were alone. She sank into a sitting position on the floor and waited for me to tell her what to do. Tears were running down the ivory cheeks now.

I sat next to her and she fell into my arms. The time of frantic weeping had come. There were no words. I held her for minutes until the emotional storm was over.

"Buchanan-san," she whispered, rising until her lips brushed my ear. "Buchanan-san, please, you love Akiko now. Akiko needs love now."

It must be something in the soul of women—when their very lives are shaken by emotional torment, physical love seems to be the only meaningful thing left for them in all the world.

There was only one woman in the world I wanted now, and she was waiting for me at the Imperial. But Akiko stood in front of me, her slender fingers gripping my shoulders. "Akiko needs love now! Now, Buchanan-san!"

I reacted without thinking. I hit her with the heel of my hand just hard enough to knock her out. She rocked back, her head bobbing crazily, and then her knees buckled and she sagged, face forward, to the floor.

I rolled her over. She'd be conscious again in seconds, dazed for a few minutes. I waited for her eyes to open again.

It was minutes before they did, and then she looked at me as if she were a spaniel whose master had beaten it.

"Akiko sorry, Buchanan-san," she said in a tiny voice. "Please no hit more. Akiko do what you want, Buchanan-san."

"I want to take you to your father."

"I cannot go to my father. He shamed of me before. Now more shame. I cannot go."

"Do you want to go, Akiko?"

"Not in shame, Buchanan-san. I can never see father again."

"You're in a lot of trouble. He could help you."

"He not help me. You help me, Buchanan-san." The tears were starting again.

There was a damn good chance she would try to kill herself today; the Japanese have the highest suicide rate of any people and Akiko Tsumi was probably the unhappiest girl in Japan.

"Akiko."

"Yes, Buchanan-san?" The small, exquisite face looked at me, crimson lips half open.

"I'll take care of you. Sleep for an hour. Then I'll come and get you. Everything will be all right. Understand?"

"Yes, Buchanan-san. You best American man. You are good."

She opened the closet panel and found a bed mat. I watched her as she spread it on the floor. I'd been right about the sleep, the girl was exhausted. She had probably lain awake through the night, wondering what the Major would do now that his wife was coming to Japan. Apparently he had told her this morning, or maybe even during the night. Then he found out what she could do. A good portion of man's troubles were over forever for Major Corbett now, but the only person I felt sorry for was his wife.

Akiko lay on the *futon*. "I wait for you, Buchanan-san."

"I'll be back in an hour. *Sayonara,* Akiko."

"*Sayonara,* Buchanan-san."

I pushed the door panel aside, stepped into the hall, closed it again.

Asahi-san was waiting for me at the end of the hall. "We speak, Mr. Buchanan. We speak now on big business."

He'd been listening at the panel. He knew now that my interest in the girl was not sex, so he'd try to find out what my real interest was. I would have to kill him before he made any shrewd guesses. I could risk myself, I could even risk Sandra, but I could not risk the secret of the RK virus.

"What name this girl? Where she come?"

"Her name is Akiko Tsumi. She is a Tokyo girl."

"Why you help this girl?"

"She's a friend of mine."

"You not make love. She want, you say no, no, never happen. Why?"

"None of your goddamn business."

He turned in a whirl of stale perfume. "I go tell police."

That was a relief. He was making an empty threat because he didn't know what move to make. He had me on the hook but he wasn't sure how to play me.

"Go ahead, you sackful of lard," I said. He wouldn't understand all of the words but he would get the point: Buchanan was not being bluffed. "I'll be back in an hour. You see that the girl is O.K. Understand?" I started down the stairs. Asahi-san would be too greedy for more of my money to take any chances with Akiko for the next hour.

I took a cab for the six-block ride to the Imperial.

There was nothing at the desk for me. Upstairs, my little box of a room was empty. I saw a note and opened it. Nothing fancy about Sandra's handwriting, big and easy, not quite a scrawl: "Mate—Were we just playing house? I wasn't. All my love, Sandra."

I folded the note. Somehow after thirty years of living I'd found the right one. I knew it the way I knew I breathed or was hungry. I was hungry, too, come to think of it. No breakfast, and I take a lot of fuel.

Downstairs I took time out for breakfast and for thinking ahead. I had Akiko but she would be a dangerous liability. Asahi-san would try to squeeze me for money, try to find out the connection between Akiko and me so he could squeeze for more. I wasn't worried about money—the RK Project expense account had no ceiling—but I had already endangered a secret possibly as important to my country as the secret of the atom bomb had been. In a way it was even more important.

The waitress brought me a copy of the Nippon *Times*, the Japanese-owned English-language morning newspaper. Yesterday's riot was the big story, two columns on the right-hand side of the front page. A picture of the overturned Buick, a fuzzy picture of Sandra Tann from the publicity section of FEN, and a lot of excited prose. Attacks on Americans were big news in Japan after the May Day riots, particularly with the Occupation about to end.

A second item, much smaller, on the front page: MYSTERIOUS MURDER OF REPORTER. "Hideomi Suruki, city reporter for the *Mainichi Press*, Kitateraocho, Tsurumi-ku, Yokohama, collapsed in the street before the *Mainichi Press* Building and was struck by a U. S. Army truck. Police revealed last night that Mr. Suruki had been stabbed by an unknown assailant immediately before he collapsed. In the confusion of the crowded street there were no witnesses to the attack and bystanders had believed Mr. Suruki's death to have been accidental or caused by heart failure until a knife wound was discovered. Tokyo Metropolitan Police are investigating."

The attack on Barham's Buick had been a gang attack. The murder of little Suruki had been a gang murder. In Japan there were only three kinds of gangs: the Reds, the black-marketeers, and maybe, now again eleven years after the Pacific war had begun, the professional assassins of the great industrial combines, the *zaibatsu*, once the richest men in the world, and the most ruthless.

The professional killers of the *zaibatsu* had gone out on commercial missions to the ends of the earth. A salesman poisoned in Bombay, a British industrialist dying from bamboo splinters in his intestines in London. They helped sell Japanese cotton goods, beer, bicycles, electric light bulbs, motor cars, silks, and heavy machinery. They helped sell them by removing obstacles, removing men or women who knew too much.

Or women who knew too much. Maybe Sandra knew too much about some revived *zaibatsu*.

Because they had revived.

When our troops took over, we planned to wipe out the incredibly powerful Japanese industrial combines. MacArthur threw the big men, and a lot of the little men, in jail. Their far-flung properties were taken away from them. We put our men in to run them. But our men needed interpreters.

Things happened to the first set of interpreters. They got drunk, or sick, or just didn't come to work any more. The next set of interpreters was a lot better. They weren't big-toothed men in horned-rimmed glasses. These were lovely girls, smooth and friendly, just as competent as the frail beavers had been, and a lot more fun to have around.

So we ran the properties of the *zaibatsu* and we were held by silken threads, guided by soft hands. The *zaibatsu* had used women to buy men for half a century. It took almost five years, but the ruthless men made it back.

Why would the Reds want Sandra Tann dead? The black-marketeers? The *zaibatsu?* She was my woman and I knew nothing about her.

I left the Imperial knowing what I was going to do. I was a man in love and a man with a dangerous, important job. There was no doubt about either of those things. Akiko would be asleep in the room over the Shamrock Bar and as safe as she would be anywhere in Tokyo until I got back. Sandra Tann might not be safe. A gang had tried to kill either her or Colonel Barham yesterday. They had killed Suruki because he had recognized at least some of the assassins in the mob. They would probably try to kill again.

I walked up the block in the bright Saturday sunshine toward the red-brown bulk of the Osaka Hotel and into the lobby, and I asked for Miss

Tann. Miss Tann was not in; they did not know when she would return.

She hadn't asked me any questions, she hadn't answered mine, but Tokyo is a poor town in which to keep secrets. She had been here almost a year, she was a dazzlingly beautiful girl, she was a personality that everybody from Korea to Hokkaido and Okinawa would know. If I could find the right source I could find everything to know about my woman, and I had to know everything. Because I believed she was in something that had her marked for death.

There was a barroom in the big Sanshin Building, Peter's, where I might find the person who could tell me about Sandra. I walked toward the Sanshin Building trying to remember names. Names of the lost people who had come to Tokyo in the first years of the Occupation and who had been seduced, who were lost. The DAC's, the civilian experts, the correspondents, the military people who had come to Tokyo and had eaten the lotus and never wanted to go home again.

For some of them it was merely the luxury of soft-footed servants and fine liquor and beautiful homes such as they could not afford in America, even if they made twenty-five thousand a year. Others loved the arrogance of being an American, of being a god in a land where the people respected gods. Some loved the country, the mist-veiled waterfalls, the intense green valleys, the villages. And some loved a woman. She would be small and delicately boned, with great, dark eyes and blue-black hair. Her skin was golden and it seemed that she offered you her body, her soul, her life in a lacquered bowl. She lived only for the pleasure and comfort she could bring you, and she was exquisite.

So they stayed, the lost ones, each for his own reason.

And like any colony of lost people, they knew one another without secrets or shame. They prided themselves on knowing the country that had seduced them, and knowing its secrets.

Vance Bogan came to my mind.

You could meet a man like Vance Bogan at the corner of Hollywood and Vine. He'd be rather goodhearted, not bright, not vicious. Just without either talent or luck, ability or relatives. He'd be starving.

But in Tokyo Vance Bogan was fat and rich and happy. He had come to Tokyo with the tide of the Army, and Tokyo turned out to be the town he'd been looking for all his life. He made lots of friends, no enemies, and stacks of money in the black-market money exchange.

Vance Bogan would know the web as well as any American could. If I could talk to him for a few minutes, he could give me the story on Sandra Tann, and somewhere within that story I could find out the reason someone wanted to kill her.

I went into the Sanshin Building. At the far end of the arcade were the steps that curved down to Peter's.

Peter's was bright with fluorescent lights. The barroom, apart from the restaurant, looked somehow more like a soda fountain than a saloon. But it was a saloon and some of the heaviest drinking by the heaviest drinkers in Tokyo was done here.

Now, close to noon, there were only three drinkers there. A lonely major sat at the bar and rolled dice with the Chinese barman. A big Australian sat at a table drinking alternately from a tall glass of straight whisky and an immense coffee cup. The third man, in a hound's-tooth sport jacket, sprawled comfortably in a deep chair, was Vance Bogan.

I went to him. He didn't recognize me, but he smiled a welcome. "Hi, fellow. How are you?"

"Hello, Vance. I'm Mate Buchanan. Few months back."

"Oh, yeah, sure. Hiyah, Mate. Have a drink." He slouched forward to shake hands. "Didn't you get court-martialed or something? I thought they were going to shoot you. Didn't, though, did they?" He was drinking a Velvet Hammer, a neat, smooth drink that would knock you out in time, but gently.

"They missed," I said. One of the things about Vance Bogan was that what mind he had was always completely open. He wasn't being candid, he simply had only a few thoughts and nothing to hide them behind.

"Let's see... Mate Buchanan. What have I heard about you recently?" He swirled his Velvet Hammer and looked around. "Oh, yeah. Riot. Riot yesterday. The *Times* this morning. Attack on an American car. Sandra Tann. You were in the fight."

"What's with this Sandra Tann?" I asked.

"She's a singer on the Far East Network. She sings real good, too. Lives over at the Osaka, of course. Been over here since—since about the time you were in all that trouble. How did that come out, huh? They put you in the can and just let you out? No, I remember. You got acquitted. Lucky."

"Sure was," I said. The barman was waiting for an order. "Canadian and soda." He whispered off.

"This dame that sings. New Yorker. Just got off the boat here one day and it turned out somebody had hired her Stateside as a DAC. Hell of a good-looking DAC, but who cares about DAC's as long as the *musume* supply holds out, huh?"

The barman slipped softly back, replaced the empty glass in front of Vance Bogan with a full one, poured my Canadian for me, and slipped softly away.

"Yeah, great singer. How'd she get in that thing yesterday? With some colonel. Didn't recognize his name, either. They're getting so many goddamn new colonels and generals over here, I hardly know anybody any more. Tokyo's going to hell, you know that? The Americans have ruined it. It was great back in '47 or even '48. Man, you could go over to Shimbashi with a couple of cartons of cigarettes and make yourself a real potful of loot."

I worked on my highball. With Bogan you just waited. If he knew it, he'd tell it when he got to it.

"That Sandra Tann, she's kind of funny. She's got a lot of talent, a lot of looks—what the hell is she doing in Tokyo? Singing over the radio for a bunch of dog faces. What did you want to know about her?" This time the question was direct. I sometimes wondered if Vance Bogan was really as simple as he seemed. He never seemed much brighter than a biscuit, but he turned out a very sumptuous life for himself.

"I met her. We had a date last night. I think she's real fine."

He put down his drink and gave me a long, slow look. "Mate, you got yourself in a lot of trouble in Korea. You got out of it, but you know that was luck, plain goddamn luck. You could have got five years. Now you're taking up with this Tann dame. You know how it is with something really luscious in Tokyo, especially if she's a DAC or some silly thing like that. Well, figure how it is with this Tann dame. Every guy in Tokyo is after her. And what does she do? She spends all her time with Japanese. Just like if we'd never won the goddamn war!"

I looked at the plump man as his lip curled over the edge of his glass. We'd won the war and the Vance Bogans had come, along with all the rest of us. They lived well, they aped the Japanese customs, they slept with Japanese girls, fell in love with them. But nine out of ten of them wore an open contempt for the people whose lives they imitated. Yet—why would Sandra Tann spend her time with Japanese?

"See her in the big bar at the Nikkatsu—fanciest place in town, makes the Imperial look like a boardinghouse—but she's always with Japs. Rich ones, too. Big wheels that should still be rotting in Sugamo prison. Goddamn."

My place here was to listen. Bogan would tell me what he knew, and often the things that Bogan could tell were things his listeners didn't want to hear.

"Other night I saw her at the Café Mimatsu—you remember the Mimatsu? Plush as hell, and that floor show—well, anyway, she was downstairs at ringside with this zillionaire Jap. Now, I'm broad-minded and liberal as all hell, you know that, but I think she ought to stick to her own kind."

If Bogan knew it, all of foreign Tokyo knew it too. They'd asked her to sing up there in the roof-garden last night, but nobody had come to the table, no old friends, no one asking for a dance. I hadn't thought of it last night, but I was thinking of it now. She should be the most popular girl in our kind of Tokyo, but even the *musume* had been more popular up there.

"What's the story, Vance? Do you know?"

He shrugged. "Nobody knows. She goes that route, and I guess it ain't illegal. But you don't want to get mixed up with her. You ain't rich and you ain't Japanese and it looks like that's what it takes."

He waved for more drinks but I shook my head. "I've got to be moving on, Vance. Good to see you."

"Have fun, Mate. See you around."

"So long, Vance."

And that's the way it goes some days.

Chapter Six

It was close to one p.m. now and a warm bright Saturday afternoon. I left the Sanshin Building and waved down a rattling taxi and told the driver to take me to the Shamrock in Shimbashi.

Akiko wasn't in the room. I saw an American, six and a half feet tall, with skin the color of chamois; a tawny tiger of a man, hands twice the size of mine, a head sloping back, long, high-bridged nose, yellow-white eyes. I knew him slightly. This was Carleton Carter, and he had been like a king in Tokyo.

"Come right in, Cap'n Buchanan. The old *honcho's* been waitin' on you," he said in a soft voice.

"Where's the girl?"

"That's what the ol' *honcho* wants to talk to you about, Cap'n."

He called himself *honcho*, Japanese for "big boss," and he meant it. I walked into the room and closed the panel.

"Get to talking, Sergeant Carter."

"That ol' stuff's long gone now, Cap'n. No more sergeant, just Carter-san."

I remembered him from Peter's, Master Sergeant Carleton Carter of the Japan Logistical Command, a tall drink in the great hand that flashed an unusual signet ring, a careless pile of yen in front of him. They called him the Duke of Shimbashi. He'd gamble on anything, loan money to anyone.

The C.I.D. had tried to get him. They were sure he was in black markets, probably in dope, too. But they'd never touched him.

"Where's the girl?"

"What you want with that li'l ol' *muse?*" Carter was laughing at me.

My knee came up hard but he twisted his body as my knee hit and nothing happened except I was off balance and in bad trouble.

One giant hand took my shoulder and clamped it, his right came chopping for my head to knock it off my shoulders. He was maybe 230, hard, mean.

I swung my head under his chin and butted, the big fist crashing into my shoulder, numbing it. He pulled away from me and his hands opened, the powerful fingers ready to throttle or gouge. I had to keep close to him or he'd have me, pounding and breaking me with those great arms. I pushed toward him and half turned inside his arms. I got the middle finger of his left hand and bent it back fast. It cracked and went loose. His right hand closed on the back of my neck, the steel fingers biting into muscles. I tried to fall against it and kicked behind him with my left leg. We both went over. I hit him in the throat and he opened his mouth.

I hooked three fingers into his mouth and pulled hard on his cheek from inside. He was digging into my neck with his fingers and there were only seconds left for me. I pulled his head up as his jaws worked, trying to reach my fingers. He pulled at my arm with his left hand, the middle finger dangling.

We were both on the floor, my body half over his, his right hand clamped on my neck, his left hand weaker on my right arm, my fingers hooked into his face and pulling. As his neck arched to his left I hit him behind the ear once, and my own head was bursting in red and black flashes and I was going out; twice, and my fingers in his mouth were tiring; three solid ones behind his ear, and his hand relaxed.

I was blind with the pounding of the blood in my head and I tried to get up. The man was out only for seconds, and as I stood up his right hand closed on my ankle. He pulled me down and rolled to his knees. My feet were toward him. I saw the flick of his right hand to his pocket and saw the knife spring open as he pulled it out. Then he was on his feet, the knife ready.

My fingers closed on the rice-straw mat and I came up as he moved on me. The mat surprised him and it caught the knife. This time my knee got him as our bodies came together, but he hit me on the side of the head with his broken left hand and I crashed against the paper-panel wall, going through it to the hall.

I didn't feel the wood strips breaking against my body as I went to the floor outside the room. I saw him through the torn wall, holding his groin with his left hand, bent half over in agony. The knife was still in his right hand.

I got up from the floor, my head exploding with pain and God knows what his broken hand must have felt like. I wanted to run but I didn't. I went back through the torn wall.

He tried to straighten up as I came through, but I hooked one up to his throat again and got him behind the ear as he went down. He was on his knees and hands, fighting to breathe, only half conscious. He still held the knife. I looked around the little room for something to hit him with. Both of my hands were loose bundles of pain now. I pushed open the closet slide. There was a brass teapot on a shelf. I took it and beat him on the head with it until he went down to the floor, his face in a puddle of blood from his head.

His fingers were clenched on the knife and my own were weak as I pulled his back, one by one. I pulled off the signet ring from his broken hand and walked out through the torn wall.

I had to steady myself before I started down the stairs. I was shaking pretty badly.

Two Japanese were waiting at the foot of the stairs. One of them wore a barman's white jacket; the other was in shoddy Western clothes. Both of them were chattering at me but I pushed them aside. They pushed easy and I walked out.

Outside it was bright with sun. A cab was bleating its horn at me. I stepped in. "Haji-basha, Ginza-nishi."

Asahi-san was going to play rough. He had brought Carter in, and that was the threat of violence. Well, now we all were playing rough.

The cab squeaked through the Saturday-afternoon crowd in the alley bazaar. I gave the driver his hundred yen and went up the stairs to the Haji-basha, where I figured on finding Asahi-san.

He was sitting in a booth. I walked over to him and tossed Carter's ring on the table in front of him.

He looked at it for several seconds. He recognized it.

"Where is she?" My voice was hoarse from Carter's cruel fingers.

A little saliva dribbled from the corner of his mouth over the lipstick and down through the caked powder. Asahi-san looked like a very tired old hag. "You very bad man," he said. I grabbed a handful of his dirty white silk suit and pulled his face toward me. The dance girls were twittering like birds behind me.

"O.K. No trouble. I take you." I let go of the crumpled silk and he puffed his way out of the booth. He waddled to the stairs and the dance girls flattened themselves back against the walls. We went down to the glare and noise of the bazaar.

I had a gun, an Army service .45, packed away neatly under my shirts in my luggage at the Imperial. I wished I had it with me now. A fight, even a brief one, uses up a man. My hands were sore and my throat felt as if it were stuffed with barbed wire.

Ken and the Hillman Minx were waiting at the far end of the alley. Apparently the boy knew nothing of what was going on and had been waiting there patiently for me since morning. He opened both doors of the Minx. I motioned Asahi-san into the front seat. I didn't want him behind me.

He spoke in Japanese to Ken and the boy started the car, pulling out into the narrow street that ran to the Ginza. I sat back and found that I was clenching and unclenching my hands in an even rhythm, partially to wear off the soreness but mostly because I was hot to go. The sleepy, satisfied animal who had been Mate Buchanan awakening next to Sandra this morning was in a rage now, a rage that had begun when I walked into the room above the Shamrock, found Akiko gone and the tigerish Duke of Shimbashi there, and realized that I had been double-crossed by thieves hungry for money in a job where money itself had no importance.

I realized why the two men had come to my room in San Francisco. Not only because Dr. Tsumi's daughter trusted me, but because this mission of mine was a one-man, lone-wolf job. The man they used had to go alone without the help of the military authorities, the Japanese government and its police, or anyone else.

One hint of the RK virus to the government and the *zaibatsu* would be in the picture, ready to blackmail 155,000,000 Americans, ready to bargain with Stalin. One hint of the RK virus to the regular military authorities and they would try to obtain it through ordinary methods, legal and orthodox. But it would take Dr. Tsumi only seconds to destroy it, and he had sworn no American would ever see the RK virus. So it was a lone-wolf job.

The Minx went steadily across the tree-lined Ginza into a narrow street beyond and then turned left. The entire block on our right now was a single four-story concrete building whose façade was broken by windows, galleries, sections of glass brick, and spiral staircases curling up to entrances in the upper floors. Ken blatted the horn of the Minx until he was able to squeeze through a line of rickety cabs and get to the curb.

Asahi-san pushed himself out of the front door of the car, his buttocks wedging against the doorframe and then rippling through. Ken ran around the back and opened the rear door for me.

"What the hell is this?" I asked Asahi-san. I knew what the big building was—the Delight Baths, a vast human zoo of public and private baths for Japanese, and for G.I.'s who loved the luxury of sprawling in a warm tub while a girl scrubbed away the dust of Korea or the weariness of Tokyo.

"Girl here. Good place nobody look." Asahi-san began puffing his way up the broad front steps toward the row of glass doors, entrances to the wonders of the Baths. Asahi-san was *ichiban* big wheel at the Delight Baths. The guides and clerks bowed and hissed, but Asahi-san paid no attention. He waddled toward the stairs and I followed him. Ken waited in the car outside.

We went up the wide spiral stairs, marble and chrome, to an upstairs saloon decorated like a little garden with dwarf trees, a flagstoned floor, and a bubbling fountain. Here Mr. Morning Sun stopped for breath and a girl came up to us, bowing and smiling.

We were in the ornate upper floors of the Delight, reserved for wealthy Japanese. This part of the Delight Baths was quiet except for the faint banjo-like jingle of samisens somewhere down the two-story colonnaded hall. In other parts of the building were long rooms reserved for Japanese chess, immense public baths for the tourists, milk baths, steam baths; restaurants, roof garden, and secrets known only to the closer friends of the owner.

"Where is she?" I said to Asahi-san.

He motioned toward the colonnaded hall. A desk was in the center of the hall, a clerk busy with a telephone and his set of reservation cards. Between the fifteen-foot imitation-marble columns were the entrances to the luxury private baths. He waved a hand and we walked into the hall of columns.

Asahi-san walked to a door toward the rear of the oval-shaped hall and knocked quickly. After a few seconds the door opened and I followed him into the room beyond.

It was a suite, one big room with Western-style furniture, a smaller room with matted floor, the bathroom itself opening from the larger room. Akiko lay face down on a narrow, western-style bed in the big room. A bath girl was giving her a massage.

Asahi-san pointed to the girl and then made a wiping motion with his hands. He reached into his coat pocket and drew out an enormous wallet. He began counting out ten-thousand-yen notes to me. When he finished we were even. He'd paid back the advance still unused on the Minx and the hundred thousand yen he'd received a few hours earlier. He wanted no more of me.

I shook my head and gave him back the Minx money. I'd still need Ken, and I was better off with Asahi-san than I would be with the commercial car agents, who would make daily reports to the police. He grumbled, sighed, and took the money. The ring had scared him. I wasn't supposed to have won that fight. He would stay scared for a day, maybe two.

Akiko turned her head and saw me. She smiled and rolled over, sitting up. The bath girl giggled and covered Akiko with a towel, a kind of polite gesture rather than any consideration of modesty.

"This fat, flower-smell man tell me better I come here. Is O.K., Buchanan-san?"

"Is O.K., Akiko."

Asahi-san began to shuffle toward the door.

"You tell Ken to wait for me downstairs. Who else knows the girl is here? Carter-san?" I walked up to the scared, soft-bellied Mr. Morning Sun.

"Nobody know. Just owner this place, and he friend."

"Carter-san friend, too?"

Asahi-san didn't want to talk about Carter. "Never happen," he said, modern Tokyo's equivalent for "No, no, don't even talk about it!"

"If anybody else bothers me or this girl, I'll cut your mouth clear around your head." He knew that one; the samurai used to play that funny joke on the peasants.

He was too worried for English. He gushed Japanese, turned around, turned back again and bowed several times, sighed, turned around again, and paddled out. The bath girl closed the door.

"Akiko's heart very heavy and cold, Buchanan-san."

I sat next to her and put my arm around her. She leaned to me.

"Your clothes rough, Buchanan-san. Why you not take off, have girl-san rub you?"

As a matter of fact, a bath sounded like just what a doctor would order.

"O.K."

While I undressed, the bath girl got instructions in Japanese and was busy in the bathroom. For a moment I felt a little ridiculous, but this fancy parlor-house setup was not lewd in Tokyo. Both Akiko and I were acting within the limits of respectable good taste.

I spent a half hour of heaven in that bath. The bath girl soaped me and rubbed me off, soaked me in nearly scalding water and then in cool water, rubbed me down, and massaged my sore neck into something near normal.

We could hear the strumming of a samisen clearly from beyond the door, somewhere in a room of the colonnaded hall. I felt the tension, the weariness, the aches of the fight leave me under the wise fingers of the bath girl. When the bath girl dressed me Akiko noticed the blood on my clothes, some of it from Carter's head when I pounded him unconscious with the kettle, but being a well-bred Japanese girl, she said nothing about it.

"Now what you do with Akiko?" she asked.

"I must take you to your father."

"Why you always say father?" she said. "You know about my father?"

The bath girl bowed to us and left the room, closing the door softly behind her.

"Yes, I know about your father," I said.

"You know about me?" Her eyes were wide in astonishment, her tiny mouth open.

"Yes."

"Where do I come from?"

"Hiroshima." I took her slender wrists in my hands. "You were burned by the bomb. You were working in a hospital within a few hundred yards of Ground Zero and you were standing on a porch. You were blown into a garden by the blast, and though you were protected from most of the heat, you got the full dose of radiation."

"Nobody but my father knew these things. Nobody but my father. Everyone else was killed." She looked at me as if I were in truth a devil. I released her wrists.

"Your father treated you. The others sickened and died. Their bodies were covered with sores, their hair fell out, they bled through their skin, and they died. But you lived, and you didn't have the terrible burn welts that the others had, even though you had been just as badly exposed."

She backed away from me.

"Your father had been experimenting with X-ray burns and he discovered something that protects and cures human bodies exposed to radiation. He had not announced his research, planning to complete it after victory in the Pacific war.

"There was no victory. Your father swore that he would keep his living antidote for radiation burns and poisoning a secret until Japan was free again, and that he would destroy it rather than see the Americans get it."

"How do you know these things?"

"We know everything."

"You don't know where my father is now!" She slid off the bed and stood facing me, a tiny, slender ivory doll whose long black hair streamed down her porcelain-smooth back.

"You are going to tell me."

She walked into the smaller room with the rice-straw floor. I followed her. Her kimono, her combs, and a new obi sash were there, and in a quick, turning movement she took a knife from the kimono. It was a big day for knives in both our lives.

"Akiko—"

She sank to the floor on her knees and bent over, the knife touching her flat stomach. She raised her head.

"*Yaro!* You took my father's son, you took his country, you took his daughter. What you did not kill you make dirty. You will not take everything. You will not find my father."

The knife, edged into her smooth skin and a drop of blood curled around it. I stood back. The knife was scalpel-sharp and she could move it three inches into her body before I could move the four feet between us.

"Akiko, don't! I love you, Akiko!"

Her lips were ugly.

"I saved you this morning. I want to marry you."

"You only want my father's secret." The knife was poised. Only one drop of blood was on the ivory skin.

"I could have turned you over to the police and they could have tortured you to find out." I was sure she would believe that; most Japanese would believe anything of the M.P.'s. "I could have made love to you, Akiko, in that room this morning."

"Why didn't you? I needed you. You would not have me!" The knife quivered as her hand shook. She was getting ready to cry, and that was a good sign.

"On a dirty *futon* in a Shimbashi pom-pom room? No, Akiko. We will get married. I will take you to America. I have friends who will get us on a plane."

"Why did you not speak this before, Buchanan-san? You are lying now?"

"I'm not lying. I will do these things if you will tell me where your father lives. I must know that."

"If I promise to tell you, Buchanan-san, will you marry me? In church with license? Take me to America?"

"Yes. Maybe I lied to you, Akiko, about love. My promise about marriage is not a lie."

The great almond eyes in the small, delicate face softened and the knife fell to the straw.

"Now I believe you, Buchanan-san. You do not love but you would marry. I will go with you. Wherever you go. We will marry and go to America. For this I betray my father. I am a pom-pom girl who wants to be married. Go outside, Buchanan-san. I will come."

I went into the larger room, opened the door, stepped into the colonnaded hall, and closed the door. The relief of saving Akiko was now overshadowed by the full realization that I would now lose Sandra. I forced the thought from my mind and tried to concentrate on the music of the samisen. It was louder now.

I walked to the end of the hall. Double doors of carved teak guarded what was probably the luxurious bath-and-party room of the Japanese section of the Delight Baths. The samisen music came from the room behind the carved doors with the intricate dragon in bold relief across them.

The double doors opened as a bath girl came out and I saw the room beyond. Sandra was standing there, wearing kimono and obi.

Chapter Seven

She saw me, too. For a moment the two of us looked at each other in a strange vacuum of time. Then the dragon doors were closed again.

As the carved doors closed I didn't believe what I had seen.

But of course I knew it was true. It was Sandra, she was here in the elaborate party room of the Delight Baths, she was in kimono and obi because she was with Japanese, and what Vance Bogan had told me must be true. But why?

Drumming through this was a greater problem: I had promised to marry Akiko Tsumi.

My promise was made out of desperation but not out of madness. We had to have the RK virus. The CIC men had impressed upon me the urgency of our need.

That's why I didn't walk through the dragon doors to find Sandra Tann and take her away. I was pledged to marry Akiko Tsumi, the ivory princess who had cut the manhood from her lover only a few hours ago. It was desperation, but it was the only way.

She came out, her glossy hair held by jade combs, elegant in traditional Japanese costume. "Buchanan-san, did you lie to Akiko?"

"Only when I said I loved you. I did not lie when I said I would marry you."

"And take me to America?"

"And take you to America."

"Not make divorce? Not throw Akiko away?"

"No, Akiko. Not unless you wanted it."

"Akiko will never want it, Buchanan-san."

The dragon doors opened and Sandra Tann came out. She was with a graying Japanese. Two Japanese girls and another man, also Japanese, were with them. Sandra nodded to me. "Hello, Mate." She wore a tweed suit now.

"Hello, Sandra." What else do you say?

They walked by us and that was all.

"That was the American girl you were with last night," said Akiko. She ran after Sandra, who turned when she heard the rapid sound of the *zori* on the terrazzo floor.

"*Dozo*," said Akiko. "*Dozo*, I must tell you. Buchanan-san and Akiko, we get married, go to America. Ask him!"

Sandra looked at me across the few yards between us. "Congratulations," she said. "He's a very nice man and you will like America." Then she turned and the five walked away, past the garden of little trees.

Akiko came back to me.

"Why did you do that?"

"Akiko not share a man with American girl ever again," she said. "I want her to know she will not go to club, get stinko, dance with you ever again."

"Let's go," I said. "We've got things to do."

I did not see Sandra or the people she was with again as we walked out of the vast, intricate building of the Delight Baths. Ken and the Minx were waiting at the curb. We got in and Ken climbed back behind the wheel after closing our door. "Where you go now, please?" he asked.

Something that Vance Bogan had said came back to me.

"Nikkatsu Hotel, Ken."

We crossed the bridge and the blue enamel walls of the sleek new Nikkatsu rose from the sidewalk to our right. At the corner was the American drugstore, full of vitamins, lipsticks, sun lamps, and antihistamines. On the other end were the offices of Northwest Airlines. Downstairs, in the basement of the Nikkatsu, arcade shops displayed pearls, jades, silks, silver, and cameras. Upstairs was the most luxurious hotel in the Far East, from Hong Kong to Hokkaido, and in the sweeping bar of that hotel Vance Bogan said Sandra Tann sometimes sat.

We got out and I told Ken to get some food. The Nikkatsu was a glow of soft colors, chrome, and enamel. We took a smooth, silent elevator to the bar floor and walked into a great, deep-carpeted room two stories high. Sandra and the other four were at a table beneath the carved mezzanine deck.

A waitress guided us to a table across the big room from Sandra.

"More whisky?" I asked Akiko.

Her dark eyes were soft and submissive. "Akiko drink what you say, Buchanan-san. Maybe you not like Akiko to drink any more?"

"You drink if you wish, Akiko." She nodded and I told the girl to bring us two highballs.

"Buchanan-san," said Akiko, "you come here to find the blonde girl again?"

"Yes."

"You love blonde girl?"

"Yes."

"But you marry Akiko just to get my father's medicine?"

"Yes."

"Maybe I change mind. What you do then?"

"Neither of us can change our minds any more, Akiko. We both keep our promises."

"You never talk to blonde girl again, Buchanan-san."

"You close your mouth and keep it closed. I'm going over to that table, and when I come back I want you to have your father's address written down here in Japanese and— Do you write English?" I put my pen and pocket notebook on the table.

"*S'koshi,*" she answered in a low voice.

"In Japanese and English. You start being a wife right now. You keep quiet until I say talk, then you talk. Like Japanese husband and wife. Understand?"

"Yes, Husband. You are right." I knew she trusted me more than she ever had before. She was about twenty-six, and for twenty of those years she had been taught to act exactly as I was telling her to act now. It must have been comfortable for her.

I walked over to Sandra's table. The two women glanced at me and then looked away. The two men stared at me as if I was about to ask for a loan. Wealthy Japanese have never been known for the humble politeness that poor Japanese use like soft armor. Sandra looked at me with a hurt little smile, but her gray eyes were warm.

"May I call you tonight, Sandra?"

"Call me at the Far East Network, Mate. I'll be there for fifteen minutes or so after the broadcast."

She made no attempt to introduce me to the others at the table, so I bowed and went back to Akiko.

There was nothing written on the open page of my notebook. My pen was still capped. The two drinks were on the table and Akiko had not touched hers.

"Where's the address, Akiko?"

"There is no address, Buchanan-san. I will take you to my father."

"Why?"

"You made me remember what it is to be Japanese girl. We go to my father."

"How long since you've seen him?"

"More than three years."

"Maybe he's dead. Maybe he's gone somewhere else."

"No. He lives. I know. Every week I go to little place in Tokyo. I ask, 'Is it the same?' They say 'It is the same.' So I know he is well and that he is still there."

"You're going to take me to him now?"

"Yes, Buchanan-san. Then we go to Shinto temple and make ready for marriage. Is marriage same as your church. Legal."

Shinto ceremonies of marriage between Japanese and Americans were perfectly legal, as many a fast-talking, angle-shooting G.I. has found out to his surprise. I didn't care. I had promised Akiko marriage and safety in America and it had been an honest promise. The RK virus was a million times more important than any hill in Korea, and I had seen good men give their lives for a forgotten Korean hill. What price Mate Buchanan? But I couldn't give up Sandra, no matter what, on her side or mine.

I finished my drink. "Let's go."

The muscles in my body were tensing. I didn't like the responsibility I was going to have in the next hour or two. Once Akiko had brought me to her father, I could not let him go until I had the virus culture. I would have to get it now, regardless of what I might have to do to get it from him.

Akiko had not touched her drink. I left enough yen on the table to pay the bill and tip. We walked over the deep carpets to the elevator. I did not look at Sandra.

While we waited for an elevator I asked Akiko where we were going.

"I tell driver in Japanese," she said. I was looking at my watch every few seconds before I realized what I was doing. I was getting ready the way you do when you're going on patrol or before you move the company up the hill.

We went down and out into the sleek main floor of the Nikkatsu.

"Wait," I said to Akiko. "We'll go out the other side. I'd rather take a taxi for this trip."

We walked the length of the building and out through the lobby of the Northwest Airlines office. Across the street was the narrow gray stone pile of the old Teikoku Building; on the eighth floor of that building was the crime laboratory of the CID, and in an office on a lower floor was the scientist who had come to me in San Francisco, waiting for me to bring him the RK virus.

I waved at a cab and it rolled to a bumpy stop a little ahead of us. Akiko gave the driver directions and he put the car in gear. We made a turn at the direction of the stiff, robot-like traffic officer at the intersection of A and Z Avenues, and we were on the street between Hibaya Park and the Palace grounds. We went straight ahead until we came to B Avenue, then turned left. Ahead was the four-story concrete mass of the old Imperial Finance Building, never quite finished, and now the barracks for Headquarters troops, the largest U.S. Army billet in the world.

"Where are we going, Akiko?"

She pointed at Finance, as it was still called. "My father has worked for the Americans for many years now. He works in that big building. Very low work—he sweeps, mops, scrubs."

Dr. Tsumi, one of the world's great research men, was working as a janitor for American troops.

Following Akiko's instructions, the driver pulled up in front of the White Duck Laundry, a straggling one-story building opposite the side entrance of the immense barracks.

I gave the driver his hundred yen and we went into the White Duck. A sergeant was waiting with his laundry under his arm while a woman behind a narrow counter clicked the items of his bill on the beads of an abacus. A girl was ironing, and the whole building was crowded with clothes, hazy with cigarette smoke.

The woman finished her total on the abacus and collected seven hundred yen from the sergeant. She saw Akiko and bowed, smiling; Akiko returned the bow and spoke quietly to her in Japanese. She answered Akiko and they spoke for over a minute, then the woman bent under the counter and handed Akiko a plastic-sheathed card. She took it and motioned me aside.

"He is in the building," Akiko explained, "but you will need a pass to go in since you are a civilian. I have a pass for you now, and all you do is show it to guard at door."

"How about you?"

Akiko looked at me as if I were stupid. "In that building there are many officers and soldiers who know Akiko Tsumi, the woman of the Major Corbett. I have been there many times."

"And you never saw your father?"

"He upstairs, where the soldiers live."

"Do these people here know who he is?"

"They think is old family servant. He call himself Watanabe now. Very common kind of name."

"How will I find him and what will I do?"

"You go to gate, show pass. Go upstairs to fourth floor. Will be many Japanese workers. You ask for Shigeru Watanabe. When you get him you bring here."

"Will he come?"

"He is used to taking orders from Americans. He will come."

"Where will you be?"

"Is little living place behind here. I will be waiting."

"Shall I tell him you're here, Akiko?"

"No, no! Just bring him. I talk to him here."

I walked out of the White Duck, across the sloping street, and up to the main entrance of Finance, where two spruce guards in shining black helmets checked passes, two ramrod-straight M.P.'s watched narrowly for soldiers who failed to salute the passing officers, and a long row of banged-up taxis waited along the curb.

A round-faced, button-eyed boy of about six was selling copies of the daily *Pacific Stars and Stripes*, the unofficial newspaper published by the American forces in the Far East. I gave him twenty yen for a copy.

My black-market pass got only a glance from the guards at the arch and I walked through to the courtyard beyond. I had come to Finance frequently when I had been stationed in Tokyo, and knew it fairly well. I walked up the stairs under the heavy portico to the central corridor and waited for an elevator. *Stars and Stripes* gave its headlines to Korea, to the peace talks there, and to some Stateside news. Yesterday's riot had a small front-page story. Major Corbett was there, too.

He was still alive. The police were searching for a young Japanese woman, Akiko Tsumi, who might have information as to the attack on the Major, and for a mysterious man who had phoned Tokyo General Dispensary with a request for medical aid to the major, and who then had vanished, possibly with Miss Tsumi. There was no mention of the kind of injury or of Mrs. Corbett's arrival.

The elevator doors opened and some soldiers, crisp in week-end khakis, got out. The operator was Japanese, as were all the maintenance personnel in Finance.

"Do you know Shigeru Watanabe?"

He gave me the usual business—the smile, the blank expression. "So sorry," he said.

"Fourth floor, *dozo*."

He closed the doors and we went up. On a Saturday afternoon everybody was leaving Finance; nobody was coming in or going up. At the fourth floor he opened the doors and I got off. I was in a long corridor. Large rooms with rows of double-decked bunks opened off the corridor, and through the open doors I could see soldiers dressing, sleeping, reading paper-bound books.

A Japanese in wooden clogs, wearing only cotton drawers and shirt, was mopping the corridor floor. I went up to him. "You know Shigeru Watanabe?"

"Me Shigeru Watanabe," he said, and kept on mopping.

I looked at him. A man of fifty, about five feet four, thin, wearing cheap, badly bent glasses.

"Is there another Shigeru Watanabe here?" The name is the Japanese equivalent of John Smith.

"Never happen," he said.

"You come with me," I said.

He put his mop in the bucket, pushed them both into a corner. "Hokay."

We started walking toward the elevator. Could this be the great Dr. Tsumi? A ragged coolie mopping barracks floors, speaking G.I. Tokyo slang, humble and servile—the doctor who had been one of the world's leading specialists in virus forms? It could happen, particularly to a doctor who had a secret to hide, and who therefore could not make a living as a doctor.

He would not go into the elevator but motioned to the stairway. The elevators of Finance were reserved for the young gods in khaki. We went down the stairs to a rear, ground-level doorway. The black-helmeted guard passed the ragged little man but stopped me. I showed him my plastic-covered pass and he waved me on. The White Duck people must have an interesting relationship with Finance, I thought.

Now I took the man by the arm and guided him around the back of the building, up a ramp, and along the street to the White Duck. Inside I took him past the desk and the heaps of dirty khakis into the door of the living quarters. Akiko was there.

His eyes opened wide and he bowed. She spoke to him in Japanese and his face was impassive. He answered her briefly and she spoke slowly now, almost lovingly. He turned and looked at me through the bent and twisted spectacles.

"Buchanan-san, this is my father," Akiko said.

"And you're a dirty, lying tramp," I said. Japanese fathers do not bow to their errant daughters.

Well, it had looked good for a while. Little Akiko had tried to pitch a curve on old Buchanan and bluff him along until he paid off. If I looked at her another ten seconds I was going to hit her, so I walked out to the front of the laundry and threw the fake pass on the counter.

Someone came in the door. An officer, followed by two M.P.'s.

"Pardon me," said the officer, a captain with the crossed-pistol insignia of the M.P.'s on his lapels, "aren't you Mr. Mate Buchanan?"

It just wasn't my day.

"Yeah, I'm Buchanan."

"Would you step over to our office with me for a moment?"

"How did you know I was here?"

He looked embarrassed. "One of the M.P.'s at the gate recognized you. There's been a bulletin out on you for several hours now. Will you come with me, please?"

The "please" had two big, husky M.P.'s behind it and both boys looked as if they could make it stick. Akiko wasn't around so I turned and followed the captain.

Some bright-eyed little rascal had probably noticed the Minx at the house behind the red tile wall this morning. They had checked out the hundred or so Minx cars in Tokyo and discovered that one had come to the Imperial for a guest there, a Mr. Buchanan. Between the Occupation forces and the Japanese police, I should have known that four or five hours would be all the time I had before they knew who had phoned the Tokyo General Dispensary.

Meanwhile Akiko—bless her little double-crossing hide—was on the loose again. It looked like a long wait for the scientist in the secret office in the Teikoku Building, unless some of the other agents came through.

I was in a bad jam, Akiko was probably lost in the jungle of Tokyo again, and Sandra Tann went to parties at the Delight Baths.

We turned and entered under the arch, the guards saluting the M.P. captain smartly.

The Provost Marshal had some kind of branch office in Finance, I remembered. They'd keep me here for a while and then ship me to the downtown office. Chances were better than even that I'd sleep in the pokey tonight.

About that time I figured out a way to find Dr. Tsumi—the way something slides into your mind and suddenly, unexpectedly the jumble all falls together in a pattern. I couldn't waste the next few hours fooling with the Provost Marshal and his junior G-men. I had thought of a thread that might lead me to Dr. Tsumi and I wanted to follow it right now.

We walked up the broad stairs at the far end of the courtyard into the main wing of the building and down the corridor to the Provost Marshal's branch office. It was Saturday afternoon and apparently my captain had been the duty officer, because no other officers were there. One fat private sat at a desk reading a tattered comic book.

The two big lads saluted the captain and left us. He went over to a desk and picked up a phone. I hit him on the point of the jaw with everything I could give. He went over. The fat boy looked surprised and started to get up. I went out into the corridor and up a flight of stairs. I was running but the fat private didn't chase me.

By the time I reached the third floor I was taking off my clothes, and at the fourth floor I stopped to get out of my trousers. Everything but my shorts, T shirt, socks, and shoes was in a loose bundle that I dumped into a trash can at the head of the stairs. My wallet was hung over my shorts and I walked down the corridor of the fourth floor of Finance looking like any other soldier going to the latrine in his underwear.

Chapter Eight

At one corner of the building, as I walked and tried to figure my moves, I found a big room filled with shirt-sleeved Japanese ironing khaki shirts and trousers and sponging clothes. My first idea had been to steal a uniform, but maybe I could work a deal. I went into the steamy room, where a couple of soldiers were waiting for their clothes. A little old brown man shuffled over to the counter where I stood.

"Give ticket, *dozo*." He held out his hand.

"No ticket," I said, shaking my head. He shuffled off again.

"Hey!" I shouted after him.

"You got ticket?" he asked, turning.

"I've got money. I need a shirt and trousers. All my clothes are dirty. *Takusan* yen."

He said nothing but shuffled along until he got to a pressing machine, and there he began working on a pair of trousers. The two soldiers got their pressed suits from a young man, paid him in yen, and walked out. The young man looked at me.

"Wattsa matter, G.I.?"

"All my clothes are dirty. I want to get the right size shirt and pants. You speak how much."

He looked at me appraisingly and shrugged his shoulders. "Hokay."

He fumbled through a rack of trousers and shirts, looked at me again, and finally brought out a pair. The shirt had sergeant's chevrons and a red-white-and-blue patch in the shape of a shield with embroidered lettering: "Pacific Stars and Stripes." The young man held out the shirt and trousers, with belt and buckle, too.

"Somebody leave long time ago. Maybe your size. Four thousand yen, huh?"

"O.K.," I said, pulling out four thousand-yen notes from my wallet. I put on the pants and shirt, and they fitted me. All I needed now was a cap, tie, brass collar insignia, and a pass. Then I could walk out of Finance like any of the other two thousand soldiers who lived there. I could buy those things in the first-floor PX—provided I had military payment certificates, the money of the Americans on official duty in Japan. My yen roll was all right for Japanese establishments, but it wouldn't buy me a package of cigarettes in the PX.

There was a stairway opposite the little pressing shop and I went down. At the third floor there was a line of soldiers waiting for the mess hall to open at four.

"Hey, any of you guys want to buy some yen?" I called out to the lads in line.

"How much you got?" a square-built Pfc asked.

"Ten bucks worth?" I countered.

"Yeah. Ten bucks—thirty-six hundred yen. Deal."

The paper changed hands and I went back to the stairs and down to the first floor toward the PX.

Two M.P.'s hurried past me. They gave me a quick glance, saw the uniform, and were satisfied. They were both carrying their .45's in their hands. They stopped at the stairway; one stayed as a guard and the other one went up. Finance was being blocked off like a gigantic masonry mousetrap.

The PX was a single long room that looked like the fancier part of a big drugstore, bright under fluorescent lights, filled with soldiers, civilians, and Japanese clerks.

The first thing I bought was a tie. They had the round brass collar insignia for enlisted men and I bought the U.S. and the crossed rifles of my old branch, the Infantry. It was a good thing that I wasted no time in putting on the tie and pinning the insignia to my collar, because a squad of

M.P.'s blocked off both exits to the PX and began working through the crowd of shoppers. If they asked for ID cards it would be the end for me. They did—but only from the male civilians. They merely nodded to the soldiers—and that was me, too.

I needed one more item of clothing to be able to walk out of the building: a cap, a plain old ordinary blue-braided khaki cap, worth about two bucks. The PX had cigarettes, watches, cameras, magazines, souvenirs, and every fool thing except military caps. I couldn't walk five feet down a Tokyo street bareheaded without being yanked into an M.P. patrol jeep, let alone get out of the well-guarded fortress of Finance.

If you need a cap, don't have one, and can't buy one, then you steal one. Stealing sounds easier than it really is: There were maybe five or six thousand little caps in Finance, but how was I going to lay my hands on one?

The guards didn't bother me as I left the PX. At the turn of the corridor, fifty feet away, was the sandwich shop of Finance. I went there and ordered a fried ham sandwich and a triple malt.

I spotted the cap I was going to steal. A corporal whose head looked about my size was talking like mad to a very pretty blonde WAC, with his cap at the far end of the table. As I went by I flipped the hat over my arm. When I finished my sandwich and malt—maybe one minute flat—he was still jabbering away to the blonde. I hoped he was making out because he sure was missing one cap.

Now there was a pretty problem: Should I follow the thread I hoped might lead to Dr. Tsumi, which meant staying in the mousetrap, or should I try to get out of the vast building and back on the streets of Tokyo? My watch showed a little after four, probably too late for my thread to Dr. Tsumi. In another hour I was to call Sandra, and what I wanted to do was to eat a big steak and get drunk.

It was decided for me. Shigeru Watanabe, still in cotton drawers and dirty shirt, walked past the doorway of the sandwich shop. I was out and into the corridor before he turned the corner. The M.P.'s had followed me to the White Duck, but it was unlikely that they had paid any attention to the old Japanese. I took the chance and caught up with him. He turned and looked at me.

My sudden guess, back when I had been walking with the M.P. captain on the sidewalk in front of Finance, was that Akiko had told me part of the truth. This old man had been a household servant of the Tsumi family. She had kept in contact with him, and probably through him knew how her father was doing. She had hoped to pass this servant off as her father because she could tell him in Japanese what to do and say, knowing that he would obey her. If I had not caught the bow with which the servant had greeted his mistress, her scheme might have worked and I would be on my way to a Shinto temple with her now—except, of course, that the M.P.'s had pounced on me. Now how was I going to wring the truth out of this wizened little elf?

If he was an old family servant he could not be bribed. He didn't seem to know much English and I didn't know enough Japanese for us to talk so that I could fool him or fancy him out of the information. There was one possibility, a kind of simple one if it worked, and if I could get out of the building.

"You stay here. Wait." I pointed to the floor where he stood. He didn't look happy but he understood.

"Hokay," he muttered.

I walked quickly to the PX. He stood there, looking at the floor. The guards were still at the PX door but they paid no attention to me. I went to the stationery counter and bought a packet of envelopes from the pert Japanese girl there.

"Will you please write a Japanese name on this envelope?" I said to her. She said she would. "Just write, 'Dr. Hideoki Tsumi, very important.'"

She reached under the counter, fished up a pen, and drew out a series of Japanese characters on the envelope. "Thank you very much," I said.

He was still standing there. I had folded over a blank envelope, put it in the one addressed by the girl, and sealed the flap. Before I reached him a group of M.P.'s double-timed along the corridor to the stairway. I wondered how many minutes I had left.

I gave Watanabe the envelope. He studied the characters and his small eyes widened in surprise. Looking up, he spoke to me in Japanese. I shook my head and took the envelope away from him. He reached for it, anxiety showing on his face. I knew now that I could trace Dr. Tsumi through him.

"No, no," I said, pulling the envelope away from him. "You bring him here. I'll give it to him."

"Never happen," he muttered. He was bewildered, an old household servant whose loyalty was to his former master but who had been trained for years now to follow the orders of the blond barbarians.

"You bring him here," I repeated. "How long will it take?"

"Tomorrow, maybe happen tomorrow."

"It must happen today. *Hayoka!*"

He shook his head, looked regretfully at the envelope, and began to walk away. I grabbed him by the arm and he shook me off. Soldiers,

WAC's, and civilians had been passing us in the corridor on their way to the sandwich shop. I couldn't use force.

"You put his address here. O.K.? Then we'll mail it."

He didn't understand. I took him by the arm and led him to the PX. "*Dozo*," I said to the pert Japanese girl, "will you ask this man for the address of the man whose name is on this envelope so that we can put it on and mail it?"

She spoke to Watanabe and he shook his head. "Tell him it's important," I urged.

They talked briefly in Japanese.

"He says to give it to him, he will take it himself. Otherwise he wants nothing to do with it," she told me.

"Do you want to earn a thousand yen?" he asked her.

"Maybe. What do I do, Sergeant?"

"I'll give this letter to this old boy, you kind of watch where he goes outside, and then meet me and tell me."

"What's cooking, G.I.?" She gave me a smile that was almost bright enough to hide the suspicion and curiosity in her narrow dark eyes.

"Can't tell you, baby. But how about it? And if you can tell me, I'll pay five thousand yen."

She pursed her mouth into a silent whistle. "Lot's of money, G.I."

"Will you do it?"

"O.K. Where do I meet you?"

"Six o'clock at Peter's. You know Peter's?"

"Sanshin Building? I know. You on level, G.I.?" Her pidgin English was a little joke; I could tell that she spoke our language very well.

"Peter's at six. Here's the five thousand yen." Watanabe could not see me open my wallet and give her five thousand-yen notes. I liked the way she looked at me.

"All right, Sergeant. I'll play detective." She took my hand, gave it a warm pressure. I gave the envelope to Watanabe. He was moving around nervously, but as soon as his hands closed on the envelope he was on his way.

She waved at me and walked after the old man.

When they were both gone I realized that I had been stupid. What would Dr. Tsumi think when old Watanabe brought him an envelope addressed to him by name and with only an empty envelope inside? He'd get the idea that things weren't square. It was too late to stop them; they were out of sight.

Maybe my stupidity had just lost a few million Americans their chance of surviving an atomic war.

Now I had to meet the pretty little clerk at the Sanshin at six. To do that I would have to get out of Finance, through the one gate open, a gate always guarded, where every man's pass was checked.

Obviously I wouldn't be able to leave by that gate. As a matter of fact, I didn't know how I was going to leave. I was feeling plenty sick about the envelope and Watanabe and I didn't have much heart for figuring an out, but I knew that since the first hurried alarm had failed to find me, the M.P.'s would start a floor-by-floor, room-by-room search that would sooner or later get me.

I had to get out. But how?

I walked the length of the corridor, seeing the bright late afternoon through the windows opening on the courtyard, and I saw my answer. Some especially eager general had been working this Saturday afternoon, a time when almost all of the Americans in Tokyo were at the golf courses, splashing around in pools, playing tennis, or drinking.

It took thirty seconds to find the stairway and door leading to the courtyard and fifteen seconds to reach the big sedan waiting before the portico doorway in the central wing of the building. The driver, a trim Japanese, was behind the wheel.

"Whose car is this?" I asked him.

"General Barbee's car."

"That's what I thought. Thanks," I said, and I waited under the portico.

There was a rippling bustle of action at the head of the stairs beyond the portico and a fast-striding tall man with two stars on his shoulders came down. The driver was out and opening the car door before I even saluted.

"General Barbee, sir—"

He spun in surprise. "Yes, Sergeant?"

"*Pacific Stars and Stripes*, sir. Sergeant White. Could you spare me time for a brief interview?"

The General looked at me, his eyes glancing at the tricolor patch on my right shoulder.

"Why, yes, son. Hop in and you can take it while we travel."

I got in and the General stepped in after me. The driver closed the door and the car rolled across the courtyard toward the main gate.

"What kind of an interview, son?"

"The *Stars and Stripes* is going to start a series on the personalities of the general officers in the Tokyo command, sir."

We went under the arch and out. The entrance was almost solid with M.P.'s and they were checking complete identification of every man trying to get out. The M.P.'s and the soldiers alike all snapped to attention and saluted as the car with the two stars on it passed through. The General returned their salutes, smiled, and turned back to me.

"I see. Now what do you want to know?"

"All I wanted now, sir, was an appointment convenient to you when I could bring our photographer and when you could spare twenty minutes or so, sir."

"Hmmm. Let's see. Monday, about sixteen hundred. All right?"

"Fine, General Barbee. Monday afternoon at your office."

"That'll be all right, Sergeant. Can I drop you anywhere?"

We were a couple of blocks from Finance now. "Right here will be fine, sir." He spoke to the driver and the car stopped.

I got out of the car and saluted him. He seemed like a mighty fine general. I watched the sedan as it went down B Avenue. I was out, but I wasn't very happy.

Now they were listening to her sing. In the red-brick barracks of Camp Crawford and in the quonsets at Chitose, in Kyushu where the wounded lay in long rows of beds, they listened to the enchantment of Tokyo Doll.

In a few minutes she'd be waiting for my call. What would I say to her? Sandra, my beloved, I almost married Akiko this afternoon, but she tried to trick me and now I don't have to. I'd like to marry you, except that I'm a fugitive, and except I don't know anything about you, my beloved. Nothing about you, Sandra, my love, beyond your voice, your laugh, your wonderful golden body, your warm, soft, easy contentment.

I was going to call her, but I wasn't quite sure why.

At A Avenue, which runs between Hibaya Park and the broad, stone-walled moat of the Palace, I turned right, thinking about my stupid blunder. By now Dr. Tsumi would probably have the envelope, and would guess at how his old servant had been tricked. Would he step to the laboratory table, or wherever he kept his RK virus cultures, and destroy them before the Americans could come to take them away? If he did, then I had done worse than fail—I had destroyed a hope that might make an atomic war less deadly.

I walked into the office of the military travel reservation bureau across from the Palace park and called Sandra at the Far East Network, and seconds later I was talking to her.

"Mate! Colonel Barham was here. You're wanted for questioning about that poor girl."

"I know, Sandra. I don't much feel like being questioned."

"The Colonel asked me if I knew where you might be. I didn't tell him you were going to call me."

"Thanks, Sandra. I've got kind of mixed up in things. I won't see you for a while."

"I'm kind of mixed up in things, too. Don't judge me any more than you want me to judge you."

"Right, Sandra. I love you." It came out like that, without thinking.

"Are you sure, Mate?"

"Sure. No matter what. How do I reach you, Sandra? You won't be able to reach me."

"Here or the Osaka. I'll always leave word for you."

"Good-by, Sandra."

"Good-by, Mate."

It was a good talk. We had said all that needed to be said.

I went out into the Tokyo evening and walked the short block to the Sanshin and Peter's. I went through the doorway into the bar and I saw him before he saw me.

He was sitting in a deep chair talking to a dark-haired, eager-faced sergeant whom I remembered from before. Carleton Carter, sprawled lazily, holding a tall drink in his right hand, his left in splints, and a large, thick bandage on his head. He was wearing a gray sharkskin suit, gray suede shoes. The sergeant was Tripper Reilly, an announcer for the Far East Network.

Tripper saw me first and remembered me from the old days. He waved. Carter looked up and the yellowish-white eyes narrowed to slits as his great body tensed.

His right hand had gone to his pocket like a snake to a hole and I knew the knife was ready.

We looked at each other.

"What's this sergeant beat you're on, Buchanan?" asked Tripper, unaware of the hate that burned in Carter's eyes.

I didn't look away from Carter. "Just a deal, Tripper. Tell you about it sometime." Carter's right hand came out of his pocket.

"Ain't the time or the place, man," he said slowly. "But there's going to be a time and place. I'll guarantee that. Mighty soon." Then he smiled broadly, his big teeth in a wide mouth, and the hunched shoulders eased back. I had been mighty lucky those few hours ago. An ordinary man would be in a hospital, but Carleton Carter was drinking tall highballs at Peter's.

"What's with you cats?" asked Tripper a little uneasily, feeling the tension.

"Poor old Carter here had a rough time. A gang jumped him over in Shimbashi."

"How're things with you, man?" asked Carter. I could see the muscles jerking in his face and hands. The man's mind was having a hard time controlling the tiger body, keeping it from springing at me.

I gave him an honest answer. "No good."

He was looking at me speculatively now. The time would come when one of us would have to kill the other, but that wasn't now, and his interest was back in my deal rather than in me. Asahi-san must have told him that I was in something big and illegal, and that they could use the girl as a hold over me. He knew now that whatever I was doing was too important for me to waste time over in talk. I had gone for him with my knee as soon as I had realized he was moving in on my situation. Carter knew all these things and they added up to a smell of big, dirty money.

"I didn't know you soldiered around," he said.

"You know how it is," I replied. A waiter had padded up behind me and I nodded at Carter's drink. "Same thing. Fill up the others."

"We're going to have to have a long talk after a bit."

"Carter and I were talking about old times," said Tripper nervously. He was in his early twenties, rather frail. "Old times in Tokyo. It'll never be the same as it was back in '49 and '50. Lord, how we lived in those days!"

Carleton Carter's yellowish-white eyes seldom glanced away from my face. I fascinated him now, the one man above all others whom he must kill, sitting easily a few feet from him, talking, drinking, still breathing, still alive.

I, too, was fascinated by him. His broken finger was splinted, the raw wounds of his head were bandaged, and I knew his body must still ache from our fight, but he also was at ease. I must have been very close to death in the Shamrock a few hours ago. I was close to death now.

"But I'm sick of it," Carter said suddenly. "The ol' *honcho's* sick of Tokyo. Tired of li'l short-legged girls nibbling on my ear, lighting my cigarettes, bringing me my things."

The waiter brought our round of drinks and I paid him. Carter drank more than half of his in a long swallow, wiped his lips with his hand.

"I'm lonely for long-gone things," he said, and now his eyes looked beyond me. He might have been half drunk; his voice had a new softness.

"It's been a long time since I've seen Forty-seventh Street, and maybe I ain't ever going to see it again. All those places bright with lights, and the chicks goin' in for a drink or maybe a barbecue rib. Man! That's so far away. Just walking along ol' Forty-seventh, seeing the cats and the chicks, maybe going to a party."

It was strange listening to that soft, deep, husky voice talking, strange that he felt that he wanted me, the man he must kill, to understand that he was lonely.

Then he laughed, a booming laugh. "But man, the kicks I've had here! This was the beat, this Tokyo beat. I used to soldier all day and steal and fight and jazz and laugh all night. Man, you never lived unless you lived in Tokyo that fine time back in '48. I've fought my way out of capers that would have sent me away for ten life beats on those hard rocks at Lompoc."

"Down, boy, down," whispered Tripper. "You don't want people hearing you. You want to go off to the Big Eight?"

"Don't talk no Big Eight talk to me, man," said Carter, his head back and smiling. "They tried to put me away in that Big Eight stockade for years and I never even smelled the place." He finished his drink. "Soldiering is all over for the *honcho*. Now I live in my big house, wear my fine clothes, eat my fine food, and I got so many *musume* waiting on me I don't even try to remember their names. I just sit around my big house and yell out, 'Girl-san!' and maybe three or four will come running. Man!"

Tripper laughed. "He's not just working his tongue, either. I've been there, and that's the way it is. He sits on the floor, he wears Japanese clothes, and he won't even talk English with you. You go to Carleton's house—and it's only one size smaller than the Emperor's palace—and you go Japanese. You gotta talk Japanese, wear Japanese clothes—man, it's a real beat."

The hooded eyes looked into mine and I could feel what he was thinking: This is all talk, this isn't important. The important thing is that I'm going to kill you.

It was almost six. The little girl from the Finance PX was due. I got up.

Carter looked at me. "You going to be easy to find, man? Because I'm going to find you."

"I'll be around," I said. "So long, Tripper."

I walked out into the lounge. She was sitting there waiting for me and she had the envelope in her hands.

"Hello, Sergeant," she said, standing up. She was a pretty little girl, as pert as a cricket.

"What happened?" I pointed to the envelope.

"He gave it to me outside Finance. He's a very simple man, maybe an old-time house servant. He talks like that."

"He is. What about it?" I was curt and impatient.

"He saw me outside the building. He said he didn't want to give the message to Dr. Tsumi. He knew what the message was—said you were going to marry Dr. Tsumi's daughter. He says Dr. Tsumi is a very bitter man, and maybe the message would kill him, break his heart. He wouldn't give it to him."

Good fielding by skinny-shanked Watanabe saves Buchanan from being charged with an error. Put it in the record books, but let old Buchanan remember he's kind of stupid to be a secret agent.

"He asked me something else," the girl continued. We were still standing, almost in the center of the bright, soft foyer lounge of Peter's. The girl was looking up at me, one of the big-eyed Japanese girls, the special kind who seem very wise and understanding and warm.

"What was that?"

"He said this daughter is in a little room behind the White Duck laundry, very scared because you went off with the M.P.'s. He said I should bring her to you."

"Where is she?"

"I went to the White Duck. She was afraid to come with me to Peter's, but she said she'll hide someplace until midnight, then she'll meet you in Shimbashi, above the Shamrock Bar. O.K.?"

"Where is she now?" The Shamrock was not my idea of a very good meeting place.

"She went to hide with friends. Why is she hiding?"

"It's a long story, baby. Midnight at the Shamrock Bar?"

"Yes. Are you going to marry this girl? She's very pretty."

I saw Carleton Carter come into the lounge and go to the telephone. It had the feeling of being a busy evening.

"*Dozo*," said the pert girl, "I asked if you're going to marry this girl."

"Why?"

"Because it's no good. I know."

"The girl is no good?" I started walking her toward the bar.

She shrugged. "What girl is good? What girl is bad? No, not her. I mean an American marrying a Japanese girl."

We walked through the doorway and a waiter led us to two deep seats in front of Peter's very imitation fireplace. I had almost six hours before Akiko would be at the Shamrock, and I had no alternative but to go back to my original mission—find Dr. Tsumi and his virus through his daughter.

"What do you want?" I asked her.

"Canadian and soda."

"Two," I said to the waiter. He nodded and shuffled away. "Why do you think it's bad for an American to marry a Japanese girl?" I didn't much care, but I had to be someplace, doing something, and this was as good as anywhere else.

"My sister married a G.I. She lives in the States now. She isn't happy. People are nice to her, everybody's friendly, but she's lonely. Different kind of houses, different kind of food, no girls like herself to talk to. Maybe it will be better when she has a baby, but I don't think so."

The waiter brought our drinks. I noticed that Carter had returned to his chair, a dozen feet away. Tripper Reilly was still there and they had been joined by two others from Far East Network.

I finished off my drink. I could feel Carter's eyes watching me. His voice boomed out and I turned toward him.

"Like this!" he said in a harsh whisper. The other three were watching him as if he was going to demonstrate something he'd been talking about. "Like this!" The right hand blurred in movement, something streaked, and I saw the knife handle quivering in the far wall, thirty feet away. It was dead center in the throat of a man's head on a wall calendar.

The Chinese manager came running, his mouth open in fright and anger. Carter laughed and looked at me. I looked at him.

"Big deal!" said the girl at the table with me, and I laughed. I thought she was a fine girl. "By the way, here's your money back. Thanks for the drink."

She laid the notes on the table and stood up. I pushed them toward her but she shook her head and smiled. "Never happen. Any way I can help the Americans, I do." A neat, pert, pretty girl with big eyes, looking down on me. "My G.I. was killed in Korea."

She whirled around and started to walk away. Then she stopped and hurried back.

"I forgot. Maybe it's important. The old man told me where Dr. Tsumi lives. I don't think he realized he was telling me. You want to know?"

"I do." I'd come five thousand miles to find out.

"He lives in the rag-picker village. You know where it is?"

"Yes." Four blocks away, between the railroad viaduct and the scum-coated canal, was the rag-picker village, shacks of paper and old boxes in a squalid row of starvation poverty. Dr. Tsumi, one of Asia's great doctors, in rag-picker village.

"O.K.," she said. "'By, Sergeant." And she was gone. I didn't even know her name.

Chapter Nine

I sat in my chair at Peter's after the girl had left and remembered what I had seen of the rag-picker village. Outcasts of Tokyo, unwanted and unnoticed, sometimes whole families of babies, children, parents, and grandparents, their grimy nakedness half covered by scraps of cloth.

Carter's eyes were still burning into me. If I got up to leave, he would follow me. Where I went he would go, until the time and place were right, and then he would try to kill me.

It was kind of funny, because I knew what Carter wanted. Revenge on a man who had won a fight he was supposed to lose. And with Carter, revenge was death. That's the way it had been before, more than once, though no one could prove it. And I couldn't ask for help or protection. I was strictly on my own. But I had to get to the rag-picker village, and take a chance on giving Carter the slip outside. I put some money on the table for the drinks, got up, and walked out of the bar. I didn't look at Carter, and I didn't hurry going up the stairs to the street.

The whole thing happened fast.

As I walked through the door to the street a sedan stopped at the curb and two big men in civilian clothes got out, took me by the arms, and put me in the rear seat of the sedan. It was that fast.

"You're under arrest, Buchanan," said the man who had been waiting in the rear seat of the sedan. One of the big men sat next to me and the other was with the driver in front.

I turned. It was Colonel Barham.

"You gave us a lot of trouble, Buchanan. We didn't find out about the clothes you bought at the pressing shop until an hour after you escaped from Captain Brady's custody. You are in very serious trouble."

The only thought I had was about the rag-picker village. I knew where Dr. Tsumi was hiding now and I was helpless.

"What is your connection with Sandra Tann?" Barham's voice was cold.

"I don't know what you're talking about or why you've arrested me."

"You're in the uniform of a sergeant in the United States Army. That's enough for a stiff sentence alone. You hit an officer who had arrested you and escaped from custody. You aided a woman who committed a frightful crime on another American officer. You are connected with an American woman whom we now suspect to be either a criminal or a Soviet agent. You're in bad trouble, Buchanan, and you'd better start talking. There are a lot of things we want to know, and we want to know them right now!"

Either a criminal or a Soviet agent. Sandra Tann.

Only I wasn't thinking about her now. I was thinking about the RK virus.

My instructions had been clear and strong. Do not communicate with the scientist who waited in the Teikoku Building unless I had the actual virus cultures in my possession. But now I knew that the precious stuff might be hidden in a shack only a few hundred yards from the Teikoku Building. And I might rot in a jail cell for months. I wasn't kidding myself—I had committed some serious crimes and I couldn't explain to Barham or any other police authority why I had done them.

"Once we found out you'd bought a sergeant's uniform and were wearing a *Stars and Stripes* patch, it was routine," said Barham. "We put out our standard net, and that includes phone inquiries to all of the indigenous places like Peter's. You didn't have a chance, Buchanan." Barham seemed quite pleased with himself.

I didn't say anything.

The sedan left the multicolored brightness of downtown Tokyo and rolled along a broad street. We weren't headed toward CID Headquarters or any of the regular offices used by the Military Police.

For a brief moment I let myself think about Sandra Tann.

"I love you, Sandra." I hadn't meant to say that on the telephone a few hours earlier, but I had said it.

"I'm kind of mixed up in things, too. Don't judge me," she had said. All I knew was that she was my woman. That's the way I was going to play it.

The sedan's tires whirred as we raced into the darkness of Tokyo. The driver was expert, tooling the car from the wide boulevard into a narrow street and then into a curving avenue where the houses were hidden behind walls of thick hedges.

He slowed and then turned into a driveway leading to a large Western-style house. The car stopped. The agent in the front seat got out, covered the door with a service automatic, and then opened it. The other agent slid out and motioned me to follow.

I walked between the two agents toward the house. Barham was behind us. One agent opened the front door and we all went in.

A Japanese servant hurried across the hall to open the heavily carved door to the living room. Inside there was a fire crackling in a big, old-fashioned fireplace. The furniture was mahogany and teak, all heavy and massive. Light came from brocaded floor lamps, and there was a chandelier with a cut-glass globe.

"Sit down, Buchanan." Barham pointed to a chair. The two agents waited until the Colonel was seated and then they took positions in chairs on either side of mine.

"You've been a lot of trouble to us and you still are a lot of trouble," Barham said. "This place is my temporary quarters and I'm going to hold the preliminary investigation here. You've got yourself involved in some very sensitive and serious matters. First, where is Miss Tsumi hiding?"

"I don't know."

"Buchanan, you've been an officer, an Infantry captain. You are not stupid. You know the kind of trouble you're in now. I can tell you this: This situation is damn important to the Far East Command. We can't afford to waste time." His cold eyes narrowed. "I might add that the horrible thing of this Tsumi woman is comparatively unimportant. I have to get that out of the way first before I can get to the really serious matters."

"I don't understand what you're talking about." That was true. Everything illegal that I had done had been connected with Akiko.

"You received a call from this Tsumi woman at the Imperial Hotel this morning. You had spent the night with Sandra Tann. You left her to go to the house in which the Tsumi woman had made an attack on an officer."

The web of Tokyo. Whatever you do, wherever you go, eyes are watching you, notes are made, the police are informed. Once Barham and the Japanese authorities had become interested in me, they could find out everything I had done or said since I stepped from the plane at Haneda.

Barham pointed a finger at me. "You phoned the Tokyo General Dispensary and then helped this woman flee the house, leaving the officer wounded and alone."

We stared into each other's eyes.

"A bulletin giving your description had gone out and you were recognized by an alert Military Policeman at the main entrance to the Finance billet. You were found some minutes later at an indigenous laundry, the White Duck. Taken into custody by Captain Brady, duty officer for the Provost Marshal section, you assaulted him in his office and escaped into the building.

"You purchased a set of used military clothing from the indigenous operators of a pressing shop on the fourth floor of the Finance building. By some means not yet known, you succeeded in avoiding the alert and left the building.

"The manager of Peter's told us, by telephone, that a man in sergeant's uniform who answered our bulletin description was then in the bar and we arrested you as you left the building.

"At present charges can be drawn up against you on three major counts. You left the scene of a crime with the presumed perpetrator of that crime. You assaulted an officer in the performance of his duty. You illegally wore the uniform of a sergeant in the United States Army. You are familiar with the probable penalties for crimes of these categories. You will undoubtedly receive a sentence of ten years at hard labor. If you are included as a defendant in the brutal assault by the Tsumi woman, you may serve twenty years. If Major Corbett dies as a result of the wound, you and Tsumi may both be hanged. Do you understand me, Buchanan?"

I understood him.

"Now." He hesitated and his eyes seemed to search out secrets in my face. "Now," he repeated, "you are involved in matters even more serious. I did not believe that your interference during the attack on my car yesterday was as much a matter of chance as you pretended.

"We have the attack on my car in which you appeared as a hero. We have the attempt by the reporter Suruki to imply that he had information on that attack. We have the murder of Suruki a short time after I left you and him talking. We have you at the scene of Suruki's murder. We have you and Sandra Tann in adultery the same night that was presumably your first meeting. Her morals are admittedly questionable, but there is no evidence yet that she engages in casual dalliance that readily."

"I don't like you, Barham, and I don't like the way you talk. When you speak of Miss Tann, remember that you're supposed to be a gentleman."

He stood up in a white rage. "You're a prisoner and you'll answer questions and that's all. Understand?"

The two burly agents were both standing too.

"Now I want two answers from you, Buchanan. I will get them, understand?" He walked over to me and stuck his face two inches from mine. "Where is Akiko Tsumi? Where is her father, Dr. Hideoki Tsumi?"

I hoped my face didn't show the shock.

"I want two answers, Buchanan."

All I had to do was tell this cold-eyed colonel the story of the RK virus and my mission. Then ten or twenty years at Leavenworth, no cell in Tokyo Detention Stockade tonight. Maybe that was the right way to play it. I knew other Intelligence teams and agents were working toward finding Dr. Tsumi and his precious virus. Maybe Barham was the big boss of such a team. He wouldn't know about the lone wolf Buchanan any more than I would know about him.

"I don't know any answers." It came out the way I had told Sandra I loved her, instinctively.

"Suppose I tell you that the lives of hundreds of thousands of people depend upon this Dr. Tsumi?" Barham's stiff forefinger almost touched my chest.

"I don't know any answers."

He stood up again, walked away from me, came back. The house was dead silent except for the tick-tock of a clock on a mantel.

"You know about BW, Buchanan?"

"Bacteriological warfare? Yes, I've heard about it."

"The Reds have been accusing our forces of using bacteriological attacks in Korea and Manchuria. We have reason to believe this is a propaganda preparation for Red use of germ warfare in Korea or elsewhere. We also have reason to believe that a new toxic agent, unbelievably deadly, was discovered toward the close of the last war by a Japanese doctor, Hideoki Tsumi. We are trying to find this doctor, to prevent any delivery of his bacteria or virus, whichever it may be, to the Reds. We must find this Dr. Tsumi and destroy his cultures. We believe that either you or Sandra Tann, or both of you, know where he is!"

My mouth was open. I closed it.

"We've traced you back. An infantry captain with an excellent record who failed to obey an order. In results your action was gallant and deserving of commendation. In practice, however, you were court-martialed and given the opportunity of resigning the service.

"You return to the United States. Suddenly you apply for entry to Japan. You seem also suddenly to be well supplied with money. The day after your arrival in Tokyo you are present at what appears to be a Red attack on a car carrying Sandra Tann and myself. You immediately make contact with this woman. The following morning you are contacted by the daughter of the man we are hunting desperately. You succeed in hiding her.

"Later you telephone Miss Tann at her billet. We missed picking you up by seconds, sending a radio jeep to the building where you phoned. Your conversation with Sandra Tann indicated collusion and conspiracy.

"Buchanan, we now believe that, embittered by your court-martial, you made contact with Red agents in the United States and returned to Japan to engage in subversive activity probably directed toward obtaining the bacteriological-warfare cultures of Dr. Tsumi for transfer to the Red forces!"

I needed something to hold on to, some kind of floor to stand on. I tried to think back to San Francisco, to the night the two men had come to my room, to the week of detailed instruction that followed. Was Barham right and was Buchanan simply a stupid tool?

I didn't know what to say or think.

"Buchanan!" Colonel Barham's voice was sharp and insistent, filling the silent room like the crack of a whip. If Barham was right, the last tiny fraction of RK had to be killed or the deadly stuff could be grown from a droplet into tons of death. If what I had been told was true, we could produce tons of curative virus from such a droplet.

"Colonel, on what do you base your suspicions of Sandra Tann?" I asked. I wasn't calm or clearheaded. There was a film of cold sweat across my forehead and I had to clench my hands.

"I'm not here to answer questions. You are."

"At present I have no answers."

He looked at me for long seconds. "If I prove this Tann woman is a Red agent, will you co-operate with us?"

I thought about that one for a while. "No."

Maybe I was being stubborn and stupid. Maybe I should have told him where Dr. Tsumi was hiding. Then the Counter-Intelligence boys and the Criminal Investigation boys would sail in, and pretty soon the RK virus would be dead cells floating in a cloudy jar. They might want to keep it alive, take it Stateside so that our scientists who study germ warfare could try to find protection against it. But this was still Occupied Japan, soon to become independent Japan again; maybe they would not take the top-level State Department risk of transporting a BW substance out of Japan. They'd simply destroy it.

I had a mission, and part of that mission was to protect the RK virus and Dr. Tsumi from any American interference until the substance had been delivered to the man in the Teikoku Building.

"Buchanan, we can make you talk."

I was quite sure they could. I wouldn't be beaten or starved or drugged—but I would talk. I knew that.

"Call Hanford, Barr, Conway, Landers, and Cowles," said Barham to one of the two agents sitting as guards. "We're going to make this man talk. We'll keep him here under interrogation, emergency prolonged."

"Emergency prolonged? Yes, sir," said the big man as he got up. He didn't sound happy about it. I wasn't either.

Stubborn, thickheaded Buchanan was going to sweat something out now just because he insisted on following orders. The same stubborn

Buchanan who had been court-martialed for not following orders.

Barham was giving instructions just as if I weren't there. He wore a holstered .45 tonight and his uniform was the plain tropical worsted of an officer on duty. He took the .45 out, checked it, and carried it in his right hand. I didn't have any ideas about making a break for it. "Interrogation, emergency prolonged" still sounded better than "dead."

I wondered how I would feel if Barham was right and because of my stubbornness the Reds were given a frightful weapon to use against America.

I wondered how I would feel if Barham was wrong and because of my weakness in "interrogation, emergency prolonged" the RK virus was destroyed and sometime in the future women and children died from a radioactive poisoning that could have been prevented.

"We'll use a three-man team," said Barham to the remaining agent. "Start off with Hanford, Barr, and you. Each man take a half hour of direct, two sessions for each relief. Three hours for the team. We'll keep it up until this man talks. Notify the contacts in G-2 and the Provost Marshal's office that we have Mate Buchanan here and will hold him here under interrogation, emergency prolonged, until we have our information. He can be taken to either the Detention Stockade or to some holding area for sensitive prisoners after that, as G-2 directs."

"Yes, sir," said the agent.

A sensitive prisoner is one who touches in some way upon the "sensitive" Army functions, those of a top-secret or intelligence nature.

I sat there with my thoughts. A lot of them were about Sandra Tann. After a few minutes the five men requested by Barham showed up. They didn't bother to look at me. They were going to see a lot of me in the next few hours, or few days, if I was very tough.

They took me into an upstairs room that contained a table, four chairs, and a bed. They stripped the bed down to a mattress and a single blanket. One of them brought in a pitcher of water and a couple of glasses.

Conway brought in a Speed Graphic camera.

"Strip down to your shorts." They were all impersonal, like doctors checking a draftee in a pre-induction physical examination. What I meant to them, mostly, was a long, hard job that could be avoided if I wasn't stupid, stubborn, and scared. Actually I wasn't too scared, but I wasn't very happy.

I stripped down to my shorts. Conway took a picture. "Turn around." He took another picture. "Raise your arms." He flashed another bulb. These were pictures for the record. After I talked they would take some more pictures, evidence that I had not been worked over. It was only a question of time. They knew I was going to talk.

For my part, I wondered how long I could hold out. And why I was trying to.

"Sit down here." I sat down. Conway and the others left. Barr, Hanford, and the big man who had arrested me were left in the room. The door was closed.

"Where is Akiko Tsumi?" Barr began.

Half an hour later he offered me a drink of water and Hanford took over.

"Where is Dr. Tsumi?"

Half an hour later Hanford offered me a cigarette and asked me if I was hungry. I wasn't. The third man, Murphy, started.

"Who told you to come to Japan?"

Half an hour later I had a cup of coffee and another cigarette. Then Barr, a tall, lean man with a sharp nose, took over.

"Where is Dr. Tsumi?"

Hanford. Murphy. I had another cup of coffee and the next team took over.

"Where did you get the money you brought to Japan?" This was Landers, Cowles, and a heavy-set man named Conway. They always made a point of telling me their names.

They tried a round. Landers, Cowles, Conway. It was two-thirty in the morning now.

"Do you want to sleep?"

"Yes."

They took me to the bed and I lay on it, covered with the blanket. The team stayed in the room. Looking up at the ceiling, the room bright with light, I didn't think I could sleep. Then somebody was pulling my arm. It was Barr. I looked at my watch. Four. I got up.

"Where is Dr. Tsumi?"

At four-thirty Hanford offered me coffee and asked me why I had come to Japan. I never answered any question unless it was about coffee, a cigarette, or bed. In that kind of interrogation the prisoner can't afford to spend his energy talking. If he's trying to hold out, he'll keep his mouth closed.

At seven in the morning a completely new team arrived. I never did get their names straight.

At eight-thirty I had a bowl of cereal and some coffee.

At one o'clock in the afternoon I had two sandwiches and some more coffee and my old friends Barr, Hanford, and Murphy took over.

At four o'clock Landers, Cowles, and Conway came on, but I was beginning to confuse them now. I couldn't remember who was who.

At seven in the evening three more showed up, but everything else was the same. The same questions. Coffee every now and then. Simple meals.

They knew that it would be easy to get Buchanan, sobbing and screaming, to blurt out all the names and places he knew. The Germans used a dentist's drill a lot for that kind of work; the Chinese work on the fingertips and eyes with hot, pointed things. Even a rubber hose over the kidneys will make a strong, stubborn man talk. They knew all these things and they didn't use them.

They used patience.

I suppose they had places to go. Instead they had to sit through the drudgery of being coldly correct with Buchanan and asking him the same questions over and over, thirty long minutes twice in three hours, then coming back a few hours later.

As far as they were concerned, I wouldn't be there if there wasn't evidence against me. I wouldn't refuse to talk if I weren't guilty. But they didn't change.

I was one raw sponge of nerves. It might have been easier if I had known why I was hanging on.

I was holding to one idea. Somehow I was going to get to the rag-picker village and find Dr. Tsumi. I was going to get the cultures and take them to the Teikoku Building. Somehow I was going to do those two things.

At ten that evening they brought me my suitcase from the Imperial and told me to dress. I washed, shaved, and dressed. They gave me my wallet. Then they took me down to the big room where Barham had talked to me.

He was there now, sitting in a straight-backed chair. He looked old and used up.

"Why are you holding out this way, Buchanan? Do you hate your own country so much? Is it for money? For a woman, for Sandra Tann? Because you believe in communism?"

"I'm not a communist. I wouldn't let love interfere with duty. There's no money. I'm an American." It was a relief to talk. I had been holding back, saying nothing for hours. Now I wanted to babble, to talk and talk. Barham knew that the system works that way—only I knew it too.

Barham seemed friendly, even sympathetic. "You've got a splendid record as a soldier. I found that out when we checked through on you. Mate, what's the story here? What are you hiding? Why are you hiding it? You know how important it is to our country. Tell me about it."

Rag-picker village. Teikoku Building.

"Colonel, I can't tell you. There's nothing to tell."

He waited. The system always worked.

"Do you feel that you're in love with Sandra Tann?"

"Yes."

"Then I must apologize for some of the things I've said about her. She has been trying desperately to find you all day. She must love you, too." No sale, I thought to myself. Good try, but I know some of the emotional tricks of interrogation myself. Try direct questioning, hour after hour, until the prisoner is a tight ball of nerves. Then put his clothes back on him, treat him well, talk about the people he's fond of, the person he loves. He's so damn grateful he melts.

"We're not at all sure that she's connected in any way with the Reds. You might be able to clear her entirely," the Colonel said. His forefinger wasn't driving at me now and he was trying hard to look friendly. But now I was sick at heart because that last remark of his was too damn good an indication that they had hard, tight proof that Sandra was a Red agent. It was a tricky trap and I was supposed to fall into it.

"I've got nothing to say." When a man has nothing else left, he can hold to his pride that he is sticking to his mission. I had nothing else left.

He tried for another ten minutes. He was good at his job. Friendliness, insinuations, little half promises of help and leniency, the whole catalogue of tricks that a full colonel in Criminal Investigation, Counter-Intelligence, or Central Intelligence would know. I was dead tired and I didn't want to play.

"Very well, Buchanan," he snapped suddenly. "You're smart, you're tough, and you're in this dirty business up to your eyes. We know it and we'll nail your dirty hide to the wall. We know that Sandra Tann is a Red agent and we're almost ready to pounce on her. Now that she guesses you're in custody, she may try to run. And the moment she does, we'll get her—if we have to shoot her."

The forefinger jabbed at my face.

"Your woman is a prostitute, Buchanan. A cheap tramp who sells herself and her country."

Second act. Make the prisoner angry. Insult the person he loves, get him to blow his top. It might work. Who can tell what anyone will do ten seconds from now?

"We know about Manuki, Buchanan. We know about those fishing boats that are supposedly captured by the Soviet coast patrol."

It was maybe good that one of us knew, because I didn't. I told him so and he didn't believe me. I wasn't angry with Barham. He was doing his job and he was doing it well. I wished I knew whether he was right or not. If he was, it would have been easy to tell what I knew, tell him that I'd been played for a sucker.

"This woman comes here as a singer, a Department of the Army Civilian employee. Her personal history is given a casual check and she is cleared for work in Japan." Barham's voice was low and cold. "Not until two months ago did a routine examination of personal history forms point up a series of holes and falsehoods in her signed statement of her background. Then we began to check her closely.

"For months she has been spending her time with a former war criminal, Yoshiru Manuki. He was released from Sugamo Prison only two years ago, convicted during the war-crimes trials of having been one of the big industrialists who urged the Japanese government into the Pacific War.

"He came out of Sugamo penniless. Now he's rich gain. How did he get his money? Why does Sandra Tann spend so much of her time with him?"

It wasn't good listening for me, but I had to listen.

"Why did Manuki want to kill Sandra Tann?" He shot the question at me as if he thought this was the unexpected question that would finally crack me. He waited for many seconds.

"You were there. You knew where and when the attempt would take place. How did you know? We can trace no connection between you and Manuki, but we trace a connection between you and Sandra Tann, between you and Akiko Tsumi. We don't know why Manuki wanted Sandra Tann killed or why he planned the attempt when I was with her, but the little reporter Suruki recognized the three men who actually attacked the car as men that Yoshiru Manuki has used as terrorists before. I'll tell you what I think, Buchanan." He stood up, a straight soldier of a man in late middle age. There was no question that he was sincere, that he believed he was fighting his country's battle against a dangerous and contemptible adversary, a traitor. Me.

"I think Sandra Tann has located Dr. Tsumi and has the plague culture. I think she has quarreled with Manuki over the money she'll get if Manuki sells this virus or germ culture to the Reds. You and she are together. She found out that Manuki planned an attack on our car in front of the Imperial and she had you there to protect her.

"You and your woman are trying to double-cross Manuki. Because she has the Tsumi culture hidden somewhere, you had to protect Tsumi's daughter.

"You're tough. You're a fighter, Buchanan. But you're also a dirty traitor. I know you are. If you weren't, you'd be doing everything in your power to help us destroy the Tsumi plague, to help us get Manuki, to help us convict Sandra Tann of treachery to her country! You sit there silent."

He turned his back on me and walked away. "Take him back upstairs. You have my approval to use violent interrogation on this man," he called to the two guards waiting outside the door.

But my whole world was different now. This man Manuki had tried to kill Sandra. It had been the sheerest chance that I had been able to save her—and Barham. Whatever Sandra was doing, she was no Red agent. I knew that. And I knew something else: Manuki would try to kill her again.

I wasn't worried about "violent interrogation." I wasn't worried because I knew now I had to get out and get to Sandra.

She would know whether Barham was right about the cultures of Dr. Tsumi. I had to find that answer if I died trying.

The two agents walked into the room. They looked at me with some curiosity. I looked all right now, a little worn and used, maybe, but in pretty good shape. They had a fair idea about how I would look in an hour or so.

It was time to start trying, even if I did die trying.

Chapter Ten

It would have to be a gamble on the way colonels act. Barham was done with me, and the chances were good that he would go somewhere else now. He was probably a busy man. He would walk to the door, and his driver, who would always be waiting near the driveway with the staff sedan, would pull up to the door. The driver would get out of his seat, leaving his door open, and attend the rear door for the Colonel. The driver would be Japanese and unarmed. That's the way it was for colonels in Japan. It took no time to figure this; it was something that I knew as I began to walk up the stairs to the second floor, the two agents following me.

My ears strained to hear the sound. I heard it—Colonel Barham's feet on the rug-covered wood floor, walking to the front door. I heard the door open.

"Colonel Barham!" I called, and stopped on the stairway. If my timing was right, the sedan would be pulling up in front now.

"Yes?" If I knew colonels, it would be instinctive for him to wait for me to walk to him to speak, not to come to me.

"I'll tell you one thing." I turned and started to walk down the stairs. The agents hesitated a moment and then followed me. I walked across the floor from the stairs to where the Colonel was standing in front of the open door. I could see the sedan five feet in front of the entrance. Both doors on this side were open and I was sure the engine was running. It would be either a Ford or a Chevrolet.

"Colonel Barham, about Sandra Tann—" I was up to him now. The agents had stopped about ten feet behind me.

"Yes?" His gun was in its holster.

The way you do it is to start your spin before you start to grab the man. My body was halfway around before my arms, elbows tight to my sides, shot out and I twisted Barham between me and the two agents. I pushed him toward them and caught the driver as he was coming forward, pulling him toward me and throwing him past me toward the Colonel's falling body. Both agents had their guns out, but I was in the driver's seat before they fired.

The motor was running and I gunned it in second, my hands and face covered with sweat. I was at the open gate before they fired again. Somebody in the darkness by the gate opened up on me with an automatic rifle that took out the rear window.

A big Japanese bus was passing as I left the gateway, tires screaming in the skid turn I made. The guard with the tommy gun or whatever didn't dare spray because of the rumbling bus, loaded with civilians.

Both doors were still open and swinging. I closed the front, slowed, and caught the rear as it banged inward. The automatic rifle had chewed it up plenty.

I had maybe three or four minutes before a buzzing swarm of radio jeeps, riot cars, and armed motorcycles would converge on the sector of Tokyo where I was. The urgency of the moment had gunned up my body, but underneath the frantic alertness of the escape I was played out and tired to my soul.

Three or four minutes to go and only a guess and a prayer as to where downtown Tokyo was from the narrow street I was traveling. A broad boulevard opened out in front of me and I skidded around the corner. I could see the pyramid apex of the Diet Building in the distance and I knew my directions now.

One minute gone. A busy crossing ahead, still teeming with the last surge of late-evening traffic. The lights were against me but I shot through, curving around the rear of a streetcar, brushing fenders with a fat-bodied bus, making half a dozen walkers scramble backward in panic. They shouted at me angrily.

Down the broad street toward the multicolored glow of central Tokyo. I swung hard right on an impulse, into a dark and narrow street, then around a corner to a street bazaar, jammed across its width with strolling shoppers in a carnival of neon, music blaring from loudspeakers. I was down to five miles an hour with my hand on the horn as I cut through.

Three minutes gone. I would have to abandon the car in another minute. They'd have road checks any second and my chances would be better on foot than in a car.

I was out of the bazaar street now and I gave a last spurt of speed before I stopped by a dark warehouse and parked the car in a shadow.

Now I was on foot, and I was probably the most desperately hunted man in Japan. I was wearing civilian clothes, I had money, and I could think of only one place I might hide—the Shamrock, if I could get there. I recognized the glitter of lights on a street ahead. It was Tenth Avenue, a bustling affair of shops, *pachinko* parlors, and bars, and it led to the brawling Shimbashi district.

All I had to do was walk with the crowds, not too fast, not too slow. Stay well away from the curbs, away from the traffic lane of the slow-moving prowl jeeps. The eyes of the men of the 720th would be restless, eager, searching out each white face in the brown tides.

I felt like a man working a machine that required four hands. Part of me was trying to be smart about avoiding capture. Part of me was anxious for morning, when I could go to find Dr. Tsumi. Part of me was a ball bouncing back and forth—would this RK Nirus save lives or bring death? And the heart of me was with Sandra Tann—the traitorous tramp that Barham believed her to be, or a lovely girl in deadly peril?

The broad white horizontal line across the front of a jeep a block away warned me that it was an M.P. patrol. I turned into the nearest *pachinko* parlor, an open-fronted store with fancy artificial garlands of gilt and red paper in front of it. The place tinkled and whirred with the noise of the *pachinko* machines; the players were quiet. I bought sixty yen worth of metal balls, found an idle machine, and began to play.

There was one other American in the place, an Air Force captain a year or two younger than myself. He saw me and waved a hello. Both of us played our machines for a minute or two and then he walked over and smiled.

"Maybe this game's got something, but I sure haven't found it. Let's go have a drink." He had a face like a good-natured chipmunk. A drink sounded like a real fine idea to me, and for a moment I felt the risk didn't matter.

"You've got yourself a player," I said.

"Jerry Clark. I'm a stovepipe jockey over for those five." The jet fighters zooming toward the Yalu and Mig Alley are "stovepipes" to the boys in the business.

"Mate Buchanan. I used to have a company of dog faces." If he recognized the name, so what? I don't know much about being a fugitive.

"Yah, you guys got all the best of it." We were walking out of the parlor as Jerry talked. "Always got a nice fat hill to sit on, and mud in your ears so you can't hear anything but chow call." He seemed like a nice guy.

Out on Tenth he waved at a cruising taxi. It was eleven now and Tokyo was beginning to curl up and go to sleep.

"Better go to a native joint," he said as he held the cab door open for me. "The clubs cut off drinks in a little while. Got any ideas?"

"The Shamrock. It's across the viaduct, over in Shimbashi."

"Good with me. But can you tell our boy Junior here where we want to go?" He motioned to the driver, who was grinning up at us.

"Shimbashi." The driver nodded and the taxi took off, clutch chattering, brakes dragging, and a little puff of steam coming up from the hood.

"You still working for Uncle?" asked Clark.

"He kicked me out," I said truthfully. "I'm just over here because I'm nuts about rice and fish heads."

"Greatest dish in the world," agreed Jerry.

"How's business in the Alley?" I asked.

His bright chipmunk face looked sober. "If they had fly boys for their stovepipes we couldn't spot them any points. They've got some good ships but they don't know tactics. Still, they score sometimes. The guy who was supposed to come to Tokyo with me on this one got his three days ago. So I'm just taking it easy floating around on vodka until I go to Tachikawa. What's with you?"

"Well, it's like this," I said. "I've got myself in a lot of trouble and I don't know how to get out."

The cab slowed down and the driver turned around for more instructions. We were in the bright lights and dark alleys of Shimbashi. The Shamrock wasn't more than a couple of hundred yards away.

"O.K.," I said. I gave him a hundred yen and we climbed out. The cab rattled along the street and we were alone.

"Jerry—"

"Yeah, pod'ner?"

"I might run into trouble at this Shamrock joint. I'm not the most popular customer they've got. It could be mean."

"Good. If they've got enough vodka I'd like me some mean trouble tonight. Mighty hospitable of you, Mate."

"Knife, gun, blackjack. They put their heart into it."

He smiled. "Sounds like a dance at the juke joint back home in Oklahoma on a Saturday night. When I go back I'm going to become the biggest vodka bootlegger in the state of Oklahoma. Figure I'll run the cornlikker boys right out of business. Then I'm going to give the state back to the Indians. Let's go, pod'ner."

We walked to the Shamrock.

The bar was almost empty. A sailor sat on a little bench, his arms around a Japanese girl, a platoon of empty beer bottles in front of them. The bartender looked familiar and then I remembered him. He'd been one of the two jokers who had tried to stop me when I left the Shamrock after my fight with Carleton Carter. When he saw me he smiled. Still I decided against having any mixed drinks at the Shamrock.

We sat at a little table and two girls appeared from behind the bar. Clark ordered a vodka, I took a bottle of Kirin. The girls pointed to themselves and Clark nodded. When they came back with drinks for the four of us I took my bottle by the neck and walked to the stairs. Nobody tried to stop me.

I went up the stairs. It was dark and quiet. I walked slowly along the hall. The panel of wood and paper that I had smashed through during the fight had been repaired and light glowed through.

The door slid open easily. Akiko was there, lying on a *futon*. Carleton Carter lay next to her, snoring loudly. Akiko's eyes widened as she saw me. She sat up, moving slowly and gently, her finger over her lips. Then she stood up, a lovely ivory figurine. Carter's great body looked powerful, even in sleep. His shoulders and biceps were thick cords of muscle. He still wore the splints on the broken finger and the bandage on his head.

I relaxed my fingers. Unconsciously they had tightened on the neck of the heavy bottle when I saw Carter.

Akiko walked to me, put her hands on my arms, and looked up. She pushed at me gently and stepped outside the door, sliding it back.

"Why you come here now, Buchanan-san?"

"Looking for you."

"Too late to look for Akiko. I wait last night until dawn, then I not wait any more. You not come here again."

"Akiko, you lied to me."

"Was only a little lie, Buchanan-san. I cannot take you to my father.

It was only a little lie.”

“Akiko, was it true about Hiroshima? Were you burned? Did your father cure you?”

Her eyes became almost slits. Her lower lip curled down. “Maybe that was lie, too. Why should Japanese girl ever tell American man truth? I not say I was burned. You say that to me. I say nothing. You say you marry me. Is this marry me?” She pointed to the closed door behind her. “Your wife sleep with other man. Now you say, ‘Tell me truth, Akiko.’ I tell you truth. I belong to big man who sleeps. I wake him up and tell him to make you go away!”

“Well, pod’ner? Who is the little lady, or am I intruding?”

Jerry Clark was standing at the top of the stairs. It was dark in the hall and he could barely see us.

“You go away, Buchanan-san. Never come back. *Dozo.*”

I turned. There was nothing to be gained here and there was no refuge here.

“Good-by, Akiko.”

“*Sayonara*, Buchanan-san.”

Clark waited for me at the head of the stairs. He was looking at Akiko.

“Man and boy, that’s the cutest little thing I’ve ever seen,” he said, nodding at Akiko, a pale shadow in the darkness as she slid the door open. She was outlined in the light for a moment, and then she was gone. “They keep that up here for a bingo prize or something?”

“She’s no prize,” I said. “Let’s get the hell away from here.”

“Anything you say, pod’ner.”

It was not yet eleven-thirty.

“Would you do a favor for me?” I asked Jerry as we stood in the doorway of the Shamrock.

“How much? Which girl of mine? What shirt? The only thing of mine you can’t have is my vodka concession for the state of Oklahoma.”

“I want you to phone a girl.”

“This is a favor?”

“You phone her as yourself, just in from a K base for five days. You want to see her tonight. Very important. But you have to act as if you’re an old friend. And as soon as she answers, you say this is the boy that wants to play house. Those words—play house, for real. Got it?”

“Sure. I call this girl, tell her I’m Jerry Clark and I want to play house for real and I’ve got to see her right away. No offense, Mate, but have you gone into some kind of business?” He was laughing. “By the way, who is this girl?”

“Sandra Tann. She sings on the radio.”

"Sandra Tann! The Witch of Tokyo? You want me to call her? You mean I'd be talking to some babe on the phone, and the babe really and truly is the Witch of Tokyo in flesh and blood? You know her?"

"Yes."

"I'll tell you what I'm gonna do. You know that concession, my vodka rights to the whole state of Oklahoma? My dearest dream and my life's ambition—I'll trade you that just for one beat-up li'l old introduction to Sandra Tann!"

"Jerry," I said, "you are now talking to the new owner of the vodka rights of the state of Oklahoma, because if she's home you'll see her tonight."

I was sounding lighthearted enough, but I wasn't. I was alone and desperate, hunted, uncertain of everything that mattered in my life. The only possible refuge through the night had been the Shamrock, and Carter was there, Carter and his woman, Akiko. It figured, but I hadn't figured it.

Now I had to reach Sandra. If she was on the wrong side, I'd find it out, and maybe I could find out what Dr. Tsumi's secret really was. If she was on the right side, somehow she was in danger of her life. I had to see her but Barham had told me she was being watched, that her phone was tapped. A lot depended on the way Jerry Clark made the call, but if I meant anything to Sandra she'd remember what I had said about playing house for real.

"There's another joint down the block. Phone her from there. She's at the Osaka."

"Lead me, boy, lead me."

We walked down the cobbled street to the joint.

I faded into a doorway as two Shore Patrol boys came out, swinging their billy clubs. Jerry didn't notice. He went in and four minutes later was out again.

"I've got to explain about the state of Oklahoma to you," he said. "Now, when you start your vodka business there—" He noticed the strain showing on my face. "I'm sorrry, Mate. She must have caught on right away, whatever those magic words of yours were. She's going to meet us in the sandwich shop of the Dai Ichi. Ten minutes. O.K.?"

The Dai Ichi, the great building that still housed the top command of Headquarters, Far East, ran on a twenty-four-hour basis, and for the convenience of the staff there was an all-night luncheonette in the basement. Clever Sandra—it was probably the only place open at midnight in all Tokyo.

It was reasonably safe for me, too. The Military Police never checked it, as far as I knew, and some of the Provost Marshal's offices or the G-

2 sections were in the Dai Ichi. My problem now was: How close did G-2 shadow the Tokyo Doll?

We got a cab and rolled out of Shimbashi, down Fifth and over on A, around the corner at the intersection of A and Z, toward the Dai Ichi.

The cab stopped before the long, square-columned portico of the building.

"You know where they keep the hash house here?" asked Jerry.

"Follow me, boy." I started up the short flight of steps as Jerry paid the driver. It was an odd feeling to be entering this eight-story square granite building. Mate Buchanan, tonight the most hunted man in Tokyo, walking into the building that housed the center of American command in the Far East.

We went inside to a Federal-Reserve-Bank-sized foyer severe in marble. It was almost midnight but two messengers were hurrying through and guards patrolled the lobby. I led Jerry through a back corridor and down a flight of marble stairs.

The sandwich shop looked as if it were in the basement of Radio City rather than in Tokyo. Half a dozen WAC's, another half-dozen soldiers, a couple of majors, and three civilians were standing at the high, chairless tables, munching on toasted cheese sandwiches and drinking malts. I didn't remember any of them, and I hoped none of them remembered me.

"Catch me a roast beef on rye and a big Coke, please," I said to Jerry. "I have no MPC."

"Roger." He went to the counter and came back doing an expert job of balancing two sandwiches, a malted, and my Coke. "Used to pop sodas for Walgreen's back in Tulsa," he explained, smiling.

"Jerry, there's some fast curves being pitched tonight," I said, taking my sandwich, "and all I can say is you'll be doing me a lot of good without getting any explanation."

"Pitch away, pod'ner. I'll cover short."

"Good boy. When she comes in, you walk right over with the big hello. Will you recognize her?"

"I'd recognize the Doll on radar."

"Fine. This is the old reunion, just two good friends meeting while you're on R and R."

"How good friends?"

"Not that good."

"Tilt. O.K., then what?"

"You take her upstairs and grab a cab with her. I'll be in the cab."

"You cute little rascal!"

"She'll probably be followed."

"Intrigue! Couple of Russian spies, you two?"

"There are those who think so. O.K.?"

"O.K. Then it's clippety-clop to the Soviet Embassy, I suppose, or do you put the H bomb together in some cellar?"

"We play it by ear from then on."

"I hope it's the Soviet Embassy. They probably have faucets for the vodka there."

"There's a better than even chance you'll get yourself in a jam, Jerry."

"Jam-spam. After the dull routine work of cooking over a hot jet all day, I'd love a jam. You know what?"

"No. What?"

"I've got to get me another ambition, now that I've given you my vodka rights in Oklahoma."

I laughed and then I saw her in the doorway. Jerry did too and he acted quickly and smoothly, a hint of the competent, steel-hard young man he really was. He walked swiftly to the door, one hand out, smiling.

"Sandra, my lovely!"

She smiled at him and they almost embraced. I faded toward the other door and slipped across the corridor. She would be followed, but the followers could not show themselves. I waited at the bend of the corridor, listening for footsteps. A man, walking deliberately. I stood, tense, beyond the corner. The man's footsteps halted. Seconds passed and then he must have entered the sandwich shop. There probably would be a second agent waiting upstairs. I tried to remember the complicated ground plan of the Dai Ichi. A stairway at the end of this corridor. A door at the far end of the entrance. Slowly and quietly I went up. The marble foyer was clear, only the guard and an enlisted messenger. I went outside.

Cabs waited through the night outside the Dai Ichi. I got into the first one and told the driver to wait. His English was good and he understood me. I sat in the back of the cab and waited.

After about ten minutes the tall, golden Sandra and Jerry came out of the doors between the square granite columns. He waved to the cab and I told the driver, "O.K.!" A moment later Sandra and Jerry were in the cab.

"Where to?"

"Around the Palace and back to the Osaka Hotel."

As the cab pulled out Sandra and I were in each other's arms.

Love is one thing, and other things are other things. Somewhere there was a tired Buchanan, not bitter but not warm with love, either, who thought coldly: This is all fine, but there's some question about you, my

Sandra, and dare I trust you at all? It would take the cab less than twenty minutes to circle the Palace grounds and turn in at the Osaka. I moved back from the girl, turned, and looked out the rear window. There were several cars behind us. One or two of them would certainly be trailing us.

"What's happened, Mate?"

Jerry sat on the far side, trying to be as inconspicuous as possible.

"Barham's had me on the grill for a day."

"Oh, Mate, my darling. Because of that girl?"

"Only *s'koshi* bit. Other things."

"Maybe me?"

"Yes."

"What did he say?"

"I'll give you two names. Tsumi. Manuki."

She was silent. Then, and it seemed long later, "Do those names mean anything to you, Mate?"

"You tell me."

"I don't know anyone named Tsumi."

"And Manuki?"

"He was one of the men you saw me with at the Nikkatsu."

"And the Delight Baths."

"And at the Delight Baths."

"Why did Manuki try to kill you?"

This time I heard her breathe in sharply.

"Did Barham say that?"

"Remember the reporter Suruki? The one who was killed? That's what he was trying to tell Barham at the Imperial bar. Somehow Barham found it out later. I don't know how. Those three—the man with the knife, the man with the torch, the man with the acid—they were Manuki's men."

"Pardon me, folks," said Jerry. "I hate to interrupt, but I do want to say you folks have fascinating chats."

"Why should Manuki try to kill you?" I asked again.

"I can't say, Mate."

Now for the most important thing. "Did you ever hear of Tsumi?"

She waited a long time. "Yes."

"How?"

There was no answer this time. I tried again.

"Did you know this girl was Tsumi's daughter?"

There was a change. If not for me, at least for Sandra, something must be falling into place. I could feel it. "I saw her name in the *Stripes*. It's not an uncommon name. I didn't make the connection."

I waited her out. Finally she spoke again. "Mate, do you know this man Tsumi?"

Lie and see what happens. "Yes. That's why I helped his daughter."

I didn't answer. I was sure that Sandra somehow knew which was right—whether the RK virus prevented radioactivity burns, or whether it was a new and deadly biological-warfare weapon.

An M.P. car screamed past us as we rounded the Palace grounds toward the Kojimachi section. Our driver turned and grinned at us. "Is many raids tonight! Everywhere M.P.'s go in. All hotels, everywhere! Big fun!"

Yes, big fun.

"How do you know Dr. Tsumi, Mate?"

Oh-ho, Sandra knows that Tsumi is a doctor. "Why does Tsumi interest you, Sandra? Does he interest Manuki, too?"

I could feel her tension. Then she reached out and took my hand and held it for a moment.

"Remember what we said on the phone when you called me?"

"We said quite a bit."

"In very few words. One of the things I said was something about going along with each other, no matter what."

"I remember."

"I want to add something to that, Mate. There's going to be another day, somewhere ahead. That's the important day, not these days now. No matter what we both must do, or be forced to think of each other, remember the important day."

We both were silent. The cab was headed toward the Osaka now.

"Mate, I'll duck in for a second and I'll be right back out. Wait for me, please."

The cab stopped in front of the Osaka entrance. Jerry got out and held the door for Sandra. She looked at me for a second and her eyes were glistening. Then she slipped out and went into the hotel.

"Do you want me to stick around?" asked Jerry.

"Get in!"

He did and asked in surprise, "What gives, pod'ner?"

"Driver. Get moving, *hayoka!*" The driver was surprised, too, but he gunned the cab away from the curb.

"Unless I'm very wrong," I said to Jerry, "our girl friend is calling the cops right now. She is being a good citizen and calling the cops to get me."

"A real pretty girl like that?"

"A real pretty girl like that."

The cab was turning the corner at the Nomura Hotel, a block away, when I looked back and saw the M.P. car racing in toward the Osaka. I swung the cab door open, and the driver slowed.

"So long Jerry. Thanks." I jumped out. "Keep going, *dozo!*"

The cab moved on. I ran to the tennis court next to the Dai Ichi Hotel and flattened myself against a wall. The M.P. car, siren howling, rounded the Nomura corner and streaked down the road. They'd catch the cab in the next few seconds.

So my Sandra had called the M.P.'s. Good fast work—she must have called radio central and they'd sent a radio car within thirty seconds of the time she'd entered the Osaka. In a couple of minutes the whole area would be alive with police.

My Sandra.

Chapter Eleven

The irony was that as I stood in the shadows of the tennis court I faced a wall behind which was the village of the rag-pickers.

Dr. Tsumi was only a few hundred feet away. Behind me, at the corner of the block, was the Osaka, where Sandra would be waiting now to hear that Mate Buchanan had been caught.

I turned back, walking past the Nomura, paralleling the railway viaduct. My chances of escaping a police trap did not look good. Tokyo is a city so crowded that there are no forgotten crannies, no overlooked spaces where a man may hide. It is also a city so well policed that nothing breathes without a policeman somewhere near and ready to note anything unusual.

And it is a city that freezes into stillness at midnight. There are no little cafés or all-night coffee shops, no bars bright and gay behind closed doors. As I hurried along in the shadows by the viaduct I heard the weird sound of a Tokyo night—the *soba* man pushing his little food cart and blowing his eerie melody on the *cheremella*. It was the haunted call of a devil bird, a few notes in a minor key.

I had to hide. I had to find a place to sleep. The twenty-four hours I had spent under interrogation had tired me until my nerves screamed for quiet and sleep.

Why had Sandra turned me in? Why had I been so sure she would? The questions cut across my panic and my weariness like the flash of a knife.

She had made a point of talking of a day ahead of us, and her eyes had glistened with tears when she left me. But then she had gone right to the desk phone and called the police radio center.

Because I had talked about Dr. Tsumi and Manuki.

The *soba* man's fluting grew distant and I felt alone in the night. On the other side of the road, opposite the viaduct, was a three-story building whose windows glowed with lights. I remembered it, the Nippon Times building, and on the third floor were the editorial offices of the *Pacific Stars and Stripes*.

There was a narrow stairway and I went up, past the offices of the *Times*, through a swinging door with the sign "Stars & Stripes," and up a narrower stairway into a large cluttered office. It looked like a newspaper office—a helter-skelter of littered desks, wallboards covered with clippings. A sergeant in crumpled khakis was asleep at a desk. The night man, probably. I was much in favor of his being asleep.

Somewhere around there would be a Japanese security guard, complete with notebook and maybe a gun. All American installations had these guards and they were conscientious. Right now he was probably on his rounds through the building. I had to find a closet.

The sergeant was snoring. Behind a haphazard row of filing cabinets was a short hallway, and at one side of it was a door. I hurried over and opened it. It was stocked with newspapers, old copies of the *Stripes*. I closed the door behind me and curled up.

The door was outlined by a crack of light; otherwise the closet was black.

After a few minutes I heard the sauntering footsteps of the security guard. I tried to peek through the crack around the door and found I could see into the large room fairly well, although the row of file cabinets blocked part of my view. The security policeman was in uniform, a spruce little guy who carried a flashlight and no sidearm. He sat down at a desk near the head of the stairs and began to fill out some paper. I watched him for a little while, and during that time the sergeant must have awakened, because he came over and talked to the guard, then went into a room on the far side of the big one. There was a faint clatter coming from it, probably teletypes clicking out the news.

It happened suddenly but it worked out all right. Two big Military Policemen walked into the big room from the stairway, billy clubs swinging, holsters unbuttoned. I could see them fine and I didn't care for it. The lads of the 720th were making a close check of the area and I was sure that it was bottled up tight by now.

I peeked out, my muscles knotted, while the two big boys talked to the guard. If any one of the three had suggested a shakedown search of the *Stripes* office I'd be in the wringer, but the guard must have assured them that he was on top of his job. It didn't figure for him to suggest that the M.P.'s check up on the property he was guarding. The M.P.'s took him at his word and left. My muscles loosened up to a warm custard.

The thing to do was to think things out slowly and carefully. I might not have another chance to be in a quiet place without anybody nipping at my ankles for quite a while.

When I woke up it was a sudden shock. The last thing I remember was getting ready to think things out; now there was a rumble of conversation outside the closet and it felt like morning. I looked at my watch. Damn right it was morning; it was after eight.

I wondered where the men's room was. I needed a shave, but the shave could wait.

Now what do we do? I peered through the crack. There was a man in civilian clothes sitting at a desk and talking to a WAF sergeant, a blonde girl who was laughing at whatever the guy was saying. He was in his mid-thirties, wore horn-rimmed glasses, and needed a haircut.

A khaki cloud blotted out my view for a moment and passed.

As I began to get my bearings on peeking through the crack I saw others, a trim little Japanese girl, an immense man wearing captain's bars and a petulant expression, another captain who was dapper and looked something like a worried poet.

It wouldn't go over at all if a crumpled civilian needing a shave suddenly dashed out of a closet and asked where the men's room was. These were newspaper people and they would know all about Mate Buchanan, what he looked like and how the Provost Marshal was pushing Tokyo through a sieve to find him.

About this time my mind chose to remind me that my girl had turned me in to the cops last night, and that if I hadn't suspected that she would, at this moment I'd be in a little room getting interrogation again, this time without patience.

All this was true, but right now Buchanan had a personal matter to take care of.

My eye was still close to the crack. Two men passed, soldiers, but they weren't wearing regular shirts, just T shirts. A third lad, near the wire room, was also in a T shirt. Apparently it was permitted for the working staff of the *Stripes*.

I was down to my T shirt in five seconds. I wadded my coat, shirt, and tie behind a stack of papers. I pushed the closet door open a few inches, waited as long as I could, and then emerged from the closet, carrying a great pile of newspapers reaching to my face. Nobody seemed to pay me any notice.

Where was it?

I walked past the row of cabinets, carrying my stack of papers. Around a corner I heard the blessed sound of somebody flushing one. I dogtrotted in the direction of the sound. There was a swinging door but it didn't have any signs saying who it was for and the flushing noise had been indeterminate. I went through the swinging door, still carrying my two-foot pile of papers, and they were heavy. Inside there was another swinging door marked, "Men." I have never felt better in my life.

I came out hidden behind my stack, but this couldn't go on forever. The staff was apparently used to seeing new men wearing T shirts and doing useful work wandering around, but I couldn't spend the rest of the morning carting a pile of newspapers. My trousers were a light gabardine that might pass for khaki or tropical worsted. I took a chance and put the papers down near the file cabinets. Then I smelled something I couldn't resist. It was freshly made coffee and it was somewhere near. I followed the aroma like a bird dog.

There was a little room at right angles to the men's room, and inside was a coffee bar. A slender young Japanese boy was pouring out a couple of cups for two customers, one wearing sergeant's stripes and a New York expression; the other was in a T shirt and wore a listening expression. They both looked me over carefully when I came in.

"Hi," said the lad in the T shirt. It was a friendly hi.

"Hi," said the sergeant. He looked through the bottom of his glasses at me. His name was Marv something, it turned out, and he was the drama, music, book, and art critic of the *Stripes*.

"You just new here?" asked the boy in the T shirt.

"Yeah. Almost brand-new."

"It's a good shop. Great crowd."

"Infants and would-be Great American Novelists," said Marv.

My coffee was down now and I was a new man. A hundred yards away was one end of rag-picker village. Two blocks away was the Osaka. Four blocks in the other direction was the Teikoku, where a man was waiting to hear from me.

"Well, I gotta leave," said Marv. "Glad to have met you. Got to get back to my novel before somebody finds some work for me."

"You working downstairs?" asked the other lad.

"Yeah." I hoped that he would turn out to be working upstairs, but I was wrong, fortunately.

"If you need some overalls I can lend you a pair."

"That's swell," I said, and I meant it.

We walked down some stairs in the rear. His name was Ted. I told him my name was Murphy. It's a good name. The typesetting and stereo-casting room was on the first floor. Japanese from the Nippon *Times* did all the lino-typing, but several Americans, mostly in overalls or printer's aprons, were working away on pages of type. Ted gave me a pair of ink-stained overalls. He walked away as I put them on over my trousers.

I went to the door and waited until one of the Japanese hurried by.

"You know Ted?" I asked him.

"Ted? Hokay!"

"Here, you give Ted this. O.K.?" I gave him five thousand yen from my wallet. He took it.

"Give Ted, huh?" he asked.

"Right," I said, and walked out the door into the bright morning of Tokyo. Ted would get the money for his overalls.

This was Monday, the beginning of the work week in Tokyo, just as it is in Toledo. It was the beginning of the end for me. I was walking toward the opening in the viaduct, the underpass that led to the rag-picker village and Dr. Tsumi. The thinking I had intended to do in the closet last night I was doing now.

Sticking up like a hurricane warning signal was the fact that I wasn't sure now about that man who waited for me in the Teikoku Building. The Reds have used better and smarter men than me as stooges, credentials and White House letters can be forged, and Red intelligence is a web that matches our own. Maybe in Asia it's even better.

I walked under the rumbling viaduct. Beyond it were the straggling huts of the rag-pickers, strung along the muddy bank of the stinking canal. On the other side of the canal were the buildings of phoenix Tokyo, tall new buildings, block-long department stores, acres of night clubs and cafés.

The two Japanese police at the far end of the underpass gave me the quick glance they give all living things and looked away. I turned and went down the wet, slippery path on the other side of the railway viaduct, the path that led to the little shacks built of flattened cans, scraps of wood, and paper cartons. It was a busy path; rag-picker village had a main street, a village life of its own.

Naked boys watched me with great, unblinking eyes. An old man looked at me with fear. A young man looked at me with scorn—an American walking among the outcasts would do so only because he wanted something from them.

I called to the young man and he looked at me, mouth hanging open, lower lip curled down.

"Tsumi? You know Tsumi?"

He shrugged and turned his back to me. In a way these rag-pickers were the proudest of all the Japanese, because they did not cheapen themselves with pretense. There was no way left by which they could cheapen themselves further, so why bother with pretense?

Two men who wore only ragged scraps of cotton around their loins were coming toward me on the path.

"Tsumi?" I asked. They looked at each other and whispered. The skinnier of the two motioned toward a shack.

"Tsumi," he said.

I wanted to run to the hut but I made myself walk.

It was about six feet square, maybe five feet high, built of fragments of the wreck of Tokyo—shards of tiles, pieces of buildings that had burned in the great B-29 fire raids or that had been blown apart by H bombs seven years ago.

A man in tattered shorts and a clean white cotton jacket stood in the opening of the shack. He wore glasses whose frames were held together with string. Both lenses were cracked and chipped. He was thin, with knobby knees and a turkey throat. I knew it was Dr. Tsumi.

I had found him.

They had told me I would be on my own when this moment came. I was to use combat judgment, doing what seemed to fit the situation best, knowing that there was no margin for error, no second chance.

I walked past him, stooping to enter his hut. He did not try to stop me.

The hut was a pitiful affair. His sleeping mat was neatly rolled. There were two boxes that must have served as his table and his storage lockers. Nothing else, not even a tea kettle. The boxes were open; one held books and photographs, the other had a few clean and mended cotton clothes. There were no medical instruments, no jars of virus cultures.

"Dr. Tsumi?' I said, coming out again.

He bowed. There was no resentment of my intrusion, no surprise, nothing.

"I have come from America to find you."

"You have found me." His English had a hint of Oxford.

"I need your help."

"An American needs help from a Japanese?"

"You are a great doctor. You made a great discovery."

"The man who discovers fire tells the man who discovers water that it is a great discovery?"

"What was your discovery, Dr. Tsumi?"

We stood there in the mud and smell by the side of the scum-rimmed canal, a thin and elderly Japanese in the scant rags of a beggar, a tired

American in overalls.

"What could a Japanese discover? A new way of humility toward the hairy conquerors?"

He wasn't being real friendly or openhearted, and I'm no expert on the refinements of politeness.

"What the hell is wrong with you people?" It wasn't what I intended to say, but it was what I was feeling. O.K., there was Hiroshima. There was a Pearl Harbor, too. My dad raised me to figure I might have a whipping coming from the kid I punched, and if I did, I had no right to cry.

"What is wrong with us? Most of us are children. Who are you?"

"My name is Mate Buchanan. I came to Japan to find you and work things out with you."

"I have nothing. I want nothing. What could you work out with this forgotten outcast?"

"Would you come to a teahouse with me now?"

There was something here. I wasn't sure what had happened, but I knew enough of the Japanese to sense something important and unexpected. If this bitter man had acted according to expectations, he would not have admitted his identity, he would not have answered me in English. He had expected me—and he wanted something from me. If he didn't he would have shrugged and turned his back on me. I wanted something from Tsumi, and he wanted something from me. I was sure of it.

He looked at his shirt, his tattered drawers. "How could this be?"

He was willing to go through preliminaries, sparring with me. He would go to the teahouse and he had already made up his mind that he would. In a couple of minutes he'd tell me about it.

"Let's go. I need some tea myself." I had the feeling I had made it.

He bowed. "One moment, please." He went into his shack. About three minutes later he came out again, and he looked pretty good—blue cotton wrapper, clog sandals, a little fan.

Dr. Tsumi and Mate Buchanan walked out of the mud and slop of ragpicker village. I wasn't sure if he knew it or not, but I would not let him go again until I had the secret of the RK virus.

We crossed the canal on an old bridge only partially repaired after seven years from the time it had splintered and cracked from some nearby bomb.

There was a small teahouse near the corner of the block on the other side of the canal. We went in, and it was a shoes-off place. I slipped into the felt sandals, Tsumi removed his clogs, and we were led to a small table by a bowing girl. Tsumi sat on his haunches and I did the best I could, squatting on the rice-mat floor.

He fluttered his fan. I offered him a cigarette from a crumpled pack in my trousers and he took it, saying, "Thank you." He was warming up and it puzzled me. The girl brought us each tiny, shell-thin cups and poured our tea. There was a plate of rice sweets and Tsumi nibbled on one.

If this was the man who hated Americans so much that he would rather destroy his lifework than allow Americans to benefit from it, he was being very friendly now.

"You ask what is wrong with us?"

"Yes, Dr. Tsumi."

"We must first admit that there is something wrong with the Japanese. Once I did not think so. But now I am older."

I sipped my tea.

"Mr. Buchanan, what is good about the Japanese?"

"The way you treat your children when they're small." That was one score on the credit side I'd give them without argument. Fathers and mothers alike, they are the warmest, kindest, jolliest parents I've ever seen, and their children are probably the nicest and happiest in the world.

Dr. Tsumi smiled. It was a friendly smile. I wasn't worried about the conversation. The fact that Tsumi wanted to start out on big, broad generalities about the Japanese people was a sure sign that he wanted to come to a definite point about something else. In his own good time.

"And that may be our fault, too, Mr. Buchanan."

"Ah, so?"

"You Americans say we Japanese are impassive, no?"

"The inscrutable Oriental." I smiled.

"But we say that you are impassive, you Americans. You do not laugh as easily or as loudly as we do. You do not have violent angers. You do not care about learning to love."

He sipped his tea and I waited.

"You become more like your own machines. Always your white faces are set and cold, showing no emotion. Machines that live and grow rich and rule the world. Machines without passion, without anger, without hatred. Americans.

"And we Japanese? We have the highest suicide rate in the world. We are children, and like children we are hot with anger, warm with love, easily frightened, easy to laugh. Like children we are sensitive and easily hurt. Like children we put on our toy swords and stomp and march and say, 'Look at me, everybody!'

"This is why, Mr. Buchanan: The only time of contentment and full happiness a Japanese ever has is when he is a child. Then there is softness and love and he does not have to pretend. A little boy thinks this is the way the world is and the way his life will always be.

"Then it is over, suddenly. He goes to school. He puts on his uniform and he marches into the cold, gray schoolroom, where there is no softness, no laughing, nothing but the rule. The one rule—a Japanese must always do what is expected. So for the rest of our lives, underneath, we want only to be children again."

He looked at me with a curious interest, as if to see whether I had interest in what he said. I did, although I had other things on my mind, too.

"We have so little in our lives that our emotions, our feelings, our senses are much more important to us than to you who have so much."

"You know America?"

"Quite well," he answered. "I was there often before the war."

"How did you feel during the war, Dr. Tsumi?"

"I thought we would win. Naturally."

"Why?"

"I had seen your people shortly before the war. Discontented, restless, divided. You complained about everything, you blamed your government for everything that was wrong in your lives. You are the most wasteful people in the world. I did not see how you could fight, much less win."

"And after the war, Dr. Tsumi?"

"You know where I was. In Hiroshima. I was like a dead man. I did not believe what I had seen. My son—my son was dead and his fleet was buried in the silt at the bottom of the sea. I was like a dead man."

"And now, Dr. Tsumi?"

He looked at me for a long time.

"And now things are very different. First I hated. For years I was a ghost who fed on hate. I had been proud of my work. After the event at Hiroshima I swore that I would hide myself and my achievement until Japan was free again, and I could help my emperor in the way of the Yamato people once more.

"Here in the street of the beggars I hid, and no one knew me or saw me except my faithful Watanabe. It was strange. My Watanabe worked for the Americans as one who mops and the money they paid him made him seem like a rich man among his class. I, his master, lived with the beggars, and yet I would not take money from Watanabe.

"Then came the peace treaty, and I sat by the canal and tried to understand it. Two days ago I made a decision. Yesterday I walked many miles to Waseda University, to the laboratory of an old friend who is a professor at Waseda. He saw me as if he saw a ghost. He had believed me dead.

"Yet the trust I had given him nearly seven years before had been respected. He had my cultures, living after these many years. He had tended them and the virus was alive and strong. More, as he had promised, he had not examined them or made research on the virus. In a scientist, who must always live with the curiosity raging within him like a tiger, this was no small thing. But he had promised me and he had kept his trust. Now after these long, hate-filled years of the Occupation, I was like a man alive again.

"I must apologize. When you came to me, when you walked like a samurai into the home of a peasant, I was angry. But there is no longer anger in my heart toward Americans. If Dai Nippon lives again, it will be because Americans have protected us from the Russians. I know this now."

"Where are the cultures now, Dr. Tsumi?" This was the jackpot question.

"Many years ago I knew a powerful man, one of the great industrialists. Months ago, when I had not yet found my decision, I wrote to him and told him what I had, but not yet where I was nor where my virus cultures were hidden. I said in my letter to him that if he was able to take my virus and protect it for the Japanese government he would tell me so by a small announcement in a certain newspaper. An announcement that was merely the Chinese characters for Great Future. He did so.

"When I left my friend at Waseda University I carried my cultures in a special protective case. Walking, I brought this case to my faithful Watanabe at the building of Finance, where he works. I could see that he was disturbed about something, but he did not wish to tell me what it was. However, I commanded him, and at last he told me of you and of a person I had considered dead. He said that you were to marry this person by Shinto rites, and that to protect my secret she had told him that he, my old servant, was Dr. Tsumi, her father.

"I knew that you were hunting for my secret. How you knew of it I can only guess. This person must have told you or my friend the great man—no others knew.

"My decision was made. I sent Watanabe with my virus to the great industrialist, who will develop it for Japan, and for the Americans as well.

"Now, where is this person, my daughter?"

"Who is the industrialist?"

He looked surprised. "Mr. Yoshiru Manuki."

Chapter Twelve

Why can't living be like climbing a clean, rocky hill so that you can be tired and body-sore, yet look back and down, seeing only the straight, hard road that you have climbed? Why does it have to be a swamp?

I put down my cup and stood up. The old man was looking up at me now, still waiting, already a little frightened by what he saw in my face.

"Mr. Buchanan, where is my daughter? I no longer hate anyone. Now I must see her."

"When was the last time you saw Yoshiru Manuki?" I asked.

"Many years ago, before the war. A rich and respected man. You tried him as a war criminal and put him in Sugamo Prison, but I read later he was released and is once again rich and powerful. Since you Americans released him from prison, I am sure that he is friendly to you, and you are friendly to him now. How else could he grow rich again so soon?"

"Who knew of your work?"

"My daughter, my friend of the Hiroshima hospital who died that day, some assistants who likewise died that day. No one else, until I wrote to Manuki."

"What will your virus do?"

That was the wrong question. The eager eyes seemed to film over.

"Will you come with me to Manuki?"

"No. Where is my daughter?"

"The police are hunting for your daughter. She is hiding."

For a brief instant there were surprise, pain, fear in the old face, and then there was only impassivity. "Why do the police hunt for her?"

"For three years she has lived with an American major. Saturday morning she wounded him with a knife."

"And you would marry her? For you she used this knife on the other?"

"Not for me. For jealousy."

"For honor." The little man stood up. We would not be friends again. It had been brutal, but at least it had been without pretense. I was sick of pretense.

"If you want me to take you to her, I will. I think I know where she is."

The little old man bowed. I paid for our tea and we put our shoes back on. I was tired and dirty, and empty inside.

I don't know why I was taking the old man to the Shamrock. It might be a death trap for me. I should be using these precious moments to get to Manuki—but I thought Akiko needed her father.

The Shamrock looked tawdry and foolish in the sunlight. Dr. Tsumi peered up at the sign through his cracked glasses and I knew that he realized what he might find there.

There was no need for me to go into the trap.

"She will be here. Upstairs. If she isn't, they will know where she is. Good-by."

"There are many things I do not understand, but thank you, Mr. Buchanan."

He bowed and turned toward the door of the Shamrock. An Army truck pulled up at the curb behind us. I started to walk away.

I flicked an insect on the back of my neck and then I felt the point. It was no insect.

"Hi, man, what's doing?"

I knew better than to turn. Carter had one arm loose around my shoulder, the enormous hand hiding the knife that touched the great artery of my neck. "The ol' *honcho's* been looking for you. Go on upstairs."

Dr. Tsumi had opened the door, unaware of the incident on the sidewalk behind him. With Carter's arm still around my shoulders, I walked after the doctor. Inside, at the stairway, he turned and saw us.

"Jes' keep goin', ol' Papa-san," said Carter. "We're comin' up too."

Carter was wearing a green-gray G.I. fatigue uniform. He was taking a tremendous risk for some reason—wearing an Army uniform, driving what must be a stolen Army truck in broad daylight.

My eyes found the bandage on his head and he noticed. "Yeah, man, you did that. You ain't going to die easy and you ain't going to die slow. Get on. You know what room. You and me been there before."

Dr. Tsumi watched us in bewilderment.

"You tag along, Papa-san. Who is you, anyway?"

"I look for my daughter, Miss Akiko Tsumi."

Garter showed his big teeth. "Li'l ol' dried-up prune of a man like you made a daughter like that one? Get movin'." The slender knife glittered in his hand.

We climbed the stairs and walked down the little hall. I slid back the panel door. She was in the room, wearing a kimono now, her blue-black hair high and glossed, her face a powder-white geisha mask. When she saw her father she bowed down, down until her head touched the floor at his feet. She waited there, silent, bowed.

The old man talked to her in Japanese. Carter listened.

Slowly the girl lifted her head, looked up at her father. He smiled. She bowed again, rose, and went to a corner of the room, where she sat on the rice-mat floor. She did not look at me.

"You go over and squat next to your li'l girl," Carter said to Dr. Tsumi. He stood by me, his eyes six inches above mine, the knife poised upward. "You, man, you and me got two kinds of business. First you tell me what you're looking for in Tokyo. That's one kind of business. Money business. Then we got a different kind. I'm going to make you scream and beg to die for a long time before you die. That's blood business."

I knew there'd be a pretty good fight before any of that happened, but this wasn't the time for a move. The knife would move faster than I could, the arm that held the knife was stronger than mine.

His powerful shoulders hunched and his face came close to mine. "I killed three-four boys, maybe mor'n that. But only one ol' boy got treated mean. Boy took some money from the *honcho* and lost it gamblin'. He lasted about four hours, but it must have seemed like maybe four years to that boy. I didn't know how much a person could suffer till I tried to find out on that boy. But you is goin' to be a surprise even to me. The *honcho* guarantees that, Mr. Buchanan. You gonna surprise even me, the way you goin' to carry on!"

The hot eyes moved back, away from mine.

"Now let's talk business. Why you in Tokyo?"

My body ached to fight, but my mind told me I was still too young to die.

"It didn't work out. A deal. It fell through."

Akiko was talking to her father in Japanese and Carter froze as he listened. I wondered if Akiko knew how well this American could understand her language.

Dr. Tsumi was answering. Carter caught a name and spoke rapidly to him in Japanese. Both father and daughter looked surprised, probably at Carter's fluency in the language. Then the Doctor and Carter talked rapidly between themselves and Akiko was silent.

Carter looked at me again and laughed. "Man, this is funny! You know what? This stuff you came over to get that this li'l chick's ol' man invented, you know who's got it? Ol' Papa-san Manuki, that's who's got it. And you know who Manuki is, boy? He's my partner. I get it, he sells it. You know who he sells it to, Mr. Buchanan? He sells it to them Chinese Reds. You know what he sells? He sells medical stuff and radio gadgets and things they want real bad. You know what we get? We get morphine and heroin and gold. Papa-san Manuki and the *honcho* got a mighty nice business."

He laughed again and brought the knife to my throat and his great lips curled away from his white teeth. "You are a dead man. I don't need you for nothing now. What you wanted I'll have. You know where it's going? Same place the rest of the stuff goes. Do you like that, Mr. Buchanan?"

He stepped away from me and with his bandaged left hand he pulled back a sliding closet door. There was an Army grease gun on the closet shelf. He scooped it up with his left hand and cradled it in his arm. The grease gun is a cheap, ugly automatic weapon that throws .45 caliber bullets like a garden hose.

"I come back here to pick this up, man. I got a truckload of stuff downstairs, and it's the big load, 'cause it's the last one. The *honcho* is going to make this trip in the li'l boat personally. I'm goin' to live in Shanghai or one of them good towns and I'm going to be the biggest *honcho* that town ever saw."

Now I realized what the yellowish-white eyes showed. Carleton Carter was high on marijuana. I could smell the stuff still here in this room from last night or this morning.

He worked the grease gun under the loose jacket of the fatigue uniform.

"Let's you and me go down to my truck. We're going to see my partner about that stuff this li'l ol' man sent him. You is going to explain just what that stuff is and how much it's worth. Then we goin' downstairs in Mr. Manuki's house and I'm goin' to have my fun."

I was quite willing to go down to the truck. I had to see Mr. Manuki myself.

He ordered me behind the wheel, and it was a nightmare ride. Driving a stolen Army truck, wanted by the police myself, captive of a marijuana-crazed giant who was looking forward to torturing me within a few minutes, headed for the home of the man who was reputed to be the lover of my woman.

The back of the truck was loaded with cases and cartons. Sometime early this morning Carter must have taken this truck to an Army warehouse where soldiers in his gang had high-value medical supplies or other equipment ready to be loaded on, and the truck passed by the guards at the gate on forged trip tickets.

He gave me directions, and at last, in the outskirts of Tokyo, we turned into a tree-shaded alleyway that gradually became a steep grade up a green-shrouded hill. We drove down the other side of the hill into a forest of pine that concealed big houses, looking like dragon ships of teak and tile. The alleyway had become a rough path now and the truck wheels bounced in the ruts.

"Slow, man, slow," said Carter. He had flipped the safety lid of the grease gun as we bounced along the road. Now he had the weapon ready for action and his eyes were searching the tangled shrubbery ahead of us. He reached over with his bandaged left hand and clicked the horn four times. A double gate in a high stone wall opened.

"Get it in there," he said. I swung the truck through the gateway. Two Japanese in peasant clothes stood there ready to close the gates after we entered. A dirt road curved between high trees and I followed it until it ended in a big, barnlike building with a curved, pointed roof.

"Take it right in."

I drove into the building, into the shadows and the warm, fetid air.

"O.K. Get out." Carter had swung his door open and climbed out, the grease gun covering me. He circled around the front of the truck, the snout of the gun always pointed toward me. I got out of the cab.

"Walk straight out of this place and turn right, then keep going. If you try anything I'll shoot your legs off." The grease gun could do it, too.

I walked out of the darkness into the light, turned, and walked toward a series of vast interconnected buildings, obviously the palace-like home of a very wealthy Japanese. It was one of the fabulous Oriental estates that have a luxury almost unbelievable to a Westerner. We passed servants working in the grounds. They bowed silently, paying no attention to Carter and the ugly grease gun.

"Up those stairs and into that big room," said Carter.

I walked up a broad, low flight of steps to the open gallery that surrounded one enormous room in a building almost separate from the others. The sliding panels were back and the room was open.

"Get your damn shoes off, you dirty Western peasant," snarled Carter.

I walked into the room barefooted. The cool rice-straw mats felt pleasant to my feet. A very low table of ebony was the only furniture in the room. Two strips of painted silk, a carved jade and porcelain lamp, a dwarf tree in a glazed pot, these were the only decorations. The room was serenely beautiful, and through open panels at the far side I could see the cone of Fuji above a cotton-ball mass of clouds.

"Sit down at that table."

Carter sat across from me, the grease gun pushed beneath the table.

Two little maids in black Western-style uniforms hurried across the floor from a door at the rear of the room and bowed to Carter. He spoke to one in a crackle of Japanese. She bowed and they hurried away again.

"Man, you relax and enjoy yourself. We gonna have tea, and we gonna wait for Papa-san Manuki. When he comes you gonna tell us all about this medicine and then you and me gonna go down into the big stone-walled hole under one of these rooms where you can make all the noise you want. Now you try and act life a gentleman, because my ol' friend Mr. Manuki don't like trouble and messing 'round. Understand?"

He lit a marijuana cigarette and cupped it in his hand while he inhaled.

The two little maids returned with a teapot and cups.

I drank tea and looked at Carter. The giant had things on his mind, too. Even the marijuana did not keep him from being fretfully nervous and his enormous fingers drummed on the mirror-like surface of the ebony table.

He came in like a brisk businessman, smiling with his eyes heavy-lidded. He wore a white silk suit and white suede slippers. It was the man I had seen with Sandra at the Delight Baths, somewhat tall for a Japanese, his hair graying. This was Yoshiru Manuki.

Carter stood up and the two men faced each other, bowing. Then they spoke together in Japanese. Manuki glanced at me and I knew he recognized me from the Delight Baths and from the Nikkatsu. I didn't get up.

Manuki walked over to me. "My name is Yoshiru Manuki," he said. His English was almost as good as that of Dr. Tsumi.

"My name is Mate Buchanan. I was brought here under threat and I'm holding you responsible for my safety." I wasn't as stupid as I sounded. I didn't want either of them to get the idea I might have wanted to come here.

"Oh, certainly, Mr. Buchanan. You are my guest. Do not be concerned about anything."

Carter was standing a few feet from the low table, his lips curled back from his teeth.

"You may have some interesting information for me," Manuki said. "Yesterday, very late, an elderly servant came to my gate. He carried a case that contained some sealed jars. They were sent by a Dr. Tsumi. I remember Dr. Tsumi as a famous research physician in the years before the war. In fact, he was my guest on several occasions. Several months ago I received from Dr. Tsumi a long message explaining that he had made a discovery of considerable value and asking me if I would handle it for the Japanese government when the Occupation was finally ended. Now Mr. Carter tells me you are interested in this discovery of Dr. Tsumi. Whom do you represent, Mr. Buchanan?"

"Myself. No one else."

"It may not surprise you to know that I am aware of the interest shown in you by American Military Intelligence and the CIC. You were questioned by a certain Colonel Barham of the Intelligence branch and you escaped from his custody. Is that correct?"

I wondered how thoroughly honeycombed with spies our Tokyo command offices were. No matter how carefully they were checked, there were always some who reported to the Reds, to the *zaibatsu*, to the secret and underground Imperial Japanese Military Intelligence, and maybe to all of them at the same time.

"Yeah, your spies gave you the correct story."

"It would seem, Mr. Buchanan, that you are a more important man than one might guess from your record. An infantry captain, court-martialed, with little money, and then you return to Japan. Why?"

"I went through this with Barham. His guys are tougher than you'll ever be."

"However, you escaped from them. You will not escape from me."

"How come all this stuff on me? You didn't even know Carter had me until a couple of minutes ago."

"Quite correct. I did not expect Mr. Carter to bring you to me. I expected that you would be brought here by the Tann woman."

That was a nice boot in the belly.

"She tried to turn me in to the police last night."

"That was before I received the cultures of Dr. Tsumi's virus. Now that I have those, everything is changed."

I didn't say anything.

"I will communicate with the Tann woman and the two of you will be my guests for lunch. We may work out something of interest."

He clapped his hands sharply. A bespectacled man in a formal morning outfit came hurrying and bowed. I guessed him to be one of Manuki's secretaries. Manuki gave him some instructions and he bowed again and hurried off. And this Manuki had come out of Sugamo only a couple of years ago, supposedly flat broke. I wondered how many tons of stuff stolen from the Army and sold to the Reds it had taken to make a millionaire out of him again. Also I wondered why Manuki referred to Sandra as "the Tann woman." It didn't sound very cozy.

Carter walked over to the table, bent over, and scooped the grease gun from beneath it.

"Man," he said to me, "don't try to run away. You can't go ten feet from that table without Mr. Manuki's permission. You're gonna be right here when I get back. The last thing I'm gonna do in Japan before I get on that boat tonight is kill you."

He walked out to the gallery and down the broad, shallow steps into the garden, the grease gun cradled in his bandaged left arm.

Manuki sat down at the table, folding his legs under him. One of the maids trotted out with some more tea. Manuki shook his head and waved the tea away.

"Whisky," he said, and she hurried off.

We came and we conquered, in our own peculiar ways. The girl brought two highballs and I was mighty glad to get mine.

"There is little point to discussing serious affairs with you now," said Manuki, his sharp-featured but soft face shadowed as he sat, back to the sunlight streaming into the severe, serene room. "When the Tann woman arrives we shall dine."

He seemed certain enough that she would come, just as the bespectacled secretary had come running when he clapped his hands.

"Where are the culture jars?" I asked.

His eyebrows snapped up and he put his highball glass down. "You wish to see them?"

"*S'koshi* bit," I said, shrugging my shoulders. Little bit—hah! The most important jars in the world as far as I was concerned.

"Very well," and he clapped his hands sharply. Another little joker with big teeth and striped pants under a morning coat came clippety-clop. He must have had a platoon of them hidden around waiting for him to clap his hands. He gave this one instructions and there was some more clippety-clop.

In a few minutes the fancy-dressed lad came back lugging a square case made of aluminum, about the size of a portable typewriter case. The case was put on the rice-straw matting and opened. Inside were three jars, pint-sized, covered with a tricky metal gadget of some sort, and a large jar that contained a reddish-brown powder. Each of the three jars was half filled with a murky, jelly-like liquid.

This was the RK virus!

Now all I had to do was get my hands on the case and fight my way out, get through Tokyo to the man in the Teikoku Building, and call it a day.

"The deadliest substance in the world," said Yoshiru Manuki, looking at the jars with a fascinated horror that showed through even on his masklike face.

"What?" It was an involuntary question. Somehow I had never really believed what Colonel Barham had told me.

"Don't you know how deadly this virus is?"

I waited.

"It is a mutation of psittacosis, parrot fever. Those jars there, merely emptied by plane into the winds that blow on Tokyo from the sea, would kill ninety per cent of the whole population within five days. Air-borne, completely infectious, almost invariably fatal. The deadliest substance in the world. You Americans can have your atomic weapons. The nation that has this virus can rule the world."

My world had finished falling down around me. "Is that what Dr. Tsumi wrote you?"

"Tsumi wrote me a lot of nonsense intended to fool anyone who read his letter. I learned the real truth the way you must have learned it." His eyes were hard.

"Which is?"

"I am convinced that you are either an agent of the American Central Intelligence Agency or, like the Tann woman, an agent of the Soviet Union. After our lunch together I will know. What we do then depends on the two of you. The Tann woman has made her own deal; now I want to hear your deal. If it isn't good enough, I'll let Carter have you. If it satisfies me, you will leave here safely. Do you understand?"

I was looking in sick horror at the three murky jars.

"Do you realize, Mr. Buchanan, that you are now the guest of the most powerful man in the world? Yesterday I was merely rich. When that ragged, elderly servant came to my gate last night he brought me power beyond any riches.

"A doctor makes a discovery. Through the long years of the Occupation he hides it, and then because he was my guest many years ago, he sends me—by an old man, on foot—the secret of world power, the completely deadly weapon. It can be spread by guided missiles, a rain of tiny missiles beyond the ability of any nation to stop. It can be smuggled in on a little boat. There is no way of fighting it.

"The virus, once released into the air, lives only a few hours outside of the human body. After about five days the virus loses its power to reinfect. A nation attacking the United States with this weapon does not risk starting a world-wide epidemic. City by city, America could be destroyed, just as you destroyed Japan."

"What about Dr. Tsumi?"

He smiled. "Carter brought me the information that Dr. Tsumi and his daughter were together in a room in Shimbashi. It may not have been important, but it was not worth dismissing, either." He glanced at his watch. "By now they are both dead. Several witnesses have been arranged to give evidence that they were murdered by Mate Buchanan."

Akiko, the ivory princess with blue-black hair. Certainly she had been selfish and foolish. Somewhere today a woman still wept because of what the girl had done to her man. But she had been lovely, and she had tried to bargain with Carter to save my life.

And the only reason I was in Japan on this mission was because that girl felt a fondness and a trust for me.

Dr. Tsumi had said, "We Japanese are children," and "My virus will be used for Japan and for the Americans as well. My hate is gone." It was the "great man" that he trusted who had ordered him murdered.

The aluminum case with the three murky jars was only a few feet away. Barham was right. If Barham was right, then I had followed a lie from that hotel room in San Francisco. Barham and Manuki agreed—those jars contained a new terror for the people of the world. Barham and Manuki agreed—Sandra Tann was a traitor to her country.

I forced myself to let my fists unclench. The knuckles had been blue-white.

"As you know, Mr. Buchanan, there are places still for such as you. With money Macao can be very sweet, or maybe Jokyakarta. Even Saigon or Shanghai, if the Russians will mark you as one of theirs. With money life is most pleasant in those cities. Liquor, women, maybe a pipe or a needle if boredom becomes oppressive. The kind of life you would like." He smiled. "Even without money, merely living might seem sweet. There are no other places in this world for you now, Mr. Buchanan. The Americans will hang you. Carter dreams of you, bound and helpless, while he walks toward you slowly. He is a very cruel man, almost Oriental at times."

The next little maid brought us two more highballs.

"So you will tell me who pays you, who sent you to find the virus, and how much they will pay me for a few drops of the living stuff. You will tell me these things and then I will decide what I wish to have happen to your life.

"Sugarno Prison was not very pleasant. It might amuse me to think of you, not me, sitting in a cell. Only you will be waiting for the steps of those who will come to take you to the hangman. The popped-out eyes, the tongue like a toad in the mouth, the neck stretched and long so that it is funny and you laugh to see it. I might be amused. Or I might smile at the thought of you this evening in the cellar with the big, patient, careful hands of Carter working on you while you scream.

"But then again I might enjoy knowing that somewhere under the sun of Asia you sat, drunken, dirty, hopeless, an outcast. But alive, Buchanan, and with your eyes and your fingers, and the soft parts of your body—not as Carter would leave you."

"Listen, Manuki, for the last couple of days everybody's been telling me how tough they're going to make things for me. I'm tired of it. When this girl gets here we'll talk. Until then I don't want you boring me with your Oriental torture routine. When you get above pulling the wings off flies, you're out of your league. Now shut up."

He looked hurt, and it looked damn funny. I laughed.

Then Sandra Tann walked into the sun-bright room.

Chapter Thirteen

She wore a sea-green linen suit, her hair was tied with a narrow ribbon, and she strode into the room like a long-legged queen.

"It didn't take you long to get here," I said, standing up.

"Mate! Are you all right?" She walked up to me, her arms out.

"I'm O.K., but everybody's trying to tell me how I'm going to get fried. Including your pal here. Manuki just told me that he's had Akiko Tsumi and Dr. Tsumi murdered." I was looking into her cool gray eyes. As she understood what I said her hands went to her face for an instant and her eyes closed. Then she looked at the man in the white suit. There was something more than contempt in her look.

"You are not bothered by a trifle like that?" said Manuki, still sitting. There was contempt and hatred in his eyes, too, as he looked up at the girl.

"Why kill them?"

He shrugged. "Why not? They had no importance, once I got the virus. They could have gone to the Americans and talked. Simpler to have them dead."

"Where is Carter?"

He gave an ugly laugh. "You would want to know that. He has business for tonight's shipment. He brought in the last load when he brought in this Buchanan. He is going to kill Buchanan tonight and I am going to watch it. You too?"

Sandra turned to look at me, her face perfectly still. "You've got yourself into a very rough game, Mate. It would have been better if the M.P.'s had got you last night."

"How did you make such quick time here?" asked Manuki, getting up at last.

"I didn't. I took a cab here from the Osaka nearly an hour ago."

"I thought you were going to wait until Buchanan called you and try to get him here. I sent for you a few minutes ago." Manuki's face was bland and expressionless.

"I left word for Buchanan with instructions on how to get here. How did Carter find him?"

"Buchanan found Tsumi somewhere and brought him to a place in Shimbashi where his daughter was hiding. Carter had her for the last two nights and he went there to get a gun. Buchanan was there. Is Buchanan one of your people?" Manuki sounded bored.

Sandra's eyes were staring at the aluminum case. "No," she said, almost absent-mindedly. "I have no people. I've told you that. Just me."

"Once I believed that," said Manuki with a strange bitterness in his voice. "Once I believed other things about you. It doesn't matter."

"Is that the Tsumi virus?" asked Sandra, a metallic tenseness in her voice.

"Yes. Three cultures, and the food to keep them alive. The food is a human blood extract."

"You fool!" Sandra bit out the words, and there was almost panic on her face now. "Don't you know what the stuff can do? A few invisible specks in the air of this room and all of us would be dead in hours."

He backed away, sudden fright showing on his face. "I had one of my experts look at the jars. He said there is a double seal. Nothing can escape through the filters."

"Your experts," said Sandra with scorn. She still stared at the culture jars with fright graying her face. "Get them out of here!"

He was trying to look unconcerned, but it didn't work. He clapped his hands and one of his stooges showed up. He gave orders in Japanese, and the case was closed and taken away.

"Where did he take it?"

"To the storeroom with the rest of the shipment for tonight."

Sandra seemed to dominate him, although he struggled against her. She was regal and curt with him, he was sullen and resentful toward her.

"We will lunch and discuss business," he said.

"What business?" asked Sandra. She was carrying a large handbag of yellow linen and she swung it idly.

"Who pays me for the Tsumi virus? How much? I want gold in a Macao bank, no other payment. No heroin, no yen, no British pounds. Gold in a Macao bank."

"How would I know?" said Sandra, swinging her bag from one outstretched finger.

"I know you're a Soviet agent. You have no secrets from me," said Manuki.

"You know nothing," said Sandra. "Without Carter and his gang you'd be stealing cameras on the Ginza."

"I will not give Carter the virus to take on the boat. You were the one who knew the secret of Tsumi, you know who wants it and how much they will pay!" His voice was shrill.

"Suppose I do. What deal do you wish to make?" The bag stopped swinging.

"One culture jar. The gold equivalent of one million American dollars."

"You're a dreamer." Sandra laughed.

"Buchanan! This is your chance," said Manuki. "Who are your people? How much will they pay?"

"It seems that you've got a load of merchandise and no buyers," said Sandra. Her back was to Manuki as she looked out the window toward Fuji.

"The Communists would pay anything for this," shouted Manuki. "The most terrible weapon of all! There would be no way to protect a country against it!"

"True," said Sandra, and she swung around to face Manuki, "but it's odd merchandise. Once you've sold it, you can't sell it again. Your buyers won't need it. From the first drop they can grow vatsful of the stuff. So you will sell one culture to the Soviet, one culture to the Americans, maybe one culture to the British or the Japanese."

"I'm a merchant," said Manuki, and he nibbled on his finger.

"Very well, Merchant," said Sandra, and she walked up to him, her head high. "Maybe there can be a sale. But who trusts the other? No one. My people will not pay a sen until they have the virus, all of it with not one single virus cell held back, and until they have tested it in their laboratories to make sure it is as described. That takes time, many weeks. On the other hand, you would not trust us with it unless you had cash in hand. So?"

Manuki looked troubled. "But you are the one who knew exactly what the virus was, you are the one who told me," he said.

"Information is one thing, proof another," answered Sandra. "For that much gold we must have proof."

"Buchanan," he said, putting his hands on the straps of my overalls, "you came to Japan to get this virus. You know now that I have it. Unless I save you, you die tonight. Bargain with me, Buchanan."

"Stick your head in a honey bucket," I said. I was only half listening now. If I could get to the shed.... If the truck was still there.... If I could drive right through those gates....

At least I could keep the Tsumi virus from the Communists. It would be worth a chance, slight as it was. But I'd have to wait for the right moment.

"Manuki," said Sandra, and I could see the tightness of strain on her face, "there is only one deal, only one way to deal."

My own attention was drawn back sharply now.

"Make your own deal. Take the cultures to the Soviet military officials at Harbin or Port Arthur. I will introduce you and I will report that you have brought all of the virus. That is most important."

"Harbin or Port Arthur! Ridiculous! How would I get there?"

"With Carter, on the fishing boat."

"That stinking tub!"

"A million dollars, gold."

"They might kill me, take the virus away and shoot me. No."

"Never happen," said Sandra. "You are important. You are a principal supplier of stolen American military equipment. You are a principal smuggler of Chinese heroin and morphine. You are too important to be harmed. Make your own deal—or give the stuff to me and I'll make the deal."

The merchants of death, I thought. Haggling over the gold to pay for a million corpses. I began to think about trying to kill them both, here and now, with my bare hands. Manuki first, maybe a cut with the side of my hand across his eyes. It kills. I know; I killed a Red lieutenant near Chorwon that way. Then Sandra. Then Sandra....

Neither one of them was watching me now. They were still haggling.

"I trust you?" Manuki waved his hands in front of him, palms forward. Sandra laughed and turned her back to him again.

"If I go, you will take me to the right people, you will make the guarantees?"

"I will take you to Lebedeff. When the laboratory tests are completed and satisfactory, you will have your million in gold."

Manuki shook his head. "But that fishing boat. So dirty, so rough."

"There's no other way, and it's safe," said Sandra. "How many fishing boats have the Russian patrol boats seized in the past year? Hundreds. How many of them were yours, carrying hijacked loot?"

"Maybe twenty," said Manuki. "But the Americans know now why the Russian patrol boats arrest the Japanese fishing boats and take them to port. They know it is a device for smugglers."

"They suspect," corrected Sandra. "It's still safe."

Manuki shook his head again. Then he looked at me.

"You are something I do not understand," he said. "You will not talk, you will not bargain. Even when you know now that I have the stuff and that you will die, you do not try to bargain. But you came to Japan to get it. I cannot understand you."

I was edging toward him. I could kill them both inside of thirty seconds, but my first move would have to be the right one. One shout and the room would be filled with his men. He was about six feet away now. Too far. Manuki first, Sandra second.

"Look out, Manuki!" Sandra almost shouted.

Manuki clapped his hands before I could move. Two men hurried into the room, both in the formal Western clothes his secretaries wore. As they came in Manuki shouted instructions. There were two guns covering me after the first word.

The Witch of Tokyo. I wondered if I could have killed her if I'd had the chance.

He came in silently from behind me but I felt his presence.

Carleton Carter strode by me as if I weren't there. He went to Sandra and stopped. "Hi, you gorgeous chick," he said.

"What's doin', man?" she replied.

Manuki had turned away, a look of defeat and bitterness on his face. Carter and Sandra looked at each other. It was a look that I knew well. I had seen it that night in my room at the Imperial.

"Maybe Manuki is coming with us tonight," said Sandra.

Carter scowled. "Why? You and me don't need nobody else except the crew, and they better have sense enough not to bother us."

"Us" is what the man said.

"Manuki wants to take the virus to Red territory and make his own deal." Sandra sat on the edge of the ebony table, knees and legs together.

"You afraid somebody gonna cheat you, Papa-san?" asked Carter. "You cheated enough people to know about that. Including me."

"What are we going to do about this one?" asked Manuki, pointing at me.

Carter looked lazily and arrogantly at the two secretaries, each still holding a gun. He smiled and moved like a serpent striking. It was too fast to follow, but a second later he held two guns and both secretaries were on the floor. Carter tossed the guns back to them, one at a time, and laughed. Sandra was swinging her purse from one finger, smiling a little.

Manuki had hit the floor when Carter moved. Now he rose, and he was puffing and shaky. "You fool!" he blurted.

Carter shrugged. "I have to keep checkin' on the ol' *honcho*. I was a little slow. Now what was you saying about my meat here?"

Yoshiru Manuki was trying hard to be calm again, but Carter's little stunt had shaken him. "I asked what we do about Buchanan."

"I kill him, man. Pretty damn soon now, too."

"Maybe not," said Manuki. "Supposing he's Central Intelligence Agency? We know he's not CID or Counter-Intelligence, but we don't know about CIA. We don't have a line there."

"Let the cat be J. Edgar Hoover or somebody. Don't matter to the *honcho*. Three, four days from now some ol' kid playin' around gonna find what the rats left of him on some dump. My chick and me, we're gonna be halfway to the mainland by then. In a week we'll be in Shanghai and living high."

"With guns you show off," sneered Manuki. "But I am the smart one, I think of the money."

"I think you're right," said Sandra, sliding from the table and standing up.

"What do you mean, I'm right? You don't know yet what I'm talking about," complained Manuki.

"You're going to suggest we sell Buchanan to Red Intelligence. It isn't often that they get a CIA boy to work over. He'll know codes, the names of agents, maybe the names and locations of Central Intelligence people in China and North Korea. They'll get all that out of him. It might take a week or so."

Manuki's little moment of triumph had melted away as she spoke.

"That's right. That's what I was going to say. This Buchanan is somebody. He's either Red or he's American Central Intelligence."

"He's not Red," said Sandra.

"How much would the cat be worth?" asked Carter, looking at me with his hot, yellowish-white eyes, his hands in his pockets.

"Nothing, maybe. Or maybe ten, twenty thousand American dollars." Sandra shrugged. "It depends on what they got out of him. They'd pay, if he talked."

"Supposing they don't get anything from him, suppose he's just a stooge?" asked Manuki.

"Then they kill him. It's worth the gamble. We'll all be there. You, peddling your damn virus; Carter—"

"And you, chick," smiled Carter. "Ol' long-legged blonde-headed gal. Only worry you gonna have is will my health and strength hold out. I ain't even gonna look at you until we get to Shanghai and we go to the biggest hotel and get the biggest set of rooms and we ain't gonna come out for a month. Just have 'em send whisky and steaks in." This was my Sandra he was talking to, and she looked as if she was in complete agreement with his ideas.

I had worked my way behind Sandra, putting her between me and the others, including the two secretaries, who were standing well apart now. This was going to be it. One quick try. If I could get to the truck....

My arm locked under her throat hard. She was a shield in front of my body and I was gambling that she had a gun in her linen purse. I noticed that it had swung heavily. As my arm swung up under her chin my right hand was reaching into the open throat of the purse. My fingers touched the flat cold metal of a gun.

Then my body exploded in pain. I held to her for a pain-streaked instant and then I stumbled back, bent over. She had kicked back and up hard, like a *savate* fighter. It hurt too damn much.

I was trying to hold myself and I could hear them laughing.

If I could ever get my hands on her I could kill her. I knew that now. I'd been stupid, standing spraddle-legged as I tried for her gun.

The pain was just waves rippling out from the center now. Mostly I was weak, almost too weak to stand. I could see her as I lifted my head.

"Don't ever try to touch me again," she said without heat.

Manuki was smiling as if he had a private joke about this all to himself.

"That was mighty beautiful, chick," said Carleton Carter.

Everybody was having a hell of a good time except me.

"Very foolish," said Manuki. "You could not get beyond this room. Many men guard this place. Do not try it again. You may be valuable to us alive."

"We'll take him with us tonight," said Sandra.

"You mean I don't get this cat?" asked Carter.

"Ten thousand dollars," murmured Manuki.

"How we split it?"

"Three ways?" replied Manuki, looking at Sandra.

"Half to me. You split the other half."

"Why half to you?" Manuki was annoyed and it showed.

"Who takes him to Soviet Intelligence? Who bargains with them?" returned the tall, golden girl.

"You sure we can get money for this piece of meat?" Carter looked at me. I was coming back into things now. At least I could stand up straight, and the weakness was fading.

Sandra shrugged again. "If he's CIA, and I think he is. If they can make him talk."

A maid entered the room and bowed, spoke a few words; bowed again, and was gone. The two secretaries bowed out on instructions from Manuki.

"We will be served our luncheon," said Manuki. "I am sure that you will enjoy it. You too, Mr. Buchanan. I have said that you were my guest."

I was the guy who had just struck out and all I was waiting for was my next turn at bat. Sandra had a gun, I knew that now. The only gun in the room that I knew of.

"I'm going to wash a bit," said Sandra, and she walked out to the gallery and down the steps.

"I tell you one thing," Carter said to Manuki, "this Buchanan has made things mean for people today. Tokyo is tight, man. What I mean, tight. They're checking the town house by house today. Tokyo police and the M.P.'s. They figuring on finding this cat."

"They will not check this house." Manuki smiled a little.

"Sure won't. Man, you done fine since we started. Remember two years ago when one of your boys come to me and say a *honcho* wants to talk to the Duke of Shimbashi?"

"We talked at the Haji-basha. I remember."

"Ol' Asahi-san. He treated you like you was Mr. God. That ol' woman-man, he's made himself a lot of loot during these fine years. He's the one who put the finger on this cat for me."

"I know." Manuki clapped his hands. One secretary came, got his instructions, and took off.

Carter laughed. "When my girl got this cat in the crotch I like to have busted."

I sat there quietly and listened.

"You sure thought my li'l chick was gone on you for long time," said Carter, looking sidewise at Manuki. "Remember first time I met her. You brought her here for dinner, big crowd, everybody traveling first class because you was making time with the Witch of Tokyo. You so proud of her you like to blow up."

I could guess now at the reason for Manuki's coolness toward Sandra. "The Tann woman"—I bet he hadn't called her that then.

Carter rubbed his face with an enormous hand. "Then li'l by li'l that chick begin to notice the ol' *honcho*. For a long time I couldn't make out even *s'koshi* bit. And now—all you gonna do is go along on our honeymoon, man. What a beat that is, huh?"

Manuki must have seen something funny in it because he laughed, but I got the idea that it might not be the same thing that amused Carleton Carter.

I saw the five men as they came up the steps. There wasn't going to be any move. One of them carried Carter's grease gun. They stationed themselves around the room.

Sandra came back. She looked at the guards and chuckled. "You need five men to guard a man that one woman could handle?"

Neither Manuki nor I looked real pleased with that remark. I hated her pretty thoroughly at that moment.

A series of maids showed up and went to work. This apparently was going to be a number-one meal in Japanese style.

The four of us sat at the ebony table and the first course was served by two girls in kimonos. I could tell by the formalized gestures, the careful exactness of each movement, that they were serving in precisely the prescribed fashion determined by several centuries of Japanese etiquette. It's a fascinating thing to watch when your mind is on it and you're in pleasant company.

Sandra was lovely. I looked at her across the table. Something in her beauty was like the serene beauty of this room—a feeling of quiet elegance. It was a dead cinch that Buchanan couldn't tell anything about women from looking at them.

"Remember the important day, Mate. It's ahead of us." She'd said that.

She meant it when she said it. I'd swear to it. A couple of minutes later she'd called the cops to come and get me. Why?

Red agents don't operate that way. The only reason she would have to call the Military Police would be to get me out of the way.

Get me out of the way for what? I was working on some tricky dish of shrimp with chopsticks now, but I wasn't thinking of food.

Tsumi's virus? She didn't know where Tsumi was hidden, she hadn't recognized Akiko Tsumi on the roof of the 64th Engineers' Club. The only connection she had with Dr. Tsumi was that both of them knew Yoshiru Manuki.

One other thing. She had been the one who had told Manuki that the Tsumi virus was a deadly disease. If that was true, how had she known it? Because she was a Red agent? The Reds had not known of Dr. Tsumi——or if they had, they would either have known where he was hiding or they would have got the same story that we did, the story of his daughter and the idiot girl, both of them cured of radiological burns.

Therefore Sandra must be lying about the virus. And if she was lying about the virus, she would be lying about the other things as well. She had met Manuki and let him make a play for her and then had moved on. She had twice tried to protect me—once by getting me arrested and once by telling Manuki and Carter that my live, healthy body would be worth much gold to Russian Intelligence. Somehow, all the pieces were fitting into place.

Sandra's kick had saved me from being shot to death outside by Manuki's guards. But why was she going to China with Carleton Carter?

Then I noticed the dish on the table before me. I recognized it and my thoughts came to an abrupt halt.

It was blowfish, the epicure's delight. There's only one thing about it—the fish contains a poison sac, and unless this sac is removed before cooking by an expert who knows exactly what he's doing, the whole fish becomes an utterly deadly poison. One bite of blowfish whose poison sac has been cut, and you're dead.

I looked at Manuki. He was smiling.

Chapter Fourteen

Each of us had been in Japan enough to know what was before us. In the home of a friend we might have eaten blowfish with enjoyment. But we were in the great house of Yoshiru Manuki, who had tried to kill Sandra Tann three days ago, the Manuki who hated her because she had not become one of his women, and who hated Carter.

I looked first at Sandra. There was a smile for Manuki—a smile of queenly contempt. She took a bit of fish in her chopsticks and I almost shouted at her in panic until I realized why she had smiled in contempt. Manuki wanted to see us frightened. This was the Orient, where pride is valued more than life.

Manuki looked away as Sandra finished the fish on her plate. I ate mine as she did hers. Manuki's gesture had turned out to be a defeat for him rather than for the Tokyo Doll. Then I saw that Carleton Carter had drawn back from the table, his eyes hooded, his fish untouched.

Before the maid came to take it I saw him stealthily flick a piece of the fish into his handkerchief and put it into a pocket of his fatigue uniform.

The dinner was finished. No one had spoken.

I was excited now. Sandra Tann had met and fooled Manuki, learning his secrets; seemingly intent upon my destruction, she had twice saved my life. She treated Manuki with scorn and made him do as she wished. She had concealed the secret of the RK virus by disguising it with another story, making it seem valuable to the Reds without letting Manuki and Carter know how desperately the United States wanted it.

I was certain that I was right about the tall golden girl. How she had learned the truth of the RK virus and how she had found the connection between Dr. Tsumi and Yoshiru Manuki I did not know, but I could see now that she was fighting a clever, skillful, and desperate fight for America. Somehow she was arranging the destruction of Manuki and Carter's black-market web that fed Red China with American goods.

We were standing now and Carter was looking at me.

"I hate to see this cat still walking like a man," he said, and he sprang like a tiger. I saw his right fist moving toward my neck just as it hit.

There was an explosion of light and a fraction of an instant when I knew I had been hit, and then I was gone.

At first I seemed to be awakening from sleep and then the throb of pain broke through and I could put the pieces together. Carter had hit me behind the ear and I had been knocked out. How long? A few minutes maybe, possibly half an hour if he'd connected just right. The whole side of my head and neck hurt and I couldn't move my arms or legs. And then I felt the tightness and bite of the cords on my arms and legs. I was on the floor, face down, with wrists and ankles bound.

I could see legs a few feet away. Carter's fatigue trousers, his feet in felt slippers. The long curve of Sandra's legs.

"O.K., chick. Like you say." It was Carter's voice. "But just let me get this li'l ol' dog here and find out something." He whistled and I heard a slow, hesitant pit-pat on the rice straw. The pit-pats came close to me and now I heard the pant of a dog's breathing. Something wet sniffed at the side of my head. Then the dog went past me. It was an aristocrat of dogs, a Samoyed. Carter was talking to it and I saw his big hand come down, ruffling the fur of the dog's neck. He played with it for a few seconds and then the hand disappeared. It came down a moment later, and there was a spread handkerchief with a morsel of blowfish on it.

The dog sniffed and then gobbled the piece.

It stood there and it seemed a carved statue of a dog. Then it toppled over, its legs stretched out in stiff awkwardness. It was one completely dead dog.

"See, chick, see?" Carter's voice was a whisper now. "I was the only one that wouldn't touch that damn fish. That fish on the ol' *honcho's* plate was rub-out fish. I'd be stiff and dead like that ol' dog now. See what I mean, chick?"

His big hands came down and picked up the dead animal.

"Gonna hide this cold meat now. Don't want ol' Papa-san to know that the *honcho* knows about that fish. After I hide this I'm gonna get my grease gun from that guard."

"Manuki should be back soon," Sandra said. "What are you going to do?"

"You and me, we'll go in the truck. I'll throw Buchanan in the back." He stood there, rocking on his feet. "Papa-san will go in one of his big cars. Probably he'll just have a driver along. He'll have that virus stuff in his car. We'll meet down on the beach near the boat. When his car's gone, I'll cut out his belly and throw him in the sea. O.K.?"

"O.K.," said Sandra.

Carter's legs disappeared from my range of sight and I heard his slippered feet going away.

"Sandra!" I whispered.

"Yes?" she walked close to me, and I looked up beyond her curved legs, up the slimness of her body to her face. She looked down at me and there was no expression.

"Untie me, Sandra. Then give me that gun you have."

She walked away from me. Her footsteps stopped just beyond the area I could see and then she ran back, bent over, and kissed me. Her long fingers were soft on the ache of my head and neck for a moment and then she was gone again.

It was all I needed. I knew that somehow we two would fight our way out of this.

I heard the soft, heavy footsteps of Carter. "Manuki show yet, chick?"

"He's coming across the garden now."

"Remember, we don't know nothing about that fish or that dog."

"We go now. I am ready." It was Manuki, his voice flat and lifeless.

I felt Carter's hands on me and then I was high in the air, slung over his shoulder, head down at his back. He was a fearfully powerful man.

We went out of the room to the gallery, down the broad steps, and toward the barnlike building where I had parked the truck earlier. Carter carried me as if I were a bag of grain. I could see the shadow of the building on the ground. It must be late afternoon now, and I could feel a hint of rain in the air.

He threw me into the back of the truck and my body crashed against the rough, hard edges of crates. I was face down on the dusty boards.

Sandra said, "I'm going back. I forgot to phone the studio. They'll be expecting me in a few minutes and I don't want them starting a search for me."

Carter's voice said, "O.K., chick."

There was silence for a couple of minutes.

Manuki's voice: "Carter, you trust that woman?"

Carter's voice, strangely soft: "Don't bother me with that talk, man. Just don't bother me."

Manuki, and there was a rising elation as he spoke: "Where did your girl sleep last Friday night?"

"At the Osaka. Where she lives. What you trying to do, man?"

"She slept at the Imperial. You know Micki, the assistant there. Micki will tell you. Call him."

"You got another phone besides the one she's using?"

"In the little house by the gate."

"I'm gonna call, and if you're foolin' around—"

I heard Carter walking away. Then Manuki came to the rear of the truck. I felt his fingers in my hair. He lifted my head and we looked at each other.

"Mr. Buchanan, I dined today with three enemies. I had hoped to have that woman for myself for a little while. But since I cannot have her, I will at least have no enemies. Not that woman, not that barbarian giant, not you."

He flung my head back to the floor with a hard push.

This time I did not hear Carter return.

"Yes?" said Manuki, softly but with a ring of hatred in his voice.

"Why didn't you tell me before? She was with this Buchanan in his room at the Imperial Friday night. Micki told me, and he wasn't lying."

"Now what are you going to do?"

"I'll tell you what I'm gonna do," said Carter. "She's calling somebody now. I don't know who. She thinks we're going to Zushi and then to the beach. We'll go the other way—'bout a mile farther down the beach. If she plans to cross us—have some hijackers or the law there—we'll be a long ways off. We can signal the boat or have one of your guys go meet 'em and tell 'em where we're at."

"Very good reasoning. If she arranges a trap, it will close on empty air. Yes?"

"And there's going to be some killing on that beach. Quite a bit of killing."

"No ten thousand dollars?"

I could hear Carter spit. "So the chick was with Buchanan. My, my. There's two people I'm goin' to really enjoy killin'."

"The Tann woman has a gun."

"Ain't no gun gonna stand against my baby with the big tin belly and the big long clip. But I ain't gonna use no gun. I'm gonna use a knife and my hands."

"Here she comes."

"Hi, chick. How you doin'?"

"Fine, Carl."

"Let's go. You understand where to meet, Manuki?"

"I understand."

"Come on, chick, climb in."

I heard the doors of the cab slam, the engine start. We began to bump along the garden road toward the gate, and then we were out on the rough road.

There was a cool wind, suddenly, and the spatter of rain on the canvas roof. I began to work at the cords on my wrist. Somebody had done a smart job of tying them. They were so tight that my hands were as numb as dead clay. I tried to rub the cords against the rough edge of a box, but the cords were too hard and smooth, the box wood too soft.

I remembered the little metal clips on the overall straps. There was about half an inch of saw-tooth metal inside to bite into the cloth straps: If I could reach that I would have a cutting edge.

It meant pushing at the snapped-down clip with dead fingers, trying to work my thumbnail under the clip when there was no feeling in my thumb. But I finally did it.

Slowly and patiently I sawed the cord against the half inch of serration. The rain lashed into the back of the open truck. I wondered how much time I would have.

The cord parted. I pulled the cut cord away from my wrists with my teeth and then I fought for feeling in my hands again.

There were ten thousand white-hot needles stuck into my right hand and then into my left. They were alive again. For minutes I flexed my fingers, worked life and feeling back into my hands. Then I struggled with the knots that bound my ankles and lived through the ten thousand hot needles in my feet.

It seemed like a long time, but I was free again with hands and feet that worked. We were rolling along at fair speed now and through the open back of the truck I could see that we were on a curving road through the hills that fringe the ocean south of Yokohama. It was dark now, and still raining.

I began to move slowly, one foot on the tail gate, then hands on the wet canvas of the roof. My body was stiff and awkward. I pulled myself over the edge of the canvas and up on top. The rain whipped at me.

Now I was flat on the sopping canvas roof, my head just behind the space between the cab body and the cargo space. My knees were drawn up, my hands spread-eagled to grasp the pipes of the frame.

I tried to look into the cab from my perch. I could see the rectangular rear window of the cab, and in the faint light of the dash I could see Sandra's knees, and then as my eyes searched out the darkness I could trace the outline of the grease gun resting on Carter's lap, its snout toward Sandra.

The truck was grinding down a steep grade now, and in its lights ahead I saw the sand of a beach and I could hear the pounding of the waves.

The wheels pushed into sand and the truck stopped.

I pulled myself up, crouching now just behind the cab, facing to the left, where the door would open when Carter came out.

The door opened. I was breathing hard. Carter's head was outlined against the glittering rain above the headlights. I could tell by the way he moved that he was carrying the grease gun.

I was down in a jump, both hands extended, crashing into Carter, bowling him half over and away from the truck, grabbing at the gun.

He had felt me coming and he had looked up, the gun half raised, just as I hit him. My fingers slipped on the short barrel, already wet in the lashing rain. His left hand would be nearly useless with that broken and splinted finger, but as we reeled together he hit at me with the fat housing of the grease gun and got my right elbow. My whole right arm went dead.

My knee came up but he turned his body and I missed. My left hand closed on the gun, clawing at the barrel, and I pushed it up. My right hand smashed into his face and came away bloody. He was swinging again, his right arm high, the left hand holding the trigger housing of the gun, all outlined in the glitter of the headlights as we stood almost directly in front of the truck.

I ducked up to his body, clinching, and his fist crashed down at the back of my head. I was blinded, staggering. My left hand clutched at the bandaged splints and I jerked hard. The gun fell, rolling against my leg as it hit the sand. His terrible right fist exploded on my side.

Each of us stumbled backward, our feet unsteady in the deep sand, both of us hurt, each of us with only one good arm. The broken finger was flopping on his left hand, but my right arm was coming back to life again.

I had a quick glimpse of Sandra just beyond the pool of light the truck headlamps made in the rain. The grease gun was on the sand between Carter and me.

Carter's face was bloody. He came for me like a tiger plunging, both hands out. I grabbed at him and pulled him on me, rolling backward into the sand, kicking upward with both feet as I went back, pulling him on top of me. He went over, but not cleanly. My right arm wasn't working right yet. His great fingers dug into my hair and his left hand moved over my face, fingers searching for my eyes. Both of us were on the sand.

I bit into the heel of the hand. He pulled my head back by my hair, trying to free his hand. My teeth scratched bone.

He screamed, pulling his mangled hand from my mouth. He tried to stand up in the sand, but I was quicker and I smashed my knee into his already battered face. He went over, rolled, and got to his knees, then put his hands to his face. He was making thick, burbling sounds through the blood.

I stood up. Sandra was there and she held the grease gun. I took it from her, cleared it to check action, and then I put a burst of six into the giant as he rose.

Carter's body spun backward as the slugs hit him and he crumpled on the sand.

The old *honcho*, the Duke of Shimbashi, the terrible Carleton Carter was dead.

I stood there, the gun hanging slack in my hands, and I was all used up. The side of my head and the ribs on one side were toothaches of pain; there was blood on my face, my throat, my hands.

Sandra came to me and I could feel her fingers on my face. "Mate, Mate, Mate."

"I'll be right... couple minutes."

She held me in her arms and I was glad to be there. Then we walked together back to the cab of the truck and got in. It was warm there. Sandra kissed me, but very gently.

I was holding the grease gun across my lap. "Manuki's coming here," I said, still short of breath. "He expects to find Carter. We were to be killed here by Carter."

"I'm not surprised," Sandra said. "Carter took my purse—with my gun in it—and emptied the gun when we started. No explanation, and I didn't dare protest. I was sort of frightened, Mate."

"Manuki told him about us. About Friday night."

"Manuki hates me. I spent months building him up, and then when he thought he had me I pretended to move over to Carter. His first blaze of jealousy showed in the attack on the car when I was with Colonel Barham."

"Who are you, Sandra?"

"No harm in your knowing now—but I shouldn't even have kissed you back there at the house. I had to play my game alone, and the most I could do for you was kick you that time. Outside you'd have been killed. Manuki's place is a regular fortress. That and telling them you could be sold to the Reds. I couldn't help doing that much, though I was supposed to play a strict lone hand. It's hard to, though, when you're in love."

"Who are you?"

"Central Intelligence Agency. Mission? Originally to get the ring smuggling goods to Red China. Later, the RK virus."

"You, too?"

"I didn't know who else was on that job. I'm guessing you were."

"Through the Tsumis."

"We learned about it through our agent planted in Manuki's office. He read the letter from Dr. Tsumi and reported to us. I was the agent assigned to get Manuki, so I got the RK job, too, from that end."

"You know what the RK virus will do?"

"Tsumi's letter said it would prevent and cure cell damage in the human body caused by radioactivity. I convinced Manuki that the Red spies in Japan knew that what Tsumi had was a new and terrible disease."

"Colonel Barham?"

"CIA works alone. Barham's Counter-Intelligence people ran across my trail without knowing I was CIA. Somebody around Manuki must work with them, because I know CIC has the disease-virus story and not the true one. Barham really thinks I'm a Soviet agent. After tonight my CIA people will brief him on the truth."

Headlights from behind the truck brightened the beach.

"Manuki!" I said, and my hands tightened around the grease gun.

"It's all right, Mate. I phoned my contact at the network offices. They'll be here, too. Manuki's through. The Navy is co-operating to pick up the smuggling boat offshore, and the Air Force is doing a sky patrol out there with night fighters, pinning Manuki's boat on radar."

A big car, a Cadillac like Asahi-san's, swung in on the sand near us. I waited. The rain had lessened while we talked. Now it stopped suddenly and the night was still.

After a minute Manuki walked out of the darkness to Carter's body, looking like a mass of wet rags on the sand. He prodded it with his foot. He started to run back toward his car. I jumped out of the cab and fired a burst of three in the sand in front of him. He froze, his hands jerking up.

"No, no! Don't shoot! I have much money, I pay!"

I walked up behind him and poked him with the snout of the gun. He fell forward into the sand and dug at it with his hands as if trying to make himself a hole to crawl into. I tossed the gun back of me and picked him up.

His driver was running toward us. I wished I hadn't been so brave about the gun. My hands and arms were sore, but I figured I was good for a couple of more rounds. I spun Manuki around jand sank one right in the middle of his round face. Something splurted and he went over backward, yelping like a kicked dog. I got ready for the driver.

"Hold it," said the driver in surprisingly crisp English. "I'm Lieutenant Matsuoka, Security Police." He had a gun on me by now and my hands went up. He wasn't big, but he looked plenty willing and able.

He came up to me, gun still pointed right where it should be.

"He's all right, Lieutenant," said Sandra.

"Miss Tann," the crisp little guy said, saluting her. Manuki would enjoy finding out that his personal driver was actually a Security Police detective.

"The Japanese Security Police have been working with us," Sandra said to me. "This is a CID function, as far as they're concerned, but the Lieutenant and two others in his department were given high-level clearance on me."

Manuki was sitting on the sand, holding his face and giving high-pitched yelps.

"Where are the others?" Sandra asked Matsuoka.

He pointed back to the road. Four sets of headlights were coming down the grade toward the beach. I ran to the big Cadillac. The aluminum case was on the floor in back, wrapped with three blankets to protect it from bumping.

The RK virus. My mission was accomplished.

I turned around. Manuki was surrounded by men now, some of them in the uniform of the Japanese Security Police, others in U.S. Army uniforms. All of us spun toward the sea as three powerful searchlights suddenly went on, sweeping across the water. One of them picked out a big fishing boat and the other two converged on it.

It looked as if Sandra's mission was accomplished, too. We rode back to Tokyo in Manuki's car.

"This is how it was, Mate," said Sandra. "We had to get to Manuki. We had an agent in his office, and I guess CIC did too. Drugs were being smuggled in, American war and medical supplies were being smuggled out. We didn't know how and we couldn't get evidence. The chiefs decided that a big production job should be done on Manuki himself. They decided to reach him with glamour.

"I almost became a night-club singer once before. Then my brother persuaded me to try CIA. They brought me over to Japan with a partially faked personal history in my records and the Tokyo Doll began to sing. It went over pretty well, too.

"Then it was arranged that I should sing at a party where Manuki would be. He has a yen for tall blondes, and he went for me. I was coy, but I was friendly too. For a time it looked as if he was making good time with me. Then I let him suspect I might be something more than a singer—maybe a Red agent.

"Last week I made the switch to Carter. Partly to get Manuki out of my hair, partly to set up a deal like tonight. I told Carter I wanted to get back to the Red mainland and that I'd like to go with him.

"Then I met you. You know how I feel. I showed it our first night together. The next day Manuki tried one last time to sell me. He threw a big party at the Delight Baths for lunch—all Japanese, and I wore a kimono. I hadn't realized that I'd already made him jealous enough to try to have me killed."

"Three things out of all this, Sandra," I said. "One, the RK virus. Two, a girl named Sandra Tann. And three, something I hadn't learned yet back there on a hill in Korea. A soldier completes his mission or dies trying. No exceptions."

I held her as if I would never let her go. I didn't intend to.

"Where to, sir?" said the driver.

"Teikoku Building." There would be someone there waiting for me.

THE END